THE CHOSEN

A BLACK ARROWHEAD NOVEL
BOOK THREE

DANNIKA DARK

ALSO BY DANNIKA DARK:

THE MAGERI SERIES

Sterling

Twist

Impulse

Gravity

Shine

The Gift

MAGERI WORLD

Risk

NOVELLAS

Closer

THE SEVEN SERIES

Seven Years

Six Months

Five Weeks

Four Days

Three Hours

Two Minutes

One Second

Winter Moon

Seven Series Companion: An Insider's Guide

SEVEN WORLD

Charming

THE CROSSBREED SERIES

Keystone

Ravenheart

Deathtrap

Gaslight

Blackout

Nevermore

Moonstruck

Spellbound

Heartless

Afterlife

Quicksilver

Evildoer

Forevermore

Crossbreed Series Companion: An Insider's Guide

THE BLACK ARROWHEAD SERIES

The Vow

The Alpha

The Chosen

First hardcover edition. 2023

ISBN 9798857460139

Formatting: Vellum

Cover design by Dannika Dark. All stock purchased.
www.dannikadark.net

A BLACK ARROWHEAD NOVEL

THE CHOSEN

USA TODAY BESTSELLING AUTHOR

DANNIKA DARK

CHAPTER 1

"We're almost there," I said to the large wolf ambling at my side.

A frosty wind blew rain against my back, but I kept my eyes on the neon lights ahead.

I'd been hitchhiking since leaving South Dakota, but it wasn't easy with a wolf companion. We spent most of the journey on foot. Once in a while, a pickup truck gave us a chance for respite. With a limited amount of cash, I had to be thrifty, which meant napping in bathrooms or sheltering in unlocked cars. A surprising number of people staying in motels didn't lock their vehicles, likely because they were tired and distracted. It didn't seem right to invade someone's personal space, but I didn't have a choice. Food took precedence over comfort, so squandering money on a motel room was out of the question.

If the rain wasn't bad enough, the evening hours made the blistering cold unbearable. We needed shelter, and soon.

I neared the two-story lodging and only counted four cars. Someone had parked a bus the size of a Greyhound horizontally in the parking spaces by the road, but it didn't have a company logo on the side.

Once we arrived at the far end of the motel, my eyes lit up. "We hit the jackpot. There's a restaurant attached. Who wants a hot meal?"

Catcher whined and sat by a room door. I stepped out of the rain and squatted beside him. *Poor guy.* Most of the water rolled off his thick coat, but his muddy paw pads must have been hurting. He normally traversed through the grass except at night, when he stayed glued to my side.

I dried his wet face. "I don't know if they have steak. If not, I'll bring you a couple of juicy burgers. How does that sound?"

He woofed softly.

Chuckling, I stood up. "*No tomatoes.* I promise. Be back soon."

While I didn't speak wolf, I knew exactly what he liked and what he didn't.

Catcher only tolerated being separated from me because he wasn't allowed inside restaurants. People could tell he was a wolf. Some panicked, while others lectured me on why you couldn't own a wild animal. I couldn't exactly explain to a human that it was impossible to own a Shifter. While a Breed restaurant would likely allow him entry, I'd been deliberately avoiding those establishments.

I approached the door beneath the neon sign that read BURGERS & COCKTAILS. To my surprise, the quaint diner was bustling with customers. The eatery had a long wooden table down the center and cheap chairs, and a few tables against the walls. The dark-blue wallpaper clashed with the orange carpet, and despite the cold weather, the ceiling fans were spinning.

Several customers at the middle table swung their gazes up at me. When I flipped my hood back, water dripped down my waterproof jacket. My cheeks tingled from the warm air as I moved toward the counter. Two cooks were chattering in the open kitchen while food smoked and sizzled.

I scanned the menu on the wall.

Hmm. Hamburgers, chili, hot dogs, chicken fingers, french fries, and macaroni. Is that it? Damn, those burgers are pricey. The hot dogs are reasonable, though. I bet they don't make their food from scratch. Probably buy it frozen and thaw it out the night before. But who cares? I'm starving. Chili sounds perfect, and I need protein.

An older fellow appeared behind the counter and wiped his forehead. "Hi. What can I get you, miss?"

I unzipped my jacket while doing math in my head. We were extra tired tonight, so Catcher deserved a hearty meal. "I'll have two burgers. Hold the tomatoes."

"Anything to drink?"

"Can I also have two hot dogs—no buns—and a bowl of chili? Does that come with crackers?"

Someone behind me chuckled.

"Yep. We top it with cheese and onions and put crackers on the side."

"Perfect. Can you take the tomatoes out of the burgers and include them with the chili order instead?"

"Not a problem."

I glanced at the drinks. "Is water free?"

He gestured to a drink dispenser on the right. "Water's over there. No charge. It's the honor system. If you want anything else, be sure to pay."

I pulled out my wallet. "How much?"

"Your total comes to thirty dollars and ninety-eight cents."

After he accepted my money and handed back the change, he asked, "What's the name?"

I drew in a breath and hesitated before answering. "Uh, Penelope." That wasn't my name, but names didn't matter. I was ordering dinner, not registering to vote. "Can you put the burgers and hot dogs in a sack?"

He frowned.

"It's for my friend," I added, putting the change in my wallet. "He wanted to lie down."

"You got it. It'll be a wait. We have a full house tonight."

I turned and selected a table against the wall. As soon as I set my coat over a chair, I shivered.

A man at the center table peered over his shoulder at me, his black cowboy hat shadowing his eyes. It wasn't one of those giant ten-gallon hats, but it fit him nicely.

"It sure is wet out there," he said in a husky voice. To my surprise, he didn't have a Southern accent to go with that hat.

The back of his T-shirt had a scenic view of mountains and a river inside a circle. I wondered what it meant.

Not in the mood for idle chat, I scanned the room. Six people shared his table—five men and one woman. Two men were dining alone on the other side of the restaurant. Three kids at a table up front argued over a phone while their parents ignored them. Behind me sat an older gentleman. At the table nearest to the door, a couple talked in hushed tones.

The glass door swung open, and a gust of wind chilled the air when a customer entered. Drops of water clung to his knit hat, and I thought it was odd he had on sunglasses at night.

I faced forward and noticed a restroom sign. Since my food needed a while to cook, I shot out of my seat and headed past the fountain drinks. Once inside the private restroom, I locked the door and hung my backpack on a hook.

My reflection startled me. These past four days had taken a toll on my appearance. If the dark circles under my eyes weren't awful enough, my dark-brown hair hadn't seen a brush since the previous Thursday, and it showed. The shaggy cut barely grazed my shoulders, yet it still looked like the end of a mop because of all the humidity. I flattened it against my head, remembering how it had once reached my waist.

Who am I?

A stranger stared back at me.

After using the toilet, I cleaned up with a few supplies in my bag, including shaving my armpits, even though no one would see them, and tried to feel like a human being again.

"What am I going to do?" I whispered to my reflection. "We're running out of money."

I sure didn't want to settle in Nebraska.

The hand drier on the wall caught my attention, so I stripped off my wet pants. Goose bumps erupted down my legs. Since it was one of those hot hand dryers, it didn't take long to warm up the room and dry my pants. Then I changed socks so my feet wouldn't squish around in my shoes. Sometimes it was hard to see puddles at night. The area was isolated with no businesses, only a gas station and a motel.

I could barely keep my eyes open. "One crisis at a time."

Once I put my clothes back on, I returned to the main room and stopped by the drink fountain to fill a plastic cup with water before returning to my table. My meal was waiting for me. Instead of sitting down, I set my heavy backpack in the chair, put on my coat, gathered the Styrofoam containers, and headed outside.

I ran to Catcher, only he wasn't there anymore. Sometimes, he wandered. When I entered a covered breezeway by the stairs, I peered into the shadows. Catcher's tail thumped against the concrete repeatedly from the other side of an inoperable vending machine.

He hopped to his feet and salivated when he sniffed the containers.

"It's practically sizzling," I said, squatting in front of him.

Catcher smacked his lips when I popped the lid open and he caught the heavenly aroma.

"I'm going back inside to eat and warm up. I won't be long."

He gobbled down the first burger.

"Slow down." I chuckled at his enthusiasm. "You're worse than a vacuum cleaner." After opening the second burger container and setting it down, I waved a third at him. "Surprise! I got you a couple of hot dogs. Do you want them now, or should I save them?"

He took the container between his teeth and regarded me with those hazel eyes.

"Fine. But there's not much around here. You found nothing on your last hunt, so maybe we need to save just one."

He growled and set the container on the ground.

I lifted one hot dog and offered it to him before closing the lid. "I'll put the rest in my bag. It's busy in there, so stay out of sight. Okay? Nobody's going to mess with a stray dog."

His lip curled. Though I was only making a point, he hated it when I called him a dog. Most Shifters blacked out when their animal took over, but alphas didn't. Even though Catcher wasn't an alpha, some wolves could remember their entire shift. Wolves understood tone and body language along with a limited vocabulary. Just not complex sentences. Catcher seemed to comprehend what I was saying, though I couldn't be certain since I'd never met him.

He slowed down on the second burger. I collected the empty container and pitched it into a trash can before returning to the restaurant. After stuffing the hot dog container into my backpack, I sat down and gobbled up the tomatoes that should have gone on Catcher's burger. Then I spooned hot chili into my mouth at record speed. It wasn't enough to satiate my hunger, and I felt like a hypocrite for warning Catcher not to eat too fast when I couldn't even follow my own advice.

"Mmm." I tore open the crackers and ate two, the crumbs sprinkling into the empty bowl. The fellow in the knit cap was staring right at me from across the room, his dark shades resting on the tip of his nose.

My stomach sank when I noticed his yellow eyes. He picked up his beer bottle and pushed his sunglasses up before taking a drink.

What is a Chitah doing in here? This can't possibly be a Breed joint, not off the highway.

Calm down. Immortals wander into human places all the time. Play it cool before he smells your panic.

Chatter from the center table about cars and motorcycles filled the room.

If Catcher scented Breed, he might come bursting through the door.

I didn't know any Chitahs personally, but they were supposedly protective of women.

Supposedly.

Many worked as trackers, and I'd heard stories about them carrying out hits.

"Good night," one couple said to the larger group. The man sounded British, though it was hard to confirm from two words.

They must have been passengers on the bus. I could only surmise that the driver had pulled over to sleep, which meant they were traveling a great distance.

"Can I buy you a beer?" The man in a black cowboy hat stood across from me, his fingers eagerly gripping the chair. He had a square jawline like Henry Cavill and smoldering brown eyes that could undress a woman in a glance.

"Sure."

I couldn't afford to turn down anything free.

"What about a basket of fries instead?" I leaned back, hoping he'd consider the suggestion.

His eyebrows shot up at the request. The stubble on his face suited him. His age was hard to pin down—late thirties, possibly. He was handsome but not too handsome for his own good.

I'd seen my reflection in the bathroom, so clearly his only motive was to find company for the night.

"And what do I get?" he inquired.

"To sit down. Isn't that what you want?"

The man swaggered to the register and put in his order. Then he leaned against the counter and gave me a cocky grin—the kind that said, "You have no idea what you're in for."

Cocky men, I could handle. I'd lived with enough of them.

He returned with a basket of fries in one hand and a beer in the other. "Penelope, huh?" When he caught my perplexed expression, he explained, "The guy called out your order when you were in the bathroom. I'm the one who brought it to your table."

I shook pepper onto my fries and ate three. "Thanks."

"Do I get a tip?"

"Sure. Never do favors if you're only expecting a reward."

He frowned and sat back, crossing his arms. "That's not what I meant."

"I know. What's the logo on your shirt mean?"

He glanced down. The logo also appeared on the front. "Montana."

"Why are you advertising where you're from? Do they pay you for that?"

A guy at the center table sputtered with laughter.

"Where are *you* from?" Mr. Cowboy Hat asked.

I savored more of the hot fries before answering. "The North Pole."

"I hear it's cold up there." His eyes flicked to my backpack, then to my fries. "Been on the road long?"

"Are you with the tour bus?"

He rested his arms on the table. "Where I come from, we don't answer a question with a question."

"Then ask me something interesting. My travels aren't worth talking about."

More chuckles came from the center table. They were all listening.

"Mind your beeswax," he chided them, never moving his eyes from mine. Then he leaned in close and lowered his voice. "What's your real name?"

A fry slipped into the basket, and I accidentally bit my finger. Concerned about where the conversation was heading, I stood and zipped up my coat. "I need to get some shut-eye."

He sat back and tipped his hat at me.

"Nice chatting with you, Montana. Thanks for buying a lady fries." I pushed in my chair. "Good luck on your adventures."

I didn't say it with sarcasm. After all, he'd bought me food and a drink. I lifted my heavy bag, collected my fries, and left him the beer.

The corridor was just a short distance through the rain. Not only had Catcher devoured his meal, but he'd turned the container into confetti as well.

"You are worse than a toddler on a sugar high." I collected all the pieces and chucked them into the trash. Then I sat on my knees and wrapped my arms around the wolf's neck. "We can't stay out here," I told him, thinking about the Chitah. "It's too cold. I need to find a warm place tonight." After pulling away, I opened my backpack and took out the container with the hot dog. I added the fries to it and packed it up. "Stay here. I want to check out something."

I dashed across the parking lot toward the bus. The door was on the opposite side, so I walked around. *Aren't buses supposed to stop at bus stations when traveling across cities?* It must have been an independent company.

Cupping my hands around my eyes, I peered into the dark vehicle. Of course, it wouldn't be unlocked, but it was worth a try. I noticed a covered lock next to the door. My heart sank until I tried pulling the door anyway, and it opened. *What luck!*

Don't get excited yet. The bus driver might be sleeping inside.

I boarded the empty vehicle. "Hello? You left your door open."

The last thing I needed was to get thrown in jail with no one to bail me out.

No bags were in the overhead storage. Passengers must have taken their carry-ons to their rooms. Perhaps the driver forgot to lock up or assumed no one would steal a bus. *Is it even possible to steal a bus without the keys?*

Once I verified the bus was vacant, I stood at the door and whistled. Catcher bounded up to the vehicle, then ground to a halt. Standing in the drizzle, he sniffed the open doorway.

"Hurry up. It's empty, and you're letting in a draft."

He growled at the strange smells mingling in the stale air.

"It's just us," I promised him. "Please, Catcher. I need to sleep somewhere warm and dry. It's only nine o'clock. That means we have plenty of time to sleep and head out before anyone notices. They're not going to wake the passengers at three in the morning to leave." My eyelids were growing heavy.

Catcher reluctantly boarded, and I shut the door. While walking ahead of me, he sniffed every seat on his way to the back. The open space by the tiny bathroom appeared to have had the seats removed. Deciding I'd rather stretch out on the floor, I tossed my backpack down and sat. Once I removed my wet coat, I turned it inside out and rolled it into a pillow. Then I put on a grey sweater for extra warmth.

I didn't need a blanket. I had Catcher.

After checking things out, Catcher shook his coat and then lay down beside me. Though he was wet, warmth radiated from him like a furnace.

I dried his fur with a T-shirt from my bag. "You shouldn't have come on this trip, you know."

He turned his head and licked my chin.

"I'm not a kid anymore."

But it didn't matter. As long as he sensed I needed him, Catcher would remain my watchdog. Now I was a twenty-eight-year-old woman with a protector.

I rested my head on my jacket. "Soon, we'll be somewhere warm. Sunshine, blue skies—no more long and unbearable winters. Lots of opportunities. You'll see."

He groaned and put his head down. Catcher enjoyed running through the snow, so warm weather didn't sway him.

"The north has nothing for me." I slid my arm over his body and yawned. "People think I'm crazy for wanting to live in a pack. Do you think I'm crazy?"

His tail thumped once, and he whined.

"My mom once told me a pack is the safest place you can be. Oh, Catcher. I just want a family again."

Catcher was the only one who made me feel truly safe, but he couldn't be my watchdog forever. He had a life of his own to live.

Maybe I should have left him behind, but the thought of traveling alone terrified me.

My thoughts drifted to a crystalline memory of a trip I'd taken with my parents to Mount Rushmore when I was nine. I remembered little about the mountain and everything about the car ride—my mom singing the *Grease* soundtrack, and my dad complaining that she was distracting his driving. He wore mirrored sunglasses, and he slid them down and rolled his eyes at me in the rearview mirror each time my mother hit a high note. That trip was shortly before my dad died from a heart attack. Mom never sang in the car after that. When he died, a part of her died with him.

Funny how my early memories were filled with sunshine, and all the memories since became cloudy skies and winter. Perhaps our minds play tricks on us and we paint all the good stuff with sunshine.

Seems like a million years ago since I was that little girl. I'd barely gotten to know my father, so I clung to what memories remained. Those were the days of innocence—long before I had my first heartbreak, my first job, my graduation, my first pack. Long before Mom died of cancer.

Long before I found out I was a Potential.

CHAPTER 2

Startled awake by Catcher's vicious barks, I bolted upright. I knew all his vocalizations, and the fear of him mauling a human terrified me.

Before I could stand, the barking abruptly stopped.

"Catcher?"

He trotted back to me, his eyes alert and his tail straight. Something was up.

I rubbed my eyes while I stood.

"Catcher! Why didn't you wake me? It's already dawn."

I'd slept all night. *No wonder* I felt rested.

The top of someone's head poking out from one of the seats made me freeze.

We weren't alone.

Time to go.

Thunder rumbled as I lifted my bag and jacket. Sensing my intent, Catcher hustled to the front of the bus. I moved past the gentleman on the right, and as soon as I reached his seat, he spoke.

"You should stay."

I paused in the aisle. "I don't have a ticket."

"You don't need one." His voice had a rich timbre, one that made my hair stand on end, and when I turned, I recognized the dark sunglasses.

"All buses need tickets," I pointed out.

"Not this one."

Intrigued, I set down my bag and sat in the seat across the aisle. "What do you mean?"

He lowered his sunglasses so that I could see his citrine eyes.

A knot formed in the pit of my stomach from his powerful gaze.

His nostrils flared as he took in my scent. "Your travel buddy's more than just a wolf. Isn't that right?"

Lying to a Chitah was an exercise in futility. "Yes. How did you keep him from tearing you apart?"

He lowered his armrest. "Shifters and Chitahs aren't so different. I just let him believe he's in charge so that he doesn't feel threatened. That'll keep him off my ass."

Chitahs, especially the trackers, wore running shoes. I glanced at his black sneakers, unable to mask my concern. It was difficult to tell anything about him. He wore a soft leather jacket, a black button-up, and skinny jeans. *Does he have any weapons?*

He took another deep breath. "Your emotions are making me dizzy, but what I can't figure out is your Breed. You're *not* a Shifter."

"So?"

He faced forward and laced his fingers over his stomach. "I'm curious about why a wolf would spend his time running around with another Breed."

For all the guy knew, I could be a Relic, a Mage, or even a Sensor. Since it was impolite to ask someone's Breed, most people liked to suss out the truth if they couldn't visibly identify a person.

My heart thumped. *Was he sent to find me?* My gut said no. I glanced out the window at large puddles in the parking lot and thought about how run-down and dirty the motel looked in the daytime.

"You should stick around," he said again. "I smell a storm coming."

An invitation for a mysterious bus ride from a Chitah? No, thanks. Especially if the bus is on its way to Breed jail. The guy had a borderline-hostile expression, and those sharp cheekbones weren't doing him any favors.

I stood. "I appreciate the concern, but we have to get moving."

He put his sunglasses back on. "Best of luck, female."

When he didn't follow me off the bus, I sighed with relief. Strangers could be sources of help or threats. Women went missing all the time. Catcher protected me, but that also meant fewer rides.

After putting on my jacket and flipping up the hood, I whistled for Catcher, who was peeing in a patch of grass. He trotted toward me, more alert than usual. The Chitah had him rattled.

"I know," I said, hiking up the road. "But if he were after us, he would have done something by now. Let's get moving. We have a long day ahead."

Two hours later, we'd made progress. Rain assailed us like enemy fire, and lightning threaded across the sky like cracks in a glass dome. The crashing thunder spooked Catcher, making him crouch each time it happened. After a while, the rain blew sideways into my face. My hood didn't do much to stop it either.

I tried thumbing a ride from two semi-trucks, but neither stopped. One trucker honked as he barreled down the road.

Catcher barked at me when I attempted to sit down and rest after a sneeze attack.

"I know! But where? We're in the middle of nowhere."

Open plains surrounded us. There were no gas stations, no farms, no restaurants, no nothing. If it weren't raining, Catcher might be able to sniff out a local farm where we could seek shelter in a barn or shed. As it stood, visibility was nonexistent.

"*Why?*" I shouted at the sky. "Why do you punish me? I never complain!"

Catcher barked at me.

"Fine. I complain to *you*, but that doesn't count."

Whoever was in charge sure didn't want me to catch a break. *What if this is a sign to go back?*

God no. I could never go back.

Catcher barked behind me. I looked over my shoulder at headlights from a large vehicle heading our way. A trucker had told me they had a policy about picking up hitchhikers, which was why most of them passed by. I didn't want to get anyone fired, but I also had no wish to die in the middle of nowhere. Traveling on foot wasn't something I'd ever done, so nothing had prepared me for the utter exhaustion or the blisters on my feet.

I stood and frantically waved my arms. "Please, stop!"

After coughing a few times, I lowered my arms and gave up. "Get out of the way. He's not slowing down."

Catcher moved off the road with me as the vehicle sped past us. Surprised, I saw it was the bus from earlier. After it shot by, the brake lights flashed, and it came to a stop.

I looked down at Catcher. "What do you think? Don't give me that look. We're going."

Air hissed from the bus like an angry dragon. The rain battered my face, making me quicken my step to the door.

When it opened, people were arguing.

The driver faced the passengers. She seemed young for a bus driver and a little punk rock with the sides of her short black hair shaved. "Listen up! While I *appreciate* everyone's concern, I need you to remember that this bus is registered to Naomi Burns. That means this baby is all mine," she said, patting a seat lovingly. "You're a guest in my house. If you want to challenge what I do with my property, you can take your ass outside and tell me all about it while I speed away to our next destination." Then she directed her comments to me. "Where're you headed?"

"How far can you take me?"

"Girl, I can take you all the way to Texas. Where's your next stop?"

"Anywhere that's dry."

She tipped her head to the side and studied Catcher. Then her eyes flicked up to me. "Is he..." She looked at Catcher again. "Tame?"

"He'll be fine. I promise." I wiped the rain off my face. "How much to get me to the next town?"

Naomi shook her head and stared up at the ceiling. "I must be out of my mind. Thought it was one of those huskies."

"He's tame," I assured her.

That wasn't entirely true, but Catcher wouldn't attack an innocent person.

She waved me up. "Come on in—no charge. Just keep the, uh... *dog* in check."

Catcher growled.

"I'll get the door," she said.

I stepped onto the bus and looked around at the familiar faces I'd seen in the restaurant the night earlier. A quick head count revealed there were about ten people, eight of them men. A few gave me icy stares. Others shifted in their leather seats to settle in for the long ride. Because of how spread apart the group was, I couldn't find a private spot.

"One surprise passenger is enough," someone in the back grumbled.

Naomi shot up in front of me. Her voice agitated, she said, "Our last stop was a *designated* pickup location. My job is to get you from A to B to C. I wasn't given any special orders about who's allowed and who's not. Now, shut your punk ass up before I put you out in the rain." She held her stance before turning to the front. "I have snacks for everyone at ten. My treat." Naomi nodded at Catcher, who was still standing outside. "Is he coming in?"

I locked eyes with Catcher. The bus was our best option, and he needed to recognize that.

With a growl, he reluctantly boarded. I let Catcher walk ahead and pick out our seat since it was better that he decide where neutral ground was.

After shaking water off his coat, he hopped onto a window seat across the aisle from a couple. I shoved my wet backpack into the tight overhead storage, then took off my jacket.

"Gracious! You're soaked to the bone," the pretty woman said. Her champagne curls were loose and soft, as if she'd taken them out of big rollers and ran her fingers through them.

I squeezed out the ends of my dripping hair before sitting.

The lady stood and pulled out a travel bag.

When the bus accelerated, I watched Catcher to make sure he settled down. He sat stoically, in full protection mode.

I ran my hands over my wet jeans.

"Here, take this." The woman offered me a white towel.

"Thank you so much." After soaking up the water from my hair, I pushed the towel against my pants to pick up some of the rain.

"No one should be out in weather like this," the woman said. "My name's Joy."

Finally settled, I gave her my attention. Joy was beautiful and soft-spoken. She strongly resembled Marilyn Monroe and was probably in her midforties. A deep scar on her forehead stretched from her hairline to her right eyebrow, and she didn't cover it with makeup or her hair.

Her blue eyes sparkled with curiosity.

"Nice to meet you," I replied.

"This is my... husband. Salem."

The man by the window acknowledged me with a cursory glance. A few strands had come loose from his top knot. His beard was combed straight, though it wasn't cleaned up around the edges. The aloof look in his eyes told me he wasn't a people person like his wife.

"Are those knitting needles?" I asked.

"It's a hobby I picked up." She lifted the green yarn on her lap. "I'm working on a scarf. It helps pass the time."

"That takes patience."

"There's a bathroom in the back," she said, gesturing behind us. "Do you have anything dry to wear? I can lend you something that might fit, but you should get out of those wet clothes."

That seemed like a good idea, except that I would be leaving Catcher unsupervised. If anyone provoked him, nothing would stop him from going for the jugular. "I'll change at the next stop."

"Are you sure, honey? You'll catch your death." She looked at her husband. "Salem, tell her she'll catch her death."

"I think you mean death of cold," he remarked. "A cold is a virus, so you can't catch it from the rain."

Joy stroked the base of her throat while staring at my wet jeans. Her brow knitted. She seemed like a compassionate old soul.

Deciding to put her at ease, I said, "I'm just glad to be out of the rain."

"It's something, isn't it? It feels like we're on Noah's Ark."

"And I brought the animal," I quipped.

Joy had a bubbly laugh that made her cheeks rosy, but she kept her mouth closed like a cork on a champagne bottle.

"Do you mind if I use this on him?" I asked her, holding up the towel. "It'll pick up dog hair."

"No, of course not. Go right ahead. I'll shake it out."

As I brushed the towel over Catcher, he licked my cheek but was too antsy to sit still. When I wiped his large paws, he sprang over me and sat down at the front of the bus to monitor everyone.

Typical Catcher.

Joy touched my arm. "How long have you had him?" she asked, her voice brimming with concern.

"Years."

Her eyes widened, and she snapped her hand back. "You can't be serious!" Then she looked at her husband. "She can't be serious, can she?"

Joy was clearly a person who didn't agree with owning a wolf, so it was best to avoid further discussion. "I think you're right about my wet clothes. I should change." After folding up the towel, I handed it to her. "Thanks. I really appreciate your kindness."

When I stood, I collected my backpack, then I headed to the rear. The sound of Catcher's toenails clicking against the floor behind me rattled my nerves.

Please, please, don't chew off anyone's face.

Avoiding eye contact with the passengers, I made it to the tiny bathroom and shut myself inside.

Great. No light.

Changing pants without tumbling out the door took finesse. After peeling off my wet jeans, I managed to slide on my black cargo pants. When I heard a clamor, I opened the door to check it out.

A few men were on their feet.

Catcher snarled, his body rigid and his posture aggressive.

But they weren't looking at him. They were looking at me.

I stood beside the wolf. "As long as you don't provoke him, he won't bite. We'll sit back here. How's that?" I sneezed and looked down. "Catcher, please sit."

"That isn't a pet," a muscular man growled. "She's walking around like it's a fucking pet!"

Thunder crashed above us like a bomb, and Joy shrieked.

"Maybe things aren't what they appear," the Chitah suggested.

The muscular guy with all the tattoos glared at Montana T-shirt guy. "You sat with her."

Montana shook his head.

Then something occurred to me. Unable to say it aloud, I approached the Chitah and whispered, "Is everyone here like you?"

A smile played on his lips.

After straightening up, I gave everyone a thorough appraisal.

Chitahs and Vampires were easy to spot, but most Breeds looked like everyone else. Sometimes I could pick up on behaviors, but I hadn't spent enough time around these people to even guess.

"He's not a pet," I informed the mob. "He's my watchdog."

A handsome blond man lifted his fedora before sitting. "All aboard the crazy train!"

Catcher nudged me from behind, but I wouldn't let him pass until I defused the situation.

"We'll mind our business if you mind yours," I said. "We just need a ride to the next stop—wherever that is."

But the muscular guy wouldn't let it go. He stroked his beard as if trying to smooth the untrimmed mess down. "I say we dump her *and* the mutt."

Catcher snarled and barked so ferociously that everyone except for Montana and the wrestler-looking guy sat down.

When the bus lurched to a stop, I realized our short ride was coming to a predictable end.

Naomi strutted to the center of the bus and stretched out her arms on the seats beside her. This time, her voice was level and friendly. "Ladies and gentlemen, please fasten your seat belts and place your bags in a secure location. I'm not playin'. Miss, if you want to debus, that's your choice. You're *more* than welcome to stay until we pull over for lunch. I don't make a point of throwing people out in a biblical flood." She turned her attention back to everyone else. "Estimated arrival time in Wichita is less than five hours, depending on the weather. We should make it to Dallas by tonight, as long as we keep to my schedule. My job is to stop at the designated locations and pick up *anyone* who wants to board."

"She didn't ask to board," Mr. Wrestler pointed out.

Naomi held a mirthless smile. "If you wanna sit here and argue, we can do that. I'll charge an extra fee for our late arrival to the alpha who hired me. How 'bout that?"

The two men sat down without another word.

I approached Naomi. "Did you say Dallas?"

I'd never been that far south, but I'd heard there were a lot of packs in Texas, so the temptation was strong. Especially if it meant getting as far away from home as possible.

She canted her head, her brown eyes dancing with amusement. "There's plenty of room. I'm getting paid by the day to pick up however many passengers we can fit in here. No sweat off my back."

"Would that be okay? I'd love to go to Dallas."

Naomi gave me a skeptical appraisal. "You're more than welcome as long as you can keep these boys in line while I'm driving." She jumped when a thunderclap made the windows vibrate. "Lord help me, I don't get paid enough for this. Your friend can sit wherever he wants, but you can't stay on the floor. It's a safety issue. Sorry I called him a dog, but you looked human. Can't be too sure these days."

"Thanks."

I wanted to dance down the aisle. No more hitchhiking, no more sleeping in the cold, and best of all, Catcher could get the rest he deserved.

After ushering him to the back, I knelt before him. With my hands wrapped around his snout, I stared into his hazel eyes so that he would know we were having a serious talk.

"I need you to stay back here. I'm fine. I promise. No one's going to try anything stupid on a bus filled with people. This is your chance to get some sleep. We'll be in Dallas soon."

His tongue slipped out between his teeth, and he licked my chin. I kissed his nose and stood. Instead of returning to the front of the bus, I chose the seat closest to him and put my bag by the window. When the bus began moving, my nerves calmed.

After a few minutes, Montana approached without his cowboy hat on. Keeping his hands in the pockets of his tan coat, he watched Catcher, who growled at him from the back. "Mind if I sit?"

I shrugged.

He made slow movements while he sat down across the aisle. "I take it that's your friend who ordered the burgers."

"Oh, that reminds me." I reached into my backpack and pulled out the container with the hot dog. After tossing it to Catcher, I started on the fries.

Montana frowned. "Are those from last night?"

"They're stale, but my stomach doesn't know the difference."

"If he's your watchdog, why doesn't he hunt for you?"

"He hunts for himself. I can't skin or cook a rabbit. Besides, we were eating pretty good until the past two days. I have to keep track of my spending."

The handsome man was studying me much too hard.

I stared back. "Ask."

"Are you a Shifter?"

"No."

He peered behind the seat at Catcher. "I don't get it. Watchdogs only watch our own kind."

That meant Montana was a Shifter.

"Why doesn't he shift?"

I sneezed and wiped my nose. "Because he won't. I can't make him."

"That's dangerous."

"Not for me."

Montana wiped his face as if frustrated by my answer.

I looked at his tan coat and lace-up boots. Maybe I'd come to the wrong conclusion about him the night before. I just saw him as a nosy man who wanted to get into my pants. The nosy part, I'd gotten right, but he didn't seem like a bad person. "What's your name?"

"James. Thanks to you, everyone's calling me Montana now. What's yours? Because it sure as hell isn't Penelope."

"What makes you say that?"

"Because you don't look like a Penelope."

I chuckled softly. "What does a Penelope look like?"

His gaze raked over me. "Not you. What's your name?"

"I suppose Penelopes are pretty girls with wavy blond hair and big blue eyes?"

"There you go again, answering a question with a question. Tell me your name."

"Trouble."

His eyes twinkled. "Is that with a lowercase or capital *T*?"

I nibbled on my bottom lip to stop myself from laughing. "It's Robyn."

"How do I know you're telling the truth?"

"May lightning strike me dead if I'm not."

Just then, a clap of thunder rattled the bus while rain hammered against the roof.

James chuckled, and it turned into a rolling laugh. He gave me a sexy smile. "I guess if you're still alive, I'll have to take your word for it."

"Where's your final destination?" I asked, curious about their journey.

"Austin, I think. To be honest, I'm not really sure. They didn't publish an address in the ad. I called the number, and they arranged for a bus to collect everyone."

It sounded like a job. "What about your cars?"

"Had to sell them or leave them with someone."

I cleared my throat. "And all your personal things?"

"People either put it in storage or sold it. I think most folks like the idea of starting over. There's no guarantee we'll get to stay. It's a trial period." He scratched the top of his left hand, drawing my attention to a scar. *No, not a scar. A burn mark shaped like the letter* C *with two lines on the bottom. Maybe* CH?

"What's down there?"

James turned his gaze out the window. "A second chance."

Following an awkward silence, he got up and returned to his seat.

Second chance. That wasn't really what I was looking for. I only wanted one chance at choosing my own destiny.

James reappeared and extended his hand. "Here. Think nothing of it."

After he walked away, I stared down at a family-sized bag of peanut M&M's.

CHAPTER 3

When we reached Wichita, Kansas, Naomi dropped us off at Kentucky Fried Chicken so that she could gas up or service the vehicle. Behind the building, 18-wheelers were parked by a grove of trees, which was a good place for Catcher to wait. I trusted him. Wolves knew how to take care of themselves.

After leaving him, I walked inside and noticed everyone lined up at the counter. Instead of joining them, I took a seat at a curved counter with tall chairs. Having a full night's sleep had made such a huge difference. I hadn't felt this relaxed in a week—actually, much longer than that if I counted the stressful period before I'd left home.

The Chitah appeared to my left and folded his arms on the counter. "You should get in line and order."

"I'm not hungry."

"That's a lie." He dipped his chin, revealing his golden eyes over the top of his sunglasses. I'd never seen a Chitah with dark eyebrows, and though his eyes were beautiful, they watched me like a predator's.

"Naomi's cookies filled me up."

He had striking features. With the knit hat covering his hair, and the sunglasses shielding his eyes, no one would know he was a Chitah, especially since he wasn't the desired height of six and a half feet. He fell on the shorter side at around five-ten.

But he was no less intimidating.

"Cookies aren't a meal," he said.

"The truth is I'm saving my money. I can't spend everything I have, and this place is out of my budget. Maybe you guys should have considered that some of your passengers might not have money to throw around. No big deal. I might walk over to the gas station and check out their selection."

He stood there for a beat before returning to the counter. Eventually, everyone received their meals and picked a table in the spacious room.

James stole the chair to my right and placed his hat on the counter. "Mind if I sit here?"

"Not at all. Thanks for the candy. I left the bag in your seat."

"They were a gift."

"I know. But too much chocolate makes me sick." I smiled at his full tray. "Hungry?"

He removed his plate of fried chicken, green beans, and corn from the tray. Then he opened up a box of extra chicken. "Take one."

"Says the guy who expects favors in return."

He picked up a chicken breast and set it on a napkin in front of me. "You look hungry enough to gnaw the rubber off a tire."

A pang of guilt for eating the man's lunch didn't stop me from devouring that delicious fried chicken in less than thirty seconds. When there wasn't any meat left on the bone, I wiped my greasy fingers on the napkin.

"Why are you being nice to me?"

Setting down his soda, he said, "With green eyes like yours, it's hard not to be."

I stole a glance at his hat. The distressed material appeared to be felt, and the brim wasn't wide, but it suited him so well that I couldn't imagine him without it. "Are people really calling you Montana? I'm sorry about that."

"I'm not."

"Should I call you James?"

He picked up a chicken leg and rested his elbows on the counter. "A new start deserves a new name."

"Then Montana, it is. What's in Austin? Or is it a big secret I'm not allowed to know? You mentioned an ad, so I'm guessing it's about a job."

Montana swallowed a mouthful of chicken. "There's an alpha starting up a new pack. He put out a call for anyone who wants to join. Serious inquiries only."

Surprised, I twisted in my seat. "Why would you travel so far? Alphas start new packs all the time in every city."

"Yeah. Green alphas. Most of them are young, and they usually bring over people from the old pack. Shifters my age want a reputable leader who's resourceful and trustworthy. Someone a little more qualified."

"You don't even know him. He could be a complete psychopath."

Montana choked on his corn, then washed it down with soda. "I doubt it. Do you think I'd travel this far on a whim?"

I nibbled on a seasoned crumb. "What's so special about this guy?"

"Ever heard of Shikoba?"

I shook my head.

"He's a gemstone dealer among the tribes. To say he's successful would be an understatement. His son is the one starting a pack. If anyone has prospects, it's this guy."

"I thought the tribes didn't let outsiders in."

Montana cleaned the meat off another chicken leg. "There's an online Breed news site in Austin, but anyone with a subscription can view it. The woman who runs it inspired people to create their own private sites. Anyhow, the details were slim. I asked around, and not many people were interested."

"I can see why. Some random guy—"

"No, that's not it." Montana wiped his fingers on a napkin. "For one, he's Native. Plenty of Shifters don't jell with Natives because of history and land disputes. The rest don't understand their ways and have concerns about why he's breaking away from his tribe. The vast majority of people don't want to leave their homes. They've got family in nearby packs. Shifters grow roots. I bet he's already screened the locals and ruled them out, so he's casting a wider net to see what he can catch. I respect that. It shows he's not gonna settle for local leftovers."

While I didn't know the man, Montana didn't strike me as impulsive. *What is his story?* Packs could be selective. Some Shifters sat on waiting lists for powerful Packmasters. They waited until a young Shifter left or someone mated outside the pack. He could have also been rejected for some reason.

I rested my elbow on the counter and tucked my fist against my cheek. "You don't have the same concerns as everyone else?"

"Maybe I'm just... curious. A guy like this has connections. Do you know what kind of power those tribal leaders wield to lead hundreds of people? They keep their shit organized like beehives."

I waited for a minute while he finished his green beans. "Why do you think he left?"

"It could be Shikoba had one more alpha than his tribe needed, so someone had to go. I don't know, but we'll find out soon enough. Under that leadership, an alpha would have gleaned a ton of knowledge. His father would have groomed him, and that doesn't always happen with young alphas in the packs." Montana set down his fork. "I've got nothing to lose."

I gestured to the room. "So with all the training he had under his father's leadership, he's going to take in a bunch of random strangers?"

Montana wiped his mouth and turned to face me. "Alphas are selective. I don't think he's taking in everyone who shows up on his doorstep. My bet is there's a screening process or background check."

Montana's light-brown eyes reeled me in. They were the color of whiskey or tea, and my heart quickened when his tongue swiped a crumb on the corner of his mouth. "I'd invite you to come, but you're not a Shifter."

He wasn't just stating the facts—he was fishing around, trying to figure out my Breed. Immortals were always sizing one another up to see where they ranked in the supernatural food chain. Some Breeds were natural enemies. I had a feeling Montana was curious what Breed a wolf would be protecting and why.

I discreetly surveyed the room and lowered my voice. "So these people might be your future packmates? What do you know about them?"

Montana held his cup in front of his face while looking at the couple on the left. "You already met Joy and Salem. They seem all right. She does most of the talking, so I haven't gotten a feel for him yet."

I noticed that while Joy was enjoying her coleslaw, Salem hadn't touched his meal. "Why isn't he eating?"

"He doesn't eat until she's almost done."

"Why?"

"Beats me." Montana steered his gaze to the corner. "The guy in the sunglasses over there, I don't know anything about him. He boarded this morning."

"He came into the diner last night."

"I didn't notice."

"That's because you were too busy trying to hit on dripping-wet customers."

Montana chuckled. He had a pleasant smile, though it quickly vanished. "The blond guy wearing the shirt that says INTROVERT, that's Virgil. He's a wild card. Introverted, my ass."

The man in the brown fedora, which lacked a hatband, was the one on the bus who'd made the crazy-train comment. He looked like the sort of fellow who would buy a plot of land, build a cabin, and grow marijuana.

"The two guys sitting across from him are cousins."

One guy's head was shaved all around the sides and back but not the top. He bleached the ends of his brown hair and styled it in textured chunks. Unfortunately, I couldn't see his neck tattoos at this distance. It was hard to judge a man by his looks, but what I *did* notice was his warm smile. For me, a smile revealed a person's true self.

His cousin, on the other hand, was Lucifer in a leather jacket. He had long brown hair, a goatee, and arctic-blue eyes that made my pulse jump when he looked at me. I avoided men like him. People didn't acquire that steely-eyed gaze for no reason.

Montana broke his fluffy biscuit in half. "The blond guy with the undercut is Archer. I doubt he'll make the cut. The long-haired fellow is Krystopher."

"He doesn't look like a Krystopher."

"Whatever you say, *Robyn*. He spells it with a K-R-Y and goes by Krys. That's how he introduces himself to everyone."

"Everyone at that table should form a band." I tucked my chin into my palm. "Why do you think Archer won't make it?"

"He's only got one arm," Montana replied, his voice barely above a whisper. "Not many Packmasters want tripods. It's better if they're already in a pack when they lose a limb. I guess he wasn't, so that works against him."

I hadn't noticed he was missing an arm, especially since he was sandwiched between Krys and the wall. "What about the wrestler?"

Montana's eyes skated over to the muscular guy sitting in the center of the room. "Deacon? He's got—"

"Anger-management issues? I gathered. It's forty degrees outside, and he's dressed like he's going to the beach for spring break."

"I think he's a beta. He gives off beta energy, and he's always calling the shots like he's trying to lead the group. The thing is, we're not a pack. Nobody here should be making decisions for others, but since he doesn't do well with pushback, everyone goes along." Montana sucked his drink through the straw. "You can't trust a beta who's wound up that tight."

I watched the couple sitting by the windows on the right. The young woman held my interest because of her enviable lengthy hair. Her cornsilk-blond tresses reached her waist. I'd recently chopped my long hair, and cutting it felt like dismembering a part of myself, especially under the circumstances.

"Something isn't right with those two," I finally said.

Montana put down his chicken. "What makes you say that?"

"They don't seem like a couple in love. Look at their body language. She's always turned away from him, even though he's sitting next to her."

"That's because they're siblings."

I furrowed my brow at his coal-black hair and beard. While I didn't know their exact heights, I was five-seven, and the woman had seemed about the same when I was standing behind her on the bus. He was a little shorter. "They sure don't resemble each other."

"My sister was half black. Don't you have siblings?"

"No."

"They might not share the same parents. Or maybe they each favor a different one."

I sat back. "I'd make a terrible detective."

"Don't beat yourself up. It's not as easy as it looks. That's Ian and Serena. They're from England, but that's all I know. They keep to themselves."

I twisted my head and sneezed three times into my sleeve. Without thinking, I grabbed my used napkin and blew my nose. When I faced forward, Montana was giving me a peculiar look.

Most Breeds didn't get allergies, and they sure didn't get sick. Relics were the exception since they were closest to humans genetically.

I rubbed my nose. "There must be pepper in that chicken."

When he reached up to touch my face, I recoiled.

Montana tilted his head ever so slightly at my reaction. "There's a crumb on your nose. From the chicken." He dusted it off and sat back. "You're an interesting woman, Robyn. Tough and timid all at once."

I pulled money from my wallet and left it on the counter. "Can you order a piece of chicken? It's for Catcher. Boneless is better, if they have it."

"Where are you going?"

"I need to round him up before he wanders." I zipped up my winter coat, which was puffed out because of my sweater underneath. "Do you think it's warmer in Dallas?"

"Weatherman said it's sixty-five today."

"Sounds dreamy. Don't wait for me. Once I find him, we'll be on the bus."

If Naomi decided to leave soon, I didn't want to get left behind because of Catcher. At least the rain had let up.

When I reached the back of the restaurant, I jogged across to the far end of a large parking area. There were a dozen semi-trucks, and I guessed they used the stop for sleeping or eating.

"Catcher!" I called out.

The trees were tall and the brush dense. It was hard to tell how deep it was, but I sure didn't want any ticks. Off to the side was a hotel and a large field. *He could be anywhere.*

"Don't make me walk in there," I muttered.

My sharp whistle startled a bird out of a tree. Catcher would never cross a road unless he was chasing prey.

"You looking for someone?" a man with a gruff voice asked.

I twisted around and spotted a middle-aged guy waltzing over from the parking lot. He combed his brownish-grey beard with his fingers.

"My dog ran off."

"Dog, huh?" He cackled. "Yeah, they'll do that."

I whistled again and listened for his howl or bark.

"You want me to help you find him?"

"No. He's not good with strangers. But thanks." I hiked through the tall grass and weaved between two bushes. Beyond that, the shrubs were too high. I whistled again.

A twig snapped behind me. When the man approached, my stomach knotted.

Since I wasn't a Shifter, I rationalized everything like humans often did. While my instincts were sharp, my brain kept spinning with all kinds of theories. I had assumed he was a trucker I'd woken up. And maybe he was. But he also could have been some pervert looking for an opportunity.

Or maybe he was a nice man helping me find my dog.

Get out of here, my inner voice said.

I veered right to walk around him.

"Hold up." He caught my arm. "Where're you going? Told you I'd help you look. Don't you want me to find your dog?"

I tried to wrench my arm away, but his grip tightened.

"There's no need to act like that. I'm a nice guy doing you a favor. Is that any way to treat someone?"

"I don't want your help."

"Maybe you do, and you just don't know it yet."

Catcher lunged from the brush and knocked the man's arm away. Instead of ripping him apart, Catcher protected me. His ferocious barks and snarls sent the man reeling backward.

"Get him away from me!"

"You'd better take off while you can," I warned him. "He hasn't had his lunch yet."

"You shouldn't have that thing. It ain't right." The man stumbled over a root and fell onto his back.

When I clicked my tongue, Catcher sat down and growled. It was against the law to kill humans, even in wolf form. I hoped he knew that.

"Let him go," I said quietly but firmly.

But Catcher lunged, his front legs spread as if he were going to attack. The man scurried backward, scrambled to his feet, and fled. To my relief, the wolf didn't chase him.

Catcher circled around me, sniffing the air to make sure I was okay.

I coughed to clear my throat. "I could have outrun this guy, you know. His cholesterol would have killed him before he caught up with me."

Catcher snorted.

"You just love disagreeing with me," I said while trudging through the brush. "Next time, don't make me come get you. What took you so long? Did you find a girlfriend out there? Some sexy little poodle?"

Catcher jumped against me before running ahead.

Despite my playful admonishment, I couldn't imagine what I would do without him. Catcher had sacrificed years of his life as my guardian. But he was right. That one snort told me he didn't think I was ready to be on my own. I needed to trust my instincts and toughen up if I wanted to live with a pack again.

If only I weren't human.

CHAPTER 4

The bus ride from Wichita to Dallas was lengthy. Joy lent me a magazine to thumb through, but like everyone else, I disappeared into my thoughts. Though Dallas sounded great, I didn't have a single connection, let alone know anything about the local packs. It would take time to identify the reputable ones, and they might not be interested in a trusted human. The odds of anyone taking me in were slim. Packs mostly stuck with their own.

I'd seen exceptions, usually someone mating a different animal or interbreeding. Other times, that person was a valuable contributor. I had to figure out what I could offer a pack and how to sell myself. *What if I joined this group? What do I have to lose?* Even if they rejected me, I would have already established a few connections. Joy and I could keep in touch, and she could give me inside information on the area packs, assuming she was accepted. It wouldn't solve my immediate need for shelter and work, but the Packmaster could point me in the right direction. If I wanted to live with Breed, I needed to work with them. The uncertainty left me anxious.

One crisis at a time.

That was something my father used to say and a motto I lived by.

After parking the bus, Naomi got up and beamed. "You have arrived at your *almost*-final destination. Naomi needs a drink."

Virgil stood and stretched out his arms. "Where are we?"

"Collin County."

"Is that Dallas?"

She pulled a bag from behind her seat. "Close enough. This is the last designated pick-up location. It just so happens I know the gentleman who runs the motel, and he gives discounts for Breed. Now, with that said, if anyone wants to save money and sleep on the bus, I'll leave it unlocked. But if you change your mind, tell me as soon as possible." She turned a sharp eye toward the long-haired Krystopher, implying he might have been the reason the bus had stayed unlocked the previous night. "We're only a few hours away from our final destination, so we'll leave bright and early. The Packmaster doesn't want anyone rolling in on his property at three in the morning, and I get it."

Virgil looked at the dark parking lot. "You said drinks. Where's the bar?"

She reached for her purse. "It's underground. I want everyone on their best behavior. The motel is brand-new and open to humans. He can't discriminate if he wants to stay in business. The bar, however, *is* Breed only. You can shift outside, but stay in the woods." She pulled a tube of lipstick from her purse and applied it without a mirror. "Do me a favor and don't start any trouble in the motel. The cops would love nothing more than to lock your asses up. Naomi doesn't bail people out of jail... *or* the pound."

"How do you get to the bar?" Virgil whined.

"There's a trail behind the motel that leads into the woods. When you reach the end, keep going until you see the barn. That's it. Just go right in. They only serve alcohol. If you're hungry, you'll need to order a pizza delivered to your room. They got two vending machines in the front office. Naomi also doesn't lend money."

Joy pulled her bag from the overhead. "I'm still full from dinner. I could pop right out of these pants!"

A few people chuckled as they collected their things. We had stopped near the Oklahoma-Texas border for Mexican food. Spicy food didn't agree with Catcher, so I'd walked over to Sonic for hot dogs. Feeding a wolf wasn't easy. They had voracious appetites and required a certain amount of food each day. I hoped he could do some real hunting either around the motel or at our next stop.

I left my bag on board. Even if someone stole it, they wouldn't make off with much more than dirty clothes, an extra pair of shoes, a map, and a sketchpad. I kept valuables, such as photographs and money, in my purse.

Catcher and I were the last off the bus. While everyone headed to the motel to check in and put up their bags, I walked around the building and crossed the parking lot.

"There's a highway nearby," I informed him. "Don't get lost, okay? After I check out the bar, I'm heading back to the bus for some shut-eye. Will you be back?"

Catcher woofed before loping off. He had to hunt, and the night air was making him restless.

Once I found the barn, Catcher dashed into the dark woods. He wasn't a pet. We didn't cuddle, and I didn't make a habit of petting him in a way that implied he was a subordinate. If he lay down next to me, it was to either keep me warm or reassure me. I didn't teach him tricks or give him commands unless it was to prevent an incident. All I could do was hope he made smart choices.

There weren't any lights to guide a person to the barn.

"What am I doing?" I asked myself. "If I'm in a horror movie, this is the part where the audience is screaming for me to go back. But here I am, walking around in the dark woods and going into a barn."

I jumped back when a man yanked the door open.

"Whatcha doin' out here?" he asked.

I glanced at the flashlight in his hand. "Is this the bar?"

"What's the secret word?"

I blinked. "Forget it."

He cackled. "Come on, darlin'. I'm just havin' a little fun. You wouldn't believe how many people try to guess." After closing the door, he shined the light on the floor and guided me to a closet in the middle of the barn. "We have to keep nosy humans from wandering in here. Especially kids and dog walkers. This place is for the locals, but sometimes, we get travelers like you passing through."

"How do you know I'm not local?"

He leaned against a wooden door in the heart of the room. "I know *all* the locals. We get 'em from Fort Worth, Dallas, and even a few in Rockwall."

"Aren't there other Breed bars they can go to?"

"Tons. Most of the customers used to live around here. They like to pop in every once in a while to hang out with their buddies."

"My friend is running in the woods. Is that okay?"

He gripped the handle. "So long as he doesn't venture past the piss lines."

Shifter wolves marked territories, so I knew exactly what he meant.

The man twirled his flashlight. "Have fun."

"Don't you get cold standing in here all night?"

He shined the light in his black Vampire eyes.

I stepped back. "Why do you need the flashlight?"

Vampires had impeccable night vision, from what I knew of them.

"So you don't fall on your ass. Unless, of course, *you* can see in the dark too. Would you like me to turn it off?"

I walked through the door to get away from him as quickly as possible. "Thanks."

Though it wasn't loud, I could hear music coming from below. Wall lanterns in the stairwell guided my way. A strong drink sounded good. *I've gotten myself this far and deserve a reward.*

The concrete steps emptied into a wide hall with a padded door. When I opened it, the smell of stale cigarettes and pine air freshener drifted out. Low lighting created a relaxing atmosphere, as did the slow country song playing. I was temporarily distracted by the wall décor of bull horns, license plates, old photographs, and the state flag of Texas.

I shimmied up to a barstool on the right and sat. It was fairly busy, so I waited patiently, listening to music and people-watching.

A stout bartender with a bushy red beard greeted me. "Haven't seen you in here before. What'll it be?"

A gin and tonic was my usual, but I wanted something different. "What's good?"

He cracked a smile. "Can't visit Texas without having my world-famous margarita."

"Sounds perfect. Do I look like I'm from somewhere else?"

"Not everyone around here has an accent. But I'm assuming you're with her, and that means you're from out of town."

I twisted around.

Naomi strutted in just as cool as could be in her leather pants. The sleeves on her button-up were rolled to the elbows, and hoop earrings swung from her ears. Her red lipstick matched her blouse, which shimmered like silk. "Hey, y'all! Naomi's here."

A few in the back whistled.

She scooted into a chair next to me. "Russ, I'll have the usual."

"Comin' right up, sweetheart. We missed you!"

"I might need to expand the company and hire drivers. Life is keeping me busy."

"I hear that."

Naomi was giving off a vibe that drew people to her. "So, what's your story?" she asked me. "A girl walking in the rain with a wolf? There's gotta be a story."

"I'm just looking for change."

"Aren't we all?"

The bartender switched on the noisy blender.

I leaned in close. "Can I ask you something?"

"Shoot."

"Are you also joining the pack that everyone's going to see?"

Naomi stirred with laughter. "Girl, no. Do I look like I belong in a pack?" She gave me a cocksure smile. "I'm a human. I've been transporting Breed for years. It's good money. *Easy* money."

"Isn't it dangerous?"

"I get a few bad apples, but most people who take the bus aren't depraved. They're people looking for a new life in a new town. They're escaping something... or someone. I've learned how to handle my passengers. My bus, my rules. I also keep a pistol by my seat."

Russ set a red drink in front of her. "House special."

That usually meant they spiked the drink with sensory magic.

She took a sip and wiggled in her chair, her shoulders hunched. "Naomi's been missing your touch."

He laughed, his eyes turning into slivers. "Rules haven't changed. You get one beer after that. No more."

"This is all I need," she assured him.

"You always say that, then I catch women buying you drinks."

She scoped out the room. "Chill out, Russ. Pickings are slim tonight. But you know I don't discriminate against men."

"*One* beer," he reiterated.

When the group from our bus filed in, the bartender and server kicked into action. I noticed Virgil ordering the same drink as Naomi. He tried asking for a second, but the bartender sent him away.

Naomi set down her glass. "Back to the story. Not everyone has a car, especially in big cities. Airline tickets are pricey. If you want the truth, most immortals don't like traveling with humans. Especially Shifters. Can you imagine if someone's panther wanted to come out on a plane? It's risky and happens to the best of them when there's turbulence. Then they have to get a Vampire on the scene to scrub everyone's memories. But these days, humans love taking videos on their phones. Everything is a story to them. It's all about the likes and shares. They don't know no better." She sipped her drink. "Technology is either going to force Breed out of the closet or put them in positions of power where they get rid of all these video phones. You watch."

"Maybe coming out wouldn't be so bad."

She snorted. "I used to think like you. I have no problem with immortals, so why should anyone else? Don't give humans credit they don't deserve. You see how divided they are. Beatin' each other's asses at the grocery store for a parking place. It would be a war. If humans don't slaughter you all, they'll dissect you in labs to get some of that power. That's a world I don't want to live in."

"Is it only Shifters you transport?"

"Not always, but they're my best customers. That's why I ripped a few seats out of the back of the bus. Sometimes I'll get a family or pack who reserves the entire bus. People like their privacy. Since we can't stop for hours at a time so that they can shift, I let them do it in the back. As long as they don't piss on my bus, we're cool. But I don't have time to pull over whenever someone gets the itch to switch. Throws off my schedule."

The bartender set a margarita in front of me. I licked the salt on the rim before tasting the drink. "Mmm."

"What did I tell you?" he said with a wink. "Give a shout when you want another."

I took out my wallet. "This is all I'm having." I glanced up at the prices he'd listed on the wall and set down the bills along with a tip. Most Breed bars handled cash. Some allowed regulars to have an account with them with a line of prepaid credit. A few accepted credit cards, but mostly, those were ones that also served humans.

Naomi bumped my shoulder. "Have a little fun. You look like you need it."

I spotted the Chitah sitting by the entrance, his sunglasses still on. Something had plagued my thoughts ever since the conversation I'd had with Montana. "Is it okay if I sleep on the bus?"

She collected her drink and hopped to her feet. "There's a blanket over the back of my seat that I cover my lap with. Just don't get it dirty." Strutting off, she called, "Hey, Walter! How's my favorite plumber? Hope you brought your dancing shoes, because Naomi is feeling *good* tonight!"

I carried my margarita to the table. "Mind if I sit?"

The Chitah popped open the cap on his soda bottle.

Taking a seat, I wrinkled my nose when he poured a package of salted peanuts into his Coke. "Why are you doing that?"

"It's a Southern thing."

I hadn't picked up on any distinguishable accent. "Are you from the South?"

"Nope. I saw it in a movie."

The music changed over to Willie Nelson.

"What's your name?" I asked. He didn't seem to be the friendliest guy who wanted attention, but I had questions.

He lifted his head, revealing his masculine jaw. "Lucian." The name rolled off his tongue like a purr.

I drank my margarita, which was in a wide-brimmed glass. "I'm Robyn. Robyn Wolfe." After removing the lime wedge from the rim, I sucked on it, then set it on a napkin.

He chuckled softly and gulped down his soda. "Robyn Wolfe but not a wolf. I can tell you've never had a margarita."

"Can I ask you something?"

"A question doesn't require permission. It's either answered or ignored."

I touched the narrow stem on my glass. "Why are you going to Austin? Are you with this group or just hitching a ride?"

"I chose to come. Whether I'm *with* this group remains to be seen."

"But you're a Chitah. Montana said a Packmaster placed the ad."

"And?"

It was hard to read him with those sunglasses on. I could only go by the annoyance coloring his tone. "Um... I just didn't think a Chitah would want to live with Shifters."

He leaned in close, tilting his head down enough that I could see his golden eyes. "You don't think they'll *want* a Chitah."

"And you do?"

"An opportunity worth having is a chance worth taking." He took another swig of his drink and crunched on the peanuts. "I read that on a fortune cookie."

I glanced over at Joy and Salem, who were seated near Montana and Virgil. "If you want to live in a pack, you need to run with the pack. These might be your future packmates, and you're isolating yourself from them."

He looked over his shoulder in their direction, then shook his head. "I need to get there first. Then we can mingle."

When Lucian faced forward again, something occurred to me. He didn't *want* the others to know he was a Chitah. His average stature didn't make it obvious, and he concealed his eyes behind dark sunglasses.

Why would a Chitah choose to live with a pack of wolves? As curious as I was to press him on the matter, it wasn't my place to judge. In fact, Lucian inspired me to say something aloud that I'd been mulling over. "Do you think they would mind if I tagged along? I want to check it out."

He canted his head. "Do you need their permission?"

"Not really. Only the Packmaster's opinion matters."

"Raise hell." He held up his cola and tipped it against my glass.

Deacon's heavy footfalls closed in. He flipped a wooden chair backward and straddled it, folding his arms over the back. "You two are getting cozy. Mind if I join?"

I turned my head away and started coughing.

"Are you okay, female?" Lucian sounded concerned, much to my surprise.

After I cleared my throat, I sat back and patted my chest. "It's just a tickle in my lungs. I think I inhaled a grain of salt."

When I noticed the two men, the tension was palpable. The baleful look Deacon gave Lucian puzzled me. Then I remembered what Lucian had said.

Only Chitahs used the term *female* with frequency.

In a flash, Deacon ripped off Lucian's sunglasses.

Lucian launched to his feet and glared at the Herculean Shifter.

"Lucian, *no*," I warned him.

Deacon gave him a sardonic smile. "Ho-ly shit." He chuckled while rising to his feet. "You don't even make the six-foot mark. What are you? Five-ten? I should call you Five-and-Dime." He snatched Lucian's knit hat, revealing the blackest hair I'd ever seen. "It just keeps getting better and better. Are you sure you're even a Chitah?"

"I'm more of a Chitah than you are a beta wolf." Lucian threw a punch so fast that it looked like a missile.

It struck Deacon hard but not enough to knock him down. Lucian's eyes were still golden, and his fangs hadn't punched out. Chitahs displayed those traits to intimidate enemies, so it mystified me when he backed up a step and gripped his chair.

Virgil appeared, amusement dancing in his intoxicated eyes. He tucked his thumbs beneath his studded leather belt. "Pump the brakes. This is a refined establishment," he said mockingly. "Collect yourselves and—"

Deacon charged and knocked Lucian backward. The two men collided with the wall.

Virgil rounded my chair and put his face next to mine. "What mischief is this?"

"Lucian's a Chitah."

Casually seating himself next to me, Virgil watched Deacon grip the Chitah by the throat. He looked highly entertained, like a man in a front-row seat at WrestleMania.

I knew better than to break up a fight between different Breeds. The Shifter could shift in the middle of it, and the Chitah could flip his switch. I winced when he punched Lucian in the gut, but then Lucian kneed him.

Virgil hissed and grabbed the Coke bottle. "That violated the man code."

Lucian grabbed Deacon's hair and reeled back his fist like a snake about to strike.

Naomi jumped into the scene. "Nope! No, you *don't*," she said loudly. "You're here by invitation. Is this how you're gonna do me? If you two don't get your shit together, you'll be walking. *Capisce*?" She shoved Deacon aside without getting between them. "Now, what in the name of baby Jesus is going on here?"

Deacon shook his head. "He isn't stepping one foot on that bus."

Virgil spit out the soda. Using his tongue, he pushed a peanut out of his mouth. "I say we kick him off for drinking this pig swill."

I stood. "Everyone needs to calm down and mind their own business. If Lucian wants to join a pack, it's his right."

"Shut the hell up," Deacon spat. "This isn't *your* business."

The rest of our group joined the ruckus.

"Maybe it is," I fired back. "Because I'm going too."

"The hell you are," he snarled.

"Everyone, hands up!" a man roared.

We all turned.

Two masked gunmen blocked the front door, aiming their rifles, which were possibly automatics, but I knew nothing about guns.

One of them shot the bottles behind the bar, causing Russ to duck. "Hands up, I said!"

We all slowly put our hands in the air.

The taller man did all the talking. "If any of you motherfuckers move one inch, I'll blow your head off. I might start with the person sitting next to you. My friend is gonna walk around with a bag, and I want all your money, your jewelry, and anything else you got on you. If you hold out on us, I'll put out your immortal light. Starting with the bartender. Empty your till. I know how much money you're raking in, so don't even think about holding out."

His scrawny pal put his gun in everyone's faces as he neared the bar, then got behind it. "Hurry your ass up!"

Breed establishments were sometimes targets for robbery, usually after hours. They didn't have to worry about the cops getting called, and business owners stored money in safes and ran it over to their bankers once a week. *This place is an easy target. But how the hell did they get past the Vampire? And what's to stop them from eliminating all witnesses?*

Sweat touched my brow as my heart pounded in my chest. I saw Joy clutching Salem, and everything felt too real.

The gun fired again, striking someone who was making a run at them from the back of the room. A woman screamed and ran to his aid. The injured man shifted into a wolf and back to heal.

Virgil stepped forward, holding his hands high. "'Scuse me. I'd like to leave."

"You *what*?" the tall man growled.

Virgil slowly reached into his pocket and pulled out his wallet with two fingers. "It's all yours. I'll step outside while you gentlemen work this out."

The second man at the bar cackled. "Keep it up, and we'll do you like we did that wolf outside. Right, Dale?"

"Shut the fuck up!" the first gunman shouted, clearly pissed that his partner had given up his name.

My mind went blank. *The wolf outside.* A buzzing filled my ears when I thought about Catcher being shot.

He could be bleeding. He needs my help!

Without thinking, I grabbed the ashtray from the table and struck the gunman in the head. Bullets sprayed the ceiling, and everyone standing within a ten-foot radius sprang into action.

Virgil howled before jumping into the fray. He disarmed the man while Deacon punched him over and over. The man blasted Deacon with what I guessed was Mage light, and Deacon flew off.

"Mage!" someone shouted. "Get a stunner!"

Virgil kicked the Mage in the head, putting him in a stupor. Then he pinned one arm to the ground.

"Everyone, stop!" The second guy at the bar aimed his weapon at the bartender, who held his hands up and had his eyes closed. "I'll kill him dead!"

Montana sat on the gunman's other arm, ripped off the mask, and shoved a gun into his mouth. "I'll put a bullet in his brain!" he shouted to the second robber. "Put down your weapon and things won't have to get ugly."

"You let my brother go!" the man shrieked.

Montana kept his eyes pinned on the man lying beneath him. "I'll let him go if you lay down your weapon. If you think I'm fucking around, keep talking. Three, two..."

"Fine! Okay!" The second gunman held up his rifle.

Before the weapon touched the bar, Archer—the tripod—vaulted over the bar and crashed into him. Bottles smashed on the floor.

Russ's face was a ghostly white. He turned his attention to the wounded customer in the back. "Everyone, stay calm. I'm calling the Regulators, so I need everyone to stay put. Next round is on the house."

Montana raised his head. "Got any zip ties?"

I DIDN'T STICK AROUND LONG ENOUGH to see the conclusion. My feet carried me up the stairs as fast as they would allow until I flew into the barn. The flashlight on the ground pointed away from the Vampire lying on his stomach with a stake in his back. Though I needed to find Catcher, I couldn't abandon the friendly doorman.

Once on my knees, I gripped the stake. "I'm sorry if this hurts. Brace yourself."

My stomach turned when I pulled it out.

The Vampire gasped and sat up. "Son of a bitch!" His fangs punched out.

I sprang back, my heart galloping.

After kicking the stake out of the way, he shadow walked to the basement door and disappeared like black ink sliding down a drain.

I grabbed the flashlight from the ground, fumbling it in my shaky hands. Blood at the entrance caught my attention. I shined the light where it had spattered onto the grass and dirt. My light finally landed on a wolf lying motionless, its fur stained crimson.

I shut my eyes in anguish. Those men had sprayed him with bullets. He'd tried to escape, but someone finished him off with a bullet to the head. I stroked his soft fur, heartbroken that he'd died alone. It hadn't even been a fair fight.

"Hey! Robyn! You shouldn't be out here," Montana warned me. "There could be more of them." He slowed his approach. "Is that..."

I sat back on my heels. "No. It's not Catcher."

Montana crouched and examined the body. "*Animals,*" he growled.

After a sharp whistle, I waited for Catcher to show. "He would have heard the gunfire."

"Maybe. Maybe not. He might have thought it was a car backfiring."

"Why aren't you in there securing things?"

"Two jackasses took over. They're taking credit for the second gunman."

"For what gain?"

"My guess is they want the Regulators to make a note of it."

I took a deep breath, held it, released the air slowly and repeated the process twice more. Then I coughed a few times.

"Is something wrong?"

"It helps to slow down the heart," I said before standing. "I feel like I'm about to pass out from all the adrenaline."

"Did you mean it back there?" Montana stepped in front of me and canted his head. "About going with us?"

"If Lucian is going, I don't see why not. I'm not a wolf, but I used to live in a pack. Even if it doesn't work out, it sounds like a great location."

"What do you know about it?"

"Nothing. But if this guy is the son of some hotshot leader, he wouldn't pick a terrible place to start a pack."

"I guess that's one way to look at it." He lifted my chin with the crook of his finger. "What you did in there—that was brave."

"You're not going to tell me it was stupid?"

"Stupid is when a person lacks intelligence. Like the men who thought they could get away with robbing a bar filled with Shifters. Brave is when someone shows courage. That was you, taking on a Mage with an ashtray."

"It was a knee-jerk reaction." I rubbed my temple. "I never instigate fights. That wasn't me. But when I thought they hurt Catcher, something took over, and I had to do whatever it took."

He leaned close to my ear. "That's what it is to be a wolf."

"Secure the area," Deacon ordered from behind us. "Do a full perimeter check, and make sure your wolf doesn't go on the attack unless provoked. Remember, we got humans around here."

It seemed Montana was right about Deacon taking over like a pack beta would.

"Montana, you too," he barked.

Clenching his jaw, Montana did a slow turn. "We have a casualty. Let the bartender and motel owner know. It might be someone local. If not, they'll need to trace his vehicle."

"You let me handle that," Deacon said, his tone laced with arrogance. He gave me a scathing look. "You could have gotten someone killed with that stupid stunt."

Montana edged closer. "That stupid stunt saved your ass."

Deacon ran his fingers through his brown hair and gave him an admonishing stare. "The Packmaster will hear about how this went down. We'll see if he wants impulsive people in his pack."

I narrowed my eyes. "So that makes you the pack snitch."

When Deacon brought up his hand, Montana stepped between us.

I backed up enough to see Deacon tapping his finger against his lip.

"Guard the corpse," he said before stalking off.

I disliked the way he was browbeating everyone into submission.

Montana faced me but kept his eyes trained on Deacon. "Careful what you say to him. Now that you're joining us, you'll need to be less confrontational until you know how things shake out. If the alpha accepts both of you, then you don't want to get off to a bad start with the pack beta."

I looked over my shoulder. "I know. But the beta's job is to keep the pack in line and be the mediator, not snitch to the Packmaster. Otherwise, people won't trust him with personal issues."

"If he wants to waste the alpha's time with pack drama, let him. That'll get him nowhere." Montana took off his hat and stared at the wolf. "Can you find a blanket or something to cover him until the Regulators arrive?"

I nodded before whistling one last time. "If you see Catcher, keep an eye on him. He'll get aggressive if I'm not here. Especially with all the blood."

Montana gave a small smile. "Better hurry, then."

CHAPTER 5

After the Regulators conducted their investigation, they questioned us for hours. Luckily for us, no one at the hotel called the cops. Some bar patrons were ready to go back to their drinks and dancing, but the owner shut it down. The deceased wolf's identification was in his vehicle, so they were able to contact his family.

Catcher didn't show up until four in the morning, whining, barking, and scratching at the bus door. When I let him inside, the blood on his snout showed that he'd recently fed. I reassured him with soothing words while cleaning his face. Smelling the dead wolf and the unfamiliar scents had worked him into a frenzy, and it took a while before he calmed down and we finally fell asleep.

I stretched hard, and in that moment between asleep and awake, I realized the bus was moving. Catcher barked when I opened my eyes.

"All right," I grumbled before standing up.

"She lives," a man, one I didn't recognize, said. He was leaning into the aisle to gawk at me. He had no hair on his head and a white stripe down his brown beard.

Oh my god. Am I on the wrong bus?

Joy peered back at me before heading over with a plastic container in her hand. "You were sleeping so hard that we left you alone. Your friend wouldn't let us near you." She gave Catcher an admonishing glance, and he thumped his tail happily in response. "We stopped for breakfast, and I saved you something. I hope you like biscuits."

"Thank you." I accepted the container. "Are we close?"

"Almost. Isn't it exciting?" Her eyes seemed bluer than normal, and I realized the sun was out. "You might want to change," she whispered. "First impressions and all."

I admired Joy's leggings and pretty grey long-sleeve blouse that fell off one shoulder. Her hair was styled, her nails painted, and she smelled like a fragrant bouquet.

After doing a quick scan, I noticed the Chitah wasn't on board. "Where's Lucian?"

Joy shrugged. "I haven't seen him." Lowering her voice to a whisper, she said, "He shouldn't have thrown the first punch at a beta. Maybe it's for the best he's not here." After patting my arm, she sashayed back to her seat.

I sat down by the window and watched the trees whiz by. It wasn't at all how I imagined Texas. "Is this Austin?" I asked loudly enough that Naomi could hear.

"No, ma'am." Naomi steered off the highway. "We're about an hour or so northwest. Close enough to drive to if you get bored. Hope none of you are city folk," she said with a chuckle.

After two bites of biscuit, I closed the container. I didn't have an appetite. My throat was a little sore, and my hips hurt from sleeping on the floor all night. When I offered Catcher the food, he whined and nudged my hand, so I put the container in my bag.

Did I make the right choice? Attempting to join a pack I knew nothing about seemed risky. *Is this guy even a trustworthy Packmaster?*

The dirt road we were on narrowed, and when we hit a pothole, Joy let out a squeak that made a few people laugh. The bus eventually slowed to a stop.

"This is as far as I go," Naomi announced after putting the vehicle in park. "I can't take you down the drive, or I'll never get her back on the road. Made that mistake already. You'll walk from here. It's been a pleasure, ladies and gentlemen. Be sure to search above, around, and below your seats to collect your things. I don't return found items." She stood and opened the steel door. "Welcome to Storybook, Texas."

When everyone stood, I noticed our group had increased by two. The husky biker with the stripe down his beard was new, and the gaunt man sitting next to him had one of those skinny little mustaches that looked painted on. When he smiled at Joy, I spotted a gold tooth. *How does he keep that thing in his mouth when he shifts?* From what I knew, Shifters didn't require dental work. They could heal through shifting. *Is it an implant or painted?* Either way, I couldn't stop thinking about it. Sometimes Breed magic eluded me.

"Follow me," Naomi instructed everyone. "I'll get your luggage out of the carriage."

When the bus emptied, I grabbed my bag and the blanket I'd slept on. Catcher walked ahead of me and hopped off.

Naomi reboarded. "Change your mind?"

"No, I'm just dragging this morning. Thanks for everything, Naomi." I handed her the blanket. "I feel like I owe you for not leaving me back there in the rain."

"Girl, you don't owe me anything but a recommendation. Next time you hear someone needs transportation, be sure to recommend Naomi Burns. I have a website and everything!"

I gave her a one-armed hug.

"You be careful out there," she said. "Some of these packs are no place for another Breed."

I lifted my backpack. "Don't worry about me. If things don't work out, I'll find someplace else."

"You gotta have guts to start over. It'll work out, one way or another. If you can't get in with this pack, just do what Naomi does."

"And what's that?"

"Hustle. Figure out what people need, and provide a service. Fake it till you make it." She wagged her finger at Catcher. "You take care of my girl."

He *woof*ed in reply.

When I rounded the front, the rest of the group had marched ahead of me down a private drive that was flanked by bushes and trees. Some were massive live oaks, while others looked like bald cypress. The woods weren't the impassable kind with dense brush, and there was a beautiful glade on the left with trees spaced apart. It was hillier than I expected.

Naomi honked her horn, which gave me a start. She pulled in behind me before backing the bus up and turning around. I was certain she would take out a few bushes in the process, but she made it. What an adventurous life she lived, meeting all kinds of people and traveling. On top of that, she was a human hauling around immortals.

Montana slowed his pace until I caught up with him. "Need a hand with that bag? You look beat."

"It's hotter than I expected." I set down my bag and removed my sweater. Beneath it, I had on a blue V-neck shirt. After I tucked my sweater into the bag, I smiled at Montana's T-shirt. "I guess you want the alpha to know where you're from."

We moseyed up the dirt drive, both of us quiet. Like everyone else, we were soaking in our surroundings. The hot sun and cool air on my skin created a wonderful combination. I could only imagine what summers were like. *Am I cut out for this?*

"What do you think?" he asked.

"I've never lived in the country."

"It's a different way of life." Montana put a swing in his step. "You get used to it. Nice and quiet."

"Is that where you're from? The country? I took you for a city boy with that flashy gun of yours."

He took off his hat and fanned his face with it. "Let's just say I've seen both sides."

When Catcher became distracted in a field of yellow wildflowers, I snapped my fingers. He joined us again, zigzagging around while he sniffed everything. Since we were on Shifter territory, I didn't want him out of my sight.

"Who are the new guys?"

Montana adjusted the bag on his back. "Remember the two jackasses I was telling you about at the bar? The ones who were trying to take all the credit for the second gunman? That's them."

"Super."

I slowed to a stop. "You should go on ahead. Catcher's going to be a minute, and it's important that you make a good first impression."

He put his hat back on and tipped the brim before quickening his pace to rejoin the group.

I bent down and stroked Catcher's soft fur. His hazel eyes were like two beautiful jewels that changed colors in the light. "Let's give this a try. Maybe it's a sign. Of all the people to pick us up, it was a bus filled with Shifters. That's gotta mean something, right?" I cupped his snout and kissed his nose. "Be on your best behavior."

Catcher gave me a silly look and jumped before going back to all his sniffing. There was no point in giving him orders—Catcher was going to do what Catcher was going to do.

The dirt drive led to a house that had a paved lot on the left. The area directly in front and to the right was grassy. A wide sidewalk led from the porch steps to the parking area. It wasn't a palatial castle with pillars and ornate architecture, but the spacious two-story luxury home was a marvel, blending in seamlessly with its surroundings. The exterior was a combination of wood and large stones.

But what made me apprehensive were the missing windows, front door, and roof. Blue tarp covered the second floor, and one area didn't even have a wall. A few people walked to the side to further explore.

South Dakota had plenty of beautiful spots and mountains, just not where I was from. So for me, Texas was a big change. The picturesque land had enormous oak trees with twisted branches. Some looked a hundred years old. Beyond them were grassy pastures.

Sparrows sang in the trees, and two noisy blue jays voiced their complaints about our arrival. A large white pickup truck was parked next to a small black one. In the shade sat a green Toyota sedan.

A lovely Native woman strolled through the doorway with a wagon behind her. In the wagon were water bottles and snacks. She walked it down the short steps and left it. While some men were eyeing the snacks, others were ogling her. Shifters loved women with thick hips and large behinds. But her blue harem pants and baggy crop top suggested she didn't invite that kind of attention.

"My name is Hope," she announced, breaking the ice. "Help yourselves to refreshments. If anyone needs to use the bathroom, we don't have a working toilet yet. We set up a temporary outhouse down that way." She gestured to the right. "Or you can shift and do your business. You'll have to remain outside for now. Tak will be out in a minute to speak to you and answer any questions you have."

Joy's hand shot up. "My name is Joy, and this is my mate, Salem."

Hope flashed a smile at them. "It's a pleasure to meet you both. Official introductions come later. In the meantime, relax and have a look around."

"Thanks!" Joy said, reaching for two water bottles. "You're the sweetest."

Hope chuckled before turning back inside. "Spread the rumor."

I opened a bottle and gulped down the drink. While everyone spread out, I went through my bag, found Catcher's metal bowl, and filled it with water.

Montana stared at the unfinished house.

"What do you think?" I asked quietly.

"Needs work."

I snorted. "That's the understatement of the year." I moved off toward a flat stone where the willowy girl was sitting. Her long, angelic hair draped over her shoulders like a shawl. Despite her young appearance, she didn't dress her age. Her peach-colored skirt covered the tops of her black lace-up shoes, and her cream sweater was too warm for the weather.

I took a spot next to her and watched Catcher lapping up his water. "We haven't met. I'm Robyn."

She gave a nervous smile. "Serena."

"Where are you from?"

"England... originally. We moved when I was a child, so that's why I don't have a strong accent. My brother, Ian, does."

"I noticed."

Ian struck me as sophisticated and not just because of his posh English accent. He wore a blazer with his turtleneck sweaters, and people didn't dress like that in the small town I'd lived in. He smelled like fancy cologne and had a certain air about him, like he thought he was in a class above everyone else.

I handed her a package of miniature donuts. "You and your brother keep to yourselves."

She opened the chocolate donuts and ate one. "He hasn't made up his mind about everyone, so he thinks we should keep our distance." After a second donut, she pointed at Catcher. "Is he really your watchdog?"

"He sure is."

Her eyebrows drew together, and I could tell she was trying to work it all out. "Why doesn't he shift back?"

"To be honest, I don't know."

"He's a handsome wolf. His coloring is different from most of the brown wolves I see."

When she caught me looking at her, I had to say something. "I like your hair."

"I like yours much better. Maybe I should cut mine."

That took me by surprise. "I recently did. Trust me—you'd regret it."

She held up a third donut. "Sometimes I like the idea of being someone else."

Ian stalked up and knocked the donut out of her hand. "That's quite enough. Too many of those sweets, and you'll get fat."

Serena handed him the remaining package and stood.

"I'm Robyn," I said.

Ian nodded at me and led Serena away.

Though Shifters were especially protective of their siblings, I didn't like the way he spoke to her.

I picked up the donut from the ground. Since chocolate didn't affect Shifters, I tossed it to Catcher. He practically inhaled it.

Virgil had climbed onto a stack of lumber and was doing a handstand. His T-shirt slid down to his chin.

Archer rested one leg on a board and watched him. "What the hell are you doing up there?"

With perfect balance, Virgil walked around. "It's good for circulation. Plus, it keeps my muscles rock hard."

Archer shook his head and laughed. Up close, I could see the tattoo around his neck. The crown of long, sharp thorns circled all the way around.

Virgil got back on his feet, his shirt still twisted around his torso. "You should try it."

Archer put his foot down, the empty sleeve of his leather jacket hanging at his side. "That's a hard no for me."

Curious about the rest of the property, I strode past them toward the back and noticed two tents set up. The firepit had a metal stand over it and two black kettles.

A shirtless man with long brown hair swung an axe, making the log on the tree stump split in two. He tossed aside the pieces and put another one on the stump.

"Hi," I said from a safe distance. "Are you the Packmaster?"

He swung the axe again.

"That ain't no Packmaster," Deacon muttered, easing up beside me.

"Isn't the alpha supposed to be Native? *He's* Native."

"Clearly, you don't know jack shit about alphas." Deacon turned to face me. "If he were the alpha, do you think he'd be back here chopping wood while complete strangers walked on his property? You can bet your sweet ass the alpha's upstairs, watching us through one of those openings. He wants to make an entrance. Besides, a Packmaster would never have his back to strangers without packmates at his side." He clucked his tongue and gave me a dismissive look. "You should go home before you embarrass yourself."

I branched away from him toward a well. The cover over it looked new, as did the water dipper inside the bucket. At least we had a reliable source of water.

Virgil strutted over, his shirt half-tucked in and his fedora gone. He flipped a quarter in the air and caught it. "I *wish* this house was finished. Think that'll come true?"

I snatched his wrist. "Don't throw that dirty coin in there. It's not a wishing well."

"You're a sassy one. I can tell we'll get along just fine." He leaned over and peered in, his dirty-blond hair hanging down. Then he sang a little melody into the well before sitting up with a grin on his face. "I love the acoustics."

"What do you think about this place?"

Virgil tapped the bucket. "I've never lived on a farm before. Not the Old MacDonald kind."

"Is there going to be running water?"

"This one's for drinking." He slapped the post that held the cover. "I guarantee there's a well pump that'll move water into the house."

"What if we run out?"

Virgil chuckled. "A well means there's an aquifer running underground." He put his arm around me and rested his head on mine. "Think we'll have to squeeze some teats?"

I elbowed him away.

Virgil laughed, revealing a dimple in his left cheek. "That's what they do on farms, city girl. Milk cows, shovel manure, breed horses. You know what the best part about this is?"

I glanced up at him. Virgil was tall, probably over six feet. By the twinkle in his eye, he was definitely a troublemaker. "What's that?"

He directed his attention to the group wandering around the backyard and adjusted himself. "Everyone's on their best behavior. Personalities are only a tenth of what they actually are. I was the first one on the bus, and each new person made everyone clam up a teensy bit more. It's like we're all on a first date and not sure if we're gonna get laid." Virgil squeezed my cheeks together with one hand. "We'll see how things shake out once everyone settles in. I love drama."

"If this is only a tenth of your personality, am I going to need a seat belt for the real thing?"

"You might need a straitjacket."

"Can I borrow yours?"

Virgil's eyebrows shot up, and he swaggered off. "I have zero regrets about coming here. Zero!"

I followed him. The biker-looking guy with the white stripe in his beard sounded local, and he introduced himself to others as Wayne. The goth with the gold tooth scoped out the property.

Montana joined my side. "I wonder how many acres he has."

Still watching the group, I asked, "Is everyone here automatically in? I'm getting nervous about this. You didn't mention what the ad said, and I'm not sure what I think about some of these people."

"Anyone in particular rubbing you the wrong way?"

I turned my back to the group. "I briefly met Ian."

Montana frowned. "From the brother-and-sister duo?"

"What did you think of him?"

"Didn't talk to him much. They always eat alone. Everyone's mostly kept to themselves on the bus. We realized it was better that way. Headstrong personalities in a confined space... Well, I guess you saw how that almost went."

"This is a strange way to form a pack. If people show him different faces, how's he going to know from a group of strangers who the psychos are?"

Montana chuckled. "I guess that'll be his test as a Packmaster. He can't go by referrals or reputation like usual. If he doesn't know how to pick the best packmates, then he's not a leader worth following."

A vibrating brassy sound made everyone turn toward the house.

When the noise faded, Joy asked, "Was that a gong?"

A tall man emerged from the open doorway. I realized the doorframe was taller than average, as was the guy. His rugged build wasn't the same body type as Deacon's but one that came naturally. While he didn't have muscles like well-formed boulders, he looked like he could break a picnic table in half all the same. His brown skin and long hair, which was either tied back or braided, signaled that he was likely the Packmaster. The enormous silver-and-turquoise necklace he wore was like nothing I'd seen.

Yet none of that was as attention-grabbing as his tribal tattoo. The designs marked the entire left side of his face.

A metal bucket swung from his hand as he walked barefoot onto the deck in a blue sarong. Before descending the steps, he grabbed a lawn chair.

We silently watched him shake the chair open and sit down. The aluminum legs creaked beneath his weight. After pulling an orange out of the bucket, he started peeling away the skin. Up close, the scars on his right shoulder appeared to be claw marks from a large animal, like a tiger or a bear. He had smaller scars elsewhere though nothing as striking as that one.

Whether or not it was his style, wearing a sarong for our first introduction seemed like a strategic move to display his battle wounds.

"Take one," he offered, his voice deep and commanding.

No one dared decline his generous offering, and there were exactly enough oranges for everyone. Naomi must have filled him in on the total count before arriving, so that was his way of telling us that he was well informed.

"Sit." He placed an orange slice in his mouth.

We glanced around before taking a seat in the grass like children gathered around their teacher. Despite any snacks people had taken from the wagon, everyone started eating their oranges, including me.

Catcher trotted over and cautiously sniffed the air around the alpha. I tensed, nervous he might behave unpredictably in this new environment. Catcher must have sensed Tak's power, as wolves often did around alphas. He crouched, his head low, before trotting past him. Then he did something so unexpected that I wanted to crawl into a hole and die from embarrassment.

Catcher separated his hind legs and started dragging his ass across the lawn.

I sat there with an orange in my hand, unable to rebuke my watchdog in front of others.

The alpha narrowed his eyes.

"That mangy mutt doesn't have any respect," Deacon bit out.

The Packmaster tossed another peel into the empty bucket. "Nothing wrong with a wolf scratching an itch. He's doing what comes naturally." His eyes twinkled, but his countenance remained stoic. "Did everyone take refreshments from Hope?"

Wayne chuckled. "If that fine little wolf's in the pack, count me in."

The alpha tossed the rest of his peel into the bucket and widened his legs, threatening to reveal more than I wanted to see. "That's my mate. Now that you know, you'll treat her with respect. If not, I can get real uncivilized." He gobbled the last orange slice in his hand and licked his fingers. "I'm Tak of the Iwa nation. As you can see by the tents, you're not the first group to arrive, but you are the last. Needn't worry about food or water. But you will sleep outside."

"I don't mind a little construction," Wayne said, tossing his orange peel into the bucket. "Sleeping on the floor suits me fine."

"It doesn't suit me," Tak replied. "Only packmates sleep under my roof. You're a guest until you prove otherwise. We have a well for drinking water, and if you wish to bathe, there's a stream nearby. Idle hands bring trouble, so you'll keep them busy finishing the house." He looked to his left, where part of a dilapidated barn stood a short distance away. "I also need a new barn for my horse."

Wayne wiped the grass off his hands. "Wait a second. How do we know you didn't bring us out here for free labor?"

Tak gave him a withering stare. "I will consider each man and woman as a packmate." He placed his fist over his heart. "My word is my bond. Manual labor reveals a lot about a person, not just their skills but also how they work with others, how they follow orders, how committed they are to excellence, and—"

"How we need an indoor toilet," Hope added. She wheeled a metal gong onto the back deck and gave it a light tap with a mallet.

Virgil laughed like a hyena, and the tension broke.

Tak glanced over his shoulder at her. "I was just getting to that, beautiful."

"The noxious smell coming from the outhouse beckons your attention. It needs another treatment. A woman shouldn't have to do such things," she said, giving him a playful stare before returning inside.

When Tak turned back around, he was smiling.

And I knew immediately that I liked him. Maybe it was a sixth sense, but a smile had never led me to the wrong conclusion about a person. He was a beast of a man, yet his warm smile and the way he reacted when his mate spoke to him suggested he wasn't as intimidating as he looked. While careful with her words in front of other wolves, she also put him in his place as her mate. His reaction to her remark wasn't annoyance or anger, which was more than I'd seen with some couples. He didn't put his ego before his mate, and he wasn't hotheaded like I imagined all alphas to be.

He smoothed a hand over his head and continued addressing the group. "You'll rotate duties, such as the aforementioned."

"What about food?" Deacon asked. He looked like a man with a hearty appetite.

"I've heard grubworms are healthy." When his remark fell flat, Tak gave a boisterous laugh. "The land provides us with nourishment. I'll supply the rest. No one starves around here."

"Where are the others?" I dared to ask. "The ones who've been working on the house."

The group slowly got up and dropped their orange peels into the bucket.

"One or two are still here," he said obliquely, implying there was more to the story. "Who wants to take care of this bucket for me?"

Wayne looked like a roly-poly struggling to right himself as he hurried to his feet. After hiking up his tight jeans, he lifted the bucket and walked off to a tree, dumped the orange peels, then returned to his spot.

I shot up and grabbed the bucket. "Dumbass," I muttered.

"Bitch, you better learn your place," he spat.

Bitch was a word I'd heard often in my last pack. When I was growing up, it was a bad word. But with some Shifters, it didn't have a negative connotation. With this guy, it clearly did.

"Show a little respect," I said over my shoulder. "This isn't our property." After collecting all the peels, I returned with the bucket and sat.

Tak stared at me.

"It'll attract ants," I explained, breaking the silence. "Besides, we can dry it out and use it for kindling."

The alpha said something in a language I didn't understand, then he gestured to Wayne. "You can go."

The husky man looked puzzled. "I took care of it, didn't I? That's what you told me to do."

Tak rose to his feet. "Gather your things and leave."

"For what?" His voice had gone up two octaves.

"For breaking my first rule. This land isn't your trash can."

Wayne stood. "That ain't hardly fair. We *just* got here. What I do with a bucket of orange peels has nothing to do with what I bring to a pack."

Tak arched an eyebrow. "That's up for debate."

Wayne unzipped his pants and pulled out his penis. An arc of urine sprayed the ground. "Here's what I think of your land."

Crossing his arms, Tak said, "How thoughtful of you to water my mate's flowers. Waste not, want not."

After grabbing his bag, Wayne marched toward the alpha. The guy with the gold tooth stayed seated, so they obviously weren't friends.

"Just so you know, this is some bullshit. You're not the big bad alpha everyone made you out to be." Wayne reached around to his back. "But this sure is a sweet piece of land you got."

He swung his arm forward with lightning speed and aimed a gun at Tak. Joy gasped. I frantically searched for Catcher, afraid he might get involved. If he was shot, he could die if he didn't shift.

Something whistled through the air, and Wayne bellowed. The gun fired toward the house before it fell from his grip. An arrow had penetrated his wrist.

Tak kicked the gun away. Montana seized the weapon and aimed it at Wayne.

"Hope!" Tak shouted.

"I'm okay," she said, still inside.

Tak stalked toward Wayne and put his large hand around his neck. "You're lucky I don't slit your throat." When he squeezed harder, Wayne's face turned purple.

"Then do it," Wayne dared him, his lips peeled back. "If you have the balls."

Tak looked down at him as if he were a bug under his boot. "Do you think you're the first brazen wolf to snap his teeth at me? To think he can steal my land? That's why there's an arrow in your arm. You threatened my life, shot at my mate, and attempted a land grab. I have a right to inflict whatever punishment I deem fit." Tak shoved him back a foot. "But I won't besmirch my soil with your cowardly blood."

Deacon jumped to his feet, grabbed the back of Wayne's collar, and gripped his good arm.

"Don't even think about returning," Tak warned him. "I'll mount your head on my new mailbox."

Deacon escorted him to the side of the house.

A big lumberjack-looking guy approached from the front. "I've got it."

Catcher barked and trotted after them, no doubt taking on the task of walking that good-for-nothing as far out as he could.

Tak waved at the burly man. "That's Bear. He's the chef, so if you want to eat, you'll get on his good side."

Deacon strutted toward the group as if he were the one who had shot that arrow.

While everyone collected themselves, I twisted around and scanned our surroundings. Up high on a tree branch, a woman with bright-turquoise hair lowered her bow. She looked my age or younger, but with Shifters, it was impossible to tell. She nodded once at Tak. There didn't appear to be anyone else hiding in the trees.

Tak returned to his chair. "As I was saying, I believe in sustainable living. That's the life I came from, and it's the life I want to live. Does it mean we can't have electricity or television? No. I like music as much as everyone else. But the more dependent you are on others to eat, the weaker you are. It doesn't mean we always hunt for our meals or make our own soap—that's where trading comes in. Trading is good for building relations with tribes and packs. I have around twelve hundred acres, which is plenty for a group our size. I also own a smaller piece of land closer to Austin. My pack will start small, and that means we'll depend on purchased goods. My mate and her friend own a shop in Austin selling high-quality jewelry and clothes—all their own designs. That's sustainability. Because of their entrepreneurship, we have a steady income."

"That's a long commute," I remarked.

"It's not that bad." Hope joined us and sat on the steps behind her mate. "A little over an hour, depending on traffic. We used to run the store by ourselves, but now we're too busy managing the business side. That gives us time to create new designs. I miss it, though. But who knows? We might open a second location. Storybook may seem isolated, but the Breed population is quite high."

"My mate worries about finances," Tak added. "That burden shouldn't fall on her alone. A pack is only as strong as its weakest member, so I expect everyone to find a meaningful way to contribute to our success. This land is not a resort. If you have dreams of kicking back and not having to do anything for the rest of your life, the road is that way," he said, gesturing to the left.

Hope's lips eased into a grin. "Behind you."

Tak frowned while he got his sense of direction. "Before we go any further, I want you to know about where I come from. My people are my life. I brought shame to myself and my family long ago when I had a drinking problem. That weakness and my reckless decisions caused a woman to die. I never hid from my mistake. In fact, I marked my face with symbols from my people to remind them that I strayed from the pack. When you think of only yourself, you're not with your pack anymore. You've chosen yourself before others. My father respects and supports my decision to form a pack outside the tribe. He also has a deal negotiated with my mate's business. Family is important. I left mine to build another. They'll never let me lead because of my past, but I feel the calling. If this is an issue with anyone, you know where the road is. I have no secrets."

Hope got up and stood behind him, putting her hand on his scarred shoulder.

"This is my destiny," he continued, a breeze rustling the leaves in the branches. "This isn't the way I imagined forming a pack, but my mate placed an ad in the paper, so here we are."

Virgil snorted.

Hope lifted her chin. "I simply talked him into it."

"After you posted the ad," he grumbled.

"I've lived in Austin all my life," Hope explained to us. "I know all the local packs, and the available wolves don't fit in with our home. Some are too young. Others are irresponsible or unreliable. In time, the good ones will feel a calling to move on and change out. We'll set an example, which will create interest. Patience is a virtue. I just wanted to speed things up to see what might happen. I trust my mate's judgment."

He stroked her hand. "She says I'm picky."

Hope turned around and slowly hiked up the stairs. "I would never say such things." She hit the gong before going back inside, which made Tak chuckle.

"Did you build this from the ground up?" Montana asked.

Tak half turned and stared at the unfinished house. "The ranch was already here, but we stripped it down for many reasons. The foundation needed work and cost me a pretty penny. The pipes were bad, and the layout was all wrong. It also had termite damage."

Virgil crossed one ankle over the other and leaned back on his hands. "Do you have a professional making sure you're up to code? I've done construction work, and I can tell you that your porch is lacking the proper support. You need to get the rest of the frame up so you can start on the roof. Unless you want issues, hire a professional to make sure the house is watertight."

"And you're that expert?"

Virgil dipped his chin. "I didn't claim that title."

Tak leaned forward, resting his elbows on his knees. "I sent two people home because they claimed to know what they were doing with the fireplace. Don't assume arrogance will win you a seat at my table. If we have to tear down something you did and start all over, we will. But you won't be there to help." Tak stood and stretched one arm across his broad chest. "Today, you can settle in—let your wolves run. If I hear any fighting, I'll lock you in the outhouse. Tomorrow, we'll see what you each have to contribute."

CHAPTER 6

TAK PROVIDED EACH OF US with a tent, and we spent a good chunk of the afternoon picking our spots and setting them up. Mine was red, and I chose the softest patch of grass I could find. Each tent had vent holes, which allowed us to zip up the flaps and still breathe.

After my first outhouse experience, I hiked up the steps and knocked on the back wall.

"Come in," Hope called out from another room.

I stepped into the back hallway and turned right until I entered an unfinished kitchen.

When Hope joined me, she was wearing a pair of overalls and a white T-shirt, and her cheeks were flushed. She wiped her forehead. "I was just finishing up the hearth. We're supposed to get the doors delivered today, so there's much to do. Are you thirsty? We have cups, if that's what you're looking for."

"No, thanks. Actually, I was hoping I could talk to, uh... Mr.—"

I panicked, wondering if I'd forgotten Tak's last name.

Hope smiled. "He doesn't have a surname. You can call him Tak. Stay right here, and I'll get him."

As she left, I looked at the dusty footprints all over the concrete floor.

Tak walked in wearing tan cargos instead of the silly sarong. He must have worn the giant necklace for show, because he no longer had it on either.

"Is there something you need?" he asked.

I glanced behind him before lowering my voice. "I need to speak to you about something. Privately."

He jerked his head toward a hall. "Follow me."

We reached the front of the house, and I admired the enormous stone fireplace on the right wall. It had a massive hearth and was a spectacular addition to the room.

He brushed his hand over the stone. "We built this using the rocks on our land. My mate is working on the finishing touches."

"It's beautiful." I glanced at a doorway on the right side of the room, along the same wall as the fireplace. "What's in there?"

"That will be the art room. For creatives who need a place of inspiration to work, design, and inspire."

"I'm Robyn, by the way. You didn't ask our names earlier."

He took a seat on the hearth. "I've had a few walk out during the first speech. Now I don't waste my time with early introductions."

I sat on the opposite side and faced him. "This was supposed to be easier, but someone else from the bus isn't here. Now I'm the odd one out. You're obviously a smart man, and I'm sure it didn't slip past you that I'm not a wolf."

He stroked his chin. "And?"

"Well, I'm guessing since I'm still here, that means you're not excluding people based on their animal."

"I knew you weren't a wolf the second I laid eyes on you." He leaned in closer. "But what I'm interested to know about is the wolf you're with."

"Actually, I'm not even a Shifter. Full disclosure—I'm a human."

He chewed on his lower lip.

"Though I didn't grow up with a pack, I've lived with one, so I understand the basic rules of pack life. To be completely transparent, I'm not here because of the ad. I was hitchhiking in the rain, and Naomi picked me up. Imagine my surprise when I realized the bus was filled with Shifters. I don't know if that means something or nothing at all. But if my being human is going to be a problem, it's probably best to send me away now, before I get comfortable."

Tak's eyebrows knitted, and he leveled me with his gaze. "If you were living with a pack, why are you here now?"

I averted my eyes. "It wasn't the right one."

"And the wolf?"

Dusting off the stone next to my leg, I replied, "That's Catcher. He's my watchdog."

I braced for the inquisition. *Why does a human need a watchdog? Why would a woman of my age? Why would a Shifter even commit to such a thing?*

"Hmm" was all he replied. "I'll have to meet him and give him the speech when he shifts back."

"That's another thing." I stood and faced him. "Catcher never shifts back."

Silence filled the room as he sat thunderstruck.

"Your intention is to bring a wolf I've never met into my pack?"

"He's tethered himself to me. As long as he's a wolf, we're a team. If you take me, you'll have to take him too."

Tak shook his head. "That's not how it works. Both of you will have to prove your worth on equal ground. I understand that if I offer you a spot and not him, you'll stay loyal to your watchdog. That's noble." He stared at the dusty floor as if deep in thought. "I can overlook this because a man has no control over his spirit animal. That's not for me to decide. As a wolf, he'll need to prove to me that he's a valuable asset. That he's family."

"Understood. Does that mean we can stay? You'll consider us?"

"I'll consider you, little Robyn." He chuckled and scratched his head. "I've never been comfortable around humans, so it looks like my ancestors are testing me."

"Thank you."

"Tell me why you'd rather join a pack than live with your own people. This world is dangerous for humans."

With my eyes downcast, I put my hands in my pockets. "To be honest, it wasn't a lifelong dream of mine. I've been living with a pack since I was sixteen. It wasn't the right pack, but I saw how a group of strangers could come together and be a family. I suppose Catcher played a big part in my decision. He's the only family I've got. It's not fair to him if I don't choose a life."

Tak paced toward a saw bench. "Are you doing this for him? To free him?"

I rubbed my nose. "That's not the reason, but there could be some truth to it. Catcher's not just my protector. He's the brother I never had. The friend I always wanted. But I feel guilty. Maybe if he thinks I'm safe, he'll finally turn. Then he can live his life and make his own choices."

"My tribe believes there's no greater honor than when a person gives their life to protect another. In some ways, that's what a watchdog does. My people have a different name for them that translates to guardians. Often, they meet as strangers and forge a bond that no one can sever. Your spirits have intertwined for a reason. He will protect you and fight to the death. Never pity a man who sacrifices his freedom for someone else."

Toenails clicked against the floor as Catcher trotted inside.

I noticed his dirty paws and concerned expression. "We were just talking about you."

Tak knelt and looked him square in the eyes. "I'm the alpha, but you already know that."

"I'm not certain he's awake in there."

"He understands all the same." Tak's brown eyes focused on Catcher. "If you each prove your worth, you're both welcome. But if I only choose one, then you two must decide whether to stay together or split apart."

Catcher woofed quietly, lowering his tail.

"You sleep outside." Tak pointed at the door. "One puddle on my floor and you're gone."

When Catcher whined, Tak laughed and rose to his feet, putting his hands in his pockets. "Is there anything I should know about your group?"

"Like what?"

"You tell me. One of your people pulled a weapon on me and could have shot my mate."

"That guy boarded last night when I was sleeping. We've never spoken."

"And the rest?"

I stroked Catcher's soft ear. If Tak was testing me, I sure didn't want to fall into that trap. "You're probably a better judge of character than I am."

Tak walked by me and leaned way down to whisper into my ear, "Good answer."

"CATCHER, *STOP IT*."

He shoved his nose beneath my back, urging me to get up. All I wanted to do was sleep. The sun had already set, bringing the temperature down. Wood from the campfire crackled, the glowing flames lighting up the red fabric of my tent.

I coughed and threw my arm over my face. "Just let me sleep. I'm not hungry."

He whined again. Then he barked, not once but a series of sharp, loud, incessant barks.

"Are you coming out for dinner?" Montana asked.

I peered at his cowboy hat, which poked through the tent opening.

"You can have my plate," I grumbled, the thought of food making my stomach turn.

Catcher flew out of the opening and jumped on Montana.

Irked by his uncharacteristic behavior, I groggily sat up. "Catcher, stop it. That's rude."

"You don't look so hot." Montana leaned in and touched my face. "Holy shit, you're burning up."

Catcher barked.

"It's just this outdoor camping stuff. It's new to me."

Joy peered in with a lantern in hand. "I asked them to save you a plate. Are you hungry? Gracious! Your face is flushed. Are you sick?" She looked at Montana. "How is that possible?"

I touched my fiery-hot cheek. When I coughed, I realized it wasn't allergies or a lingering sinus infection I'd been struggling with over the past few days. Only Relics could get sick, and I didn't want to mislead anyone. "I guess the cat's out of the bag. I'm a human."

Montana leaned back, his mouth agape. He apparently didn't see that one coming. "And you're sick?"

"I'll get Salem." Joy whirled around and disappeared.

"Don't make this into a big deal," I begged him. "It'll make me look weak. Tak already knows I'm human." I coughed again. "So much for telling everyone later."

"I thought you were a Relic. Packs need Relics, and that made sense. Why the hell are you here?"

"Why are *you* here?" I fired back. "Second chances, remember? Do I deserve it less because I'm not immortal?"

God, this isn't me. I'm never this snappy.

Salem crouched in front of the opening and nudged Montana aside. Then he set an electric lantern next to me and opened a black bag.

I rubbed my temple. "Great. It's a party."

Joy peered over his shoulder. "Salem's a healer in your world."

He took out a bulky thermometer. "I worked in the medical field with humans. I have experience in emergency medicine and surgery, but pathogens aren't my area of expertise. Especially without lab work." He ran a thermometer over my forehead until it beeped.

Joy's eyes widened at the glowing red light from the digital reading.

"What are your symptoms?" he asked.

I continued rubbing my temple, which throbbed as if someone had struck me in the head with a baseball bat. "This is the most I've ever heard you speak."

"Symptoms."

I cleared my throat. "A mild cough. The fever only started today. I might have had a low-grade one earlier, but I don't know. I was tired this morning—more than usual."

He put something on my index finger while Catcher kept pawing and nipping him. "What about appetite?"

"None to speak of. I haven't been eating much for the past several days."

"Your immune system's worn down. Do you have a stiff neck or a rash?"

"No."

"Sore throat?"

"A little. I thought my sinuses were draining. My head is killing me. I think if I get some sleep, I'll be fine."

"Not with that fever. It's too high. We need to get it down before you become dehydrated or start having seizures." He dug around in his bag and found a bottle. When he popped the lid, he offered me two green tablets.

"This isn't Tylenol." I smelled the tablets, leery of taking something that didn't come from a pharmacy.

"These are better for you. A Relic gave me the formula. No side effects on your organs. It'll lower your fever and fight infection. Any vomiting?"

With all the immortals staring at me like I couldn't handle a fever, I was mortified. "Only once. After I drank some water."

He rubbed one of his eyebrows, appearing frustrated. "It could be a number of things. The flu, a virus like streptococcus, or even an infection. Have you cut yourself recently? Any soreness or swelling I should know about? Belly pain?"

I shook my head.

"Take the pills."

When I tried to swallow them, I thought I would choke. They lodged in my throat until I washed them down with a second gulp of water.

"Keep them down long enough to dissolve," he advised me while returning the bottle to his bag. "After thirty minutes, start sipping water. You need to stay hydrated, but don't drink too much at once. Especially if you feel nauseated. I'll check back in an hour. Tell me if you experience any new pain or symptoms. If your temperature goes up any higher than what it is, we'll have to take you to a hospital. But I don't know where the nearest one is from here."

"No, no hospital. It's not that serious. They'll charge me two thousand dollars for a shot and some ibuprofen."

"It's your decision, but if this worsens, I can't do anything without the proper tests."

When my lip quivered, I looked away before anyone noticed. "Thanks for the pills."

Salem and Joy's footfalls grew distant until they rejoined the others by the campfire.

Montana patted my shoe. "Mind if I come in?"

I scooted back. The tent was roomy for one but cozy for two.

He took off his hat and crawled in next to me, one knee drawn up and the other tucked in. "I think I'll keep an eye on you for a little while. What's got you upset?"

"I don't want to be the weak link. My first night here, and now everyone's talking about me in whispers at the campfire. I should be out there bonding with you guys." I swiped my tears away.

"The fever is screwing with your emotions." He patted the blanket. "Lie down, and let the medicine do its work."

Too drowsy to quarrel, I collapsed onto my back with a thud. Sweat dampened my shirt as if I were sitting in a sauna. After tucking a rolled-up sweater beneath my head, I curled onto my side to face him.

"That's a surprise," he remarked under his breath.

"What?"

"Salem. If he knows as much as he claims about medicine, that'll be a valuable asset."

"Packs use Relics for healing."

"Sure they do. But out here? If there are any, I doubt they have any openings. How many do you think would accept clients if that meant commuting all the way from Austin? If there's an emergency, that's a long time to wait for help. A packmate who's a healer—that's peace of mind if a kid gets hurt."

Catcher whined outside the tent opening.

"It's okay," I assured him. "Can you turn off that lantern? It hurts my eyes."

Montana found the switch and turned it down to a low level. Then he pushed up his short sleeve to scratch his shoulder. He had strong arms, the kind that could lift a woman off her feet without him flinching. His features were handsome—a mix between hardened and soft, like somehow, I could see both the good and the bad. *And my god, his brown eyes.* When he looked at me, it was like looking into infinity. The way he watched me was reassuring, and I felt comfortable in his presence. Perhaps we'd known each other in a past life.

Those arms...

He furrowed his brow. "Why are you looking at me like that?"

"You're handsome. I didn't notice it before." My eyes closed, and everything seemed wavy and distant, like a dream.

When I opened them again, his face was in front of mine. I'd never seen such soulful eyes on a man. The lines on his forehead suggested he worried a great deal. *About what? About who?*

He touched my hand, and when he did, I got butterflies. "You're gonna be fine."

"But you *are* fine." I closed my eyes again, my skin as cold as ice. It made me shiver even harder. Maybe my fever had finally broken.

THE NEXT THING I KNEW, my body floated, weightless.

"Keep her down," Salem instructed.

Disoriented by the talking, I opened my eyes and realized someone had submersed me in water. "What's happening? Why am I in a tub?"

Archer put his hand on my forehead. "You need to get her fever down." He looked over his shoulder at Salem. "We should take her to the stream. The water's cold."

"Too cold," Salem pointed out. "It'll cause her to shiver, which generates body heat. The lukewarm water will provide adequate relief."

Archer got up and marched out.

"But the pills," I argued, still trying to figure out if I was having a nightmare. "I just took them."

"That was over two hours ago," Salem informed me. "Usually, they work right away."

Tak folded his arms. "Have you ever given them to a human?"

"No, but they worked as expected on an adolescent Shifter. I've had them for a while. It's possible their efficacy is reduced, or perhaps I need to adjust the dosage for a human."

Lanterns illuminated the partially constructed room, which lacked drywall. Then it became apparent I was in a clawfoot tub.

Naked.

"I'm naked!" Water splashed over the edge when I covered my chest and plastered myself against the edge.

Virgil hopped off a workbench. "If only I had a nickel for every time I've woken up and said the same thing."

"Everyone, out," Tak commanded, inviting no argument.

Archer returned and handed a bundle to Tak. "Clean clothes. Let me know if you need anything else."

I buried my face in my arm.

"Everyone includes you," Hope insisted, then came the sound of a kiss. "Let me take over from here. I think you've all seen quite enough tonight."

"Whatever you say, Duckie."

When the footsteps grew distant, a sponge dabbed my left shoulder.

"Does this bother you?" she asked.

"My skin feels sensitive." When I peered up, she sat down in a chair and handed me a bottle of water.

My focus drifted to the scars on her forehead and jaw. They looked like bite marks.

Following Salem's advice, I sipped the water. "Were those pills he gave me safe?"

Hope squeezed the sponge, then pressed it to my forehead. "The pills might have knocked you out more than the fever. He said they worked on you as a sedative. Something about it being a side effect of fighting infection."

The archer with the turquoise hair waltzed in and bent forward. She wore black leggings paired with shorts. "What's the verdict?"

Hope smiled at her. "She'll live."

The friendly young woman sat on the edge of the tub. Her beautiful freckles were small and scattered on her face. So far, it seemed her personality was as colorful as her appearance. "A human joining our pack. The mind boggles. Don't worry—we don't exclude your kind. In fact, one of my aunts was human. Now she's a Mage. True story."

I handed Hope the water bottle and wiped back my wet hair. "This isn't the first impression I was going for."

Hope's friend laughed, and her demeanor put me at ease. "I like her already. I'm Melody, but everyone calls me Mel."

Sweat trickled down my forehead. "I'm Robyn. You're an excellent shot."

She twirled her wavy hair, which fell past her shoulders. "I'm not a professional, but nobody goes hungry around here." Melody got up and sashayed to the opposite side and squatted. After resting her arms on the rim of the tub, she drew in a sharp breath and held it for a beat. "You know what I'm really interested in hearing about when you get better?" She flicked the water with her finger. "That mark on your hip."

I rolled onto my back and held my arms over my chest.

"It just so happens one of my aunts has that same mark," she said in a hushed tone. "I know what you are, and according to your reaction, so do you. Look, even though we're strangers, you can trust us. Your secret's safe with me."

"And me," Hope added. "We understand the risk of others finding out, but do you?"

I thought about the birthmark, which didn't look like a birthmark. It had a distinct shape of a spade, like in a deck of cards. I'd always kept it hidden because if the wrong person saw it, they might discover I was a Potential. Most didn't know about us, but that didn't eliminate the threat of someone taking my choice away—or worse, selling me on the black market. My mother had warned me about the dangers, and I used to think she was exaggerating so I would keep it a secret. Then I heard stories about the black market and realized to some, I was a valuable commodity.

"Have you always known?" Melody asked.

I coughed, then flicked my eyes between them. *Can I trust complete strangers?* As Hope was the Packmaster's mate, surely she understood the value of trust. Since they knew, it seemed pointless to lie. Maybe the fever had me delirious, but I needed to confess it to someone.

"No. My parents were trusted humans. They shielded me as a kid. It's hard for a child to keep a secret that big, so I didn't learn about Breed—or about me—until I was a teen."

Hope exchanged glances with Melody before frowning at me. "Are you just here to find a mate?"

I wiped my face, which was still hot. "God no. If I only wanted to turn, I would have slept with someone ages ago. It's not that hard to find a willing man."

"You've got that right," Melody said. "Not that I'd know anything about that."

Hope gave her a wry smile. "I remember differently from days long past."

"I'm a saint." Melody waggled her eyebrows. "That's my story, and I'm stickin' to it."

"I hope to be a Shifter someday," I admitted. "For whatever reason, I feel connected to wolves. Maybe that means something. But if it happens, it'll be out of love. I don't want to use someone just for that."

"But you could," Melody said, not showing any judgment. "Then you could get it over with. It would be easier to join a pack if you were already a wolf."

"I like doing things the hard way." A smile touched my lips. "Love matters."

As a Potential, I had something in my DNA that allowed me, a human, to change into the first Breed I had sex with. And I would remain that Breed forever, regardless of who I slept with afterward. For me, sex wasn't recreational. I didn't have one-night stands or affairs. Living with a pack had made it difficult to maintain a relationship with humans. They weren't allowed to learn about the Breed world, so I could never bring them home. That inevitably created problems and raised suspicion.

Melody's wet finger squeaked against the rim of the tub. "What if you fall for a Vampire or a Chitah?"

"I'd still want to live in a pack. If you accept me as a human, would you throw me out if I became something else? Or if I stayed a human forever?" I closed my eyes, weak and exhausted. "Will it matter?"

"She needs to rest," Hope said. "I'll get Tak to lift her out."

CHAPTER 7

I LAY IN A MEADOW, surrounded by rolling waves of orange flowers. Their petals were fanning in and out like butterfly wings. My skin warmed from the loving rays of the sun, which hung in the lilac sky like a champagne-colored orb. In the distance, a lone wolf howled, the note stretching across the horizon like a memory.

When a rumbling sound vibrated against my body, the butterflies took off to the skies until they blocked the sun. In the gathering darkness, an unfamiliar fragrance swirled around me. I moved my head, and something prickled against my nose.

My eyes opened, and the dream faded. I was wrapped in a tight embrace. While I could have easily shoved the person away, their heartbeat thumping against my palm was a comfort I'd never known. It didn't matter who it was. I was just grateful for the warmth.

I nuzzled my face against their bristly neck. When I drew in another deep breath, their heady scent stirred something deep within me, and my skin flushed all over. While my original fever was gone, I was experiencing a new fever of a different kind.

His hand grazed down my back and found a home at the base of my spine. "Are you awake?" he whispered, his breath hot against the shell of my ear.

Oh god, was I.

When I leaned back, I was startled to see Montana. Though his brown hair was too short for bedhead, one of his eyebrow hairs was sticking out of place. I wanted to smooth it down.

"Feeling better?" he asked. "You're not hot anymore." His gaze darted to my mouth.

I licked my dry lips. "Then why are you holding me?"

"After all that rambling you did last night about how hot I am, it seemed only right."

"What?" I scooted farther back and rubbed my eyes. Montana's morning voice was even sexier than his bare chest.

He eased up on one elbow, and I stole a glance at a round scar on his abdomen. Montana didn't have any visible tattoos, but he was marked all the same. Maybe not by choice, but the brand on his hand carried a story I wondered about.

"You don't remember much, do you?" he asked. "Salem said that might happen. After we knocked your fever down, he was afraid you'd get too cold with the nighttime temperatures. I was the next best thing to an electric blanket, especially since there's no electricity."

Still weak, I forced myself to sit up. My head still hurt but not nearly as much. My stringy brown hair stuck to my face, and I brushed the tangled mess away with my fingers. "What time is it?"

"We missed breakfast." He reached for a bottle of water and handed it to me.

I gulped it all down and then gasped for air.

"Human, huh?" Montana sat up and located his T-shirt behind him.

"My parents were trusted humans."

"Is that so?" He nodded, staring off. "That makes sense. What did they do for a living?"

"My dad was in the military, though I don't know much about what he did exactly. He watched for unusual Breed activity that the military stumbled on and reported it to colleagues."

"Breed colleagues," he said.

I screwed the cap back on the empty bottle. "I didn't find out what they did until I was older."

"That must have been an interesting conversation."

"My mom relayed a story about lightning balls, a strange phenomenon that people have been seeing for centuries. They appear in random places, and nobody knows what causes them." I searched my bag for socks. "Apparently, a group of Air Force personnel captured one on video. After an internal investigation, my dad found out it was actually from a Mage." I hiccupped because of all the water I'd drunk.

"People who make those energy balls are called Wielders."

"Huh. Anyhow, they tracked down the guy responsible, and it was a new Learner. He was practicing, and I guess he wasn't making sure they were extinguished. My dad worked with a team to destroy the video. The military keeps stuff like that confidential, but out of context, they might get the wrong idea and think they're top-secret weapons from enemy countries."

Montana balled up his shirt. "Or they might dig a little more, find the Mage, and run every type of experiment on him."

"Exactly. Everyone who saw it had their memories scrubbed by a Vampire. My mom didn't want to make the Breed world sound magical, because she was afraid I wouldn't take it seriously. I learned that you guys are like us, only we pose more of a danger. In ancient times, humans probably thought you were devils."

"They did. Usually the religious fanatics. Now there's more at stake. Governments would think we were a danger to national security. The idea is tempting for the young ones who don't remember what it was like to be out. I'm not that old, but I've heard the stories. People don't change."

"No, they don't." Still groggy, I rubbed my eyes.

The previous night had made me miss my mom. It reminded me of the times when I was sick and she doted on me.

Montana ran his fingers through his hair. "And your mom? She also worked in the military?"

"She was a pediatric nurse."

He gave a sympathetic smile. "I'm sorry."

I realized I'd been talking about my parents in the past tense. He must have picked up on it. "They died when I was young. First my dad from a heart attack when I was nine."

"And your mom?"

My gaze shifted to my backpack and the case of drawing pencils poking out. "Cancer. She didn't get along with her family. In the last year, we moved in with her best friend, who was a Shifter. She helped take care of my mom, but mostly, I think my mom wanted to be sure that someone was there to take care of me when she was gone. I remember hearing discussions between them late at night, and her friend didn't feel like she could raise me. My mom promised her it would only be for a few years, then I'd be old enough to leave."

Montana glanced at the zipped door, which Catcher was scratching on. "Where does he fit into the picture?"

Since I was a Potential, my mom had paid Catcher to protect me. But I couldn't tell Montana that secret.

"She wanted another layer of protection in case her friend wasn't up to the task, so she hired a watchdog to guard me. I think she was afraid I might fall into the system and get bounced around in foster care." I cleared my throat. "She told me if something ever happened to find a pack. They would protect me."

His eyebrows knitted. "From what?"

Again, I couldn't elaborate on that. Though my mother had never given me a reason, I later suspected she wanted me to join a pack so that I would remain in the Breed world. Maybe she trusted Shifters more than any other Breed and assumed I would one day give up being human.

"We only stayed with Tasha for three weeks after my mom died." I twisted my back to stretch. "You don't want to hear all this."

Montana captured my wrist. "I do." Then he drew back and gave me his full attention. I'd never told the full story to anyone, and it felt strange.

"Tasha tried, but she had her own busy life. She wasn't ready to take on a teenager who was as awful as I was."

"You'd just buried your mother."

"Yeah. I wish I could have been better, though. I lashed out. Catcher lived with us, so he was always on the offense. Tasha and I were fighting one night about something trivial. I hadn't done the dishes, and she'd been working a fourteen-hour shift. She was tired, I was hormonal, and we got into a screaming match. Catcher didn't know what was happening, and he bit her. Not a severe bite, just a warning. That was it. She said she couldn't do it anymore and cried. Tasha loved my mom like a sister, but I don't blame her. She wasn't ready for that kind of responsibility."

"Did you run away?"

"She couldn't give me what I needed, and because of her work hours, I spent too much time alone. So she found a pack for me to live with. My mom had told her that she didn't want me going into foster care. That if something ever happened, I needed to go with a pack." I worried my bottom lip and crawled toward the tent opening. "It was just the wrong pack. Tasha's a bear, so it wasn't her fault she didn't know the good packs from the bad."

When I unzipped the tent, Catcher flew inside and cleaned my face with his tongue.

"I'm okay. I promise." To give him the assurance he needed, I scratched beneath his chin and kissed his wet nose. "Why didn't you let Catcher in here to keep me warm?"

Montana sat up and cleared his throat. "I'm taller. You needed more real estate."

Wagging his tail, Catcher nudged me, his eyes bright and his body wiggling with energy. He nipped my shirt and pulled on it before letting go and dashing off.

"You should do as he says and eat something." Montana put his hand on my forehead.

I closed my eyes, enjoying the press of his hand—not just the physical contact but the concern behind it.

"Can you walk?"

I suddenly noticed my oversized long-sleeved shirt. "Whose clothes are these? They smell like coconut."

"Archer's. Unless you want those sweatpants to fall off in front of everyone, you might want to change."

I palmed my face when I had a flashback of the bathtub the previous night.

"Don't sweat it," he said. "That was the most excitement we had all day. If you're worried about everyone seeing you naked, they came in *after* Tak put you in the tub."

I stared daggers at him. There hadn't been any bubbles in that water, so they'd seen enough.

Montana rubbed the back of his neck. "We're wolves, Robyn."

"I know. It's just that I've never had to be naked in front of people. Not a whole group all at once. Since I don't shift, there's not a reason to show off my body."

"I disagree." A sinful smile touched his lips for a second before he wiped it away. "What do you think about Tak?"

"I like him."

"Man, that energy. Can you feel it as a human?"

"No."

Montana rubbed his eye with the heel of his hand. "It laps off him in waves. I don't think he'll have trouble with any of the wolves submitting when they meet him."

"I need to change. Can you make yourself scarce?"

"Are you sure you want me to leave? I know how hard it must be for you not to be near all this... hotness," he said while crawling out of the tent.

"I was at death's door! I was practically hallucinating."

He laughed in the distance while I zipped up my tent.

"Someone thinks he's hilarious," I muttered while pulling off my clothes. "Why did I say all that to him? I must have been out of my mind. The last thing I need to do is hook up with someone joining the same pack. Nothing but trouble if the Packmaster found out."

James didn't bother putting his shirt on. The warm sun and cool breeze were idyllic. He could get used to this. He could also get used to his new nickname. In fact, he hadn't felt like James in a long time. It was common for immortals to change their names, especially if they were hundreds of years old. Sometimes names became outdated or linked to a family the immortal didn't want to be associated with. In his case, he no longer wanted to remember the pain of his old life. After a deep breath of fresh air, he let go of James and embraced his new identity—Montana.

"Heads up!"

Montana turned and caught an apple in his palm.

Deacon's thin long-sleeved shirt looked painted on.

"What's with all the apparel?" Montana asked.

Once Deacon reached the old oak, he sat on one of the lower branches that touched the ground. "I don't want the alpha to think I'm trying to outgun him." He flexed his arm before biting into his own green apple. "How's the weakling?"

Montana bristled. He'd spent time around humans and liked them enough but never thought he'd be defending one. "Her name's Robyn."

Deacon's eyebrows rose while he chewed his apple. "You don't say. Forgot it already. You need to get your shit together if you want to stick around. She's weak. Can't go around associating with the omegas. That'll put you at the bottom of the totem pole."

"And why do you care where I rank?"

Deacon took another bite and chewed. "Because a beta needs a good wolf he can trust right below him. You're the only one showing promise. The tripod doesn't have a chance in hell of making the cut, but his cousin might. Or the other new guy. You might have competition, so step it up."

During the bus ride, Montana had wondered where he might rank in the group, assuming everyone was chosen. Wolves more than most Shifters relied on creating ranks within a group to keep order. It was necessary for the stability of a pack. If something happened to the beta, they needed a temporary stand-in who could lead the group until they found a replacement. Positions were challenged by dominant wolves and occasionally switched up, but going into a new pack, no one wanted to be at the bottom.

And that was exactly where Robyn would be. He didn't like it. For one, she wasn't a Shifter. And her not having a skill to contribute didn't bode well.

Deacon flicked the core of his apple onto the ground before standing. "Think about it. But if I have your back, you'd better have mine." He gave him a hard pat on the chest before returning to the group.

Montana took a seat on the mossy branch. Joy and Serena were washing and wringing clothes in metal tubs. Virgil was still inside with Tak, looking at the construction and offering an opinion. Archer had found the long axe and gone to cleave wood. As Montana studied the area, he noticed a few old trees near the house posed a threat. At the very least, some branches needed to come off. Oak was good not only for burning but also for building.

"How's it going?"

Montana regarded the blue-eyed Native man who had sneaked up on him from behind. He must have either been of mixed heritage or come from an unusual tribe. Montana had once heard about a falcon tribe who had blue eyes as a common trait.

"It's going," he replied.

The man straddled the branch to his left. "Nice hat. You'll need that out here to shade your head from the sun. I'm Lakota Cross."

"James Vance, but I go by Montana. Are you local?"

"Cognito originally." Lakota pulled a tall weed from the ground and played with it. "Are you a city boy?"

Montana chuckled. "Half."

"The other half is better. I spent my childhood in both places, but if you want to live in the country, be prepared to work. The jokers before your group didn't make the cut. Some gave up, and he banished the rest. You might want to start apartment hunting before the prices jump."

"I was wondering where he keeps his horse. Some of these trees need to be cleared out, and a horse would be useful."

Lakota flicked the weed into the wind. "The horse doesn't have a barn, so it sleeps with his father-in-law."

Montana got a good vibe coming from Lakota. But another strong vibe came through in his voice, even when joking around, and he couldn't overlook it.

Lakota was a beta.

"What are you going to do with a felled tree?" Lakota stood and brushed off his pants. "That creates extra work. Right now, there's a skeleton he calls a house that still needs a roof."

Montana bit into his apple. "That tree on the right is too close. One strong storm will make that branch slice through the house like a knife through butter."

Lakota stared at it for a while. He wore a white T-shirt with a wolf's head, which suggested he had a sense of humor. Except for the occasional belt buckle or necklace, wolves didn't usually advertise themselves on clothing. "You should be the one to persuade him. I hear the wifey likes that tree and wants to put a swing in it."

"She might be happier with a new table. We can do plenty with that wood besides burning or composting it."

Lakota pursed his lips. "You'd need professional saws and a kiln to dry it out. In case you haven't noticed, we don't even have a roof."

"You keep saying that." Montana stared at his apple. "We may not have the equipment, but I'd be willing to bet someone around here does. Might be a chance to negotiate and build a rapport with the locals. There has to be a sawmill close by. We could use that wood for the barn. Save some money. By the looks of it, he's been purchasing a lot of materials."

Lakota patted his arm. "Sounds like you've got yourself a project."

"Feel like helping?"

Lakota laughed and strode away. "We have one axe and no chainsaws. Feel like guessing my answer?"

Montana suddenly had all sorts of ideas about what he would do with the land. But those thoughts disintegrated when Robyn emerged from her tent, and his mind drifted back to the night before. After she'd taken the pills, Montana watched over her with confidence. But when her fever spiked and she fainted, Salem and the others had taken over. *Could I have done more?*

Once her fever broke, Salem had expressed concern. Since it was too cold outside, someone needed to keep her warm. Montana was the first and only to volunteer. He could have shifted and let his wolf do it. Hell, he could have let Catcher do it. But since he'd first laid eyes on Robyn, all he could think about—all he could wonder about—was how she would feel in his arms. Though she was pretty, it had nothing to do with her looks.

And she was a real looker—shaggy dark hair, green eyes, and a perfect nose that wasn't narrow and had a subtle slope. Though she had a lean frame, she had arms that could wrap around a man and squeeze him tight. She was a no-fuss girl who didn't doll herself up. But the intensity of her gaze was otherworldly, as if she could look right into a man's soul.

But good looks weren't worth a hill of beans without a personality. He'd met plenty of pretty girls with ugly hearts. Robyn was not only kind but also intelligent. The fact that she looked after her watchdog showed how loyal she was—how selfless. And he loved the way her nose scrunched when she laughed.

His spirit wolf had been the first to notice her when she walked into the diner. The first time they locked eyes, his heart quickened. He decided to talk to her but got so nervous that he said all the wrong things. Knowing the full story, he thought about how she'd ordered more food for her watchdog than for herself. She'd fed him before she had a single bite, even though she was soaking wet and freezing cold. He was set to guard her, yet she put his needs above hers. That was loyalty.

Her not being a Shifter was acceptable, but not being Breed was another matter.

Surely his wolf knew it was wrong to pine for a human. If it was just an infatuation, he didn't understand why the hell his animal was getting involved. Maybe Montana had been out of the dating game too long, but damn if his wolf didn't want to claim her. And when she'd nuzzled against him this morning, the chemistry was undeniable. Suddenly, *he* was the one sweating all over.

Montana could still smell her vanilla scent all over him.

The voice in his head wouldn't shut up. *How could I have missed all the signs that she was sick? The way she'd skipped meals or only ate small portions, always making sure her watchdog was well fed. How far did she walk before running into us that night in the rain? Where did she take shelter?* Thinking back, he remembered her coughing a few times. *Why didn't I offer her more than a bag of candy or a bite of lunch?*

She needed sustenance for her recovery, and that made him want to hunt.

Montana's skin vibrated, the muscle contractions visible. Before anyone saw him losing his shit, he stalked toward the brush and shifted. Once in wolf form, he looked back, listening to the voices behind him. His wolf craned his neck and howled, yearning for her to call back.

Like a spark of lightning, he raced through a field in search of prey.

CHAPTER 8

Salem sat beside me on the porch steps. The crisp air had him dressed in a dark-green cardigan over a Henley shirt, a casual but conservative style that suited his demeanor. Though his hair was long enough to curtain his face, he tied it back in a knot. Salem wasn't as gregarious as his mate, but his compassion showed through his medical care. As crazy as last night had been, he made me feel cared for. Salem wouldn't be my first choice as a drinking buddy, but I felt comfortable talking to him. He seemed like an amiable guy—one I could confide in.

"How are you feeling this morning?" he inquired.

"Better. Especially after Joy force-fed me three sausages, a biscuit, and two eggs."

He chuckled softly. "She has a kind heart. I want you to take it easy today and stay rested. If you push yourself to prove something, you'll wear your body down. It's good you're getting some sun. Vitamin D is nature's gift."

I froze when he touched my forehead.

"Hard to tell if you're feverish with the sun on your head." Salem lifted my eyelids in an impromptu examination.

"I don't feel hot, just a little run down. One crisis at a time. Right?"

"Come see me later. I'll do a full workup and check your blood pressure. From the looks of it, you're on the mend. The medicine is unique because it fights fever and infection simultaneously."

"Why not give something like that to humans?"

"Their drug companies are proprietary and wouldn't be interested in drugs that work without side effects."

"I'd say those pills had a pretty big side effect."

"Only because of the dosage. I've never given them to a human before." Salem reached into his pocket and handed me four small packets. "I had a few of these electrolytes in my bag. Add them to your water and be sure to stay hydrated."

"Thank you."

He stared off at Archer, who was swinging an axe. He split the log every bit as expertly as the man from yesterday. I wondered how much more effort he had to put into certain activities with his limitations. Swinging an axe with one arm seemed dangerous. He held it differently and widened his stance when he brought it down.

"Someone needs to take that away from him." Salem smoothed down his mustache and beard. "I don't know how to sew a foot back on."

I chuckled while wiping a scuff on my shoe. "It's so quiet out here. I'm not from the big city or anything, but you get used to the sounds of cars, planes, and air conditioners. This is peaceful."

"I don't think we're on a flight path." Salem turned his gaze up to the sky. "I hope this works out."

"Same. You two shouldn't have any trouble getting in. It's easier for mated couples. Have you let your wolf out?"

He stroked his bottom lip. "I think it's best if we let our wolves out one at a time to avoid conflict."

"That's a good idea."

"This is an unusual situation. Usually, the alpha introduces new packmates to his pack, but none of us are pack. We'll have to be careful."

Salem seemed like a pragmatic man and not just because of the medical aspect. No one else had mentioned anything about letting their wolves run and what the plan was. Maybe they assumed everyone would get along fine. If any of them attacked another, it could cause serious injury or even death. Not exactly a great impression for anyone serious about joining the pack.

"This is the craziest thing I've ever done," I admitted.

He stroked his beard. "Wish I could say the same."

A beeping horn halted all activity and chatter. It continued tapping in rhythm, like Morse code. Everyone headed to the front to check out the commotion. A powder-blue Vespa zipped up the drive, the rider wearing a white helmet and goggles.

Tak and Hope remained on the front porch, and I saw no sign of Melody. The rest of us stood off to the side.

The scooter rolled to a stop. After the rider cut the engine, she removed her helmet and dismounted. At first, I thought she was an older woman because of her silver hair, which was cut in a pixie style and longer on top. Then she removed her goggles and revealed a youthful face.

She straightened her pink shirt and dusted off her jean capris. "I am *so* sorry I'm late," she said, her accent as country as could be. "I was gonna be on that bus, but Daisy got herself impounded for illegal parking. I couldn't just leave her behind."

Hope crossed her arms. "Daisy is your partner?"

"She sure is!" The woman patted the side of her scooter, which had a white daisy painted on the side. "We go everywhere together. We've been through things. Now... I *know* your ad said you were doing pickup only, but I figured she's small enough I could squeeze her somewhere in the back of the bus. Maybe on top with a little rope and ingenuity."

Everyone watched for Tak's reaction, waiting for him to return inside.

A slow chuckle sounded, then he rocked with laughter.

She walked right up to them and curtseyed. "My name's Mercy. I popped right out of my momma with this silver hair, and she said, '*Mercy* me!' So that's what she called me. You can't make it up."

Tak bent over laughing, his hands on his knees. "I'm going to piss myself."

Hope elbowed him. "We expected a few late arrivals," she said with a friendly smile. "You're welcome to stay on our land. The Packmaster here will give you the official speech before you settle in."

"I'm grateful to be here. Especially after what I went through last night. I know I seem like a handful, but I swear I'll fit right in like a bee in a hive. I get along with everyone. Just ask anyone."

Virgil put his arm around me. "Looks like I have competition for the most likeable packmate."

Mercy swung her gaze around. "Real nice place you got here. *Real* nice." She waved at her captive audience. "Hi."

Some of us raised our hands. Others mumbled.

"Where should I put Daisy so she's out of your way?" Mercy asked. "I'm sorry, but I couldn't sell her. Wouldn't bring much to the pot anyhow. She's got a few miles on her, and we were clutching each other tight all the way down I-35."

Hope gestured to the vehicles to the left of the house. "Anywhere over there is fine. Watch where you step. We've tried to pick up all the nails, but it's a work in progress."

Mercy glanced up at the tarp. "Your builders are doing a great job. Looks like she's gonna be a beauty."

"We're the builders," Tak informed her.

"Holy mackerel! Do I get to help? Please say yes! I've laid down flooring and cut tile, and my favorite thing to do is paint walls. You should have seen my last apartment."

"All that comes later," Tak said, adopting a serious tone. "You can leave your things out here. They're safe. Come with me."

Mercy glanced in our direction and waved again. "Bye."

"Ain't she a peach?" Deacon said with a chuckle. "Dibs."

That word triggered something in me, and I stalked off. My heart pounded as memories of the final days in my former home flooded back. *What if it happens again?*

I walked behind an oak tree and calmed myself with deep, focused breaths.

"Is something wrong, female?"

I looked up at the Native man from yesterday.

"I'm Lakota," he said as if reading my mind. "You're Robyn. Now that we've met, are you ill?"

I shook my head. "It's not that. I just needed to get away for a minute. This is a weird situation."

Grinning, he said, "This group isn't as bad as the last one. They were pretty rough."

"What made you stay?"

He squinted up at the tall tree. "Sometimes your wolf knows when it's home."

I peered around the tree.

Lakota stepped forward. "What troubles you?"

"This isn't a pack yet. What protection are we offered?"

"From who?"

I wiped my tousled hair out of my eyes. "None of us really knows each other. I've got a ball of nerves in the pit of my stomach."

"That's because your watchdog isn't around. When you were sick, people helped. On my word, you're safe. No harm will come to any female on this land, not as long as I'm here."

His words comforted me.

"Rumor has it you're a beta. Is it true?"

Lakota regarded me a moment before switching the subject. "It's a bold choice joining a pack when you're not even Breed."

"I belong in a pack."

"Are you sure? It's a crazy experience growing up in a house filled with wolves. Maybe you need to find a herd of deer."

I paced out a few steps until the wind was in front of me. "What kind of Breed did you grow up with?"

The wind was blowing his hair all over the place. "I'm a wolf."

"If you say so. But you don't act like a wolf. Well, not entirely."

He rubbed his chin.

When I realized I'd put my foot in my mouth, I added, "I didn't mean it as an insult. Ah, sorry if it sounded that way. It's just that I rarely hear Shifters use the word *female* as freely as you do. Not all wolves grow up in packs, so I figured you might have had a less conventional home."

"You're human, right? I guess to you, none of our homes are conventional."

I smiled. "True."

"Don't miss lunch. Packs that eat together stay together." He swaggered off toward the house.

Constant tapping from inside the house overlapped as the hammering started back up. People had jobs to do. Archer split wood while the long-haired Krystopher carried the pieces to a covered woodpile. Joy was clipping wet laundry onto a makeshift clothesline.

As much as I wanted to help, Salem had a point. If I pushed myself too soon, I'd be useless. Better to take the day off and replenish my strength, so I grabbed my backpack and took out my dirty laundry. I spent an hour sitting in the sun, washing my clothes against a washboard and ringing them out. I paused each time, sipping water and soaking in the sun. Puffy white clouds dotted the sky, and the azure blue reflected in the sudsy water like a Monet painting.

In this peaceful moment, I imagined this place as home.

. . .

Two hours had passed. I found a low branch of an oak tree and sat down to draw. Montana's wolf returned when I wasn't looking. When Archer was ready to shift, he did it privately in the field, beyond the tree line. I could barely see him. With a front leg missing, he didn't run fast, but his animal managed to get around just fine.

"What are you doing?" Montana asked.

I looked up from my sketchpad. "Just fiddling around."

He stood over me and turned his head. "That's real good." Then he glanced over his shoulder at the barn. "It doesn't look like that, though."

"No, but it's how I imagine it should look."

"May I?" He lifted the sketchpad and stared at it. "This is detailed. You did all this from memory?"

"I guess. My mom used to say I had a way of seeing things as they should be. She's the one who encouraged me to draw. It relaxes me."

"Mind if I borrow this?" Montana abruptly stalked off.

My pencils rolled to the ground when I hopped up and chased him. "Wait a second! Come back with that."

Montana's long strides toward the Packmaster put distance between us.

My pace slowed when I reached them.

Tak's brown skin glistened in the sun as he sat on the porch steps. "You did this?"

"It's just a sketch."

He flicked his gaze toward the barn and furrowed his brow. "That's up for debate."

"What do you mean?"

Tak gave me a pensive stare. "It's evocative. Like you crawled inside my head and pulled out my vision. This drawing is exactly how I pictured my barn. Do you work in architecture?"

I shook my head. "I doodle."

Tak threw back his head and laughed. "'Doodle,' she says. You even added the weathervane, which shows me you were paying attention to my thoughts about not being dependent on technology. People use their phones for information that's all around them. Do you know what this silo is for?"

I took the sketch back from him. "I see them on old barns."

"They used them for storing grain. We don't need one of those for now. We'll use the barn for storing hay and tools. I'll need to educate everyone on safety precautions so that my barn doesn't go up in flames. Do you think you can sketch a stable with six stalls? Something modern."

"Don't horses sleep in the barn?"

Tak smiled. "City people have many fantasies."

Hope appeared behind him and descended the steps. "Mind your tongue. Your mate is a city girl."

He held his smile and intimately admired his mate's figure. Then he steered his gaze back to me. "Your ancestors blessed you with the gift of vision. Use it. I want the stable away from the barn. It's safer to store the hay in a separate place from the animals. That's the way my people do it. Over there," he said, pointing at a clearing. "Draw me something large enough for six mares. Don't forget windows. They'll need coverings to protect them from getting broken."

My eyes widened. "Are we riding horses? I thought I could buy a car when I saved up enough money."

Tak grinned. "Horses are optional. I need a place for my pretty girl, and she might want a mate. If they produce ponies, I could sell them."

I tilted my head to look at my sketch. "How do you keep the rats out?"

Montana smothered a grin and turned away.

Then I remembered that a pack of hungry wolves didn't have to worry about getting a barn cat.

Tak stood up and stretched. "If we need milk, we can buy a cow. They get easily spooked in a pack, so we'll have to buy from a breeder who raised them around wolves."

"What about meat?" Montana inquired.

Hope appeared disinterested in the conversation and collected a bucket by the porch before heading to the well.

After watching a mockingbird dive at his mate, Tak slapped his ankle, where ants had gathered for a bite. "Sustainability doesn't mean we have to do everything ourselves. Our wolves can hunt, and I've seen deer on the property. That's plenty of meat we can freeze. No need to have a slaughterhouse. If we require any beef or pork, we can trade for it or buy."

"Or raise a pig," Montana suggested.

Tak waved his hand. "No pigs. They're a nuisance. Chickens and goats are fine for cheese and eggs, but we'll need to keep them penned."

Montana squared his shoulders, and I thought about how handsome and confident he looked in that cowboy hat. He gestured to the rotting structure. "I'd like to ask your permission to lead construction on the barn. I was thinking about taking down some of these trees and repurposing the wood." He pointed at the one nearest the house. "This one needs to come down. I heard your mate is attached to it, but the branches could split your house in two."

The alpha swung his gaze up to the mighty oak. "She loves that tree. But you're right. I've brought this issue up with her, and we're at a stalemate."

"We could use it for a table or something special. I'm sure she'd appreciate having a piece of your property inside the house as a centerpiece." Montana jerked his chin at a grove of trees. "You also have deadfall and widow-makers that should be cleared out. Some of those will look a hell of a lot better if the lower branches are trimmed off."

After pacing a few steps, Tak pinched his chin. "Her mother makes furniture. Perhaps we'll conspire to build something that will earn her forgiveness."

When Hope returned with the heavy bucket of water, Tak collected it from her. "Rest your feet."

She wrapped her arms around him and kissed him softly on the chin. "Only if you promise to drive me to the city. I need supplies, and

I'm sure our guests would like to purchase clothes and basic necessities."

He walked up the porch steps and set the pail down. "You needn't worry about a thing. We'll go this afternoon."

That promise filled me with excitement. I had enough money to buy essentials. "Should I make a list for you? I've got paper. I can get everyone's requests."

"Don't be silly," Hope said, the wind caressing her beautiful hair. "There's plenty of room in the back of the truck."

CHAPTER 9

Although there were a few shops nearby, Tak wanted to drive to Austin that afternoon to run errands. Not all of us went on the ride. The alpha didn't want to leave his property unguarded, so Deacon volunteered to stay along with Lakota, Krystopher, Joy, and Gordon—the guy with the gold tooth. Bear also remained behind to work on meal prep and cleaning. Catcher chased the truck to the end of the drive, but he couldn't go. A wolf in the city would be nothing but trouble.

We all fit in two trucks. Melody drove the small black one with Virgil in the passenger seat. Serena and Ian rode in the truck bed without complaint. Mercy and I rode with Tak and his mate since they had a back seat. Archer, Salem, and Montana sat in the bed.

I thought Mercy might talk my ear off, but her drive from Dallas on a scooter must have wiped her out. As soon as we buckled our seat belts, she was out like a light.

I listened to Tak and Hope talking about their families, and he mentioned his father had generously gifted them a large sum of money after their mating ceremony. Hope wanted to invite him down once the house was finished, then they talked at length about what needed to be done.

Finding an existing home with a pack's specifications and land requirements wasn't easy. Shifter houses were constructed differently from human ones. Not only did they have more bedrooms, but the private quarters were smaller too. Dining and other common rooms had the most square footage. Even if termites and age hadn't gotten to the house, he would still have had to knock out all the walls to build enough rooms for a pack.

Hearing their plans and dreams filled me with mixed emotions. On one hand, I felt like an outsider. On the other, the idea of finding a real family gave me butterflies in the best way. Despite his menacing facial tattoo and frightening size, Tak was nothing like my last Packmaster. He was powerful, yet fair. Strict, yet he had a sense of humor.

He called his mate Duckie as a pet name. When he started telling me the story of how they'd met, she quickly slapped his arm.

"I was stranded," she said, "and the fates sent me a warrior in a desperate time."

Tak grinned at her. "That's *one* way to tell it. The other is that I was lost on a road just like this one. I glanced over and nearly wrecked my truck when I caught sight of—"

She held a hand over his mouth. "That's not how it happened. Don't make me switch your backside."

"Mmm." He kissed her palm. "Please do." Tak looked over his shoulder at me. "My mate has opinions about my version of that story."

"Guilty as charged," she admitted. "Why don't you put on some music?"

My eyes widened when he switched on the radio and hard metal blared through the speakers. *Not what I imagined tribes listening to.* Hope quickly turned it down, but Mercy didn't flinch. She continued snoozing with a dainty snore in the back of her throat.

Once we arrived in Austin, Tak gave us a brief tour of the downtown area. The Colorado River flowed right through the heart of the city, which had lots of bars, apartments, tall buildings, old houses, shopping, and places to eat. Hope mentioned the local packs occasionally met up to watch movies in Republic Square Park. She said it was an opportunity to enjoy all the perks of Austin life, even if it meant being around humans. Public events were a fun diversion for packmates who lived outside city limits.

We drove through the Breed district. Like in most cities, Breed purchased all the buildings on certain streets. Depending on the city, sometimes it was a large area. It also wasn't uncommon for them to buy up apartments and homes nearby. It provided immortals a safe place where they could connect with their own kind and also make sure their money went back to the Breed community.

Austin was so different from the small town in South Dakota where I'd traveled from.

After parking, we split up. I didn't have a phone, but Tak didn't seem concerned with modern technology. He instructed us to meet back at the trucks at exactly four.

I hit the jackpot at a thrift store. Sometimes, they could be pricy, but it had all the basics. I bought several summer shirts, tank tops, sunglasses, and two flannel shirts. Since Tak was putting us to work, comfortable clothes made sense. I also picked up a baseball hat, even though the blue jean material wasn't my style. After that, I visited a different store for panties, bras, socks, and a pajama set. While I was trying on a pair of brown lace-up boots at a shoe store, a group of friendly-looking Chitahs walked in, looking for custom-sized sneakers.

Another thing I wanted to do was make my tent comfortable, so I found a store that sold bedding and purchased two blankets, a pillow, and a sheet set.

"Girl, you need a wagon!" Mercy called out from behind me.

I set down my blanket, which was zipped up in a plastic carrier.

The pillow was easier to hold since it was vacuum sealed in the bag, but with my other bags, it was a lot.

Just then, Hope waved at me while crossing the street. I loved her harem pants and turquoise-colored shirt. She had a casual style and didn't fuss with makeup besides a little eyeliner. If only I could look that good naturally.

Her thick eyebrows shot up. "My gosh. I see you found everything you needed."

I snorted. "And then some. I didn't bring much with me."

Hope switched her shopping bag to her left hand. "I had to buy towels and rags. Bear also needed cooking utensils. If you forgot anything like toothpaste or soap, don't worry. Mel and I have extra supplies at the house."

I watched a kid fly by on a skateboard. Austin was so different from where Tak had settled. "What kind of name is Storybook? The bus driver mentioned it when she dropped us off."

"It might seem rural at first," she said, "but there are more Breed living out there than you think. We're just getting things up and running. Most of the businesses are on the same road, but it takes time to build in a new area without getting noticed by humans. Maybe it'll look like this someday, and we'll talk about when it was nothing but hills and trees as far as the eye can see."

A car horn blared, and two men argued through their open windows.

I set down a heavy bag. "I like your small town just the way it is."

Her straight hair rose when a car sped by. "This is nothing. You should see what it's like up in Cognito. Have you ever been there? It's a historical city, so there are tons of Breed. Probably more than humans. Their districts are so much bigger than what we have down here."

Mercy beamed when she caught up with us. She lifted two small shopping bags. "I've died and gone to heaven. I bought the cutest shoes and pants you ever did see at this store called Moonglow. You *need* to check it out. Some of the jewelry was out of my price range, but I found these earrings, and I'm wearing them to the grave." She tapped a pair of turquoise earrings shaped like hearts. "They're clip-ons! Aren't they nifty? I had pierced ears when I was a little girl, but after my first change, it was a pain to pierce them over and over again. I never thought to buy clip-on earrings, mostly because I can never find any I like. The magnetic ones always got lost, so I gave up."

Hope tucked her hair behind her ear. "They're beautiful on you. I'm honored to see my design on someone who appreciates them."

Mercy took off her sunglasses, revealing her grey eyes.

"That's our store," Hope explained. "Melody and I are the owners. She designs the clothing and shoes, and I work on the jewelry."

"How in the world do you have time to tie your shoes?" Mercy asked.

"Easy. Others do the labor, and we focus on new designs and all the business details."

"That's impressive," I said. "I wouldn't know the first thing about running a business."

She took a deep breath and sighed. "We're still learning as we go, and we've encountered plenty of obstacles. I'd love to give you an official tour sometime, but it's getting late now, and we need to get back." She gripped the handle on my comforter bag.

As Hope took the lead up the sidewalk, Mercy fell back and whispered, "I am *mortified*."

"Why?" I asked, slowing down to meet her pace.

"I should have known that was her store. Why didn't I ask? I called her earrings nifty. I should have said they were stunning or beautiful, which they are. But I said *nifty*. All I meant was I'd never seen clip-ons this special. On top of that, I said her jewelry's too expensive." Mercy sighed and shook her head. "I could just die. Right here on the sidewalk, in front of everyone."

"I think you actually made her day."

She slipped her sunglasses back on. "Think I can get a discount?"

I chuckled.

"Pump the brakes!" Virgil shouted.

I glanced over my shoulder and spotted him running toward us with his shirt pulled up to his chin. He was holding the bottom hem, and large objects were making the fabric bulge.

When he caught up with us, a plastic jar of peanut butter fell out of his arms and rolled toward the curb.

I grabbed it and tucked it under his chin. "What the hell is all this?"

"It took forever to find a grocery store," he said, out of breath. "Then I got lost. The humans were giving me all kinds of strange looks."

"Like the ones we're giving you now?" I asked.

A powerful gust of wind blew his brown fedora off.

Mercy picked it up and patted it onto his head. "Someone has a craving."

"If you're smart, you'll stock up too," he advised her. "We're in the middle of nowhere, and there's nothing worse than shifting back and not having your favorite food."

Mercy looked amused by Virgil's serious expression. "I have self-control."

"Whatever you say, Shortcake."

"You know what they say about small packages."

He lifted a leg. "You know what they say about big feet."

She stood on her tiptoes and looked behind him. "Are the police hunting you down? Why didn't you get a bag to carry all that?"

"I don't like those plastic bags. My wolf got a bag stuck around his neck once and couldn't shift back. Someone had to cut it off."

Hope set down her things. "I need to grab something before we leave. I'll only be a second."

While she rushed into the hardware store next to us, I scanned the wide, tree-lined street in search of our group. I spotted them across the road and waved.

People honked at Virgil when he crossed through traffic with his armload of Jiffy. A jar of peanut butter tumbled onto the street and busted beneath a truck tire.

Mercy set her bags next to mine. "That boy needs serious help. Say, how long have you been with these fellas?"

"Just a day or two."

"I haven't met everyone yet. Is the cowboy friendly?"

"He's all right."

Mercy fluffed her hair. "He sure likes them shirts nice and tight. That's a sign of a dangerous man."

I laughed at her strange remark.

"Don't look at me. I don't make the rules. But what you really gotta watch out for are the ones in tight pants. I once dated a man with tight pants. Turns out he couldn't keep 'em zipped, so that's why he wore 'em so tight. Can't make it up." She put one hand on her hip and tipped her sunglasses down. "What about Hot Jesus? What's his story?"

"Who?" I followed the direction of her gaze. "Oh, that's Salem. Not much of a talker. He's mated to Joy, the lady with the curly blond hair."

"Really?" Mercy didn't say it with jealousy or even surprise, more like a person finding out their best friend had just gotten hitched. "I bet they'll make some pretty babies. I'm glad we have a mated couple trying to get in. That's the stability I'm looking for." Mercy sat on a curved bike rack. "You're easy to talk to. Did anyone ever tell you that? I haven't spoken to Joy, but she seems like a sweetheart."

"You two will get along great. Serena's quiet, and I'm the serious one."

I'd always been the serious one since I had to grow up fast after losing both parents, so the weight of the world was always on my shoulders.

Mercy crossed her ankles. "You say that like it's a bad thing. Life would be way too boring if we were all the same. That's what balances everything out. And on that note, thank heaven we have some feminine energy in the group. I was worried I'd drive all this way and find nothing but a bunch of boys."

I peered through the store's window. My stomach dropped when I saw Hope kneeling with her head down. I abandoned my bags and flew into the store.

"Hope! What's wrong?"

She panted as if she had been running a mile. Her trembling hands came away from her face, and the frantic look in her eyes scared me.

"Holy mackerel. What happened?" Mercy asked.

I quickly assessed the situation. "Get Tak. *Hurry.*"

A customer walked around and gawked at us. "Is she okay?"

Hope was hyperventilating and abruptly stood up. When she knocked a few cans of spray paint onto the floor, the customer said, "I'll get the manager."

Hope shook her head.

"She's fine," I assured him. "It happens all the time."

I held her arms and kept my voice calm. "Did someone hurt you?"

She shook her head, then licked her lips. Hope wasn't acting like herself, and she wasn't making any eye contact.

"I want you to take a deep breath and hold it for five seconds. Listen to my voice."

She clutched her chest and frantically shook her head. "I can't. My heart's racing. I need to go before I shift."

"Deep breath." I drew in a breath to encourage her to do the same, which she did. "Now hold it. One, two, three… Focus on a peaceful thought. Four. And we're going to do a slow exhalation on five."

Together, we breathed out. Though it wasn't stopping whatever she was experiencing, she'd calmed down. Too much oxygen, and she might pass out.

Tak stormed in. I moved aside while he caged Hope in his arms. She rested her flushed face against his chest, her arms tucked in and her fists clenched. When the others filed in to watch, she closed her eyes and turned her head away.

"What happened?" Montana asked sharply, and I guessed everyone thought she might have been assaulted.

Tak was murmuring in a language I didn't understand, cradling her head. He noticed her knees shaking and wrapped her in a supportive hug. "Tell me what sounds you hear," he said softly.

"Terrible music," she replied.

"What else?"

"A child calling for his mother outside."

When a store worker poked his head around, I walked over to greet him. "Everything's fine. You don't need to call for help. We've got it."

The best thing about a Breed shop was not having them call an ambulance for every little crisis. He gave a cursory glance before heading back to the register.

"Hand me the keys," Montana said. "I'll bring the truck around." He noticed my baseball cap before catching the keys flying at him.

Salem leaned in. "Is there anything I can do to assist?"

Tak slanted his eyes toward us. "Give us room."

We filed out the door and waited on the sidewalk. The second the white truck rolled up, Tak emerged with Hope in his arms. When the black truck parked behind it, everyone returned to the vehicles with their bags. Melody's group drove on ahead of us while we stayed in the truck. I sat directly behind Hope.

With the motor humming, Tak leaned toward Hope, clasping her hand.

"She has episodes," he said at last. "You know them as panic attacks or anxiety. They don't happen often, but she's a warrior." He reached over, and I guessed he was caressing her cheek or brushing a lock of hair away from her face.

Mercy shot me a concerned look. It was unusual for a prominent alpha to choose a mate with a condition many regarded as a weakness.

I wasn't sure how to broach the topic without their being offended. "Has she ever sought treatment?"

"We tried," he answered, revealing his unmarked profile. "The Relics suggested medicine, but Hope is against medicating herself."

"I know it helps some people," Hope added in a weak voice. "But these happen infrequently. Why take medicine daily for something that only occurs every few months? Perhaps I make the episodes worse because I worry about shifting in public. That would be awful."

Tak adjusted a vent. "If she shifts during an attack, her wolf can be unpredictable and aggressive. Even in the Breed district, there are always humans around."

I leaned forward and gripped the back of her seat. "Maybe I can help. Obviously, I can't cure panic attacks, but have you ever tried yoga or meditation? There's even a simple technique you can do to slow down your heart by stimulating the vagus nerve. Splashing cold water on the face also helps, but that's not something you'd want to do in the middle of an attack."

Hope twisted around. "Would that stop them?"

"Honestly, I don't know. After my father died, I struggled with anger. My mom was a nurse, and she knew tricks to calm new mothers. The breathing techniques help when I feel myself getting worked up. I don't think it'll prevent a panic attack, but it might make them shorter or less severe. It might even stop it if you catch it early enough. You redirect your thoughts and focus, but it seems like you're already doing that." I looked at Tak. "You asked her what sounds she heard. Sometimes distractions can help center a person when they're spinning out of control. It's worth trying. If anything, it can't hurt."

Still out of breath, Hope sat forward again and pulled her seat belt on. "If you think it might help, I'd love to hear more later. I'm too tired right now."

Tak reached into the back seat and grabbed the neatly folded afghan between Mercy and me. He draped it over Hope's lap before kissing her forehead.

Mercy clutched her chest, and her thoughts were written all over her pouty face. She was touched by his tenderness, patience, and complete devotion to Hope's needs, and especially the respectful way in which he discussed her condition. He felt no shame and didn't attempt to conceal it for fear that it might reflect poorly on him as an alpha.

Tak held her hand until she closed her eyes.

CHAPTER 10

THE DRIVE HOME WAS QUIET. Through the side-view mirror, I observed Hope sleeping soundly. I'd never personally experienced a panic attack, though I was sure she must have been exhausted. Tak said she was usually unsettled afterward and slept for a long time. He was surprisingly forthright and revealed how she'd gotten her facial scars as a child—how that violent encounter with a rogue wolf had changed her. Hope had silently carried that trauma for many years, and Tak vowed that no wolf in his pack would ever walk alone. I appreciated his candor and wished I could be as honest.

But that wasn't in the cards. Burdening him with my drama wouldn't prove me a worthy packmate, and being human had already set me back a few points.

We were close to home when Tak rolled his truck to a stop. Since Hope was fast asleep, he put his finger over his lips to hush us. The radio quietly played an old song about the rains in Africa. In front of us, a bright-red Ferrari was blocking the road.

Tak got out and prowled toward the vehicle. I thought someone had car trouble until I saw a middle-aged man step out. He straightened his expensive-looking suit before shutting the car door and leaning against it.

My stomach dropped. "Stay here."

Mercy's eyes widened. "And where do you think you're going?" she hissed.

"That guy looks confrontational. I don't have a good feeling about Tak going alone."

Mercy clutched my arm. "Everyone says you're human!"

"Yes, but *that* guy doesn't know it."

We looked through the rear window at the men jumping out. Archer stood at the tailgate while Salem walked around and stood by Hope's door.

Mercy watched Montana ease up to the driver's side with his back to us. "Maybe I should go instead."

"No," I stressed when she took off her seat belt. "The alpha's mate is the most valuable thing to him. She's vulnerable, especially after what happened earlier. That's why the men are guarding her. If something happens, you might need to shift. I can't protect her like you can."

"What're you gonna do if *that* guy shifts?"

Crap my pants?

"It's not about a fight," I said. "I'm projecting an image that Tak has backup. It doesn't feel right hiding. Stay here."

Despite the issues I had with my previous pack, I'd learned a great deal about Shifter culture. My former alpha was never alone with strangers or enemies. Cutting someone off in the middle of the road instead of going to their home didn't strike me as a friendly gesture.

My heart sped up as I coolly paced toward them. Instead of joining Tak, I hung back and clasped my hands behind me, doing my best to appear confident but also nonthreatening.

The stranger acknowledged me with a cold, calculating stare. Despite his flashy car and expensive clothes, he didn't look like he belonged in this era. His hair was short on the sides and longer on top, grey mixed with rusty brown. But his old-fashioned mustache stole the show. The thick ornament covered his upper lip and curled up at the ends. It felt like he was daring someone to make fun of it.

He narrowed his eyes at our group before steering his attention back to our formidable Packmaster. "As I was saying…" His voice was as sharp and textured as a serrated knife. "The offer drops every time we meet."

His Southern drawl differed from Mercy's flavorful accent and sounded more local—like a gunslinger from an old Western.

"Not for sale." Tak crossed his arms. "But we've been over this."

"It's my land."

"It *was* your land. I have official paperwork from the higher authority with my name on it."

The gentleman retrieved a cigarette case from inside his jacket pocket. After taking one out, he returned the small case to his pocket and lit up the smoke. He didn't seem in a hurry. He pulled in a drag from his cigarette and studied Tak as if he were figuring things out.

"It'll always be my land," he said. "The higher authority needs to keep their noses out of Shifter business. That land has been in my possession for a long, long time. I'll be damned if I see it passed over to a bunch of Natives."

Tak took his sunglasses off and polished the lenses with his shirt. "We're neighbors, whether you like it or not. We should be allies. That will strengthen our community. You never know what the future might bring."

"No. You certainly don't." Despite his shorter stature, the man stepped forward and blew smoke in Tak's face. "I'll take back what's mine. One way or the other."

Tak eclipsed the smug man. "Then you'll have a war on your hands."

"You need soldiers to go to war. That all you got?" He gestured to the truck.

I looked over my shoulder at Montana, who was closing in, scanning the surrounding woods.

This guy's imperious attitude around an alpha led me to believe that he, too, was an alpha.

"We can settle this now like men." Tak raised his chin and made a fist.

"Instigating an attack against a prominent Packmaster will put your ass in the hot seat, my friend." He dropped his cigarette and smashed it beneath his leather dress shoe. "They might strip your rights to that land as punishment. Maybe I'll seek retribution by claiming one of those pretty little bitches of yours."

When Tak tensed, the man grinned.

"What a conundrum," he said. "Pride goeth before the fall."

A twig snapped on the right. Wolves flanked us, keeping their distance by the trees.

"Get back in the truck," Montana whispered.

When I spun on my heel, my soul went catatonic. A wolf jumped against the driver's-side door. It took me a second to figure out why Archer and Salem hadn't chased him off—they were defending the vehicle from an encroaching pack.

One shot by me, its fur brushing against my back. Montana pivoted to track its movement. I shuddered at the thought of a wolf savagely ripping my flesh apart.

Tak clapped the man on his shoulder as if to illustrate that he stood six inches taller. "If you set one foot on my land, I'll cut off that foot. By the way, quit smoking. Bad habit and stinky breath." Tak turned and strutted back to his vehicle with a smirk.

Shifters postured around each other all the time—even made threats. But I'd never been smack dab in the middle of it.

The man extended his arm toward me, a card between his fingers. "Don't waste your time with him. Come see me when you want a real Packmaster."

Montana put his arm around me and walked us back to the truck. "Stay calm. I got you."

I took a deep breath as the wolves continued to pace. Montana escorted me to the door and closed it once I was inside. Hope was awake and aware of the situation. She had partially rolled down the window to listen in on the conversation.

We watched the man get back in his car and speed around us. The wolves hastily dispersed in the same direction.

Archer and Montana stood by the driver's-side windows, waiting until Tak's window rolled all the way down.

Tak sighed and growled like a bear. "Of all the jackasses I have to put up with, it's a prick with a lousy mustache. How do you think he gets those curls to stay in place?"

"What did he want this time?" Hope asked.

"The same as usual."

"Something must be done about it."

"You think?"

I put my hat on the seat. "Who was that?"

Tak smoothed back a few flyaway hairs, then he adjusted the rearview mirror. "You've just met the one and only Hamish Macgregor."

CHAPTER 11

After returning home from our trip to the city, we scattered on the property. Catcher detected the scent of another wolf on my clothes and went into alert mode. Mercy slept for the rest of the afternoon, and I sketched several angles —inside and out—of a stable. Even though my old pack didn't have stables or barns, I'd seen enough of them.

That evening, embers from the campfire floated up to the dark skies. We gathered around the fire while the beef stew finished cooking. A few of the guys had dragged over a log to sit on. I sat on the far-left with Lakota, Serena, and Ian on my right. The others were seated in chairs. Catcher hadn't left my side since we arrived.

Mercy joined our circle with a blanket wrapped around her like a tortilla. "I sure hope there aren't any raccoons around here. Those things scare me." She sat in one of the chairs to the right and loosened her blanket.

Virgil crossed his legs. "Racoons don't bother me. Skunks are another story."

"You ain't never seen a pissed-off raccoon."

With an impish grin, he replied, "Skunks are the gift that keeps on giving."

A light flickered inside the house, where Bear was preparing food in the unfinished kitchen. He did the bulk of the cooking in the yard, but they stored the food inside. The wood creaked on the porch when he emerged with a large tray.

Mercy peered over her shoulder as he descended the steps. It was her first time officially meeting most of us.

Bear walked around and let everyone collect a slice of buttered bread to add to their stainless-steel plates, which resembled wide bowls. "Save room for dessert." He set down the leftovers and eased into his Adirondack chair.

Mercy, who sat to his left, canted her head. "Well, aren't you just a big ol' scoop of ice cream."

Red bloomed on Bear's cheeks, and he stroked his beard.

"Did you cook all this yourself?" she asked.

"Yes, ma'am."

"Bear took over as the group chef," Hope explained. "We never asked, but everyone loves his cooking."

"He sure looks like he eats well," Virgil remarked.

Bear ran a finger around the collar of his long-sleeved shirt. For a hefty guy, he was a man of few words.

Deacon got up to swipe another piece of bread.

"Let the females have seconds before you," Lakota snapped.

Deacon's head slowly turned in his direction. "Could you repeat that?"

Lakota held his gaze. "They're the glue that holds a pack together. Their needs always come before ours."

In the firelight, Deacon's tattoos looked like shadows dancing on his chest. "Females."

"That's what I said."

"Shifters don't use that word."

"I do." Lakota set his plate between us and rested his hands on his lap.

"Why?" Deacon asked.

"My birth parents were Shifters, but my adoptive parents weren't."

"So you weren't raised in a pack," he said in a tone that implied Lakota was inferior. "Doesn't that just take the cake?"

"My uncle was a wolf and lived with us," Lakota said, telling his story to the rest of us rather than explaining to Deacon. "I work well with others. That's important for any pack, especially when conducting business and negotiating trades. Other Breeds can be allies and provide aid if problems arise with another pack."

Deacon grumbled while he sat down in his chair.

A gong sounded, drawing our attention to the porch. Tak emerged with a large case of soda in glass bottles. "They're not cold, since we don't have a fridge, but drink up."

"Do you have anything harder?" Archer asked.

Tak let everyone collect their drinks. "I was an alcoholic, remember? I'm not stopping anyone from drinking, but I won't be the one serving you booze."

Archer popped the lid off his bottle. "Gotcha."

Using a potholder, Bear carefully lifted the hot lid from the large kettle. Everyone drew in deep breaths and eagerly held out their plates while he dished out generous helpings with a giant ladle. Conversation quieted as we enjoyed the delicious meal—well, everyone except Salem, who, as always, was waiting for Joy to finish hers.

Tak patted Bear's knee and smiled. "This is even better than the last batch."

"Just an old recipe," Bear said. "Nothing special."

Tak cleared his throat. "I'm Tak, son of the great Shikoba of the Iwa tribe. My people come from Oklahoma territory. You already know about my dark past with alcohol. Hope inspired me to leave all the comforts of home to lead my own people. When it came to acquiring land, we had several options. This one felt like home, and the price was a steal. As a Packmaster, I expect a lot out of my packmates. But I'm not here to tell you what that is. I must see it for myself to know if you belong here." He shoveled food into his mouth and chewed. "Besides running a pack, I enjoy afternoon rides in my truck, swimming nude in the stream, and beating my partner at Yahtzee."

Several of us laughed.

"Finally! Someone who knows how to laugh," Virgil remarked while toeing off his sneakers. "Some of you stiffs need to loosen up."

"My people thought humor a weakness," Tak explained. "If you ever meet my father, you'll know why. But don't let the sly one fool you. He has his own subtle brand of humor."

Melody snorted. "I'll say."

Tak sopped up his stew with bread. "Now I want to hear about you."

I choked on my potato. Lakota patted my back, and I swallowed the rest of it without chewing. It was definitely not the time to reveal I was a Potential. Hope and Melody obviously knew the dangers, but I didn't trust the rest of them.

Bear cleared his throat. "I guess some of y'all know I'm Bear."

"Or as big as one," Ian added, rousing a few more laughs.

Bear was an ideal candidate for a phone-sex operator. His Southern accent was slow, like molasses on a hot summer day. Honestly, I couldn't distinguish them all to tell which specific region they were from, but he didn't have a twang. His voice was deep, and his accent drifted through his words like an undercurrent.

Bear cleaned his mouth and beard with a napkin. "I'm from the Lubbock area. That's in Texas, for all you foreigners," he said with a wry grin.

"Are you a professional chef?" Mercy asked.

He shook his head. "No, ma'am."

"You should be," I said, enjoying how tender the beef was.

"That's mighty kind." He stared down at his plate. "I worked as a bodyguard."

That made sense. Tak had mentioned he was six-foot-seven and wanted to build taller doorframes in the house so that he could comfortably walk through them in heavy boots without knocking his head. Though Bear was an inch or two shorter, both were large men. Bear was just proportioned differently. He kept most of his weight up top, whereas Tak's thickness was evenly distributed. Bear had shoulders that could fill a doorframe.

"Just looking for a change," Bear added, a verbal cue for the next person.

Mercy jumped to her feet and set her plate in her chair. "I'm Mercy Breedlove. And before you start rolling my name around in your head, I've heard all the jokes. Save yourself the embarrassment."

Still chewing, Virgil said, "Shortcake, I'd marry a woman with that name if it meant I could take it."

Mercy waited for someone to hurl the first joke. When no one did, she continued, "I guess you can tell by my accent I'm not from New York. I was born and raised deep in the mountains of Arkansas. Left home when I was twenty-five and never looked back. I've bounced around all over the place. Miami, Tennessee, and even Michigan for a while. It's too dang cold up there. I'd been in Dallas for a year when I saw your ad. You can't imagine how exciting that was. Nobody ever posts an ad for packmates. What an ingenious idea!"

"You've got a little brown on your nose," Virgil said with a jaunty smile.

Mercy put her hands on her hips. "I *know* I look like a city girl, but deep down, I'm country. I've been a-huntin', and I can bait a line and lure the fish like the Pied Piper. Just put me near a fishing hole, and I'm a happy gal." She lifted her plate and sat back down, drawing the blanket over her lap. "I guess that's all."

I felt relieved we weren't having an in-depth background reveal.

When I finished my food, I set my plate in the grass and let Catcher lick it clean. He hadn't shown interest in dinner, presumably because he'd been hunting earlier.

Archer stretched hard, then crossed his ankles. "I guess I'll get this out of the way before dessert," he said with a handsome grin. "I'm Archer Swift. Saw the ad and had to check it out. I've heard about your tribe," he said to Tak. "I dragged my cousin down here from Oregon. As for me, I love women and cinnamon rolls with frosting." He pointed at Bear. "Hint, hint."

A few of us laughed.

Archer patted his left sleeve. "It goes without saying I'm missing an arm. I've been looking, so if anyone finds it, let me know."

Virgil spit out his drink.

After a beat, Archer met eyes with Tak. "I can't share the details behind that over campfire stories."

Tak nodded.

Leaning in his seat, Archer continued, "I also own an expensive prosthetic arm I only use for lifting weights. If anyone touches it, I'll break *your* arm. It's not a toy. A Relic made it special for me. It's not comfortable to wear all the time and not practical when shifting. But it helps me work out so I can maintain muscle mass." He flicked a glance at Tak again. "I'm not a weak wolf."

"How much can you bench with a fake arm?" Deacon asked.

Archer locked eyes with him. "Two ninety."

"But your fake arm is bearing all the weight."

"The prosthetic makes sure the weight is evenly distributed."

"So you're *really* only lifting one forty."

Archer's jaw clenched. "Half of two hundred ninety is one hundred forty-five, Einstein. I'll be happy to demonstrate how the arm works and how my shoulder takes on the brunt of the weight. How much can *you* lift with one arm?"

I smiled, impressed by his abilities. But clearly, someone wasn't.

Deacon dropped his plate and silverware onto the ground.

"I'd like to check out your prosthesis," Salem said with interest. "If you don't mind."

Archer rubbed his chin. "Not at all. You're next."

Salem gave a curt nod. "I'm Salem Lockwood. I have twenty-five years of experience working in emergency medicine for humans. Most of my career was spent as an insider for the higher authority, monitoring incoming patients to identify Breed. While I've never lived in a pack, I've worked closely with them as a healer when Relics weren't available. Some packs don't trust Relics. Joy and I are interested in a position within the pack."

"Your introduction sounds like a job résumé," Virgil quipped. Then he steepled his fingers. "Tell us something *fun*."

Salem stroked his eyebrow. "I enjoy reading."

Virgil mimicked snoring, which prompted Joy to stand.

"I'm Joy Lockwood, Salem's mate. And while he's serious by nature, I think he's absolutely wonderful. Such an intelligent man with so much compassion. More than you could ever imagine."

Archer tossed a lump of his bread at Virgil.

It seemed Joy had won everyone over with her soft-spoken nature, her classiness, and her devotion to her mate. "We've only been mated a short time, but it feels like I've known him forever." She cleared her throat. The firelight illuminated her blond hair. "I know most of you from the bus ride. For those I haven't spoken with, I'm easy to talk to. It's hard to say that I'm from anywhere since I've spent most of my life traveling from one city to the next. I even lived in Tokyo for a year."

"Doing what?" I asked, certain it was job-related.

She exchanged a private look with Salem before answering. "I worked as an impersonator."

Virgil raised his hand high. "Let me guess. Marilyn Monroe."

Everyone nodded, seeing the striking resemblance.

Joy smiled humbly and sat back down. "Did you know Marilyn

wasn't a natural blonde? I look more like Marilyn than she did. But I don't do that anymore. It's in the past."

"Why not?" Mercy asked. "You're drop-dead gorgeous. You could still rake in a fortune."

Joy set her gaze on the fire. "Gracious, no. I spent years pretending to be someone else and lost all sense of who *I* was. I made money for years after her death. But eventually, humans lost interest in seeing Marilyn. The younger ones don't care."

"What about Shifter clubs?" I asked.

Joy picked at her bread. "Shifter men don't want to see a scarred woman. You know how it is. Even with dim lighting, once they see it, they get fixated and distracted by it. Anyway, we're here looking for a fresh start in a new place. I've been on the road for over sixty years. It's time to plant roots."

A few others raised their drinks in agreement with that sentiment, including me.

Salem finally started his meal just as most of us finished.

Krystopher was sitting across the fire from me. His crystal-blue eyes watched the group with uncertainty while he stroked his goatee. Unlike his friendly cousin, who seemed to get along with everyone, Krystopher kept to himself. I thought about Archer saying how he'd dragged him along. I tried not to cast aspersions because of his leather pants and boots with chains, but he gave off the vibe of a troublemaker. He didn't smile much.

"I'm Krystopher Kelso," he jumped in. "Everyone calls me Krys. K-R-Y-S."

"Why do you spell it out?" Tak asked. "I have no need to write it down."

Virgil raised his hand. "I know why. Haven't you guys ever heard of the infamous Christopher Kelso? He spells his name the common way with the C-H."

"*Oh yeah,*" Melody sang, twirling her colorful hair around a finger. "He butchered like fifty people or something."

"Sixty-one children." Virgil pinched the brim of his hat. "Those kids had nothing in common. Relics, Chitahs, Shifters—and different ages. All in their sleep. They nicknamed him Windowman because he'd crept into their windows at night. There are rumors he was part of an assassination group. Some people think the parents were involved in something and this was a punishment. No one really knows."

Melody shivered. "What happened to him?"

"They caught him," Krys answered. "After a quick trial, they cut off his head. But people still talk about him like he escaped."

The wood snapped in the fire, making everyone jump.

Melody stabbed her last potato. "That sucks. Not that he's dead, but that you two have the same name."

"Why don't you change it?" Deacon asked. "Fuck that. I'd change my name."

Krys stared daggers at him. "Because my mother gave me this fucking name, and it's mine. Anyhow, not much to tell. I sold my bike to come here."

"If you knew how attached to that bike he was, you'd recognize the sacrifice," Archer added. "I've been listening to him complain about it since we left."

Krys gave him the middle finger and then directed his comments to the alpha. "I'm not gonna kiss anyone's ass. Either I'm in, or I'm not. Don't worry. I'll pull my weight. Everyone just needs to keep the fuck out of my tent when I'm down for the night. *Next.*" He started playing with a pendant hanging from a long chain around his neck.

"There's something I've been dying to ask," Mercy chimed in, pointing her fork at Virgil. "Why do you wear a shirt that says Introvert?"

Virgil wedged his soda bottle between his legs and tugged each end of his shirt next to the writing. "I like the duality."

"Seems like false advertising," I pointed out.

"Where's the fun in stating the obvious? I could get Shortcake here a shirt that says Shy. Or one for you that says I'm Hilarious. I'm not picking on you, but none of us can be summed up in a single word. This is a statement about labels. If you only see me as a comedian, you haven't had the full experience that is Virgil Nightingale," he said, sweeping his arms out theatrically.

The tall, thin man with the gold tooth set his plate on the ground. "I'm Gordon Pipe. Originally came down from Maine. I've worked odd jobs. Deckhand, bartender, repaired tires—you name it, I've done it." After that brief intro, he resumed drinking his soda.

When it got quiet, I decided to jump in and get it over with. "I'm Robyn Wolfe from South Dakota. Obviously, you guys know I'm human. My parents were trusted humans, so I didn't just stumble into all this. I've lived in a pack for the past twelve years. Catcher's been my watchdog since I was a teenager." I smiled at him and touched his ear. "He's loyal and protective and has a great sense of humor. He's hard-working. Even though he won't shift to human form, he'll do whatever's asked of him."

I hoped.

Ian went next by lifting his finger to draw everyone's attention. I leaned forward to see him better.

"Ian Ward. As you can tell by my accent, I'm from England. We come from good stock, and it wasn't customary for people of our status to live in a pack. A wealthy Packmaster might employ his packmates as servants to the master, but those were often people of the lower class. My sister knows nothing of that life. I've made sure she's never had to want for anything. That's why her lovely skin is so pale. Never had to work." He looked at his hands, which were browner than hers. "Serena's much younger and naïve. Twenty and not yet gone through her first change."

Serena's face bloomed red, and she turned her gaze downward.

"That's why we're in this together," Ian added, putting his arm around her.

Tak finished his food and wiped his mouth. "Twenty isn't old. In my tribe, there's no specific age when a Shifter goes through their first change. It's better if it happens later. A woman needs to experience life without all the wolves chasing her."

Among Shifters, males typically didn't pursue women until after they'd experienced their first change of shifting into their animal, which usually happened in their late teens or early twenties.

"In our family line, it's *late*," Ian replied. "Serena's quiet and won't be a bother. Isn't that right, my little poppet?" He gave her shoulder a squeeze before returning to his meal. "That's right. We'll mate you off to a prestigious Shifter in no time."

Melody hopped up and collected plates. "I'm Melody, but everyone calls me Mel. Hope and I run a business called Moonglow. That's why we want to finish this house so we can get back to work." She set the empty plates on a table behind her chair and returned. "I'm the daredevil. Nothing scares me."

"Except snakes," Lakota countered.

"I'm not afraid of snakes. I just don't like them."

"Whatever you say, *wife*." He gave Melody a fervent stare—a familiar look one only shared with their lover.

Yep. They're married.

Deacon drummed his fingers on the arm of his chair. "You're mated?"

Lakota gave a slow and deliberate nod.

Deacon's jaw clenched, and the tension in the air snapped like the wood on the fire. He must have sensed that Lakota was also a beta. Knowing he was mated to Melody, who was obviously already a member of the pack, led to only one conclusion.

Deacon released an audible breath and looked at Tak. "Have you chosen your beta?"

The Packmaster nodded. "Lakota is second-in-command."

"He's too inexperienced to lead a pack. He wasn't even raised in one. Grew up in some hippy household with a bunch of Chitahs and whatever else. I trust an alpha always stands by his decision, but you have another candidate for beta. This pack isn't established yet. I've got experience. I've got knowledge."

Lakota raised his chin. "My knowledge isn't limited to pack life. If you're thinking you're gonna get in this household and challenge me out of this position, then challenge me now." When he stood, Catcher weaved in front of me. "You've got some pair. You're not even chosen as packmate, and you think you already have a seat at the head of the table."

Deacon laced his fingers over his stomach. "I see a boy with all kinds of fantasies about what it takes to lead a pack. I respect the alpha's decision, but nothing is set in stone. Betas lose their spots all the time when they screw up or fail to follow command."

Lakota swaggered over to where Melody was sitting, and she stood to let him take her seat. Then she sat in his lap. The move was deliberate to establish rank since that seat was next to the Packmaster.

"A beta shouldn't be spying on his packmates," Deacon grumbled. "You deceived us all."

Lakota's eyebrows rose. "Did you ever ask me? Did you ask the alpha who his second-in-command was? I never lied."

"You're also not sleeping inside," Deacon pointed out, a vein bulging in his forehead. "Only packmates sleep in the house. And here you are, sleeping in a tent with the rest of us."

Melody pinched Lakota's chin. "I'll share my bed again when he gets a shower installed."

Lakota stroked her thigh, keeping his eyes on Deacon. "Where else would I sleep? Everyone's here to join the pack. The beta keeps order. Why would I retreat into the house? Why would I not be out here, bonding with my potential sisters and brothers? Why would I not be working alongside you? Why would I not create bonds and get a feel for who everyone is, even if that means sleeping out in the cold? If you think a beta belongs in the lap of luxury"—he swung his arm toward the house—"go inside and choose your room."

Deacon sat taller in his chair. "If your intention is to make this a stronger group, you need to show some authority, because I'm not seeing it. You've got *that one* scribbling pictures in her book all day," he said, pointing at me. "And some people here aren't pulling their weight." He turned a sharp eye toward Archer. "Why the fuck are you chopping wood all day and night when we only need to light a fire for meals? There's a house to build."

Montana, who had remained quiet the entire time in a chair to my left, got up. "Robyn's working on a project by the alpha's command." He strode to a table and set down his plate before returning. "Once Virgil and Tak give us the plans for finishing the house, we'll bust our asses to make that happen. We all just got here. Lots of personalities trying to feel each other out. We need to respect Lakota since he's the beta. If you prove yourself worthy, that'll speak louder than words in the Packmaster's eyes. I don't know how any of this will pan out. I just want a seat at the table." He sat down in his chair and put his hat back on. "I'm Montana Vance. I like to solve problems."

Butterflies flitted around in my stomach, not only because of how swiftly he'd defused the situation but also that he was introducing himself as a nickname I'd given him. *Why would he want to leave his name behind and let a complete stranger give him a new one?* I didn't know why, but it made me feel like I had claim over him.

"Holy mackerel!" Mercy exclaimed, sliding down in her chair. "That supper was the best I've had in ages. I feel like a busted can of biscuits."

Everyone roared with laughter, and that broke the tension. Light chatter started up again.

When I looked at Montana, he gave me a wink, and I got a funny feeling in my stomach all over again.

Catcher growled and turned in a circle. He lifted his nose in the air and howled.

"What's wrong?" I asked.

It couldn't have anything to do with those fleeting feelings I had for

Montana. Catcher wasn't psychic when it came to men I was attracted to.

Tak snapped his attention to my left.

I heard leaves rustling before I saw anything. A figure blurred into view, running at an unnatural speed. The person halted and then emerged from the shadows. My fingernails bit into the wood log as several rose to their feet.

Lucian.

CHAPTER 12

Lucian slung his bag, and it landed by Deacon's chair with a thump.

He stalked into view with a stony gaze. "Sorry I'm late. Took longer than I expected." He stopped at the edge of our circle and glared at Deacon.

I felt strangely relieved to see him, realizing I wasn't the only outcast. *Where has he been?*

Deacon shook his head. "Should have stayed right where you were. You're wasting your time here, *Chitah*."

Lakota rose to his feet and walked toward him. He and Lucian stared each other down before Lakota laughed and pulled him into an embrace. "Thought you changed your mind, Uncle."

Uncle?

Lakota had mentioned he grew up with Chitahs. *Of course!* I gave a small smile while the men hugged. Lucian still carried a cross look on his face, in addition to a fading bruise.

As Lakota leaned away, he ripped off Lucian's knit hat. "What the hell is this?"

Lucian ran his hand over his shaved head. "I'm going for a new look. I like it better this way."

"Are you sure that's how you want to tell it?"

That beautiful black hair, all shaved off. I could hardly believe it. But his eyebrows were still as black as his lashes, and the dark stubble on his scalp made his features stand out.

"This is bullshit," Deacon spat. "I guess that means he's automatically in. I thought this was a level playing field, not some family-favor thing."

"You mean nepotism," Lucian said, correcting him without eye contact. "And fuck all the way off with that insinuation."

After standing, Tak put his hands on his hips. "No one gets a free pass around here. Everyone has to earn their spot, even family." He nodded at Lucian. "Good to meet you."

Lucian inclined his head. "I'll try not to screw up again. Had to run half the way." He glanced down at his sneakers, which were chewed up and dirty.

Lakota clutched his shoulder. "Sit. And put your hat back on. You look naked."

Instead, Lucian tossed his knit hat into the fire, and it lit up with sparks. We all watched him drag his bag to an empty spot by Montana and take a seat on the ground. He drew up his knees, resting his arms over them and locking two fingers. His face glistened, his cheeks red, and I wondered how long he'd been running at Chitah speed in the dark.

"Hand him a plate," Tak said to Bear, who jumped into action.

Lucian accepted the stew and silently ate while we watched him.

Once seated, Tak grabbed a stick from the ground and tapped it against his leg. "This afternoon, some of you met Hamish, our neighbor. He's given us nothing but trouble since we purchased this land. First, I want to commend those who were there. You secured the one and only thing that matters to me and guarded her from all directions. I never had to tell you what to do. Even you."

My heart jumped when I realized he was pointing at me with the stick.

Tak nodded firmly at me, telling me he wasn't bullshitting or trying to boost my ego. "Even a human showed presence without getting involved. No blood was spilled, and no one reacted to the wolves' taunts. That would've ended in bloodshed. Hamish is an instigator—a trickster. You have to use your brain with men like him. They're dangerous."

"Who is this Hamish guy?" Mercy asked.

"Hamish Macgregor rules a neighboring pack, one all of you should know about. They owned land out here for centuries. I respect that, since my tribe has also fought to keep what is ours. When I purchased this land, the representative who sold it warned me about Hamish. He committed a serious offense by threatening a Councilman's family when he wouldn't take a bribe. The Council noticed he possessed more land than what's allowed for a pack his size. He violated trust with a man of the law. The Council gained permission from the higher authority to reclaim some of his land with no option to buy back. Tribes are entitled to more because this was always our land. My understanding is packs have a limit based on size. The higher authority can grant additional acres or take it away. In this case, he shouldn't have engaged in bribery."

Montana put his hat on his lap. "I wonder who else he might be bribing."

Tak's brown eyes fixed on the fire. "He feels entitled to my land and offered to buy it from me under the table. No paperwork. By law, he's not allowed to have his name on more land than he already has registered. Each time we meet, the price drops and the threats increase."

"Can you report it to the Council?" I asked, thinking the situation could lead to a land grab, which wasn't unheard of with Shifters.

"This is for Packmasters to settle. They don't get involved in pack disputes unless a law has been broken, and we don't need them to. The less you involve outsiders, the better. My people have battled for centuries over land rights. You can never show fear." He tossed the stick into the fire. "Fear is your enemy's feast."

"What do you want us to do if his wolves tread on your property?" Montana asked.

Tak flipped his long braid over his chest. "If his wolves wander onto my land with intent, it's within our rights to kill on sight. But keep in mind the same applies to us. Don't let his wolves bait you. Their aggressive behavior is a ruse. They'll lead you on a chase and lure you into his territory. He's cunning."

Hope got up from her chair and stood behind Tak. "This is our land now, and that means if you're chosen as packmates, you'll be expected to fight for it. This isn't the first time my family has battled for freedom." She exchanged glances with Melody and Lakota. "This is our home now. It's rightfully ours—legally and otherwise. We've made numerous attempts to work things out with Hamish and be on good terms, but he's an obstinate alpha who deserves a whipping to his backside."

Lakota chuckled. "Easy, Sis. You'll scare the others with your violent nature."

Deacon sighed loudly. "*Sis?* You gotta be fucking kidding me. Anyone else you're related to that we should know about?"

Virgil cackled. "He could be my father. I never met him."

"The spirits of our ancestors will guide us," Tak continued. "Their wisdom lives in our blood."

"Anyone here a bloodletter?" Virgil inquired.

Crickets chirped.

Tak slapped his knee and gave a boisterous laugh, which broke the tension.

"That's not how the real world works," Gordon interrupted. "Spirit guides and ancestors—that kind of fairy-tale bullshit might fly on the reservation, but in the real world, pack warfare is a threat. Some alphas will eat their enemies for breakfast and spit them out. Spirit guides and praying won't save your ass from fifty wolves creeping up in the middle of the night."

Tak tipped his head to the side and gave Gordon an admonishing look. "First thing, a reservation is a piece of land white men forced human tribes to settle on. Human tribes have suffered atrocities, as have our own. My people were fortunate to hold on to what was always ours, but that doesn't mean we don't have enemies trying to steal it. Not long ago, a trusted official attempted to frame my people in a pathetic attempt to revoke our land rights. Second, living in a tribe doesn't mean I'm naïve to what goes on in what you call the *real world*. My people are educated."

"On tribal stuff, maybe." Gordon leaned forward and held his gaze. "All I'm saying is your knowledge is limited."

Tak casually flicked something off his chest. "I speak three languages fluently, including English, French, and my Native tongue. I'm now learning my mate's language on her father's side. If any of my future packmates have a primary language, I will learn it out of respect. I may not understand your ways of trashing this world with your waste, but I'm well versed in non-Native history and culture. We learn about all Breeds—their strengths and weaknesses. How much do you know about *my* culture?"

"To be honest, I don't really give a shit," Gordon admitted. "You've got an enemy down the road, and I want to know what you're going to do about it. I think we need to strike fast and hard."

"And here I thought only Vampires thirsted for blood. Your words tell me you know nothing of how leaders handle disputes. We are peacemakers, not instigators. Hamish is an arrogant, greedy man. He covets what is mine. But a man is not an enemy on principle alone. There is always a chance you can negotiate, find common ground, or even change their view. Only when a man seeks to destroy or take that which you love, honor, or regard as rightfully yours does he declare himself an enemy."

"He stopped you on the road, didn't he?"

"If your neighbor covets your fancy car and offers to buy it, are you going to slip into his house in the middle of the night and murder his family because you think he *might* steal it? That is a barbaric way of living. If Hamish or his men instigate violence, I want to know about it. No one takes action without my command. Say I follow your advice and slaughter a Packmaster. What reward do you think I'll reap? Rights to keep this land? Do you think the Council supports preventative measures? How would it affect my mate's business? How would it affect whether packs will do business with us going forward? If I were stripped of my rights as Packmaster and this pack dissolved, how easy do you think it would be for *you* to find a decent pack? Your names would be sullied."

Gordon huffed and sat back. "If one of those assholes crosses my path, I'll slit his throat."

Tak stretched out his legs. "You can collect your bags and leave."

"The fuck? For what?"

Montana leaned forward. "You just admitted in front of everyone here you'll disobey the Packmaster's orders. Do you need an explanation?"

Gordon got up and kicked his plate into the fire. Then he flipped his chair over and stalked off, cursing and shouting at Tak while he ripped apart the tent.

Tak motioned for Lakota to follow Gordon, who was tossing his things around and spewing insults, then nonchalantly laced his fingers over his stomach. "Do any of you think my father became a powerful leader through violence? A hot-tempered alpha can't be trusted. Violence is a last resort. There are better ways to piss off a man. But don't confuse it with weakness. This wolf draws blood when he goes for the kill."

I cringed when Gordon threw a bottle of water at the house.

"Fuck you and your pack!"

Tak gave him a mechanical smile. "I will remember this if you're ever accepted into a local pack. I'm certain your Packmaster will be interested in how we came to meet."

That shut Gordon up fast, and he stormed out of sight.

Tak kissed his mate's hand, which rested on his shoulder. "Sometimes misfortune comes along to teach us about ourselves. When Robyn fell ill the first night, it was a gift in disguise."

"It sure didn't feel like a gift," I said.

He arched an eyebrow. "It showed me who stepped up. A pack comes together in times of crisis. When one is down, the rest must lift them up. Some of you gave her medicine, showed concern, and kept her warm through the night. Some of you couldn't be bothered to leave your tents." He stared directly at Ian.

Everyone noticed.

I cupped my elbows when a chilly wind blew against my back. The woods were drenched in darkness, and my gaze drifted as I thought about how stealthily Lucian had sneaked up on us. It reinserted a fear in my mind that my old pack might come after me. I couldn't imagine they would waste their time but wondered *what if*.

Catcher pawing on my knee pulled my attention away. He barked twice while looking toward the side of the house.

"What troubles him?" Tak asked.

I tapped beneath Catcher's chin, and he ran off toward the front. "He wants to check the area and make sure it's safe. Lucian's surprise visit put him on edge."

"How do *you* know that's what he wants?" Deacon asked, skepticism in his voice. "You're not a wolf."

"Because I'd be a complete idiot to live with a wolf for more than ten years and not learn his language. I know what every bark and every gesture means. I can't read his mind, but most of the time, I understand what he wants."

Deacon looked like he was itching to share his opinion about my knowledge of wolves, but after Gordon's unexpected exit, it was obvious that Tak was watching for cues that we weren't a good fit. So instead of berating me, Deacon kept his mouth shut.

The more I got to know Tak, the more I wanted to be under his leadership. I suspected the others felt the same. Coming across an alpha with his traits—someone who could lead without instilling fear among his packmates—was a rarity. We feared his judgment, but we didn't fear him as a person. Some alphas were brutal, not just verbally or physically, but there were packs who lived on the fringe—following archaic laws no longer practiced. Like sharing mates, or an alpha having the first claim of every new female in a pack.

The more I wanted to stay, the more I feared it might slip through my fingers. Not that this pack was the end of the line, but the thought of starting all over gave me hives.

"Deacon, tell me about yourself," Tak said after Hope sat on his lap.

Deacon grinned and stroked one of his tattoos. "I'm Deacon Shaw from Nevada. There aren't many packs in that state. Too dry and not much hunting. Most of them are rogues. I served as second-in-command for the Reno pack before they disbanded."

"Why did they split up?" I asked, curious if there had been a fight for leadership positions.

"The alpha was too old and senile," Deacon said, avoiding eye contact with me. "He was upward of nine hundred. We didn't have any alphas fit to follow. I saw your ad and knew you'd need a beta you could count on."

Tak jerked his chin at Lucian. "And what about you?"

Lucian finished his last bite of food and wiped his mouth with the back of his hand. "Lucian Cross from the Cross family in Cognito. Obviously, we're Chitahs."

That earned a few chuckles.

"Hey, I'm from there too!" Virgil's eyes lit up, and he tipped his chair to the side. "Where exactly?"

"All over. I used to live downtown. I can't elaborate on the exact location of my previous home, since my brothers do important work."

Virgil scooted his chair a foot closer to the fire and stretched out so that his feet were resting on a stone. "Have you been to Magic Hour? Or the Red Door club?"

Lucian shrugged. "I've been to them a few times. It's not my scene."

"Man, I miss it." Virgil's head lolled back, and he sighed. "I'd give my left kidney for a Coyote Burger."

Deacon cleared his throat, clearly unimpressed by their connection.

Lucian set his bowl aside. "I mostly do programming work and surveillance setup. Lakota talked me into coming down and giving this a shot. My brothers and I have been living with family in the same building for thirty years."

"And if you have all that family, why leave?" Tak inquired.

Lucian adjusted to sit cross-legged. "Jobs aren't as easy to come by. All the techies are moving to places like Cognito, New York, and other large cities. No matter how you slice it, more competition means less work. I can set you up with top-notch surveillance. Or maybe find work around here." His eyebrows slowly rose. "Or... I can sit in my room and monitor your property once I get everything set up. Either way, I prefer working alone."

"He's also done some teaching," Lakota offered.

Lucian gave him a black look.

"Keep giving me that look, Uncle. Your students may not like you, but you're smart. Just not very... affable."

Hope stood and set her and Tak's empty bottles back in the case before taking a different chair. The second she rubbed her arms to warm them, Mercy hopped up and gave up her blanket.

"Go on and take it. I'm as hot as fire. Especially after that *delicious* meal." Mercy pinched Bear's cheek before returning to her chair.

Tak clapped his hands together. "Now that we've all officially met, I'll say one thing: I don't care about your past. Everyone has a right to start a new life. My decision is based on who you are now. The exception is if you've ever harmed a woman or child. But if I invite you into my pack, you need to trust me as your Packmaster. Some of you haven't lived in a pack before. *Your* problems become *our* problems." Tak licked his lips. "Bear, did you make dessert? My stomach is begging for more."

Bear stood. "Be back in a wink." He disappeared into the dark house and, after a minute, emerged with a tray. Bear halted and then backed up, lightly tapping the gong.

Virgil howled with laughter. "I want that in my bedroom."

The tray held objects wrapped in foil. Bear set them around the embers. "I cored apples right before dinner and filled them with sugar, cinnamon, granola, and raisins."

Tak grinned handsomely, and I could easily see why Hope was attracted to a man with half his face tattooed. "We have pecan trees on the property to harvest from in the fall."

Melody grabbed another piece of bread and took a big bite. "I don't know what we'd do without you, Bear. I thought we were going to be roughing it out here with nothing but pinto beans and cornbread until you showed up."

"Is there anything else edible on the property?" I asked.

Tak pointed at me. "Good question. Plenty of dandelion. You can eat any part of it."

"I'll be sure to stick flowers in my next salad," Bear promised him.

Tak leaned forward to watch the apples heat up. "I've seen bees but haven't found the hive. Anyone interested in beekeeping?"

Joy slumped in her chair. "Please don't sign me up for that. I don't do well with flying bugs or anything sticking me."

Tak chuckled. "We also have blackberry bushes, fish, plenty of wild rabbits and deer, and honeysuckle vines. This is rich soil for gardening, and there's not much snow compared to Oklahoma." He rubbed his jaw. "I plan to build a cellar to store canned food and supplies."

"Something wrong with the grocery store?" Lucian asked.

"Nothing," Tak replied. "But a pack should always prepare for hard times. Remember that period when stores had empty shelves and shuttered their doors?"

Virgil picked his teeth. "How can I forget? I practically had to sell my body for toilet paper."

"I don't want a pack that relies on the outside world for survival," Tak explained. "How can you help those in need if you can't help yourself? Montana brought up a good point about the property. We need to work on clearing it out. Dead trees, weak branches, thorny bushes, fallen limbs—it all needs to go before someone's injured. I also noticed some poison oak we need to dig up."

"I purchased a few chainsaws," Montana said. "My thought is we either buy or rent one of those large utility trailers to haul it out. Some of it, we can burn."

"I don't want anyone setting fires on the property," Tak cut in. "We take what we need for firewood and repurpose the rest."

"What about a wood chipper?" Lakota pulled his long hair back and then locked his fingers behind his head. "I once saw landscapers with a truck they were shoving limbs into. Chewed them into a million pieces."

Tak wrinkled his nose. "Sounds like too much noise. Let someone make compost out of it. I still hear hammering in my sleep."

When the apples were done, Bear gave one to each of us while the group hashed out the details for clearing land. The apples were scrumptious, and even though my throat still hurt, the virus had miraculously run its course.

Melody licked her finger. "We have cattails. Did you know you can use them to kindle a fire? True story."

Virgil snorted. "We're in the woods. Everything is flammable."

"One more thing," Tak said as he wadded up his empty foil wrapper. "Our wolves need to meet."

CHAPTER 13

FIVE DAYS HAD PASSED SINCE the night of introductions. We'd made a ton of progress on the roof. To my surprise, Virgil took the lead in organizing everyone and making sure they knew exactly what they were doing. He also gave an animated explanation about rafters. Lucian helped with calculating the cuttings. They had all the equipment, and once we knew what to do, we went to work.

Because I was human, they wouldn't let me on the roof. Serena, Archer, and I hauled materials around to help out. The temperature stayed in the seventies, and Tak prioritized the roof since he was concerned about rain. Once they installed the underlayment, Virgil lectured the crew about safety. Apparently, someone had knocked a staple gun off the roof, which nearly struck Melody on the head. It went smoothly for a while until they started arguing about nail spacing.

Then I switched over to helping Montana and Lakota move dead brush. They worked tirelessly, cutting tree limbs with the noisy chainsaws. Even Catcher pitched in. Tak made him a makeshift harness that attached to a large wagon, and he hauled limbs to the front, where we loaded them into the trailer and pickup.

"Here, drink this." Joy handed me a bottle of water before sitting next to me on a giant flat rock in the front yard. She glanced down at her white tennis shoes. "I think my feet are swelling."

"Between the nail guns and chainsaws, I'm losing my mind." I held the cold water bottle against my swollen and scratched fingers. "Good thing I didn't have a manicure to worry about."

She adjusted the scarf on her head. "Gracious, I've never worked like this before."

Joy's cheeks were red, and she had sweat on her upper lip and forehead. Even so, she still had a natural beauty that couldn't be diminished. What fascinated me most was how she could have impersonated such a high-profile celebrity and have such a humble demeanor.

After wiping my sweaty face, I gulped down the water. The front yard was beautiful, and once the house was finished and all the debris cleaned out, it would be an absolute paradise.

"I sure hope they get the plumbing set up soon," Joy said. "I was born in 1902, but we never had an outhouse. We lived in the city, so I'm not used to this lifestyle."

"Which city?"

She gasped after finishing her drink and set the empty bottle down. "Baltimore. It doesn't even feel real to me anymore. I've seen so many places that everything blurs together. I've always dreamed about settling down." She tilted her head back when a breeze rolled through. "It's breathtaking out here. Salem and I took a walk before sunset yesterday and found a hill with a picturesque view. It's a dream I hope to never wake up from. Dirty fingernails and all," she said with a giggle. Her blue eyes were arresting, her lashes so long that she didn't need mascara to bring them out.

I pulled the bandage away from my knee where a stick had scratched me. It was bleeding again because of the bandage constantly rubbing against it. I poured water over the wound to flush it out.

"Gee whiz, that looks terrible. You should have Salem look at it."

"Not while everyone's busy. I'm up to date on my tetanus shot anyhow."

"You poor thing. All those needles humans have to get poked with. I hate needles."

I reclined onto my back and stared up at the branches. Birds flitted between the canopy of trees, and two young squirrels chased each other. "I hope they hurry back. I'm starving."

Hope, Deacon, Bear, and Salem had gone out for food and supplies. Hope didn't let her anxiety attacks slow her down. Since the group knew about them, they wouldn't panic if it happened again.

"I hear them," Joy said at the sound of a distant engine. "I hope Salem remembered to buy cantaloupe. He doesn't know his melons very well. The last time I sent him for cantaloupe, he brought me a honeydew. I don't like those at all."

"Is that your Shifter craving?"

"No, but I've been addicted to them lately."

"I hope they bought stuff for salad. I've been craving salad with red bell peppers and chicken."

Joy stood on the rock and shielded her eyes with her hand. "Robyn?"

I raised my head. When a silver GMC van rolled into view, my blood ran cold. "I know them. Go in the back and let me handle this." My water bottle hit the ground when I slid off the rock and stood.

Joy hopped down and headed toward the backyard.

Hoping it was a coincidence, I waited for a minute. Then I saw Dax's face through the windshield, and he grinned. Emotion swelled like a rising tide, and I wasn't sure if it was anger, fear, or anguish.

But I was about to find out.

Before the truck got too close, I hurried down the drive to prevent him from reaching the house. Familiar faces peered out from inside—men we used to call Dax's posse. His beta wasn't with him, though.

Once the van stopped, he killed the engine.

"Well, well, well." Dax popped opened the door and stepped out.

"Look where my little Robyn flew—all the way down to Texas. *Yee*haw."

He kept his mirrored shades on. Dax thought people were more intimidated when they could see their reflection while talking to him. He was a seasoned alpha who physically appeared in his fifties. His salt-and-pepper hair was always short and nicely styled, though the same couldn't be said at the moment for his facial hair. His unshaven face implied he'd been on the road for a while.

Dax dressed like a regular Joe. Wearing flannel shirts over white T-shirts was his signature style. I used to think he dressed down to make everyone comfortable, but the simple truth was Dax liked to throw people off. He used simple tactics to gain their trust.

"You haven't changed," he remarked. "Literally. I can always smell a new wolf." He waved the air in front of him and sniffed loudly. "You're still human. I can't tell you how thrilled that makes me." Dax pulled a stick of spearmint gum out of his pocket and folded it into his mouth. He grinned a lot—just not with his eyes. "Nice haircut."

"What are you doing here?"

"What else? Looking for my girl."

"You wasted a trip. I'm not going back with you."

He tipped his head to the side. "You know how I feel about back talk. But I'm gonna let that one slide."

I got that tingly feeling in my stomach that happens when a roller-coaster tips over the first hill. "I'm not in your pack anymore."

"See, that's where you're wrong." When he gripped my upper arm, I winced. His grin never waned, but it lost its charm. "You seem to think you have a choice in the matter. You know as well as I do that *you* are *in* a *lot* of *debt*." Dax spaced apart the last few words for emphasis, the way he often did when making a point. "So come on, honeybunch! Saved you a seat."

I wrenched away, but he didn't let go. His bruising grip pulled me toward the van doors, and I dug in my heels.

"Did you really think you could hide from me?" he asked. "I got people all over, and when I heard a report that you were questioned by Regulators in Dallas after a murder, well, I just *had* to come down and see for myself. The hotel owner was a friendly fellow. Told me all about your little traveling group and where you were heading."

I struggled in vain to free my arm. "I'm *not* going."

He reeled me in tight, and a minty smell coated his words. The angrier Dax got, the more enthusiastic and chipper he seemed. "*Of course* you are. I've fed you, taken care of you, and given you protection for *twelve years*. You're beholden to me."

When we reached the driver's-side door, I shouted, "Let go!"

A metallic noise from behind me made my pulse jump. Catcher was running full throttle, but the empty wagon attached to his harness prevented a surprise attack.

Catcher snapped at Dax's leg but not before Dax gripped the harness and threw him off. When the back doors flew open, his packmates jumped out to subdue Catcher.

"Stop!" I shouted, lunging at the men. "Don't you touch him!"

Dax yanked me back and kept a tight hold on my arm. "That pesky little shit is staying behind."

Catcher chomped down on one man's arm and tore the skin off while violently shaking it. The man bellowed.

"What's going on?" Tak boomed.

"Let her go." Montana aimed his gun at Dax's head with the steadiest hand I'd ever seen. He stood facing the side of the van, his eyes locked on my former Packmaster.

Tak walked into view and coolly gripped Catcher's harness. The wolf lunged at one man and bit his hand. When the Shifter attempted to kick him, Tak moved Catcher out of the way. Blood was everywhere.

Dax didn't allow his men to shift without his say-so, even if they needed to heal, as a way to inflict punishment. He took control to a whole new level.

Tak growled a command in his language and used his alpha power to make Catcher submit. Even Dax's packmates backed up.

Then he let go of my watchdog and faced Dax. "This is private property. What brings you onto my territory?"

Dax assessed him with a punishing smile. "I'm collecting my things. Tell your cowboy to take the gun off me."

Tak dipped his chin. "You forget where you are. My land, my rules. State your business in plain English."

"I'll do that, given it doesn't appear to be your first language." He put his free hand around the back of my neck. "This one? She belongs to me. I'm her Packmaster."

"A Packmaster doesn't own his people."

Dax slid his arm around my chest from behind, as if he were hugging me. He wasn't about to let go of me as long as there was a gun on him. As much as I wanted to elbow him in the gut, that might set off a battle. Catcher was still attached to the wagon, and several of the men in our group weren't around.

Dax's whiskers scraped against my cheek. "Are you trying to join another alpha behind my back? That would be *scandalous*. What would everyone say if they found out? Not very loyal of you, Robyn. But that's okay. Come home with me now, and we'll work it out. Before anyone gets hurt. You don't want these nice people involved in our personal business, do you?"

Montana stepped forward, but his gun was aimed up and not at our heads. With Dax standing right behind me, his face against mine, Montana might shoot me by accident.

Catcher's growl filled my ears, and my heart pounded.

Tak locked eyes with me. "Do you want to leave with this man?"

Dax's grip tightened.

"No," I said, trying to slow my breathing.

In my periphery, I spied Krys, Archer, and Mercy. On my left, Virgil and Lucian circled around the back, which trapped the men.

Dax sighed. "I'm disappointed in you, honeybunch. But if we're going to play games, I'll just get the Council to come out here and rectify the matter."

As soon as he let go, I stumbled away from him. Montana's arm hooked around me so fast that I was tucked against his side before I knew it. He aimed the gun at Dax's head, and for a split second, I wished he would pull the trigger. But killing a Packmaster was the gravest offense a Shifter could commit.

Dax patted the side of the van. "Back inside, boys. Looks like *someone* wants to get these poor, innocent people all mixed up in family affairs." He stepped inside and slammed the door while his men filed in. When he slid his glasses on top of his head, he gave me a baleful look.

Tak approached his open window. "If you step foot on my land again, blood will spill. Won't be mine."

"Your name?"

"Tak."

Dax grinned. "I'll be seeing you around, *Tak*." He laughed as if he knew some inside joke.

My blood curdled at the proprietary look Dax gave me. He was a man who always got what he wanted. I'd never seen him lose the upper hand, and that made me nervous.

He started the engine and gave me a counterfeit smile. "See you soon, Robyn. Don't fly too far. A mate has an obligation to her alpha."

Instead of turning around, he drove backward. Catcher ran after him with the flatbed wagon dragging behind him until Krys sat on it to stop him.

In one fell swoop, Dax killed any chance I had of joining this pack.

Once the van was out of sight, Montana lowered his gun. He turned and cupped my arm to examine the red marks. After his short assessment, he held my gaze. One word hung in suspension for a painfully long time.

Mate.

CHAPTER 14

After Dax's confirmed departure, construction came to a grinding halt. Catcher remained at the end of the drive while the rest of us waited for the others to return. When they did, I had some explaining to do.

While Salem patched up my knee, people carried chairs over to the shaded area where we were seated and formed a circle. Others sat in the grass, like Virgil, who was lying on his back with his eyes closed and his ankles crossed.

Salem pressed the adhesive edges of the bandage. "The surgical tape will keep it from opening up. Try not to bend it too much today. It's a minor abrasion, and you should see improvement by tomorrow."

"Thanks."

He stuffed the wrappers and used cotton balls into a paper bag before taking a seat next to Joy on the grass.

The Packmaster sat opposite me, tilting his head to one side. He wanted me to start talking.

I gripped the seat of the lawn chair and gathered my thoughts.

Welp, here goes nothing.

"I told you I lived with a pack, but that's not the full story. After my mom died, a friend of hers placed me with Dax. I don't think she knew much about him, only that he was a prominent Packmaster. Dax is great with kids. He's like everyone's favorite dad, and I never had any issues with him in the early years. I rarely saw him at all except at dinner. He was always working, always with his men, and I had things to do. School, friends, and eventually a job. I didn't go to college because most Shifters don't attend human schools, and I wanted to follow the pack way. Jobs were scarce, so I didn't earn much."

Tak stroked his arm. "Did you consider leaving the pack when you came of age? You're human, after all. Your parents knew about our world and wanted to see you taken care of, but you're still not one of us."

I flicked a glance at Melody and Hope. "As I grew older, Dax still saw me as one of the kids. He didn't consider me an equal. I'm human, I'm weaker, and that's how he treated me. Living there meant free meals and a room, so I didn't want to leave. It's also nice to have people who are like family around you."

None of the men in the group made eye contact with me. Either their eyes were downcast, or they were staring off at something in the distance. The women, on the other hand, connected with my story enough to meet my gaze.

I swatted a gnat away. "For a few years, I worked at an ice cream store. Then I did administrative work for a lighting company. Dax owned several businesses, but he didn't hire the women in our pack."

"Why not?" Mercy asked.

"Because Dax believes a woman's place is at home. The women in the pack worked hard raising kids, educating them, and doing all the housework. None of them complained. He also made sure that the local Breed businesses knew about his rules. One woman got a night job waitressing at an adult club. She didn't tell her mate."

"How did he not know?" Mercy asked.

"Because he was a drunk. He passed out by midnight. Dax made it sound as if she was seduced by heathens or something. That going out alone made women fall prey to drugs, sex, and men. In retrospect, I think she was probably trying to save enough money to escape. He didn't punish her, but he sure punished her mate." I cleared my throat. "Because I'm human, he didn't care if I got a job with humans. I was the exception. He expected me to leave eventually."

With doe eyes, Mercy asked, "What kept you there so long?"

I rubbed my face, still in disbelief that he'd found me. "I'd never lived in a pack, so I had nothing to compare it to. Joining another one didn't seem practical, unless I found a husband. Eventually, I was the only unmated woman in the pack who was over twenty-one. So... awkward. Women who hit that age in his pack and went through their first change either were mated off or joined another group." I stretched out my leg and stared at the bandage on my knee. "Single women threatened pack stability. Since none of the Shifters wanted to date me, he didn't consider me a problem. So that's why he let me stay. All my boyfriends were human." I gazed into the distance. "Sure, I could have left. But there's security in a pack." Thinking about the events of the past few years, I fell silent.

Tak leaned forward. "How did you come to be mated?"

"It happened when he was going to boot me out of the pack. He was cutting back on expenses, and I was an expense. Honestly, I think someone must have complained about me. Either that or one of the women asked him why they couldn't get a job but I could." I brushed a hair out of my eye and stared listlessly at a dandelion. "After hearing all this, am I out?"

Tak mulled it over. "You're a troubled soul, but it doesn't influence my opinion."

Sweet relief.

"Good, because there's one more thing." I took a deep breath for courage. "I'm a Potential."

Joy jerked her head back. "A what?"

Virgil flew up to a sitting position. "Holy cannoli! Are you serious?

All this time, I thought you guys were a myth. Show me the mark. I wanna see."

"No."

Tak sat back and nodded as if he knew all about Potentials. "You can't take it back. Everyone here knows now."

"Maybe it's better that way."

"My father told me about your kind many years ago when I was a young man."

Joy looked between Tak and me. "I don't understand. What's a Potential?"

The expressions on others' faces told me she wasn't the only one who didn't know. The Breed world held a number of mysteries, and I was one of them.

Hope caught her mate's attention. "Melody and I already know. We saw the mark when she was in the bath."

Tak scratched the side of his head. "I guess the secret's out—I'm not a pervert. Didn't notice it. The only body I pay attention to is yours, beautiful."

A few people chuckled.

Tak winked at Hope and redirected his attention to me. "Let me allay your fears. I'm not upset you confided in my mate. I understand your trepidation, but I'm glad you could trust your secret with *someone*."

None of the men were looking away anymore.

"I'm human," I said to Joy. "My parents and their parents were all human. But I was born with a mark that identifies me as a Potential. It means there's some genetic flaw that enables me to become Breed."

Joy's jaw dropped, and she covered her mouth.

Mercy nodded. "My mama told me a story once about a panther she met who had a mark. He said he was born human. I always thought it was one of those tall tales that Mama loved tellin'."

Montana leaned on the arm of his chair, one fist tucked against his chin.

I smoothed down the adhesive edges on the bandage. "Dax didn't see a point in keeping me if it was costing him money. I had nothing to offer him, and the money I brought in was miniscule compared to what the men earned. We had a private meeting, and I told him the truth about me. That way, he could feel reassured that I wasn't just taking advantage of them. I wanted to live in a pack and marry a Shifter, if I ever found anyone."

Archer, who sat to my left, crossed one leg over his other knee. "I think I know where this is heading."

I noticed the sleeve on his right arm was rolled up, revealing a tattoo of a bow and arrow. The bow was a curved set of wings with the feathers flowing toward the pulled bowstring. Black ink filled in the feathers, and highlights added dimension. It distracted me momentarily.

"Dax didn't want me telling anyone," I explained. "I thought he was protecting me. But it turns out he didn't want someone else to be the first. He honestly believes that if he's the one who turns me, I'll be more loyal to him than anyone. That he'll have more dominion over me than he does with his other wives."

Melody shot forward in her chair. "Other *what*?"

"So he's one of *those* Packmasters," Virgil said while bending his knees and leaning back on his hands. "Let me guess—he also likes to bed every newly mated female in the pack?"

I shook my head. "Not that I know of. But he has four wives. Well, they're more like concubines. They don't lead the household or make decisions. They mostly spend all their time together."

Tak drummed his fingers on the flat arm of the chair. "Why would he believe he'd gain control over you?"

"He doesn't know anything about Potentials beyond the rumors. I tried to explain how it worked, but he didn't believe me. He has this wild fantasy that we'll have this perfect union, and I'll give him an alpha. You see, he doesn't have any sons. That's why he has four wives. I guess you know about the odds of having an alpha being better with the first child. He's completely obsessed with producing an alpha son, but he knows it'll look bad if he sleeps with a ton of women outside marriage. With four wives, let's just say that he's gotten real insecure about it." Caged by the chair, I stood and paced behind it. "He forced me into a mating ceremony. You don't know Dax. He's got connections. He had a Councilman officiate, even though I *begged* the guy to stop."

"And what kind of man is Dax?" Tak asked.

Our eyes met. "Dangerous. The punishments on his enemies were extreme. People were afraid of him. I thought it was because he commanded their respect. I'd never had any serious interactions with him, just superficial greetings and small talk. After that meeting, everything changed. He was worried I'd sleep with someone else in the pack first, so he coerced me into silence so that no one would find out what I was. He put me in the sleeping quarters with his wives. They shared a room. I think he was hoping they'd convince me and erase all doubt, because he waited a month before the ceremony. I wasn't allowed to leave the house."

The thought of it gave me anxiety, and I bit my lip. I'd never felt more trapped than in those last weeks.

"How in the world did you escape?" Mercy asked.

I gripped the back of my chair. "Right after the ceremony, Dax let his guard down. He wanted to throw a big party and show off his new bride. He figured since it was all on paper, I wouldn't run. I belonged to him. People were drunk, and nobody was guarding the house anymore. I told him I was going upstairs to change out of my dress, but I packed a bag, stole money from his wallet, and climbed out the window. Catcher was outside. We were lucky to hitch a ride. Otherwise, his wolves would've tracked our scent."

Tak furrowed his brow. "Why did your watchdog not protect you if he sensed you were in distress?"

"Dax wouldn't let him inside for that entire month. Catcher howled under the window at night, and Dax's men chased him off plenty of times. But Catcher always came back." After returning to my chair, I leaned forward and rubbed my forehead. "I fled before we consummated the marriage. Honestly, I never thought he'd find me this far south." Unbidden tears blurred my vision, so I reined them back in. "He linked me to the incident in Dallas."

Montana cursed under his breath.

In the short time I'd been here, Tak and everyone else had grown on me. They just wanted to build a life, and Dax threatened to ruin all of that.

Tak leaned toward Lakota. "See what you can learn without tipping off the Council. If this alpha has legal rights to his mate, we should avoid getting them involved for now. I don't know all your laws."

Lakota stretched his arms. "When we're done here, I'll call my father and see if he knows anything."

Two chairs to my right, Ian groaned. "If you had a brother, you wouldn't have to worry about blokes like him. As long as Serena's with me, she has protection."

"*Rude,*" Archer bit out. "No offense to you, Serena. You seem like a swell girl. But, Ian, that was a dick move. She obviously didn't have options, so what the actual *fuck* is the point of stating the obvious?"

Ian scoffed. "Bollocks. Are we to believe he was the devil incarnate? If he was so awful, she could have left years ago."

"He fed us lies," I said to everyone. "We heard things, but he kept his nocturnal activities private. He had a group of men we jokingly called his posse. Sometimes they disappeared at night and came home without explanation. Nobody spread rumors. Dax didn't tolerate gossip. But when I got older, I heard chatter in town. People were jealous of his power, so it was hard to believe every single rumor. Maybe part of me didn't want to." I glared at Ian, who was rolling his eyes. "I didn't see who Dax really was until he stripped me of my rights. Sometimes people we trust are that good at pulling the wool over our eyes."

Archer heaved a sigh.

I gathered the courage to stand and approach the Packmaster. "I entered the last pack carrying a secret. I was young, and it probably saved my life. But I'm not that little girl anymore. I need assurances."

"What kind of assurances?" he asked.

"I need you to promise me in front of your mate and your beta that you'll protect me. That if I'm chosen, you won't let anyone in the pack, including yourself, take away the choice that's rightfully mine. Even if I never make that choice at all. This isn't about my sleeping with a Shifter for a ticket to immortality. I'm looking for people I can trust. People who will always be there for me. Protection. Family. If you don't want me in your pack, I need help finding a safe place. That's not something I planned on asking for, but everyone here knows what I am now. You must know people who can help."

Tak rose and towered over me. "I will protect you for as long as you remain on my land. No one will harm you. If anyone here attempts to violate your safety, they'll wish their ancestors had never been born. Men like Dax are an abomination and have no business leading a pack. I'm a fair man with honor, and my pack will never know such fear. Should you leave, Robyn Wolfe, I vow to see that you're given safe passage to a new location." He placed his fist over his heart. "My word is my bond."

The world quieted. In that moment, I realized how different my life could have been had I been taken in by someone like him instead of Dax.

Hope stood up and touched my arm. "You have my promise as well." She turned her attention to the group. "If any of you reveal Robyn's secret to an outsider, you've threatened her life. Potentials who remain human live in constant danger. The ones who understand what they are keep the mark concealed for a reason. Everyone here is still getting to know one another. Consider this a test of your character."

Tak adjusted his braid. "I'll see what we can find out about your rights. I'm only familiar with tribal laws."

"He can't make her stay mated to him," Mercy pointed out. "This isn't the Dark Ages."

Hope tapped her chin as if considering the facts. "No, but she's staying on our land, and we're not allowing him to see his mate. They might think we're interfering in a Packmaster's affairs. Councils are more concerned with keeping the peace than following common sense. We need time to look into this."

Seeing the uncertainty in her eyes filled me with dread. "Thanks for understanding and giving me your word. Sorry, I need to be alone for a while."

I abruptly turned on my heel and headed into the field. I could feel everyone's eyes on me but didn't care. The property had many beautiful transitions. When I reached the end of the field where trees were spaced apart, I climbed a hill. Once at the top, I stood at the rocky ledge. Blue sky stretched as far as I could see, and so did the land. The stream below invited wildlife to taste its cool waters and was larger than I'd imagined.

Will I ever be free? I wondered if Dax would have found me had it not been for the incident in Dallas.

I straightened my arms and screamed, releasing all that pent up rage. Then I picked up a rock and threw it. After scaling down the hill, I walked along the rocky edges of the water and stared at all the beautiful flat rocks. Some were large enough to stretch out on, so I climbed onto one and sat with my feet hanging over. The water was as deep as my love for this place. Working on the house had filled me with hopes and dreams.

"Found you."

I glanced up at Montana. "Hey. Have you been here before?"

He sat beside me and tipped his hat. "My wolf checked out the property."

"You can remember your entire shift?"

"Usually, I black out after fifteen minutes." He picked a small flower growing between the rocks and twirled it. "Lakota gave me the full tour."

Montana still smelled like sweat from all the manual labor, but I didn't mind.

"You okay?" he asked.

"Sure."

"Tell that to all the birds you scared out of the trees with your primal scream."

"Are you following me?"

His lips twitched. "Just wanted to make sure you didn't get lost."

That put a thought in my head. "Do you think Tak can mark his property line with a short fence or something? That way, if I take a walk, I won't accidentally wander onto someone else's territory."

Montana lightly scratched the brand on his left hand. "That's probably a good idea, if he accepts packmates who aren't Shifters. For now, don't go exploring beyond the waters."

The bandage on my knee had risen in one corner, so I pressed it with my finger. "I want to stay. I'm just afraid of what Dax might do. You don't know this man. He doesn't let things go. When you're in his pack, that's a good thing. But if you're not, he'll make your life hell if you cross him."

"What about accepting Tak's offer to move to a new location?"

"And give up the chance at all this? I don't want to quit. When I lived with Dax, I was waiting for life to happen. That's why I never had any control. People made all the choices for me. It wasn't until I left that I realized I needed to make my own choices and take control of my destiny. This is an opportunity for a good life with people I actually like. Well, maybe not everyone." I tossed a pebble into the water. "As long as Dax sticks around, we're not safe. Once Tak realizes how much trouble he is, he'll cut me loose."

A tear slid down my cheek. I missed my mom. She was the only person who had ever given me sound advice. She would have known the right thing to do.

Suddenly, Montana held my hand, and my problems melted away. I was never more present or more aware of the man sitting next to me, the one with eyes the color of summer tea, with lines on his forehead and pensive eyebrows. He had already gained a tan on his arms, though it did nothing to conceal the brand on the back of his hand.

What is it about his touch that feels different from every other man? I wanted to ask him so many questions but not if it meant breaking the connection.

He brushed his thumb tenderly over my knuckles, the rough pad stroking a corner of my heart.

After a lingering pause, he finally stood and offered me his hand. "Come on. You can't hide in the woods all day, screaming."

"I'm not hiding."

He pulled me to my feet and gave me a sexy smile. "Ready for a meet and greet?"

"What do you mean?"

After jumping off the flat rock, he helped me down. "Tak wants everyone's wolves to meet. Between all that's going on with Hamish and Dax, it's better if we get this over with now. How would that look if we shifted around them and wound up tearing one another apart? Normally in a pack, they do this one at a time with new people. So we'll see how this goes."

"You don't sound too confident." I followed him down the path and admired his form. Montana looked good from behind. "What if Catcher mauls everyone?"

He ducked beneath a low branch. "Then I hope he starts with Deacon."

My steps faltered, and I rested my arms on the branch.

Montana turned. "What's wrong?"

"My first group meeting didn't go well with the last pack. Two wolves sensed I was human and growled at me. They had to pry Catcher off one of them."

Montana lifted his hat to catch the breeze. "Tak won't let anything happen."

I ducked under the branch. "If you say so."

He stepped in front of me and tilted my chin up. "Let me make this crystal clear—*I* won't let anything happen."

Montana held my gaze a bit longer before leading me uphill. It wasn't the steepest section, so it was easy to scale. Once at the top, we made a gradual descent. Leaves and grass crackled beneath our feet.

"What if your wolf bites me?" I asked.

Montana chuckled. "There you go again, arguing with me. My wolf won't hurt you. Not gonna happen." When we reached the bottom, he put his hat on my head. "A Potential, huh? Have you always known?"

"No. My mom told me before she died."

"I guess that explains Catcher. I wondered about that. Now it makes sense."

"Remember how I told you about my mom working in pediatrics?"

"Yeah."

"She got into that because of me. They always knew what I was, and that inspired her. She thought she could find newborns with the same mark. Instead of falling through the cracks, the Breed authorities could monitor them. If something ever happened to their parents, they could be protected."

"You lived in a pack for that long, and you were never tempted?"

"No." I adjusted the oversized hat on my head. "Honestly, it scares me. My mom didn't know anything about what happens, only that it happens. I didn't trust anyone enough to find out, so I only slept with humans."

"If you marry a human, you'll stay this way. Get old. Get sick."

"I'm not scared of life or getting old." I decided to change the subject. "My turn. What kind of work do you do?"

He took my hand when I skidded down a slope. "Detective stuff. I worked in human law enforcement before that. Then I started my own business with Breed—undercover work."

That made sense. Montana seemed the type. He'd always asked the right questions ever since the night we met. He also had the right temperament. I thought about how coolly he'd handled himself with Dax and how he hadn't made any impulsive decisions. I also thought about his steady hand. He was a person who knew how to control his emotions.

We traversed through a field and caught sight of a redtail hawk searching for lunch.

"I figured you were on the run," he said. "I just didn't know from what. People leave packs all the time when it doesn't work out, but they don't go wandering off with no destination, hitchhiking in the freezing rain with a watchdog."

"My hair used to reach my waist—that's why I cut it off. It would have been easy for people to remember me. I needed to be invisible."

He assessed my hair. "Nah. I can't see you with hair like Serena's. This looks good on you."

Beneath a canopy of trees, I eased into a potentially sensitive topic. "No family?"

"Not anymore," he muttered.

I stepped over a fallen branch. "You mentioned a sister."

Montana slowed to a stop and swung his gaze up to a towering bald cypress tree with the widest trunk I'd ever seen. "Tammy was my half sister. I sometimes called her Tam-Tam, and she hated it, but it became a childhood nickname." He smiled wistfully. "She was about fifty years younger than me."

"Jeez. How old are you?"

He gave me a wry grin. "Ancient. In my seventies."

Leaning against the tree, I said, "Old man."

Montana propped one foot on a thick tree root. "We had the same mother, different fathers. Neither dad was in the picture. Our mother died when Tammy was seventeen. Boating accident. She couldn't swim. Her wolf could've, but it happened so fast, and she hit her head. It was just a random accident."

"Sorry."

He ran his fingers through his disheveled hair. "Tammy took it hard. I'd moved out of the pack decades before, so I couldn't get back in. The Packmaster wouldn't release her to my care since they considered me a rogue. They thought it wouldn't give her the stability a girl needs, and she hadn't gone through her first change yet." Montana rested his hand on his thigh. "She was a good kid. Smarter than me and wanted to work with disabled children. Shifters, I mean. Some kids are born with issues that don't affect our kind. Others get in accidents before their first change."

"What happened to her?"

He stared at a rip on his blue shirt. "She disappeared."

When I realized he was emotionally shutting down, I closed the distance between us. We might have been strangers, but the pain of losing family was universal.

I took the hat off my head and returned it to its rightful owner. After adjusting it, I stroked his left cheek. Montana had a masculine jawline and chin. His lips looked soft, and I wondered what it might be like to kiss them. Would I feel any sparks?

He reeled me in with his magnetic gaze, and my heart quickened. Then a smile tugged the corner of his mouth. "We'd better head back before they call a search party."

"Montana?"

"Yeah?"

"I hope we're packmates someday."

He cupped my cheek. "Me too."

CHAPTER 15

THE GROUP GATHERED IN THE front yard, away from all the lumber and distractions. Tak didn't want us on the paved area near the cars, since the concrete was hard and could be problematic. A sidewalk led from the porch steps to the parking area on the left, but the rest was grass.

"This is how it'll go," Tak began while stepping off the porch. "We'll do this one shift at a time. If you black out before your wolf is done, I'll bring you back. If everyone still has their fingers by the end, we'll do a group shift so the wolves can meet. That's where I expect the most problems." He gestured to Lucian, Serena, and me. "You three will need to leave at that time. The last part is just for the wolves, Catcher included."

I stroked Catcher's ear, nervous that I wouldn't be there to watch. Catcher raised his head and gave me a reassuring look.

Tak clapped his hands together. "Who wants to get naked first?"

Melody laughed from the porch steps.

"Say no more." Virgil strutted away from the group and stopped beneath the tree. After removing his hat, he belted out the opening lyrics to Queen's "I Want to Break Free" while unlacing his shoes.

Clutching my arm, Mercy exclaimed, "That boy can sing!"

Virgil had a vocal range and could easily have been mistaken for the real singer.

Tak crossed his arms. "We should put him on a singing show."

Lakota chuckled. "American Howler."

Instead of transforming in his clothes like most Shifters did, Virgil entertained us with a striptease, still singing. With nothing left but his red briefs and tall socks, he folded everything in a neat pile.

"You can stop there," Lucian informed him. "Some of us didn't pay for the full show."

Virgil flipped back his dirty-blond hair. "My wolf gets tangled up in my clothes, so he shifts a certain way, whether I'm dressed or naked. Make room."

He ran swiftly and launched himself onto a large rock. As soon as his foot touched down, he rocketed into the air and executed a magnificent full-body spin. In a tornado of magic, Virgil shifted in midair. His white wolf did a half turn before his paws hit the ground.

Catcher pressed himself against me and growled.

Most wolves were easily distinguishable from one another. They had variations in pattern and size, as well as unique markings. Their eye color matched their human counterpart. Living in the Breed world, I'd seen all kinds of strange eye colors. Virgil's white wolf had vibrant turquoise eyes, just like him, and the color was beautiful on a white wolf.

Tak crouched in front of the confused animal. "Calm your wolf," he ordered Virgil. Though I couldn't feel it, Tak was pushing alpha power into his voice.

Virgil's wolf barked several times before chasing his own tail. Then he froze, stared at Tak, and ran in a circle again.

Everyone lost it.

"He looks like the Tasmanian Devil," Archer said with a throaty chuckle.

We formed a wide circle around Virgil and Tak. His wolf edged closer to Lakota first and sniffed his hand. When he circled around Melody, he jumped on Lakota's back and barked.

Lakota pushed him off, and Virgil continued sniffing everyone. When he met Deacon, he bit his pant leg and gave it a hard shake.

"Get the hell off me," Deacon growled.

Tak sauntered over and placed his hand on Virgil's head. After a loud snort, Virgil finally let go. It didn't take long for him to greet us and show off his playful personality.

Catcher growled when Virgil drew near. Catcher was a larger wolf, so Virgil warily looked between us.

"It's okay," I said to Catcher, my nerves rattled. If I didn't get myself collected, Virgil might smell my fear.

I reached out with my palm up.

The white wolf kept his head down but drew close enough to smell me. His tail wagged like a handheld fan, and I breathed a sigh of relief. He and Catcher briefly sniffed each other before Virgil lost interest.

Finally, his wolf trotted back to the oak tree and shifted. Virgil continued whistling his song while Tak pointed at Mercy to go next.

"Can y'all look away when I shift back?" She kicked off her shoes. "I just don't like people lookin' at me all at once."

"How about we *all* do that for each other?" Melody suggested while taking her hair out of a ponytail. "I didn't think we'd be doing this until *after* we chose our packmates."

When Mercy shifted, she did it quickly and quietly.

"Wow, she's pretty," Hope gushed.

Mercy's wolf meekly entered the circle. Tak smiled and ran his hand over her black-and-grey coat. The hairs were evenly mixed, but her legs were ebony and her ears solid grey. She was smaller than most wolves.

"You're a quiet spirit." Tak let her lick his palm. He directed his comments to Lucian and me. "Sometimes our personalities are similar, and that makes for better harmony between man and animal. But it's not unusual for our wolves to be opposite. We often compensate for each other's weaknesses. They are their own being."

He led Mercy around, and she kept her tail tucked in during the brief interactions, never once showing any sign of aggression. Catcher whined and playfully nuzzled against her, but she shied away from his friendly hello. When she finally stopped in front of Bear, he pulled something out of his pocket and offered it to her.

She wagged her tail and gobbled up whatever it was.

Bear gave a sheepish grin. "I brought a little jerky."

Virgil plopped down on the grass. "Cheater, cheater, pumpkin eater."

Mercy circled behind Bear and shifted back to human form. Since Bear was a burly guy, no one could see her dressing behind him.

Tak gestured to Salem next, and he shifted without discussion. His wolf looked at Tak with soulful eyes, but instead of greeting him, he turned to Joy. She stroked his fur lovingly. He was on the leaner side, and the colors on his black-and-brown coat blended like a painting. He licked her hand, and Joy scratched under his chin.

"Be right back!" Virgil unexpectedly shot up and sprinted behind the house, which startled Salem's wolf.

He spun around and growled when he noticed the group of strangers surrounding him. His wolf had a regal walk and confident posture. Unlike the others, he held his tail high and observed each person carefully.

Montana inched closer to me while Tak and the wolf stared each other down. When Deacon tried to intervene, Tak raised his hand to stop him. Salem smelled the air, pulling in tangled scents from the strangers surrounding him.

I gripped a tuft of Catcher's fur. It only took a split second for a wolf to attack.

When Salem finally sat down, everyone breathed a sigh of relief. While he was submitting to the alpha, it was obvious that his wolf was a force to be reckoned with.

Then Virgil jogged into sight with a jar of peanut butter. Salem's wolf whipped his head around and torpedoed after him.

Virgil's eyes rounded when he saw the wolf tearing across the yard. He sprinted toward the tree seconds before Salem's wolf snapped at his leg. When he pulled himself up on a horizontal branch, he took the spoon out of his mouth. "Your wolf is a shithead."

"Why are you running all over creation?" Mercy called out. "We're in the middle of something."

He removed the lid from the peanut butter and shoved his spoon into the jar. "Priorities."

"Whatever you say, Mr. Exhibitionist."

"You're just mad you didn't stock up on your craving like I told you to."

Tak planted his hands on his hips. "If you don't get out of that tree, I'll drag you down."

Virgil ate another spoonful and looked down at Salem, who was lunging for him and barking. "Only if I get a bodyguard."

"Don't be a pussy!" Deacon shouted. "You can heal, numbnuts."

Virgil walked up the slope of the branch. "I'm sure nothing would be more entertaining than watching me get torn to pieces. As it so happens, I like this shirt."

Archer whistled, which pulled Salem's attention away. "Get your ass down here, Taz," he said with a chuckle. "We have too much work to do, so let's get this over with."

Virgil teetered as he walked down the branch. "If any of you bite me, I'll hide your food."

He slipped, his pants hooking on a broken branch, and he swung from it upside down. The peanut butter jar bounced onto the grass.

His long hair hung straight down, and his face turned red. When Salem's wolf stalked up to him, my breath caught.

After sniffing Virgil's face, the wolf walked a few steps, lifted his hind leg, and urinated on the peanut butter.

"This is going well," Montana muttered.

I gave him a nervous smile.

Hope, Melody, and Lakota all shifted at once. Both Lakota and Hope were shades of silver, but similarities weren't uncommon among siblings. Melody's multicolored wolf bounced around and jumped on everyone. Just like her human counterpart, she was fearless. Her wolf and Hope's briefly chased each other around the yard before they shifted back.

Bear went next, and he exploded into shape.

"Oh my God," I said under my breath. "He looks like—"

"A bear," Montana finished.

His reddish-brown coat matched that of a grizzly, and his stout size set him apart from the others. He turned in a circle, and everyone backed up a step.

When Tak lightly smacked his snout, I clutched Montana's arm.

Slapping a wolf? He has *to be crazy.*

"It's fine," Montana said quietly. "He's testing his temperament."

Virgil put his arm around Archer. "I haven't felt this much suspense since that time I dated a porcupine Shifter."

Mercy sidestepped toward Lakota. Her petite size made her an easy target.

Bear growled only a few times, and one of them was at Ian. Catcher weaved back and forth in front of me, denying Bear access. We had to get this over with, so I reached over Catcher and let Bear sniff my fingers.

"Hope you're not attached to those," Deacon quipped.

After Bear moved on, I noticed his large paws. He completed the circle with Mercy and Lakota. Much to everyone's relief, he had a positive reaction with the beta. When he greeted Mercy, his tail fanned back and forth. Then he nuzzled against her before abruptly taking off around the house.

Tak scratched his head. "We'll do a one-on-one meeting later with him. No sense pissing off the man in charge of dinner."

The moment Deacon entered the circle, I dropped to my knees and held Catcher, remaining calm so that he would too. Deacon was an asshole, and if his wolf was anything like him, he might start something with Lucian or me. In his eyes, we were interlopers.

Deacon ran his hand over his short beard and smiled with his eyes before transforming into a black wolf.

A low rumble sounded in Catcher's throat, and his body vibrated. He must have felt Deacon's beta energy.

Deacon's wolf met each person without Tak's guidance, and if they didn't show him a visual cue of submission, he growled or barked at them until they did. With Tak watching, the smart thing for everyone to do was avoid a confrontation.

Deacon snubbed Lucian, then did the same with me. When Catcher snarled at him, Deacon's wolf slowly looked back and delivered a lethal glare.

Once the two worked it out, I stood up and took a breath.

Tak watched with interest, but not until the two betas met did he draw closer.

Straight away, Deacon recognized his competition. The hairs on his back and shoulders stood up, making him appear larger. He jumped on Lakota and snarled. Lakota threw him an unimpressed look before shoving him off.

Melody narrowed her eyes at the wolf, but she didn't appear worried, more like she didn't appreciate someone threatening her man.

Lakota stared him down. Instead of kneeling in front of the wolf, he stood next to Deacon and dropped to one knee. When he put his head and forearm over the back of Deacon's neck, the wolf snarled.

"Lakota's asserting himself as the dominant wolf," Montana whispered to me.

While I'd lived in a pack and understood their way of life, no one had ever taken the time to explain everything to me, so I appreciated his comment. I usually watched their tails, and Deacon's hadn't curled under yet.

When Deacon snarled, Lakota growled against the back of his head. That shut him up fast, and the standoff ended.

Tak ambled over and evaluated his behavior. Deacon lowered his head and curled his tail under, showing absolute submission to the alpha. Then he shifted back and stood with his head bowed.

I quickly averted my eyes. I wasn't born and raised in a pack, so nudity was still hard to get used to. And I sure didn't want to take a gander at Deacon's toolshed. It might scar me for life.

As if reading my mind, Virgil tossed Deacon his shirt. "Do the world a favor and cover up those marbles."

Joy wrung her hands as she approached the Packmaster. "Could I request private introductions at a later time?" Her eyes flicked to the others, who were mostly chatting and paying her no attention.

Tak hitched up his cargo pants. "It's quicker this way."

Salem stepped forward and lowered his voice. "If Joy doesn't wish to participate, we should honor that. Don't you think? Introductions are only required for packmates."

After looking between them, Tak gave them a curt nod. "So be it. But if there's trouble, she'll need to stay out of it."

Archer cleared his throat. By the way his eyes darted around, I could tell he was nervous. "I'll go next."

Shifters didn't have to strip if they knew how to shift properly. But when Archer mashed his lips together and peeled off his shirt, I had a feeling he was doing it for an entirely different reason.

For the first time, we saw the amputation. His arm hadn't been taken off right at the shoulder. The remaining portion balanced with his other arm in terms of proportion. Archer had an athletic physique to be proud of, yet he never showed it off. His six-pack and pecs caught my eye more than his disability. A few averted their gaze, which felt more disrespectful than staring. While Deacon shook his head in disgust, Salem craned his neck to get a better look.

Archer nodded at Tak before his image blurred and he dropped down to a wolf. I'd glimpsed his wolf earlier, and he was a gorgeous color I'd never seen before. His cream-colored coat had blond mixed in. The white was mainly on the underside and around the snout.

From his spot on the grass, Virgil leaned back on his hands. "He looks like a polar wolf."

Tak went to greet him and crouched. Instead of grinning, which would reveal his teeth and look threatening, he stared at him. Archer's creamsicle-colored wolf grew curious and licked the alpha's throat. Tak stroked the spot where his front leg was missing, giving him a good petting. "You're a tough one." Then he petted the wolf's snout, which made Archer's animal relax.

When Tak stood, Archer hopped over to Lakota next.

"He's weak." Deacon folded his arms. "A tripod'll ruin your reputation."

Tak replied, "The only thing that can sully a man's name are his deeds."

Scratching his beard, Deacon asked, "So you're giving out pity passes?"

Krys shoved Deacon. "Shut your fucking mouth. That's my cousin you're disrespecting."

Deacon pushed him back harder, which made Krys stumble.

"Enough!" Tak shouted.

Archer's wolf ran between Deacon's legs so fast that Deacon flipped over like a pancake.

His back hit the ground with a sickening thud. "Motherfucker!"

Virgil howled with laughter. He grabbed his ruined peanut butter and set it down in front of Archer's wolf. "You get a reward."

Archer took one whiff and sneezed. He was friendly and not as standoffish as some of the others, which matched his personality. With each person, he did a thorough investigation of all their scents. Catcher whined and swished his tail once in a greeting. Did he sense he wasn't a threat? What did wolves judge one another on?

I laughed when Archer's wolf stuck his nose in Montana's crotch.

Montana sighed and stared upward.

After Archer shifted back and dressed, Montana set his hat on the ground. He winked at me briefly and shifted the second he jumped into the circle.

"Well, look who's the blacktop," Virgil said as if jealous.

Montana's fur had a mix of colors. The bottom half was white and brown, but on top, it looked like he was wearing a black cloak. It started at the top of his head and draped across his back and tail. The pattern wasn't unusual, but it was one of my favorites.

The wolf turned his gaze about. He growled at Catcher, and the two circled like old foes.

At least they aren't killing each other, I thought.

Tak bent over and braced his hands on his knees. "Come here."

Montana's wolf dutifully obeyed, and they had a friendly interaction. Tak looked pleased. While Montana might have been awake in there, he had no control over his wolf's behavior.

Once Tak straightened up, Montana trotted around the circle to check everyone out. When he set his brown eyes on me, Catcher snarled.

"Cut it out." I pinched Catcher's ear, and he gave me an apprehensive look. "I have to do this, and you know it." Wolves were vocal creatures, and Catcher groaned with frustration before moving out of the way.

Montana pawed the ground.

"He wants you to sit," Tak explained.

Sure. I'll just sit right down so he can have easy access to my jugular. "Maybe that's not a good idea."

The Packmaster walked over and stood on my right. "He's not behaving aggressively. I promise I won't let him eat your face."

Someone laughed.

I clenched my fists and slowly knelt. Catcher's head rested on Montana's back to warn him that nothing had better happen to his girl.

When I looked into Montana's brown eyes, my fears melted

away. I could see the wolf and man all at once, and a calming energy blanketed me. He sniffed beneath my hair, around my neck, and even under my arm. I laughed when it tickled, and he gave a short bark.

I tunneled my fingers through his soft fur. Montana stretched his neck and howled. Virgil joined in, and I giggled.

"You're a noisy one," I told him.

Virgil stood up and stretched out his long arms. "That means he doesn't get night patrol. The only howling I want to hear at three a.m. is between the sheets."

"It won't be *your* sheets," Archer quipped.

"*Au contraire, mon frère.* When it comes to sexploration, I am Magellan." Virgil cupped his hands around Archer's neck. "Someday, I'll reveal the exquisite mystery that is Virgil Nightingale, but today is not that day."

Archer knocked him away with a smile. "You can keep that mystery all to yourself."

"Magellan was slaughtered by the people he tried to conquer," Lucian said.

Tak patted Montana's back before returning to the circle.

The wolf's body vibrated, and I shot to my feet and turned around before he shifted. Kneeling wasn't the best position for when a man shifted back.

"I've got nothing to be shy about," I heard him say.

"You *sure* don't," Mercy added.

When I peered over my shoulder, he had his jeans on.

Tak pointed at Krys. "You're next."

Krys shared a private look with Archer, who shrugged.

Unlike his cousin, Krys didn't connect with others. He had a death stare that made a person clutch their soul a little tighter. I knew less about him than I did the others, so he gave me an uneasy feeling. *Why does someone who shares the same name as a notorious serial killer have such a dark disposition?* That wasn't doing him any favors. Neither was all the leather. I'd seen him in leather pants, but he didn't wear those while working on the house.

Krys pulled off his leather boots and gave Archer a peevish glance. "This was all your idea. Fuck you if I kill somebody."

And with that, everyone took a giant step back.

Tak stood opposite him. "Is there something you want to tell me?"

Krys peeled off his shirt, revealing a lean, sinewy body. "Yeah. My wolf is one crazy motherfucker."

Tak rolled his shoulders as if getting ready to fight. "How long do you stay in control?"

"A few seconds."

Lakota entered the circle. "That could be a problem."

Tak gave him a sideways glance. "You think?"

"Maybe I should order that iron diaper I saw on the black market." Lakota slapped the Packmaster on the back. "Wouldn't want an episode like what happened with the last group."

"What happened?" Mercy dared to ask.

"A wolf bit him in the ass."

Tak gave his beta a light shove, and Lakota chuckled. I didn't know much about how they'd met, only that they bantered like old friends.

Archer spoke up. "He knows me. Should I—"

"No." Tak fanned out his arms, gesturing for us to make even more room. "I don't want him feeling comfortable. You can't see a wolf's true spirit if he's wrapped in a security blanket."

Archer rubbed his face.

Nervous about what might happen, I walked alongside Catcher to the porch steps and stood by Hope and Melody.

What made the situation especially delicate was that Tak didn't have the full support of a large pack behind him. If this wasn't executed with enough control, all the wolves might turn on one another.

Mel chewed on her fingernail. "Should I get my bow?"

Hope kept her eyes trained on Krys. "Only if you aim at his backside. One miscalculation, and you might kill him."

Mel gave a disappointed sigh. "I guess we could do without the scandal."

"Don't be a worrywart," Hope said quietly. "Tak knows what he's doing."

Krys raked back his long hair and stretched as if he were warming up for a swimming competition. He didn't look nervous so much as defeated, as if resigned to the fact that his shift would ruin his chances.

Tak clapped once. "Let's go! The longer you wait, the more jittery you'll make that wolf."

After a minute, Krys shook his head. "Fuck. I sold my bike for nothing."

In a burst of magic, Krys morphed into a wolf. The moment his animal came onto the scene, he was snapping and snarling, his lips peeled back. His brown wolf had a black outline around his dazzling crystal-blue eyes. When he turned, everyone got a good look at the striking black pattern on the right side of his coat.

"Those look like claw marks," I muttered, craning my neck to get another glimpse of the four black stripes in his fur, which looked painted on.

Krys mercilessly barked and growled at everyone, holding his ears flat and twisting his body around like he was afraid someone might come up behind him. He lunged at Montana.

"Shit!" Montana yelled as he jumped out of biting rage.

"Forget it!" Deacon boomed. "Ain't no way that crazy ass belongs in a pack! Make him shift back."

Krys's wolf lunged at Deacon, snapping at his legs and fingers. Deacon jerked his hands out of reach but didn't move otherwise.

Tak circled the wolf so that he and Lakota flanked him, studying the vicious animal as if solving a mathematical equation. "What crawled up your trousers?"

The hair on my arms stood on end when the wolf bared his sharp teeth at the alpha.

"*No!*" Hope hissed when Tak held out his hand.

With his hand inches away from the animal's fangs, everyone froze. Without showing any apprehension, Tak stroked the snarling animal's face. Krys's wolf never calmed—it simply tolerated the alpha's greeting.

What does Tak know that we don't? As far as I could tell, Krys was dynamite with a short fuse. I would never have taken that risk.

Hunched over the animal, Tak growled into his neck while petting his side.

To say that everyone was stunned by that fearless gesture would be an understatement.

Krys's body finally straightened, but he never stopped growling. The threat level changed from "I will crush your spinal cord" to "I might just chew on your arm."

Tak nodded and got up. "We'll do this one differently. Come up one at a time. Slow movements. Don't approach him from behind."

Each person either cursed under their breath or said a prayer before it was their turn. When Hope approached, Tak intervened and uttered a warning in his native tongue. The wolf calmed long enough to smell her hand.

The strangest thing happened when it was Catcher's turn. While our introduction was brief and nerve-wracking, Catcher had no trouble. While the two sniffed each other, Krys exhibited normal behavior.

"Interesting," Tak remarked.

I separated from Catcher and returned to the spot by Hope.

"You can't trust a wolf like that," Deacon fumed. "He's not right in the head. Do you want him around your mate? Around children?"

"He won't hurt kids," Archer snapped.

Deacon shook his head. "Sure. Just women. But that's fine, right?"

Tak stroked Krys's head, and the growling started again. "His wolf has issues to work through, but he's good."

Virgil fell onto his back and laughed. "All aboard the crazy train."

Tak met our curious stares. "His behavior suggests he doesn't trust people. But he seems okay with his own kind. In a pack, you have to respect what lines you can cross with some that you can't with others.

Each deserves their own space to be who they are. I don't believe in forcing a wolf to change. You can't tame the wild out of us. Despite his fear, he didn't attack anyone. I still have all my fingers," he said, wiggling them in front of his smiling face. Then he threw alpha power into his voice when he said, "*Shift.*"

The wolf transformed. Most wolves complied with an alpha's command. They didn't understand all words, but alphas put immense energy into them.

Krys briefly remained on one knee before he stalked over to his clothes.

Tak jerked his chin at him. "Interesting marks on your wolf."

"I don't need a lecture on how I'm marked by a demon." Krys flipped his hair out from under his shirt collar. "I've heard it before."

Lakota returned to his spot.

"The ancestors mark wolves for a reason," Tak stated as fact. "My people believe unique marks are intrinsically tied to our fate. My wolf is also marked." Tak touched the tattooed side of his face. "That's why I'm here. I had a different path to follow. The spirits have given you a message, so be sure to listen."

Virgil stared up at Krys from the grass, his fingers locked behind his head. "Your wolf liked me best. He kissed me *all* over the face."

Montana chuckled while dusting off his hat. "That's the tallest tale I've ever heard."

I sat down and retied the laces on one of my boots, glad we were getting meeting the wolves out of the way. At least now I knew which ones to avoid.

Ian rubbed his hands together. "All right, chaps. I suppose it's my turn." He stripped off his beige turtleneck and handed it to Serena. "I've never done this before," he said in his refined accent. "In a group setting with an alpha, I mean. As I said, we weren't raised in a pack This is not a tradition we're accustomed to."

His sister slanted her eyes toward him and cupped her elbows. I wondered how she felt about everything, since she'd never shifted before. Her calm demeanor was impressive.

Serena sat down beside me. "Thank the stars no one's been killed."

I put my hand over my rumbling stomach. "I hope we can eat after this."

It had been an exhausting day, and I kept glancing up the driveway as if Dax might return. Honestly, I just wanted to be alone for a while. Part of the reason they were shifting was because of me.

Ian fidgeted while the others chatted with one another. Tak was giving his attention to Catcher, who wanted to shake hands. I had taught him that trick when I first got him. It embarrassed me that I'd done it because he still continued to shake hands with people he liked.

Ian shifted so fast that I glimpsed it from the corner of my eye. His dark wolf whirled around and locked eyes with Serena. Then he saw me next to her and made a wild lunge.

CHAPTER 16

I FELL BACK ON THE steps and kicked Ian's wolf in the face. He bit the bottom of my boot and tugged hard enough that it dragged me onto the sidewalk.

"Get him off!" I shouted.

Montana lifted Ian's wolf by the haunches and pulled hard, but all it did was drag me with them. Serena gripped my arms. She might have yelled at him, but I couldn't hear anything aside from growling and my blood pumping against my eardrums.

Jumping into the fray, Catcher attacked Ian. The dark beast let go of my shoe, and the two wolves twirled in a monstrous tornado of fangs and fury. Without missing a beat, Ian twisted away from Catcher and vaulted onto Montana. Before he could deliver a bite, Tak threw him off.

Ian's wolf skidded and rolled in the dirt. Then he sprang to his feet and bit the first person in reach.

A scream tore from Virgil's throat when the wolf clamped down on his forearm. The animal thrashed, and Virgil desperately punched Ian's head. Then Catcher attacked the wolf from behind. Everything was happening so fast that I was dizzy with panic.

The wolf moved like lightning, tangling with Catcher before weaving around him. When Hope and Melody saw his direction change, they scrambled onto the porch. Before the wolf could execute his attack, Lakota tackled him from the side, and they hit the ground.

"Submit!" Tak roared.

I'd never seen so much rage on Tak's face and knew it must have been because Ian had the balls to go after his mate.

Catcher hunched down, submitting to the alpha's command.

Ian bolted toward Tak and lunged for his neck. Though Tak staggered backward, he didn't fall. He struck Ian in the head with a powerful blow, and Ian erupted in violence.

Shifters didn't intervene in an alpha fight unless the alpha called them. To interfere was to question the alpha's authority.

Tak never called.

Knocking Ian to the ground, Tak growled, "You want to fight? Let's get uncivilized." The Packmaster shifted to an enormous black wolf with grey patches. I barely noticed the marking on half his face before he crippled the other wolf with a single bite. The two wolves twisted in circles before rearing up on their hind legs.

Hope covered her mouth, her eyes wide.

I looked at Serena, wondering why she didn't call Ian. Instead, she stared vacantly at the death match.

The fight had escalated beyond one for dominance—it was a fight to the death. I could scarcely breathe, and Catcher was blocking my view. The sounds that filled the air chilled me to the marrow.

Montana, Deacon, and Lakota acted like referees. Despite his smaller size, Ian relentlessly fought the alpha. Crimson blood peppered the air like tiny bullets, spraying everything in sight. Tak flipped Ian onto his back and wrapped his jaws around the wolf's throat. Instead of finishing him off, he kept his hold.

Ian shifted back to human form and shrieked.

For three more seconds, Tak's wolf kept the hold before he shifted to a standing position. Fire burned in his eyes. He stalked toward his clothes and quickly yanked up his trousers.

Ian scrambled to his own pile of clothing and managed to put on his pants before he surveyed the aftermath with a bewildered look in his eyes.

Virgil shifted to wolf form then back. When he wiped his arm and saw it was still bleeding, he growled an obscenity and morphed back into a wolf.

Tak slowly raked back his handsome mane, which was free of the braid. Red scratches marred his chest, face, and arms. Blood trickled down his jaw and onto his chest, and he swiped it with his arm. "You can pack your things and leave."

Ian touched his throat and looked around frantically. "I don't understand. What happened? Did someone provoke my animal?"

"You attacked a female," Lakota bit out while pointing at me.

Ian looked over his shoulder. "That's different. She's sitting by my sister. My wolf was merely protecting her. You can't possibly fault him for what comes naturally."

Lakota shut his eyes, his rage palpable.

A few people bent over and panted. The tension still crackled like the last bits of wood burning in a fire.

Angrily, Ian dusted off his hands. "This was a trap, it was. Is this really how the lot of you live? What rubbish. It's no wonder my family avoided such savage rituals."

Tak swaggered toward him. "Yet here you are, on *my* land, asking to join our so-called savage ways."

"I don't give a shite about living in a pack." Ian smoothed back his thick hair with one hand. "As it so happens, I'm willing to make sacrifices for my sister until she's betrothed. In your country, you worship packs. If that's the background she requires to gain the interest of an esteemed Packmaster, then I will do what needs to be done." He held out his hand to Serena. "Come on, poppet. We're better off elsewhere."

Serena took his hand and stood.

"I didn't say the woman had to leave," Tak informed him. He wiped his bloody hand across his chest. "Only you."

"Don't be absurd. She's my sister. Where I go, she goes."

Tak nodded at Lakota. "Why don't you escort him to the back while I speak with Serena."

Gripping the back of Ian's neck, Lakota growled, "You want to go after my mate *and* my sister? You're lucky you're still breathing."

Though Ian fiercely objected, Lakota and Deacon hauled him off by the arms.

I finally stood and got my bearings.

Montana touched my shoulder. "Are you okay?"

After examining my shoe for holes or blood, I blew out a breath and nodded.

"I thought I was going to have a coronary," Mercy declared. "I ain't doing that again without a football helmet."

Tak inclined his head to the group in respect for letting him handle things.

When his gaze fell back on Serena, his eyebrows knitted. "You should stay. Your brother is a dangerous wolf, but he cannot protect you like he thinks he can. He'll hold you back."

A gust of wind blew back her blond hair, and when she looked up, dappled sunlight caught in her eyes. I hadn't noticed them before, but they were pale violet.

"He's my brother."

Catcher approached her, cocking his head and whining.

Tak wiped at blood that continued running down his chest in rivulets. "I'm giving you a chance to choose your own path."

She glanced over her shoulder toward the side of the house. "Does that mean I'm in?"

He shook his head. "Each wolf has to prove themselves first."

"What kind of option is that?" Serena shook her head. "I can't. If I'm not chosen, I'll have nowhere to go. No one to protect me."

Lowering his voice, Tak gently asked, "And who do you need protection *from*?"

She backed away. "I have to go. I'm so sorry this happened." Tears welled in her eyes before she hurried off to her brother.

I felt a sharp stab of guilt for not having had more interactions with Serena. She seemed like a sweet girl, and it wasn't fair. On the other hand, I completely understood her decision. If Catcher had been the one to act a fool and get kicked out, I likely would have gone with him.

Tak squeezed his long hair as if it would magically turn into a braid. "Who's ready for the real fun?"

Melody snorted and sat on the steps. "I'm ready for a shot of tequila."

Tak looked me over. "Do you need Salem to examine your foot?"

"No. I'm fine." I inspected my boot again. "His teeth just caught on the rubber."

Tak scratched his chin. "You and Lucian, go inside. Don't go out back until Ian and Serena have left the property." He faced the group. "I want all the friendly wolves to shift first. One at a time. Then Deacon and Salem. Krys, you go last, my brother. Less drama."

Krys stripped off his shirt again. "That ship has sailed."

CHAPTER 17

Dinner was unusually quiet, especially with two vacant seats. Bear cooked up a hearty meal with the goods purchased earlier, so we ate like kings, enjoying steaks that had been chilling in a cooler.

But my appetite had fizzled. Salem treated Catcher's injuries, which weren't too severe. Even though Catcher couldn't shift, he still healed remarkably fast.

Still rattled from the chaos earlier, I retired to my tent after dinner, thankful I'd bought the comforter, because in a matter of thirty minutes, the temperature dropped significantly. While the wind whipped against the fabric of my tent, I listened to the chatter outside. The solar lantern by my feet was bright enough for me to see but not so bright that it would keep me awake.

Clutching my pillow tightly, I drew my knees up in a fetal position.

Please, make Dax go back home.

Catcher howled, and the sound calmed me, as if he could read my thoughts and was saying, "Stop your worrying. I'm here, and I won't let anything happen to you."

I jerked when the zipper buzzed like a bee.

Montana poked his head in. "Are you awake?"

"Don't you knock?"

"We've got a problem."

I pulled the covers over my head. "The complaint department is closed."

"There's a cold front moving in."

"Is he letting us inside?" I lowered the blanket to the tip of my chin.

Montana scooted inside. "You know his stance on that. Something about it being bad luck to invite strangers who aren't packmates and might have nefarious intentions to sleep under his roof. Imagine if he had let Ian in there."

"Does he think it would be good luck to find my frozen corpse on his lawn?"

Montana rocked with laughter. "We're not letting it get to that. He's asking everyone to shift. Wolves are built for cold weather. We're putting out the fire since the wind is kicking up."

"Sounds amazing. Why don't you zip up the door? You're letting the warm air out."

"It's gonna get colder."

"I thought this was spring in Texas."

Melody's face appeared. "You thought wrong! Texas weather changes on a dime. Shorts and flip-flops one day, parka and snow boots the next."

I sat up. "It's not going to snow, is it?"

"Even if it did, it wouldn't stick," she replied. "Are you cozy in here? I've got a warm blanket you can borrow if it gets too cold. Do you want to sleep with Lucian?"

My jaw slackened.

She smiled. "I take that as a no. I thought you two could cuddle up for warmth, but Tak has other ideas." She patted Montana on the back.

"Did Lakota ask his father about my situation?" I asked, more concerned about Dax than a little wind chill.

Squatting at the entrance, she replied, "It's tricky. His father didn't have a definitive answer. He said the only way to know for sure was to speak to a Councilman. Tak was going to send Lakota, but Deacon volunteered. We'll see how *that* goes."

Concern flickered in her eyes. She must have been worried about the prospect of another beta entering the pack. "Anyhow," she continued, snapping back to reality. "Catcher's down at the end of the drive. We tried calling him in, but I think he's guarding us from uninvited visitors. Which leaves you... freezing your ass off."

I lay back down and pulled the blanket up to my chin. "I'll be fine."

She rested her arm on Montana's shoulder and shivered. "The temperature's dropping to thirty-eight."

"Twenty-eight," Lakota corrected her from somewhere outside.

She sprang to her feet. "You just know everything, don't you?"

Lakota chuckled and bent into view. "Montana's wolf is staying in here to keep you warm tonight. Are you good with that? Tak thought you hit it off better with him than the rest of us."

"Um..." I wasn't sure how I felt about sleeping with another wolf.

Montana took his hat off. "You have my word—nothing will happen."

Lakota waggled his eyebrows. "I'll go see if Lucian needs a bed buddy."

Somehow, I didn't think that would work out.

After Lakota and Melody left, Montana crawled inside and zipped up the tent.

"Don't shift," I said, shivering beneath the blanket.

He moved his hat by the lantern. "I'm not gonna hurt you."

Wind rattled the tent, and I heard Mercy shriek from the biting cold.

"I've never trusted anyone except Catcher. Even with my last pack, I never slept near the wolves—not even the women. It may not seem like a big deal to you, but I'm the most vulnerable in my sleep. I don't know your wolf that well. And you can't predict what he might do if I accidentally kick him while I'm sleeping."

He sighed and bent his leg at the knee. "I get it. So now what? This isn't a cold-weather tent. It's okay, but there's only one layer of fabric. The temperature's dropping fast. I suggested the truck, but he doesn't want to leave it running idle all night."

"I wouldn't feel right sleeping in his truck anyway."

Wolves howled and yelped outside as they got their first taste of the cold front.

I sat up. "Keep me company. Two people should be able to warm it up in here."

I could have sworn he blushed.

Montana scratched the top of his left hand. "I don't think that's what Tak had in mind."

"Your wolf is the one I'm more afraid of." I flipped back the blanket. "Don't be such a baby."

Montana barked out a laugh. "I haven't seen that much flannel since I took a trip to Seattle back in the nineties."

I looked down at my red plaid pajamas. The shirt had white buttons, and the pants had an elastic waist.

"Sorry." Montana touched my foot through the covers. "I'm a jerk who needs to keep his mouth shut."

I wasn't insulted. Pajamas were my go-to sleep attire. "Take your shoes off." I scooted over to make room. "You get the cold spot by the door."

While Montana removed his shoes, I rolled away from him and tucked my arm beneath my pillow. When he settled behind me and pulled the covers up, the only sound was the wind whistling through the branches.

"I can't believe two more are gone," I finally said. "If he cut almost everyone from the previous groups, he must have high expectations."

"Let's be real—Ian set the bar pretty low. Don't let it rattle you. He's not even in the same league as the rest of us."

Montana's voice warmed me like a lover's promise. It sometimes had a rumbling quality, like an old truck motor in the distance.

"Are you having second thoughts?" he asked.

I remembered the moment when Ian had ambushed me and Catcher was distracted for a split second. "If I get in this pack, I'll feel safer than I do now."

"Safe means a lot to you."

"It does."

I rolled over and faced him. Montana was lying on his side, his hand propping up his head. He smelled earthy from bathing in the nearby stream, but his grey T-shirt still carried the clean scent of detergent.

"Why?" he asked.

How to articulate this...

"Lots of kids lose their parents. I didn't have siblings, cousins, or family members. We were so close. When my dad died, my mom changed. He was her world, and I don't think she was prepared to lose him that fast. It happened when he was at work, so she didn't get a final goodbye."

"Neither did you."

I played with a loose thread on the blanket. "I can't even remember the last thing I said to him. After he died, I clung to my mom. I had her for a few more years, then she got sick out of nowhere. God, that scared the hell out of me. My life flashed before my eyes. No parents at my wedding, no brothers or sisters to call on the phone, no holiday gatherings, no memories. Because they were trusted humans, they were estranged from their families. But they had problems with them anyhow. Her hiring Catcher was a gift. She knew how much I would need him. Not just for companionship but also protection. Finding out I was a Potential and then having to process my mother's death—let's just say I went wild after she died. I was so pissed off that they left me but also that they lied to me."

He brushed my hair out of my eyes. "To protect you. Trusted humans don't tell their children."

"I know that now, but tell that to a fifteen-year-old. Catcher provided the only affection I got after she died. He kept me safe and loved me even when I was unlovable. When I joined Dax's group, I realized I could have a family again. One I could count on always being there. Shifters live for centuries, so I'd never—"

"Have to lose anyone," he finished.

He gets me.

"I feel more alone in the human world," I admitted. "Crazy, huh? Even the guys I dated weren't enough to fill that void. Something was always missing. I can't share everything with them, so maybe that was it."

What I didn't want to admit to Montana was that human men were also a reminder that they were mortal. I could fall madly in love and then lose him in a split second, the same way my mother had lost my father. Because of that fear, I put up walls and never let anyone get too close.

Montana cleared his throat. "Were they *all* human?"

"Yes. The local Shifters weren't interested."

"I find that hard to believe."

"I never said they wouldn't have sex with me." My body shivered, so I pulled the covers over my shoulder. "I'm nervous about what'll happen. My mom never told me. Either because I was too young, or she didn't know what happens when a Potential turns."

"There wasn't anyone you could ask?"

"Santa Claus? It was the big secret. Remember?" I scratched the side of my nose. "It's not just the unknown but also the idea that the guy I choose won't stick around long enough to help me adjust."

Montana cupped the nape of my neck and held my gaze. "You deserve a real man."

The tender look he gave me lingered, and when I placed my hand on his chest, desire simmered in his eyes. I ran my hand down to the end of his shirt, beneath the covers. When my fingertips grazed his skin, Montana sucked in a sharp breath.

Touch me, I thought, willing him to obey without my saying the words. Dark hunger flooded my senses, but I could only bring myself to lightly stroke his flank.

Montana looked at me as if I were one of those breakable figurines in a store window. "You deserve a better man. I'm not the right one to turn you."

The north gale blustered against the tent, and the air chilled.

Slowly, I unbuttoned my shirt. Montana's eyes fixed on me as if I were a ticking time bomb. When I reached the last button, I pulled my top open and bared myself to him. My nipples tightened once exposed.

"Keep me warm. Packmaster's orders."

Montana stripped off his shirt. My pulse jumped at the thought of his touching me. Now I had confirmation that what we had was more than a fleeting crush on my end. The chemistry between us was explosive.

He slid his hand beneath my shirt in the back. With a single motion, he joined our bodies. My breasts heaved against his chest, and the warmth was heavenly.

"You're so hot," I whispered.

He chuckled. "That's what you said the other night."

I smiled, our lips almost touching. "I meant your skin."

Montana was noticeably out of breath, and his heart pounded loud enough that I could hear it. I nuzzled against his neck and inhaled. God, he even smelled different from humans. His whiskery jaw scratched my cheek as I moved my head to face him again.

When our lips were close enough to touch, neither of us moved, as if we both knew that the minute we started that kiss, a firestorm would blaze out of control.

Montana's lips brushed across my cheek before resting at the shell of my ear. "I want you."

I kissed his neck, and his little grunt sent me right over the edge.

"Keep doing that," he whispered. He rubbed my back, pushing the skin around like clay. I was his to shape.

Wolves filled the night with their ancient song, each note growing more distant. Montana was the only Shifter I'd ever touched so intimately, and it was as if we were under a spell.

I kissed my way up his jaw until our lips lightly touched again. We gazed deeply at each other, then Montana rolled on top. He trembled before resting his full weight on me.

Cradling his neck in my hands, I lightly scratched, and he pushed his hard erection against me.

I gasped, closing my eyes.

He radiated sexual energy.

Suddenly, I was oblivious to the freezing temperature. I felt like a calzone in a hot oven, waiting to be devoured.

Montana lowered his lips to mine, his featherlight touch teasing me with the promise of a crushing kiss that would cleave my soul in two. Instead, he traveled to my neck, and my pulse ticked against his lips like a time bomb.

I lay boneless beneath him.

Then he grazed his lips over my shoulder and down to my breast. Montana's lips teased my nipples, kissing all around them but never taking them in.

I moaned softly when his tongue slid up my belly. "You really know your way around a woman's body."

He nipped his teeth below my breast. "I memorized the map."

Remembering the wolves outside, I fisted the pillow and shut my mouth. He slid upward, his body close enough that my breasts stroked him.

Then he was over me, hovering with expectation.

I took his nipple lightly between my teeth before sucking it. *What do wolves like? Is sex with them different?* He was so uninhibited and raw. *Has he ever been with a human?*

I kissed him everywhere my mouth would reach while caressing his sides, his back, and his hips. Hungry for more, I coaxed him onto his side.

When Montana complied, my kisses stretched from his navel to his neck. I memorized every rope of muscle, every ridge, every valley, every soft bit of flesh with my hands.

God, his scent is driving me wild.

I wanted to claim him.

He cradled my neck in his hands. "You're so damn sexy."

I gazed into his smoldering brown eyes, my heart skipping wildly. "I don't think I'm ready."

No matter how much I wanted him, I couldn't get over the fear of the unknown. I was scared of what I was feeling because it was more than passion. We were caught up in something without considering the repercussions.

I might as well have thrown a bucket of ice water on him. *This is the part where he gets up and walks off.*

Montana lowered his head until our lips met. His tongue teased the seam of my lips. The kiss became molten, and when his tongue found mine, I belonged to him.

"We can do other things." He slid down my pajama bottoms.

I lifted my hips and succumbed to his suggestion. He skimmed his fingers over my panties, teasing me the way our kisses had.

Instead of ceasing, the kiss deepened, and my heart clenched.

Now I was the one trembling.

When our kiss finally broke, he caged me with his rapturous gaze. For the first time, I could see the wolf in his eyes.

"What's it like?" I asked, out of breath. "Is sex between Shifters different?"

"We don't have STDs."

I nipped at his bottom lip before stealing a kiss. "That's not what I meant. How do you like it?"

He kept stroking me. "Most like it from behind, the woman on her hands and knees. It feels natural that way because it's what our animal wants."

I melted from his unhurried strokes. Each time my eyes hooded or my breath hitched, he repeated that motion.

"What else?" I asked. "Tell me more."

Even in the dim light, I could see how flushed his cheeks were. He tugged the edges of my panties down, and I raised my hips.

As Montana touched me with his bare hand, he bit his lower lip so hard that it left teeth impressions. "When it feels good—real good—our wolves push against our skin like they're coming out." He slipped two fingers inside while his thumb stroked my clitoris. "It's primal."

I tucked my hands beneath the pillow. "Do you ever shift during—?"

"No. Our wolf spirit is awake. It watches and feels what we feel. I can't describe it." His thumb rolled faster.

I writhed beneath him. "Try."

"Feel that?" he asked quietly, his mouth close to mine. "Right before you come, *that's* what it feels like. You become one with your wolf."

"I want to be a wolf," I breathed.

He moved his mouth to my ear. "Then howl."

Montana lowered himself so fast that his mouth was on me before I knew what was happening. He dragged my panties and pajamas the rest of the way down, and I toed them off. I wanted to lock my legs around his head, but he widened them. I'd never felt more vulnerable.

He sucked and stroked me with his ravenous tongue, and a current of pleasure ripped through me. My orgasm coiled tight, seconds from springing free.

The pack howled in the distance, coaxing out the wild in me. I felt taken.

Adored.

Worshipped.

"James," I whispered.

Growling, he tightened his hold.

I gripped his hair when that coil tensed. Every brush of his tongue summoned my orgasm out of hiding, and my body erupted. A sharp wave of ecstasy made my muscles clench. When he stroked me with his hand, I cried out.

Montana lightly kissed my trembling thighs as if his hunger hadn't been sated.

I couldn't breathe.

Goose bumps erupted across my flesh from the sudden realization that it was freezing outside.

After pulling up my pajamas, he nestled beside me under the covers.

My muscles were jelly as I rolled onto my side. Montana's chest was the sun, and I gravitated toward it like a planet. He wrapped his arm around me.

Then I spent time inside my head. *What did I just do? What if we're both accepted into the pack and don't take this any further? Am I just a conquest for his curiosity? Does he think I'm easy? Does he think I'm using him? He said he didn't want sex—that he wasn't the right man. What did he mean by that? Now he's forced to hold me all night on the Packmaster's orders.*

Shut up, Robyn. Get out of your head. This can't turn into anything serious. You can't have casual sex with packmates. That's not how it works in a pack. Why did I start something we can't finish? Why does he smell like cinnamon?

Thirty minutes must have passed. I had doubts, uncertainties, and fears about what we'd just done. But I didn't feel regret.

Did he?

As the northern wind battered the tent, all my fears were allayed when Montana kissed the top of my head.

CHAPTER 18

MONTANA WOKE UP EARLY THE next morning. After a quick shift, he worked on his second cup of coffee by the campfire. What he really needed was a cold shower in that icy stream. After adjusting his hat, he stared at the remaining coffee in his metal cup. At least it was regular coffee. He couldn't stand all that flavored stuff.

His thoughts drifted to the night before. He'd never been with a human, so it felt strange to look into a woman's eyes and not see her wolf staring back. No, *strange* wasn't the right word—*intimate*.

Robyn was the only woman who'd ever made his wolf sing, the only one who made him tremble like a leaf in the wind. And the way she touched him—no woman had ever been so attentive and delicate with him. Not that all Shifter women were the same in bed, but there were rituals typical among wolves.

Maybe he'd just been with the wrong women who always expected more and treated him roughly.

She'd mastered him like a captain, and he felt like a ship losing course in turbulent weather. It had been the first time he had ever ached to please another more than himself.

Fuck. He really needed her out of his head.

Fooling around with a potential future packmate was asking for trouble. Robyn wanted to join the pack, and honestly, she needed it more than he did.

She could have easily used him to become a Shifter, which might have secured her a spot in the pack. But that was a life-changing decision, one he had no business pressuring her into. She needed to feel safe, but how the hell could anyone feel safe with him?

Montana splashed the rest of his coffee into the fire.

At that moment, Lucian walked up and poured himself a cup. He didn't seem fazed by the cold as he walked around in a tight black tank top. "I hate this shit."

"Then why drink it?"

"We don't have any energy drinks." The Chitah sat in the lawn chair next to him and yawned. "I have insomnia. Caffeine helps. So does cold weather." He took a sip. "That was some storm last night. Lots of howling."

Touching the sherpa collar on his tan jacket, Montana replied, "Yep."

Lucian slurped his coffee. "Sounded like a banshee."

While descending the steps of the house, Tak put on a jacket with Native patterns and bright colors. He lazily walked around a chair on the left and sat down while Lakota dusted off the Adirondack.

Tak jerked his head at Montana. "How did your wolf do last night with Robyn?"

Nervous about lying, Montana cleared his throat. "Everything went fine."

"Cozy enough?" His lips twitched. "Lucian here didn't want a bed warmer."

Lucian sipped his coffee loudly.

"I think I'm finally getting used to seeing your skull, Uncle." Lakota unzipped his soft leather jacket and took a seat. "When can I send a picture to everyone?"

Resting his cup on his lap, Lucian asked, "How much do you love that pretty mane of yours?"

"You haven't changed. Except that here, you don't have a room to hide in." Lakota looked toward the barn. "I think we need to tear it down and start over."

Tak stretched out his legs. "She's got good bones."

"She's got osteoporosis." Lakota studied the building. "If we're gonna tear it down, we should do it while we have the flatbed trailer."

Tak gnawed on a piece of jerky in his hand. "You people bray like donkeys over a little work. Perhaps I should have bought a private island with a cave instead."

Lakota chuckled. "Good idea. You'd be better off in the ocean, where you can't make all these enemies."

The alpha tore off another piece of jerky while staring at the barn. "Enemies build character."

"You've got so much character you could be in a book." Leaning over, Lakota tipped his chair and patted the alpha's chest.

While they bantered, Montana steered his gaze toward a figure walking across the roof. Virgil didn't have a jacket on, just a plain white tee. He waved at Montana before doing a handstand.

"That kid is gonna get himself killed," Montana muttered.

Tak twisted around and looked up at the screwball Shifter, who started singing. Montana recognized the oldie "Feeling Good."

"Should we worry about Ian coming back?" Montana asked.

Tak swallowed his jerky. "His wolf is batshit crazy, but men like him don't concern me. It's that interloper I'm thinking about."

"Dax," Montana said, the name rolling off his tongue like a curse.

The thought of anyone feeling entitled to Robyn fired him up. But what could he do? She was mated to a Packmaster, which was far above his rank.

Lakota rubbed his forehead as he reclined his head. "Are you sure you want Deacon talking to the Council on your behalf?"

"This isn't a daycare. Is that what they call it? Or nursery." Tak flicked something off his jacket. "Humans are odd creatures. If they lived in a pack, they wouldn't have to give their children to strangers. But you're right to be concerned. I don't want Deacon going alone for a few reasons. You have work to do here, though." He gestured to Montana and Lucian. "You two go with Deacon." Then he jerked his thumb at Virgil, who was on his feet again. "And take that one with you before I tie him up with rope."

FIFTEEN MINUTES away from the house, the group reached a private road blocked by a gate. The sign in the tall grass read: NO TRESPASSING, but the paw print design below it was an open invitation to all Breed. Montana jumped out and opened the gate. After they'd pulled through, he closed it and got back in the cab. They had borrowed Lakota's black truck, which meant Lucian and Virgil had to ride in the bed.

Deacon stared at a piece of paper while driving. "He said it's down here somewhere."

After half a mile, Montana pointed to the right. "Here. That's it. The Rabbit Lounge."

Deacon jerked the wheel, and a loud knocking, like shoes in a dryer, sounded in the back. After parking in the gravel parking lot, Montana got out.

Virgil marched toward them from the road. "I can tell someone didn't take a driving test."

Deacon slammed the door. "Don't be a pussy. That's Lucian's job."

Ignoring him, Lucian marched ahead and went inside. Chitahs were the butt of a lot of cat jokes.

Business meetings were common in public, especially between strangers. Breed establishments were neutral ground. Most clubs also had soundproof rooms that could be rented by the hour for added privacy. Montana was curious about the local attractions. It was good to know they had a few shops and businesses tucked away in the vicinity so that he didn't always have to drive to Austin for everything.

Virgil walked backward in front of them. "P's and q's, gentlemen. If you get me blacklisted from here, I'll haunt your dreams."

Upon first glance, the building was a typical dive. Two rows of pool tables on the left went toward a recessed wall in the back. The square tables in the middle were empty, as were the high tables to the left of the door. The few people in there were sitting in one of the cozy booths that ran along the left-hand wall.

"Montana! Let me borrow your hat," Virgil shouted from the bar on the right, sitting astride one of the saddle seats.

Montana glared at him and replied with a shake of his head. Virgil didn't always wear his fedora, and he looked like a kid who'd showed up at a costume party without a costume.

A woman in a coral-blue top and a black skirt approached their group. She was a knockout with espresso curls and luminous orange eyes. Her businesslike demeanor told Montana she must be the Councilwoman. He hoped like hell that Deacon wouldn't embarrass them by hitting on her like he had with the women in that Dallas bar.

"Which one of you is Deacon?" she asked in a no-nonsense tone.

Deacon countered, "How did you know it was us?"

The woman raised her eyebrows. "Because that's my job. I'm Eden Thompson, member of the local Council." She quickly sized them up. "You can call me Ms. Thompson. If you call me pretty lady, honey, brown sugar, sweetie, or anything similar, our meeting ends. I've got too much work on my plate and no patience for anyone wasting my time. And you are?"

Deacon cleared his throat. "I'm Deacon Shaw. This is Montana Vance and, uh... Lucy."

Lucian's lip curled in a snarl. He stepped toward the Councilwoman and inclined his head. "I'm Lucian Cross." A mirage of Chitah spotting appeared on his neck before quickly disappearing.

A smile crept up her face as she glanced at Lucian. "Deacon, come with me. I reserved a private room in the back. Your partners can stay out here and have a few drinks."

As they walked away, Lucian stalked toward the pool tables on the left and slid into an empty booth. Since there weren't any servers, Montana gestured for the bartender and called out, "A pitcher. Thanks."

Lucian sat with his back against the wall and one leg on his bench seat. With his left elbow propped on the table, he ran his hand over his shaved head several times as if still not used to it.

Montana took the spot across from him. "Some betas are assholes. Deacon thinks everyone's a threat."

The biker-looking bartender with a grey goatee delivered a pitcher of beer and two glasses. "I'm Calvin. Let me know when you need another."

They both tipped their heads at him as the long-haired man headed back to his station. His hair was as grey as his mood.

"Imported is better," Lucian grumbled.

"Well, then. Guess it's all mine."

Lucian poured himself a tall glass, then gulped it halfway down before leaning back. "Why did he send us on this errand?"

Montana finished pouring his own. "To babysit. Maybe we can't go into the room with them, but we'll know if something didn't go right. Deacon's a hothead, and Tak knows it. He's testing him."

"What the hell did Lakota talk me into?" Lucian muttered.

It didn't take a genius to figure out that Lucian was the black sheep of his family and not because of his personality. His black hair and shorter stature automatically made him a target. He must have endured incessant taunting from everyone. The Breed world could be cruel to those who were different.

It also hadn't escaped Montana's attention that Lucian had shown up on the property that first night with a shiner and a few knots on his head.

"Did you see her eyes?" Lucian asked.

"Yeah." Montana thought about how intense they were. He'd never seen eyes that color before. For a minute, he thought she might be a Chitah. They weren't quite the gold color Chitahs were known for, but they were in the same family. Then he thought about how much Deacon hated other Breeds and hoped that idiot would behave himself in there with her and not say anything offensive. That got him thinking.

Montana set his glass down and stared at it. "What happened back in Dallas?"

"Deacon happened."

Pool balls clacked together on one of the billiard tables where two men were playing.

"He didn't want me on that bus. After the Regulators left and everyone cleared out, he jumped me." Lucian unzipped his leather jacket and took it off. "Beat me unconscious. I think he used a blade to cut my hair. When I woke up, it was a reverse mohawk, so I shaved the rest. Screw him."

Montana chuckled softly. "Suits you better anyhow."

"Do me a favor and don't mention it to anyone."

Lucian's nostrils were twitching, a sign that he was taking in Montana's emotional scent. If he had confided in him to begin with, he must have sensed he could trust him.

"You have my word," Montana promised him.

Lucian was obviously worried about his reputation, especially being related to Lakota. It would make him look weak, but it could also be problematic to continue the drama with Deacon if they were both accepted.

"If you lie to me, I'll know." Lucian tapped his nose. "You can't get anything by me. On that note—"

"Do you have a big family?" Montana interrupted, sensing Lucian might trap him into a Q & A session he wasn't in the mood for. Chitahs had a built-in lie detector.

Lucian pondered for a second. "You could say that. A few others who aren't related lived in our building. Everyone has busy lives. I was closest to my sister, but she settled with a mate years ago, after she turned."

Montana furrowed his brow. "Turned what? Eighteen?"

Lucian snorted. "She's a Mage."

Nonplussed, Montana touched the brim of his hat and tried to comprehend what he'd just been told. "Are you shitting me? How's that even possible?"

The Chitah poured himself a refill. "Long story."

"That's quite a family you've got."

"You're telling me."

The conversation died, and Montana's thoughts wandered.

Why did I confide in Robyn about my sister?

Montana wanted to leave his past behind but found it difficult to lie to Robyn. She had shown him the compassion and tenderness he never felt he deserved for failing the one person who needed him most.

"You need another pitcher?" Lucian asked. "Your scent changed." He lifted his arm and took a whiff. "I know it can't be me."

When Montana shook his head, Lucian flashed a crooked grin.

"Looks like it's down to eleven," Montana noted, thinking about their group dwindling. "Twelve, if you count Catcher. Do you think he'll cut all of us like he did with the other groups?"

Touching his bristly scalp, Lucian replied, "Fifty bucks says he gives up this dream and returns to his tribe."

"Might be a good idea."

"I'm glad Ian's gone. Something wasn't right with him." Lucian sipped his drink.

Montana hadn't gotten that impression. Ian was a different sort of fellow who stayed to himself and seemed protective of his sister, something Montana could relate to in a situation like theirs. "He can't help that he's got a wild wolf."

Lucian shook his head. "I didn't like his scent. He avoided being around me."

"Well, he's out of our hair now."

"That remains to be seen." Lucian lifted his glass. "All the rejects might show up one night to exact their revenge before stealing his land. They could be conspiring somewhere."

"Why would you say shit like that?"

Lucian shrugged. "It's one logical possibility. He'll never be more vulnerable than he is right now. No pack, an incomplete home, and out in the middle of nowhere. Another possibility is that they go after his mate."

That thought gave Montana chills. He had a feeling Lucian wasn't trying to be dismissive; he just didn't have a filter between his thoughts and his mouth. Had he said anything like that around Tak, it might have earned him a beating.

Montana turned his head when Virgil's singing of "She'll Be Coming 'Round the Mountain" filled the room.

"That didn't take long," Lucian remarked. "*He's* the one who'll get us blacklisted."

Montana crossed the room toward the bar, where Virgil continued singing in his saddle. His eyes were glazed.

Virgil spotted Montana and patted the saddle next to him. "Hop on, and take a ride on the magical mystery tour."

Catching the bartender's attention, Montana asked, "What did he have?"

The bartender pointed up at a sign on the wall that listed the house special.

Montana cursed. Specialty drinks in Breed bars were spiked with sensory magic, and bartenders often charged ridiculously high prices for them. "What's in the Wild Rabbit?"

Virgil clapped Montana's shoulders and struggled to focus. "The universe. The whole universe inside a glass. It poured through my body, and everything is sliding through my DNA."

Montana sighed. "Don't give him anything else," he warned the bartender, who muttered something and turned away.

Virgil stripped off his black trench coat and stood. Then he studied Montana's serious expression. "What's your catastrophe?"

"Besides your getting shitfaced when the Councilwoman is just feet away? Not much."

Virgil pirouetted on one foot. "I am the dream weaver. I am the heart's deceiver."

Montana snapped his fingers to get Lucian's attention. After picking up Virgil's coat, he put his arm around him and patted his chest. "How would you like to go on that magical ride with our friend Lucian?"

"What's wrong with him?" Lucian asked as he approached.

Montana gestured to the specialty drink on the wall. "Stay in the truck with him until Deacon's finished. I'll wait in here."

Lucian gave him a frosty glare. "I didn't finish my beer."

Virgil clutched the Chitah by the shirt. "Story of my life. Now, let's get out of this place. Too many people anyhow." He sang "People are Strange" while strutting toward the door.

Montana glanced around the nearly empty establishment.

That kid is going to be a handful.

AFTER TWENTY MINUTES, Deacon and the Councilwoman wrapped up their meeting. She walked briskly out the door, and Deacon didn't say a word when they got in the truck. Montana couldn't ask, either, since they had to put Virgil in the front seat and strap him in so that he wouldn't attempt flying.

While sitting in the truck bed, Montana admired the bluest sky he'd ever seen. Despite the temperature, the sun radiated enough heat to warm his legs.

When Deacon hit another bump that knocked them around, Lucian slammed his palm on the rear window. "Slow down, jackass!"

The truck came to a grinding halt, thrusting them against the cab.

Lucian cursed and climbed to his feet. The moment he did, Deacon gunned it backward. Montana looked past the tailgate at a van pulling out of a driveway. It blocked them, and Deacon hit the brakes again.

"Get up," Lucian said to Montana ominously.

Gripping the edge, Montana pulled himself up. The men exiting the vehicle didn't catch his attention as much as the ones emerging from the trees on either side—all armed.

With weapons trained on them, Montana didn't go for his gun. Lucian's fangs punched out, but his eyes stayed gold. Flipping his switch now would be suicide.

"Well, well, well," Dax said after exiting the vehicle from the passenger side. "If it isn't the Hardy Boys." He leaned against the side of his van, crossing his arms.

The driver's-side door to Lakota's truck popped open, and Deacon got out. He stopped at the tailgate. "You're in our way."

Looking over the roof of the truck, Montana saw another van blocking them from the front. Armed men surrounded them from all angles. He did a quick estimate of eighteen.

Dax cocked his head to the side. His mirrored shades sat on his head. "Aren't you a *big* boy."

"What's your business?" Deacon asked, keeping his voice calm and authoritative.

Dax jerked his head in disbelief. "My business?" He laughed and patted his packmate's shoulder. "He wants to know *my* business. Can you believe that?"

"If this is about the human, you'll have to talk to the Packmaster."

"If?" Dax folded a stick of gum in his mouth and chewed. "What other reason do I have to be down here, son? Do you think I'm stopping in for a tea party? *If*, he says." Dax nudged his packmate again. "Obviously, he's not the bright one. What about you, cowboy? Yeah, I remember you. *You're* the one who pulled a gun on me. Someone's mother forgot to teach him not to stick his nose where it doesn't belong."

Montana's heart rate picked up speed. The one thing in this scenario that bothered him most was Dax's position. During a confrontation, an alpha's natural reaction is to approach the person they're confronting. It allows them to push off that alpha power and intimidate them.

But he stayed right where he was, smacking that gum.

"Why don't you take your best shot?" Dax opened his arms wide and did a slow turn. "Here I am, cowboy."

"We don't have time for this bullshit!" Deacon shouted. "Move your damn van!"

Montana wanted to tell him to shut the hell up. His gut said something was off.

Dax's wide grin was so chilling that it could have wilted the wildflowers. "Guess what I found out. You aren't actually in the pack, are you? Especially the Chitah. You're just a bunch of ragtag nobodies!"

Keeping his hand by his holster, Montana remained calm.

Dax stared at them and held a long pause before speaking. "Do you know what that means?" He bit his lower lip as if he couldn't wait to tell a secret. "That's right, boys and girls. It means you're fair game. Tak has zero rights." He took a single step forward, his eyes ripe with malice. "Which one of you wants to be my new best friend? All you have to do is bring me my little Robyn that flew away. That alpha hasn't secured your loyalty, and you sure as shit don't have obligations to the woman. *My* woman."

Deacon backed up and gripped the tailgate. "We'll pass along the message."

Dax chuckled as he climbed into the van and shut the door. "You finally got something right, big boy. Be sure to tell Tak the message is from me."

Montana exchanged a look with Lucian, who glanced down. Now

was the time for action. Montana balled his hand into a fist, and he released one finger at a time in a count.

One...

Two...

Dax put his sunglasses on and tapped his hand on the door. "Gentlemen!"

The moment Montana showed a third finger, Dax's men opened fire.

CHAPTER 19

"THAT WAS HARDER THAN I thought it would be," Hope said while shaking grass off her thin blanket. "They make yoga look so easy on TV."

"Those were the basic poses," I explained. "I'm not an expert or anything. I used to watch it online."

Because it was chilly, we'd put on sweatshirts and sweatpants, but after thirty minutes of yoga in the sun, we'd worked up a sweat.

She wore a relaxed smile, like someone getting a massage. "What was that pose we just did?"

"The downward dog."

She giggled. "I think my mate likes that one."

I glanced back at the house, where Tak was standing on the roof, staring at Hope like a dog in heat.

"Yoga helps with balance and flexibility."

She rubbed her thigh. "Some of those made my legs quiver. My gosh, I didn't realize how weak my muscles are. They're sore like the dickens."

"It's your first time. Maybe I pushed too hard. We should probably take it slower and do more stretching before we begin."

Patting her behind, she said, "My backside could use a little sculpting."

"I'm pretty sure your mate would disagree." I gathered my blanket and shook it out. "We can work on breathing and meditation another day. It's hard to do that with all *this* going on." I tipped my head at the house, where the men were hammering and firing nail guns.

"You should gather more of us on our break and make a class of it. I'd like to do it again." She swept her lovely brown hair away from her face. "I think you're a good teacher. You explain things well and make it fun."

"Thanks." I warmed at the compliment.

After putting the blankets back in my tent, we strolled to the well and drew water, which was deliciously crisp and didn't have the same chemical taste as tap water.

I leaned against the stone. "Can I ask you something?"

"One hardly needs permission."

"Did you and Tak have a big ceremony? It's just that you don't have your own pack yet, and his old pack lives quite a distance away."

While pulling on the drawstrings of her grey sweatshirt, she watched her mate walk the roof. "No, we had a private ceremony. Right here. That's why this land is sacred to us. It was a moonless night, and Mel and Lakota were witnesses. A Councilwoman officiated. That's the way we wanted it." Hope touched one of her white feather earrings—ones she'd told me earlier she made herself. The small red stones at the top were so perfectly placed that I couldn't believe she had that kind of patience.

"You didn't invite your parents?"

She shook her head. "I love my family dearly. We both do. But it was important to honor our new beginning with our new pack. No peace party." She gripped my hand. "Of course, we had a family cookout." Hope beamed as memories must have been flooding her thoughts. "We invited our family to check out the property. Tak's father blessed the land, but we still want his blessing on the house... once it's built."

I peered down at the water. "How did you know you were in love? I mean, how did you know he was the one?"

Hope tucked her hair behind her ears. "Your heart always knows who it beats fast for. But you also need to look at that person with an honest heart. It's possible to love and trust the wrong one."

"If you love them, how do you know if they're the right or wrong person? How can you tell when *that* love differs from all the rest?"

Sitting on the stone ledge, she dipped her chin before deciding on her answer. "You ask yourself this: do they lift you up? Do they protect you and give you strength? Do they support your ambitions? Do they respect your opinions and treat you as an equal? A person can love you back, but if they don't offer these basic essentials, how can love grow? My mother always told me that the heart of a man is revealed by not just what he's willing to give but also what he's willing to give up."

"Your mom sounds like a wise woman."

"She is." Hope's eyes were brimming with love. "I used to think she was talking about vices like smoking or gambling. She meant giving up things like pride, expectations, or negative traits that make a person weak. Money and promises mean nothing if they come from a man who wants to control you. Tak is my protector, but he doesn't fight my battles. Even if it means swallowing his pride. Instead, he cheers me on. In return, I do the same. He has more potential than he realizes, so I remind him of that. It has to be a two-way street. I love that man with my entire soul." She stood. "Except when he gloats after winning at Yahtzee."

I thought about Montana, and when I did, my heart squeezed tight. It felt that way every time I remembered the way he'd looked at me in the tent—the way he had touched me. At first, I thought it was only physical attraction. But I'd never gotten butterflies so many times around a man as I did with Montana.

And he had held me *all night*. Maybe that was a Shifter thing and nothing personal. I'd never been with a Shifter, so I didn't know what to expect in the bedroom.

Hope shielded her eyes as she gazed at the land behind us. "Your wolf will always know who it sings for."

I sighed. "But I don't have a wolf."

"Everyone has a wolf inside them, Robyn." She walked over and placed her hand over my heart. "Listen to your wolf."

"It sounds like you take after your mom."

Hope gave a mischievous laugh. "Tell that to my mate. He thinks I favor my father, one of the most formidable Packmasters in the Austin area. He's a man to be reckoned with." As she strolled toward the house, she added, "A man who instills fear."

I followed her. "You don't strike me as terrifying."

She glanced over her shoulder. "If Tak doesn't get the toilet installed soon, you might change your opinion."

Suddenly, a falcon swooped between us, and I gasped and jumped back. It flapped its beautiful wings before perching high in a tree.

Hope waved at it.

Curious, I followed her to the porch. The falcon startled me again when it dove toward us and landed on the railing.

Hope leisurely ascended the steps and untied a string wrapped around the falcon's foot. It let go of a tube it had clutched in its feet.

"What is it?" I asked as I reached the top step.

She opened the tube, and a small scroll popped out. "One of my suppliers likes to send messages this way. She lives with different birds."

"Why not use a phone?"

"We like to think about ways to support our community. Using messenger birds for nonurgent matters is a simple way to create jobs. They used to wear the messages around their chest, but it created problems if someone needed to shift in an emergency. Now they use the tubes and string, but they're still working on ideas." Hope read the message and smiled at the falcon. "Thank her for me. I'll be over to pick them up as soon as I can."

The falcon screeched and then launched itself skyward.

Hope's eyes brightened. "Would you like to go for a ride? I have to pick up a box of feathers, and I could use the company."

I wanted to say yes. Not only was it a privilege for the alpha's mate to invite me somewhere, but it also sounded like the outing I needed.

Then I remembered Dax was looking for me. That would put a target on Hope, which was the last thing in the world I wanted.

"I'd love to go the next time. You should probably take one of the men for protection."

While folding the paper, she said, "You're right." Then she leaned in close and whispered, "I'd rather you stay here and make a good impression on Tak. Just between us, I'd love for you to be a part of this family, but it's not up to me."

"Any tips?" I asked with a smile.

Hope played with the string from the falcon. "Show him who you really are. He's not afraid of your former Packmaster. Tak's a brave warrior. No one intimidates him. Well, except for my father. But that's for entirely different reasons. Don't let that fear overshadow your desire to stay."

A horn blared from the private road. What alarmed me was the urgency of the honking. Hope and I cut through the house and rushed out the front.

Lakota's black truck sped toward the house, kicking up a cloud of dust.

"What the actual fuck is going on?" Archer asked. He set his hammer on the railing and shot down the steps.

The horn kept honking before the driver laid down on it. I could hear a calamity on the roof as everyone rushed to get down. The truck skidded to a stop in the front parking area, and Deacon jumped out and left the driver's door open.

When I noticed his clothing, I clutched my chest. *So much blood.* The truck didn't look right, either, but none of that registered.

Archer, Krys, and Lakota jogged to the back of the truck.

After one glance inside, Archer shouted, "Get Salem!"

My stomach dropped.

Hope took off inside, calling Salem's name.

"Who's hurt?" I asked. "What can I do?"

Deacon lunged at me and gripped my sweatshirt. "You can get the fuck out of here. That's what you can do!" With a single shove, he threw me to the ground, and my head thumped against the concrete.

When I looked up, Montana was punching Deacon over and over, like a fighter in a ring, until Deacon fell against the truck.

Tak pulled them apart. "*What happened?*"

Deacon spat out a mouthful of blood. "Her mate attacked us."

Then I noticed Montana's bloody clothing, which had holes in it, and his hat was missing.

I sprang to my feet and ran toward him. "Are you hurt?" I touched the rips in his shirt.

"I shifted," he said tersely. "Dax ambushed us. He blocked the road both ways. All of his men were armed."

Tak slammed his fist on the truck. "What did he say?"

Montana's lips pressed into a mulish line, and he looked like he was about to explode. "He wants her."

"He can fucking *have* her," Deacon spat. "I took seven bullets for that stupid bitch. I had to cut one of them out of my arm."

Montana's gaze became glacial. He swung at Deacon, but Tak's quick reflexes blocked the punch. "If he lays a hand on her again, I will beat him within an inch of his life."

I turned to the back of the truck, where others had gathered. "Who's hurt?"

Out of breath, Montana wiped his face. "They sprayed us with bullets. I shot two of them. They sped off as soon as we were down. Lucian's hit, and he seems to be healing. But he lost a lot of blood. Virgil couldn't shift. He's got a bullet stuck in him."

"Get them inside!" Lakota shouted. "Clear the floor!"

"I'll get lanterns." I dashed to the backyard as fast as my feet would carry me. If Salem needed to perform emergency surgery, he would need light.

Once I'd snatched my lantern, I raided Lucian's tent for his. With an armload of clean towels, I realized we needed something else. "Water!" I shouted at Melody, who was rifling through Salem's tent. "We need clean water!"

After handing me Salem's black bag, she grabbed a bucket and ran at breakneck speed to the well.

My mind was in a scramble, and I couldn't think of what else to grab. With an armload of supplies, I shot up the steps and through the house.

When I entered the front room, they had laid the two men on the dusty floor, and it was a shocking sight. I set the bag by Salem and switched the lanterns on the highest setting.

Mercy cupped her face, her eyes saucer wide.

Lakota, Bear, Krys, and Hope were stripping off Virgil's and Lucian's shirts.

Salem examined Lucian first since he had blood all over his shaved head. He wiped it with a towel and muttered, "Superficial abrasion."

"Doesn't feel superficial," Lucian croaked. He rolled to his side and coughed up blood.

Through the window, I could see Deacon pacing out front.

Salem used medical lingo I wasn't familiar with while searching for entry and exit wounds. "Blood loss affects healing time," he said, checking the wounds on Lucian's abdomen. "Chitahs rarely die from gunshot or stab wounds, unless they continue bleeding out. An obliterated artery, for instance. But the body has a marvelous way of regenerating." He patted Lucian's shoulder. "Lie on your back."

How Salem remained unflappable in situations like this was beyond my comprehension. He spoke in a dispassionate tone, as if we were all strangers who had wandered into his emergency room.

Lucian looked at his bleeding stomach and then thumped his head on the floor.

Resting his hand on Lucian's shoulder, Lakota said, "You're gonna be fine, Uncle. I've taken worse shots than this."

"Bullshit." Lucian coughed up more blood.

"I took an arrow to the heart, and I'm still here."

Lucian attempted to smile. "Maybe your heart's too small."

Salem pulled a black wand the length of a flashlight from his bag. "This is a high-sensitivity metal detector I purchased from a Relic shop. If you have any bullet fragments in you, it'll pick them up."

Lucian wiped his mouth. "Then what?"

"Since you're a Chitah, it's too risky to remove fragments without the proper equipment. I'll have to treat your injuries differently because of your healing timeline. If this detects any metal, we'll have to locate a Relic. You'll need an X-ray before surgical extraction, if that's even necessary. Depending on the location, sometimes it's not worth removing them."

Lucian bared his teeth, and all four of his fangs punched out.

Everyone reeled back.

"Don't flip your switch," Lakota warned him. "We can't help you if you're feral."

I'd never been around a Chitah who flipped. People said that a primal side of them took over. They behaved like wild animals, unable to understand language. Usually, it happened when they were angry and ready to fight, but it could happen for other reasons.

"Chitah, I can't help unless you stay calm." Salem ran the wand over Lucian's torso. When it didn't beep, Bear and Lakota rolled him onto his side so that Salem could check his back. "He's clear. Put pressure on the wounds until I assess Virgil. If his stomach extends or he passes out, do let me know."

Melody stumbled in with a pail of water and blankets. Water sloshed on the concrete floor when she set down the bucket. "I brought these in case you wanted to lay them on something clean." Out of breath, she set the blankets nearby.

Joy stayed near Salem to assist him. Whenever he asked for something, she reached into his bag and handed it to him. Lakota, Archer, and Bear pressed towels against Lucian's wounds, and Lucian groaned loudly, pounding his fist against the floor.

I turned my attention to the window. Montana and Deacon were arguing in the front yard.

Virgil pulled his bloodstained hair away from his face. "Why am *I* the one who's always dying?" He sounded intoxicated. "I'm too young to leave this mortal plane. Not like this. I'm not even two hundred."

Salem looked over his shoulder at Lucian. "What did he have?"

"A little drinkypoo," Virgil answered. He put an inch of space between his thumb and index finger before his eyes were drawn down to his bloody chest. Then he covered a bullet hole with his hand. "Oh, *no, no, no*. The universe is leaking out. You can't let it!" He gripped Salem's collar and pulled him down until their noses touched. "Promise you won't bury me in a cemetery."

Salem freed himself from Virgil's clumsy grip.

Virgil's head bounced against the floor as he tried to hold it up. "I want to be cremated. But don't put me in the ocean. I can't swim." His eyes fluttered before his head thumped again and stayed.

Salem felt his neck for a pulse. "Still alive."

Melody sat next to him. "If they went to the Rabbit Lounge, I'm pretty sure I know what he had. The specialty drink is spiked with sensory magic."

"Good," Salem replied. "That means I won't have to administer pain medicine. He doesn't appear to feel anything."

Melody held out her hand. "Give me your supplies. If there's one thing I can do well, it's stitch. I'll take care of Lucian while you work on Virgil."

I grabbed a blanket. "Do you want to move them?"

I didn't want to say out loud that they were going to stain the floor with blood. That would be something Tak would forever think about every time he sat by the fire. Aside from that, the floor was dirty and filled with debris.

After rolling out the blankets, we moved the men onto their clean, comfortable surface.

Salem ran his wand all over Virgil's body.

When Catcher started barking, I glanced up at the window where he was standing but couldn't see around him.

Salem slowed the wand when it started beeping around Virgil's thigh. "Take his pants off."

I quickly untied one shoe while Hope removed the other, and we gently pulled off his pants, leaving him in nothing but a pair of blue briefs that left little to the imagination. One of his socks had come off, revealing a tattoo of a black cat on his right leg I hadn't noticed before. Though its body was facing away, the head was turned to look straight ahead. Its hypnotic green eyes held me prisoner.

Mercy asked what everyone must have been thinking. "Why would a wolf tattoo a cat on his body?"

Archer, who was pressing a towel to Lucian's arm, stole a glance. "Maybe it's the only pussy he can get."

Virgil raised his head from the floor. "Leave Chastity alone."

That broke the tension.

Unlike the hole in his abdomen, Virgil's shoulder wouldn't stop bleeding. He also had a bullet hole in his outer right thigh and a grisly laceration on his knee. When they were moving him around, I'd seen where the bullet had exited his abdomen on the opposite side. Injuries like those would kill a human. But with each passing second, his body was performing slow healing magic.

Just not fast enough.

Montana entered the room. "Should we locate a Relic?"

"I have this under control, but I need more light. And someone fetch me a few feet of cord or rope." Salem finished scanning Virgil. "Joy, unroll my instruments."

While they set up for emergency surgery, I switched on the lanterns. Hope held one, and I held the other.

Salem put on a pair of black glasses that looked like binoculars attached to a regular pair of glasses. "Montana, stanch the bleeding on his shoulder wound."

Grabbing a towel, Montana dropped to his knees. Salem stepped over Virgil and sat by the injured leg. He bent the leg at the knee and continued examining the site.

"Do you know where it is?" I asked warily.

He inspected Virgil's inside thigh. "Without an X-ray, I can't be certain of the exact location. Not without my laparoscopic instruments. Joy, hand me the retractors."

Tak returned with a thin rope.

"Tie off his upper thigh," Salem instructed him. "Make a tourniquet."

I'd never seen anything like it. Many of Dax's packmates had come home wounded, but their healing always happened behind closed doors.

After Tak finished, he moved out of the way.

"I can't work from this angle on the floor," Salem complained.

Hope shook her head. "We don't have a table."

"Just the one with the saw," Tak offered.

Salem stroked his beard while in thought. "Help me turn him onto his side."

Montana continued putting pressure on the shoulder wound while we rolled Virgil over. He grimaced at Virgil's back, then folded the towel over to stop the bleeding from both sides.

Salem looked at Virgil's thigh. "Hold the light where I can see."

I held the lantern as close as I could.

After putting on gloves, Salem made a wider incision with a scalpel. Then he held the wound open with retractors. Blood trickled down Virgil's thigh and onto the blanket, soaking through the beige threads.

Salem steadied his hand. It reminded me of that childhood game *Operation* with the tweezers and buzzer that scared the living hell out of children.

Virgil groaned.

"Should we knock him out?" I asked.

"No," Salem said quietly. "If we sedate him, he can't shift when I'm done. Operating on Shifters isn't about precision or even comfort. It's about speed. I need a few strong men to hold him down in case he becomes agitated."

Bear stepped in and placed one hand on Virgil's left arm and another on his right flank. Tak knelt and gripped his ankles.

"I see it." Salem's voice was the only level thing in the room. "He's lucky it didn't hit his artery."

Virgil groaned like an old man waking up from a long nap.

"Would that have killed him?" I asked.

Salem never looked away from the surgical site. "Not likely. It would just be more to mop up."

Lucian growled.

"Sorry," Melody said in a small voice. "I usually do this on purses. You're my first live subject."

"On that note, someone call a Relic," Lucian complained.

"I'll try to be gentle," she said. "Just stop breathing."

Salem was laser-focused on his job, taking his time.

Virgil had quit squirming and was mumbling something about cookies. Blood leaked out of his wounds and soaked the towels. Until he could shift, it was imperative to keep as much of that blood inside his body as possible.

My right arm trembled from holding the lantern, so I switched to using my left hand.

"Got it." Salem slowly pulled out his instrument and revealed a bullet fragment.

Everyone breathed a sigh of relief.

Except for Salem, who picked up his wand again and ran it all around Virgil's thigh. "It's clear. Let me check him once more. Sometimes they leave smaller fragments. I want to be as thorough as possible to prevent further injury when he shifts."

"I need to leave." Joy abruptly sprang to her feet and hurried out of the room. After a beat, we heard her throwing up in the kitchen.

I felt the same after seeing all the gore.

Salem finally finished his thorough examination and untied the cord around Virgil's thigh. "You may shift."

Virgil rolled onto his back, spreading his arms and legs wide. "Do I get a cookie?"

When Virgil shifted, it was a wavy transformation that looked like a mirage. His white wolf twisted on the bloody blanket.

"Shift back," Salem said with urgency.

The disoriented wolf laid his head down, his tongue hanging out and his eyes crossed.

Tak got up. "Shift!"

Virgil morphed back to himself. "You take all the fun out of it."

I crawled over to Lucian. "Is there anything I can do?"

Archer replied, "Take over. Nature calls."

Virgil stood, completely naked, his underwear twisted around his ankle. "I almost became your next haunt. I deserve a cookie. Peanut butter's my fave." He jumped across the room and only rotated a half turn before his wolf slammed against the floor on his side.

Archer snorted. "Come on, Taz. I'll get you a cookie."

CHAPTER 20

After dinner, I crouched at Lucian's tent opening. "Can I bring you anything? Something to drink?"

Lucian was lying on his back, propped up by several pillows. The stubble on his head appeared darker because of the shadows. He set down a book with a dragon on the cover next to his lantern. "I can't eat or drink."

"Why not?"

He pointed at a small scar on his belly where the skin had already sealed up. "In case things inside aren't closed up all the way. I'm not thirsty. Salem had an IV kit in that little magic bag of his."

"Is there anything I can do?"

Lucian's dark eyebrows sloped down. "Yeah. Scratch my foot." He wiggled it beneath the covers. "A bullet grazed it. I'm lucky I didn't lose a toe. It's itching like hell, and I can't bend over."

I lightly scratched his foot beneath the blanket. When all four of his canines punched out, I knew I'd hit the right spot.

I withdrew my hand. "I'm just glad no one was killed. You don't know how sorry I am. How..."

He drew in a deep breath. "That prick doesn't deserve your guilt. It has nothing to do with you anymore."

"But it does." I gripped the zipper. "Do you want this closed?"

"Thanks."

"Just yell if you need anything."

After zipping his tent, I stood and tucked my hands into my coat pockets. Virgil had healed through shifting, but the repeated process knocked him out. Shifting one time didn't drain a person's energy as much as doing it several times, especially if it was for healing. It tapped out their core energy and made them sleep anywhere from several hours to a day or two.

Once Salem had stabilized them, I helped clean up the blood. We tried washing the blankets and towels but wound up burning them instead.

I found it hard not to think about Dallas. If Catcher and I had just stayed behind, the attack wouldn't have happened. Now I faced a crucial decision.

Catcher licked my hand and nudged it, but I was too caught up in my tangled thoughts. Soft murmurs came from the fire while Bear noisily washed the dishes. Because Virgil and Lucian were recovering in their tents, Hope suggested we not cook anything on the fire. The aroma would only torment them. Instead, we'd gathered for a quiet meal of peanut butter and jelly sandwiches with chips.

And it was so quiet that the only sound was people chewing their food and swallowing water. Not until after I walked away did low chatter begin.

I knelt and looked Catcher in the eyes. "What should we do?" I whispered. "If I stay, I'm safe. But they're not."

He groaned with uncertainty. Catcher knew the obvious: at least here, we had a measure of protection. Out there, we were on our own. Yet staying came at a price.

Catcher walked alongside me to the firepit. When I plopped down in the empty chair between Krys and Archer, he sat at my feet. He wasn't typically clingy, so he must have sensed a change in everyone, especially since the conversation died the second we walked up.

Before I could open my mouth, Tak said, "I have an announcement." He stood and brushed breadcrumbs off his jacket. "I want to make a formal speech in front of my mate, my beta, and my best archer."

Melody beamed at the compliment. When she caught Lakota picking something out of his teeth with a toothpick, she lightly slapped his arm to get his attention.

Quirking a smile at her, Tak continued, "Today, we suffered at the hands of our foe, but we're not defeated. I watched how you pulled together as a group. I also observed how you reacted under pressure. Most of you impressed me, especially one in particular. Salem, rise to your feet."

Salem got up and wiped his hand over his short beard.

Tak approached him. "I've seen bullets removed, arrowheads, glass —you name it. Never with such precision and patience, especially with your lack of equipment. You're a skilled healer, and my pack could use a man like you, someone who's calm under pressure and treats everyone as equals. You're honest. I've known a few healers who wouldn't admit their shortcomings, but you demonstrated that a life is more precious than your pride." Tak clasped his hands behind him and dipped his chin. "Salem Lockwood, do you accept this invitation to join my pack? Will you follow my lead, protect your brothers and sisters, help the needy, and stay loyal to this house?"

Salem peered down at Joy, and I could no longer see his face.

The corner of Tak's mouth hooked up in a smile. "She's your mate, so she's automatically in if you accept. I don't separate life mates, and Joy has also shown me that she is caring, a hard worker, and a good assistant." He winked at her.

With pleading eyes, Joy looked up at Salem.

After a moment, Salem faced the Packmaster. "It would be our honor."

Tak gripped Salem's shoulder and rocked with laughter. "You can smile. It won't hurt."

Tak's packmates clapped loudly.

I wasn't sure if Salem smiled, but Joy sure did. She bounced to her feet and clutched his arm.

"Your wolf needs to meet everyone," Tak informed her. "That's not something you want to put off."

While they briefly exchanged words, I noticed everyone looking at one another. *Will Salem be his only pick tonight?*

Deacon hooked his arms over the back of his short chair and grinned like a man about to accept an award.

What happened with the Councilman today? So much had gone on with the shooting that it never came up.

When I shifted my gaze, I caught Montana looking at me from across the firepit. Butterflies swarmed in my stomach. *Is it possible for someone to get better looking?* I sure didn't remember feeling so attracted to him when we first met. The light dusting of whiskers on his face needed to live there forever. And sometimes he did a thing with his eyebrow in which he could slant it more than the other. Montana gave me sexy-cop-meets-cowboy vibes, and whenever he wore that black hat, I melted on the spot.

The flames crackled between us. I tried to forget about our passionate encounter, but my face heated when he tipped his hat at me.

Finally, Salem and Joy sat down.

Tak slowly walked around the fire. "I base my decisions on several things, not just one." He finally stopped. "Bear, rise up."

Bear's Adam's apple undulated as he swallowed his drink. When he stood, the two men looked like giants facing off. Bear straightened his long-sleeved shirt, a mannerism that looked like a nervous reaction.

Tak nodded at him. "I've put this off for long enough, mostly because I wasn't sure if you were fattening me up on purpose." He chuckled softly and clasped his hands behind his back. "Bear, I don't know your full name, but I don't need to. I'm also a man with one name. You were in the first group and have made it this far. I've watched you feed people you didn't like, including that jackass who burned all your cookbooks."

Bear lowered his head.

After a quiet moment, Tak looked over his shoulder at us. "This man made a special soup for my mate when she was feeling ill one night. Everyone had gone to sleep, and he started a fire and gave her something that would soothe her stomach." The Packmaster looked at Bear again. "You're compassionate. I come from a family of warriors, but bravery isn't the only admirable quality in a man. A warrior without a heart is only a weapon. Bear, do you accept this invitation to join my pack? Will you follow my lead, protect your brothers and sisters, help the needy, and stay loyal to this house?"

Bear's eyes shone, and he finally cracked a smile. "You bet."

His new packmates cheered while Tak gave him a pat on the chest. Bear's cheeks flushed when someone whistled, but he didn't wipe the smile off his face.

"Does this mean I get a say in the kitchen design?"

Tak threw back his head and laughed. "Brother, you can hang your name over that doorway if you want." He turned to his chair and sat down. "Now I'd like to move to the next topic. Deacon, tell me what Councilwoman Thompson had to say."

Deacon gave me a thorny look before answering. "She said that unless the human was being held on the land against her will, no law was broken. But if at any point the human blames you for keeping her away from her mate, the Council will strip you of your land. And you can bet your sweet ass if she leaves, that Packmaster will get her to say anything to watch you suffer."

All eyes turned to me.

I gripped the arms of my chair, anger rising like steam. "I would *never* do that."

Deacon cocked his head. "Oh yeah? Because we've all met your lover, and he's a fucking monster. You're a weak little human who could never stand up to him. You're a puppet."

I shot to my feet and directed my words at Tak. "Do you want me to leave? I don't want this for you, but this is the only place that's ever felt like... home." I wiped away a rogue tear.

Catcher growled and circled in front of me.

Archer lightly held my arm, coaxing me to sit, which I did.

"What else did she say?" Tak asked.

Deacon shook his head. "I told her about your situation. She already knew you were vetting packmates. Their hands are tied if he tries anything. The human isn't your packmate. They'll consider it a personal matter between an alpha and his mate, and you're just the unfortunate bastard who got caught in the crossfire. Trespassing on your territory without your consent is illegal, but that's where it gets tricky. She *belongs* to him. If a fight broke out and someone was killed, *his* Council would be the one to preside over the final ruling, and I'd be willing to bet he's got their loyalty in his pocket. Her advice was to either work it out with Dax or get rid of the girl. I vote for the second. She's not worth the trouble."

Tak stroked his chin. "Did Ms. Thompson mention whether the Packmaster sought their assistance?"

"Oh yeah. She met him. He claims the human was lured here on false pretenses. That she was supposed to leave home for a temporary job to work off a debt she owes him."

"That's a lie," I snapped.

Deacon avoided eye contact with me. "His packmates will testify it's true. He said he's willing to overlook the debt if she goes home. Stealing from a Packmaster is a serious offense." Deacon picked up the drink by his chair. "Until they legally sever the bond with his Council, you're harboring a Packmaster's mate. Technically, he has the right to challenge you or take compensation for the money she owes. Even if she goes to the local Council here, it won't mean jack shit. Dax could say she's under your influence."

"I'm *not* going back with him," I ground out. "You don't understand. They *forced* me into the ceremony. The Council ignored my pleas. Do you think they'll care if I want a divorce? Dax owns them. He owns everyone. And I was never in debt. I stole five hundred dollars from his wallet when I left, but that's it. Every cent I made at my jobs went directly to Dax instead of a banker, so that money was mine."

Rubbing the tattooed side of his face with two fingers, Tak kept his eyes fixed on the fire. "Why must matings involve the Council? It's a vow between two wolves. Your ways make no sense."

Hope adjusted the blanket on her lap. "It's a public declaration in case there are legal issues or situations like these. If you don't put your names in their book, it's harder to prove you're mated to that person. In a small community or with an established pack, it's known—the same way it is with your tribe. But say you travel to a different city or state. If someone killed your mate, how would the Council know whether or not you were concocting a story?"

Tak rolled his eyes. "Because I don't put my axe in just anyone."

Melody snorted.

"Going to the Council and making a marriage public knowledge is like having an insurance policy," Hope continued. "Especially for a Packmaster. That's why I made you invite Eden to our property."

He gave her a crooked smile. "I thought maybe you were getting cold feet and needed a replacement."

"Don't be silly."

Catcher put his head in my lap and stared up at me with soulful eyes. I touched his face, uncertain what he wanted to say.

"Can we get a restraining order?" I asked.

Deacon scoffed.

"Those don't exist in our world," Hope informed me. "We don't have the manpower to enforce a million laws."

Melody snacked on a bag of soft peppermints. Between bites, she said, "Not to mention we don't have enough jails. They have a limit on how many are allowed and where they can be built. It requires a ton of work to keep them a secret from humans. If the packs can't settle matters between themselves, it looks bad for the Packmasters. Like they can't manage their business."

"Cut her loose," Deacon said, acting as the voice of reason. "There's another detail none of you thought about. If the human joins your pack, she'll stay single. She can't legally mate with anyone as long as she's mated to a Packmaster."

"But I'm a human," I argued. "The rules don't apply."

"You bet your sweet ass they apply. Human or not, once you marry a Packmaster, you're in for life."

Tak sighed. "Lakota, search the area tomorrow. Find out if he's still around. Today might have been an arrogant man's final attempt to salvage his pride instead of leaving with his tail between his legs. Let's hope that's the case." He reached behind his head and pulled his braid to the front. From the way his thick eyebrows pressed together, I knew something was troubling him. "Now I want to discuss *you*, Deacon."

"Me?" Deacon shifted in his chair, his chest puffing out like he was expecting an award.

Tak gave an imperceptible nod. "I want to address your reprehensible behavior this afternoon." He slowly lifted his head and locked eyes with Deacon. "You shoved Robyn to the ground. That's not how we treat women in my tribe."

Deacon jerked his head back in surprise. "We almost lost two men because of her! She's not even Breed."

Tak quelled him with a reproachful look. "The pack looks up to a beta. He sets the example on how to behave. I've been troubled by this all evening. Up to now, you've shown yourself to be hardworking with leadership skills. You volunteered to take on an important task with the local Council. We not only gain information from those meetings but also establish a rapport." Tak stroked his chin. "I've been mulling this over, trying to decide whether I should give you a probationary period. Was this an isolated action or a display of your true character? There's one thing I want to know. What were you and Montana arguing about?"

I thought back to when we were helping Lucian and Salem. Montana and Deacon had been outside, so I assumed it was the usual Shifter bullshit between two men.

Deacon shifted his gaze to Montana like a kid about to get busted for cheating.

"Two men were bleeding out on my floor," Tak said angrily. "You're the last person I would expect to be outside, so it must have been something significant. Prying into personal matters isn't a hobby of mine, but under the circumstances, I'm entitled to answers. I'm giving you a chance to speak your piece. Let's settle this now before someone dies because of your lack of attention." Tak laced his fingers together and shifted his gaze. "Montana?"

Deacon suddenly shot up. "I'll save you the decision. *Fuck* your probationary period. I'm the best damn beta this pack could ever have. This is your loss, not mine. You'll regret it someday—I can promise you that."

Without another word, Deacon stormed off toward his tent and gathered his belongings. The rest of us sat in surprise. Why would a beta give up so easily? Especially when Tak seemed ready to forgive his actions if Deacon would give more insight.

Tak shook his head with a look of disappointment.

The gaping silence was fractured by the wood snapping in the fire. Deacon didn't scuttle off like a dog licking his wounds. Instead, he approached us with a menacing stride.

Catcher got up and elicited a growl that made the hair on my arms stand up.

Tak rose as well. His stance made me nervous that something might go down.

Catcher barked at Deacon and kept him away from the group by a few feet.

Deacon hefted his bag and glowered at everyone. "None of you deserve to be in a pack." He locked eyes with someone, and I followed his gaze to Lakota. "I'm the best second-in-command a Packmaster could want. Someone else will get that privilege." He marched away with a confident stride—nothing like the previous men, who had flounced off like petulant children.

Catcher trotted close behind to escort him off the property.

Tak remained on his feet. "I pity men like him. Deacon's a strong beta with potential, but his position meant more to him than being part of a family. I hope one day he sorts that out." Tak steered his gaze to Montana. "I won't ask what went on between you two. That's behind us now, and I hope you've learned from it. My pack has grown larger tonight, and my heart is full. Though not as full as my belly." He patted his stomach and grinned at Bear. "What have you got in that magic cooler?"

Bear ran his fingers around the collar of his shirt. "All I made were campfire brownies. I was gonna break 'em out tomorrow since we got two people laid up."

Slowly, Tak sat down. "I don't think I've had brownies before."

Bear swaggered toward the cooler. "They're made from chocolate."

Tak chuckled. "I should like to try your chocolate brownies. Perhaps I can give you a few recipes from my people. We sweeten our food with fresh berries and honey."

"I thought you just ate eggs for dessert," Hope remarked.

When he reached over and tickled her hips, his chair tipped sideways. "Only if you hand-feed me those eggs, Duckie."

Still feeling unsure of my place, I got up and circled behind my chair.

Tak peered over his shoulder at me when his mate quit laughing. "Where are you going? Wolves eat together."

"Are you willing to take the risk of keeping me here if you're not sure you want me? Dax could ruin you. Even if he doesn't, he'll try. You've seen what he can do." I glanced back at Lucian's tent. "I never thought he'd go this far, and I'm sorry about that. My head's still swimming with everything going on, so I guess I'm not clear on what you want."

He sat back again. "And what do *you* want?"

"Not to bring harm to anyone. Not to ruin your reputation or your life."

"But you want to be here."

I gave a curt nod. "I do. But Deacon was wrong about me. I'll never go back to him."

Tak crooked his finger at me.

I walked around the fire and stood before him. Even seated, he looked like a god among men.

"You would leave this pack if it meant saving others from harm. You would put *their* lives before yours. Their comfort before your happiness." He pointed directly at me. "*That's* what I want in a packmate. You only need to prove yourself to me." He chuckled. "I never imagined humans and Chitahs would knock on my door, but the spirits brought you here for a reason. Maybe to test me—to see if I'm ready to lead a pack. I won't ask you to leave because of another man's actions. That goes for everyone here. I want my choices tonight to inspire you to stand out."

"Thank you," I said to both Tak and his mate.

For reasons I couldn't explain, I wanted to rush into Montana's arms. I wanted him to hold me tight and tell me everything was going to be okay and that I had nothing to worry about with Dax. But I had to come to terms with his not feeling the same way. Sexual attraction was one thing, but love was entirely another.

Love.

I wasn't a silly woman who fell in love at the drop of a hat. I'd never told the men in my past I loved them. But the way I felt about Montana was something wholly different. It would be unrealistic to say that it was love at first sight, because it wasn't. He was handsome, self-assured, and charismatic. Men like that were a dime a dozen. But when he held my hand at the stream, I fell fast and hard.

That was it. That moment.

A space in time that crystallized in my mind.

Something undeniable in his touch warmed my heart. He showed me that despite my troubles, he was there to support me. I knew immediately he embodied all the traits I wanted in a man, including tenderness. And since then, my heart quickened at the thought of him.

How is this possible? We barely know each other.

I returned to my chair with nebulous thoughts swirling in my head, but they quieted to perfect silence when we locked eyes from across the fire.

This time, I didn't look away.

CHAPTER 21

Montana woke up before sunrise. He'd slept hard for a few hours, until a wolf howling in the distance snapped him awake. For the first time since arriving, he hadn't felt safe on the property. And his first instinct had been to fly out of his tent and check on Robyn.

After his run-in with Dax yesterday, now he understood *why* Robyn had fled in the night, cut her hair, and endured miles of walking in torturous weather to escape that monster. Dax was malevolent.

Montana had known men like him—unpredictable, patient, calculating. They would do anything to win, even if that meant destroying what they wanted most.

"It's ready," Bear called out to Montana.

Everyone had eaten breakfast except for Lucian and Virgil, and Lucian was told to rest. Bear was cooking up something special for them.

After delivering Lucian his breakfast, Montana planned to join Lakota, who was clearing out the side of the house. They had a hard day of work ahead, so the earlier they got started, the better.

Virgil emerged from his tent in a long silk kimono and slippers. He put on a pair of round sunglasses and yawned. "Yesterday was a trip," he said, looking like hell warmed over. Virgil took the bowl Bear handed him and sniffed it. "I need a few more hours before I can work."

"Tak doesn't want you on the roof, son." Bear gave him a spoon. "Not today."

When Virgil landed in his chair, soup dribbled onto his robe. He wiped it away before noticing Montana. "What happened after the gun show? It's all... fuzzy."

Montana squinted at him. "All that amnesia from one drink?"

Virgil stirred his soup with the spoon. "I paid extra for a second glass."

Montana sighed. "You're lucky he didn't blacklist you."

"Doubtful." Virgil nonchalantly tossed his spoon over his shoulder. "It was a slow day. I think Calvin was bored. Worked out in my favor anyhow. I didn't feel a thing."

Bear chuckled. "Neither did Chastity."

Virgil gulped his soup right from the bowl.

After a beat, Bear handed Montana another bowl. "This is bone broth. Salem doesn't want Lucian eating solid foods until tomorrow, so hide your M&M's."

Montana took the bowl and headed to Lucian's blue tent. "It's Montana. I'm coming in," he announced through the opening.

Lucian sat up and rubbed his eyes with the heel of his hand. "What time is it?"

"Midmorning. Here." Montana offered him the bowl. "Liquid diet for twenty-four hours."

"Thanks." Lucian slurped his soup and then grimaced when he swallowed.

"That bad?"

The Chitah turned his head and coughed. "My throat's dry, so it hurts to swallow."

"You okay?"

"I've seen better days."

Montana crawled inside and zipped the tent closed. "We need to talk."

Lucian set his bowl aside and scratched the healed areas on his stomach where Dax's men had shot him. "So talk."

Montana took off his hat. "Deacon's gone. Maybe you heard. Maybe you didn't. A couple of things rubbed Tak the wrong way. Him shoving Robyn and the fight we had afterward."

When Lucian looked up, his top fangs had descended. "He touched a female?"

"I took care of it."

Lucian shut his eyes and released a slow breath.

"Tak was asking for the reason behind our fight. Deacon wasn't talking, but then the alpha asked me. I think that spooked him. He knew if I said anything, he'd never save face."

Lucian picked up his bowl. "What did you tell him?"

"Not a damn thing." Montana sighed. In a pack, alphas didn't get deeply involved in everyone's business. The beta was the guy to go to, but they weren't officially part of the pack. "Even though he's gone, I think at least Lakota should know what happened yesterday. There's always a chance Deacon might crawl back and smooth things over. Virgil doesn't remember yesterday. I don't think Tak needs to hear this if it might change his opinion of you. Not saying he's got reason to, but the way he's cutting people left and right..."

Lucian spooned the soup into his mouth. Clearly, he didn't like talking about it, but it had to be said.

Montana thought back to the shooting. On his countdown to three, he and Lucian had hit the truck bed. Bullets were flying. Some blazed right through the metal and struck them. When Montana opened fire, the shooting ceased. Lucian jumped out, someone screamed, and more shots rang out.

It was chaos.

When Montana finally peered over the tailgate, Dax's van had driven off, taking half the men with him. The other half were running toward the second van. Blood spatters were in the truck, on the road, and on the grass. He struggled to stand, and when he turned, he saw a Shifter limping toward the van. Montana stood and fired over the roof of the truck, striking the van several times before he ran out of ammo. When the vehicle sped around them, a hail of bullets hit the truck.

After they left, Montana had stripped down to examine his injuries. Sometimes it wasn't easy to tell, but in his line of work, he'd learned to spot the difference between an entry and an exit wound. Since they were clean shots, he shifted twice. After that, he rushed to put on his pants and check on everyone.

Deacon's feet stuck out from beneath the van where he'd crawled to hide. He bellowed when Montana grabbed his ankles and dragged him out. Then Montana spotted Lucian lying in the grass. There were cuts on his knuckles, and blood covered his mouth where he'd bitten someone in a fight for his life.

It was hard to believe the same man was sitting in front of him. Lucian's cheeks had color, and he didn't look like a crime scene photo.

"The thing is," Montana continued, "Lakota's your family, and I appreciate how that complicates matters. For personal reasons, maybe you don't want him to know your business. I get it. He'll have questions. Lots of them. Especially about that haircut. But if we sit on this, there's always a chance Deacon might talk his way back in. And if you wait until then to tell your side, it'll look like you're just trying to keep him out. People might think you'd say anything to secure Lakota's place in the pack."

Lucian glared at him. "I've got better things to do than sabotage my family."

"If you keep this to yourself, it could hurt Lakota more than it does you." Montana gave him a minute to realize all the ramifications. "Who should tell him?"

"I'll do it."

"Can I trust you'll do it? If that asshole comes back and things come to a head, it'll look shitty that I didn't go to anyone."

Lucian's predatory gaze was unsettling. "My word is my bond."

That was all Montana needed to hear. He put on his hat and unzipped the tent. "You should get some sun instead of hiding out in here all day. I know you like to keep to yourself, but this is a pack you're trying to get into."

Lucian frowned as he picked up his bowl. "Thanks for the soup. And... everything."

Montana patted his leg. "Think nothing of it."

Once he was out of the tent, a cool breeze hit him. The weather had warmed up considerably. He wandered over to the well and drew water, his thoughts on Lucian's words: *and everything*.

Everything was what had happened after Deacon saw Lucian's body. "Let's get the hell out of here," he had said. "Help me load Virgil into the back in case he shifts."

When Deacon closed the tailgate, Montana confronted him about Lucian, who was still bleeding out in the grass. "We're not leaving him here to die."

Deacon had already shifted to heal and was putting on his clothes. "He's as good as dead anyhow. Let nature take its course. You and I both know we're better off without him. A Chitah doesn't belong in a pack."

"Don't leave me," Lucian rasped when he'd overheard their conversation. "Don't leave."

He had begged for his life. Maybe that was one reason Lucian seemed ashamed this morning, but there was no shame in wanting to live. Chitahs could usually recover from wounds like those, but it wasn't always certain.

Montana recalled how Deacon had put his arm around him, acting as if they were old pals. "No one has to know. If you do this for me and we get in, *you'll* be my right-hand man."

Montana had shoved Deacon away. "Help me get him in the truck."

That confrontation was the reason Deacon had left. He was afraid Montana would tell the truth about how he wanted to abandon the Chitah, who happened to be the beta's uncle, and how he'd tried to bribe Montana.

They'd exchanged curses and threats, all because Lucian wasn't a Shifter. What really happened back in Dallas between those two? Why was Deacon so dead set on keeping him and Robyn out of the pack? Just because they weren't Shifters? Sure, packs were traditionally made up of the same animal. Sometimes, they included other Shifter types. But there were always exceptions, and everyone knew it. Occasionally, pack members mated outside their Breed. Some Packmasters were more tolerant of it, whereas others weren't.

Maybe it was as simple as Lucian having walked into camp that night. Deacon hadn't planned on his showing up. And he certainly wasn't prepared to find out that the Chitah was related to the second-in-command. Suddenly his lofty goal of winning Tak's favor as beta was in jeopardy.

Montana sipped his water and glanced at the house, his thoughts coming to a full stop.

Robyn was climbing a ladder to carry something up to Krys. When she raised her arm, her short blouse rose. He remembered how soft that skin around her middle was.

He thought about her taste.

Montana swallowed a gulp of water before taking off his hat and pouring the rest on his head.

He couldn't imagine her with long hair. He loved the choppy style because it was short enough to grip when he was kissing her.

Damn, those legs.

She had on her brown lace-up boots, shorts, and that blue jean baseball hat he loved on her. *Does she like baseball?* Suddenly, he had so many unanswered questions.

When Robyn's foot touched the grass, she turned around and tripped over Catcher.

Montana chuckled. Even flailing in the air, she was the most endearing woman. When she sat up, Catcher licked her face. Robyn didn't look mad. She seemed to understand how mischievous wolves could be when they were in a playful mood. After a quick bark, her watchdog grabbed the rope on a flatbed wagon and hauled it toward the side of the yard, ready to get to work.

Montana thought about those tense moments last night at the fire. What if Robyn had chosen to leave? His chest tightened at the idea of it. He remembered the uncertain look in her eyes as to whether Tak wanted her gone. He also remembered the sheer determination to choose her own destiny and not succumb to the whims of a madman.

And if she had left, then what? Follow her? She would have filed a restraining order. If Montana lacked one skill, it was reading a woman's mind. He had better odds of learning braille with his toes.

He straightened up when Robyn waved at him. "You want some water?" he yelled.

She showed him the bottle of water in her right hand.

Smooth. Real smooth.

He wanted to shove his head into an oven and turn the gas on. No, that wouldn't be quick enough.

Robyn smiled and strutted off, leaving him to watch her tight ass in her jean shorts.

Her sweet taste. Her silky skin. Her delicious scent.

When his cock stirred inside his tight jeans, he splashed more cold water on his face. One thing was for certain—he had more incentive to stay than ever before.

CHAPTER 22

One month later.

I STEPPED OVER MERCY, WHO WAS sprawled out on the living room floor. "Where's Joy?"

"I have no idea," she said. "I feel like a deflated balloon."

"We worked our asses off today. Everyone's going for a swim."

"I may need someone to haul me down there in the wheelbarrow."

Smiling at her humor, I headed down a hall that cut to the back of the house. The staircase was located on the left wall, just before the kitchen. On the wall opposite the stairs was a large closet for coats, shoes, and whatever else.

We had accomplished so much in the past month. After completing the roof, we installed windows and finished the exterior walls. Tak brought in a professional electrician before we completed the interior. The guy was a Mage but friendly, and his team worked fast to wire the house and check the existing power lines. I'd never done that type of work before, so it was a learning experience. Then I helped lay down wood flooring and quickly got the hang of it.

Bear wanted to install the orange-gold Spanish tile in the kitchen himself, since that would be his domain. The spacious kitchen was in the back-left corner of the home. It had counters on both sides and an island in the middle. He also planned on adding wood beams across the ceiling. The windows on the south wall brightened it up—a perfect place to grow herbs. Even though there was a double built-in oven and an extra-large range, Tak came from a different world where men didn't trust electricity. On the far-right wall by the entryway, opposite the windows, he built a large fireplace for cooking.

Everything was finally coming together.

Aside from the Packmaster's private quarters, there were three bedrooms on the main floor. All were accessed by the back hall that ran from the kitchen all the way to Tak's private quarters. The first bedroom was the room to the right of the kitchen. Bear claimed it since he'd taken on the role as pack chef.

Walking from the kitchen toward Tak's room was a door to a massive storage room on the right and the back door on the left. Outside, an oversized deck was flanked by both bedrooms. Opposite the back door was a small bathroom. After that, a cozy sitting area in a recessed part of the wall offered access to the library. Tak's bedroom was on the far left, but around the corner was a bathroom and two more bedrooms. All of them were located on the left wall since the right one was where the library ended. Whoever chose those rooms would have complete privacy.

Twelve quaint bedrooms and two baths were located upstairs. Most people only used their bedroom for sleep or sex, and only a bed was needed for either of those activities. The rooms were still large enough to add more beds, should a couple have children. From what I understood, if there were enough rooms in a house, sometimes the kids all shared one.

When standing in the front doorway of the house, the grand living room was to the left. A massive stone fireplace against the far wall was the showpiece, and there was tons of space for multiple couches, chairs, and whatever else they decided on. The first piece of furniture that found its way into the house was a hot-pink couch. Melody wasn't sure where she wanted it yet, and Tak didn't seem thrilled with the idea. He said it clashed with his very existence.

To the right of the front door, a wall with a tall arched entryway connected to the activity room. That wasn't the official name for it, but the plan was to decorate it with games, billiard tables, and whatever else the pack requested. All the rooms were massive—like something out of a movie. On the other side of the activity room were two tall wooden doors that easily slid open, revealing the library.

Oh man. The library.

It jutted out from the front of the house, and instead of regular windows on the front wall, Archer and Krys installed floor-to-ceiling bookshelves. There were two rectangular windows near the ceiling and a ladder that slid along the wall. They did the same on the wall opposite the entrance, creating massive shelves that begged to be filled with tales of adventure, romance, and mystery. There was plenty of space for educational books as well, and it could one day serve as a classroom for the pack children. Each shelf had small built-in lights in the front that cast a dim glow on the spines, which would allow people to see them at night. They could be turned on or off. On the wall to the left of the sliding doors was an archway that opened to the back hall by Tak's room.

My imagination ran wild as I thought about rainy evenings spent curled up in a chair, a Tiffany lamp switched on, and a book in my hand.

But there was no sense in getting excited. Tak hadn't chosen anyone new since the night Deacon left.

At the top of the stairs, the hall ran from left to right. The window on the left overlooked the backyard. Going right led to a center hall that cut through the house. No one had a bedroom door off that center hall, since it was busy with foot traffic. Instead, there were two halls on the right and three on the left. Both bathrooms were located in one of the left halls. Each had double sinks, oversized closets, plenty of cabinets, walk-in showers, and one had a large garden tub with a view of the backyard.

At the end of the center hall was a large walk-in closet where all the linens, extra pillows, and blankets would go. Tak also designed a storage room off the first left hall that could easily be converted to a bedroom, but he insisted storage was vital in a pack.

The paint fumes hadn't quite aired out yet. Not every bedroom had windows, so we had to use box fans in the center rooms to draw out the chemical smell.

I'd asked Tak what would happen if he outgrew the house. He laughed and waved his hand at the property, which spanned over a thousand acres. Not all of his people lived in one house. His tribe had not only added on to their existing house over the years, but they'd also formed subpacks under his father's leadership. That way, alphas didn't have to leave the tribe. In any case, a growing pack was a nonissue.

The more I fell in love with the place, the more I wanted to impress Tak. I just didn't know how.

"Picking out your room?" Virgil asked with a suspicious gaze. He rested his arm against the wall, revealing sweat stains on his grey shirt from digging up flat stones and hauling them around in a wheelbarrow. "This one's mine."

I took off my hat and wiped my brow. "They're all the same."

"Or *are* they? Some measure a few inches bigger."

"A few inches don't matter."

He waggled his eyebrows. "That's not what I've heard."

"You have to get chosen first."

He pushed away from the wall and strode past me. "If you don't call your room now, you'll get stuck next to the bathroom." He pinched his nose.

An object clanged against the floor in a room around the corner.

"Joy?" I called out.

We strode toward the bathroom and overheard her talking in a flustered tone.

Virgil and I pressed our ears to the door, curious about who was in there.

"The ballcock isn't rising. I'm so sick of this thing!" she exclaimed.

Virgil pivoted until his back was against the wall. "If I had a nickel for every time I've heard that, I'd have zero cents."

Joy swung the door open and jumped back a step. "Gracious! You two scared me half to death."

Peering inside the room at Salem, Virgil asked, "Christening the house, are we?"

From the other side of the long sink, Salem jiggled the toilet handle. "Do you know anything about commodes?"

Virgil spun on his heel. "That's my cue to leave. I've got work to do. Have fun with that!" he said while rounding the corner.

"I thought this was supposed to work out of the box," Joy whined.

I walked in and peeked into the tank. "It looks like the chain twisted, so that flap thingy isn't closing. There's not enough water in the tank."

"Huh." Salem studied a sheet of paper. "I can't say I've ever had to fool with a toilet."

While leaving the room, I said, "We're heading down to the swimming hole. Wanna come?"

Joy touched her pretty blond hair, which had a few flecks of paint in it. "That sounds wonderful. I've been sweating like a pig. I can't wait until Tak gets the air-conditioning units installed."

"Me too," I replied. "Opening the windows doesn't help up here. At least it's April, right? Anyhow, they're talking about going out tonight to celebrate finishing the barn, so everyone wants to wash up. Do you think they'll let us take showers in here once the bathrooms are done?" I peered behind her. "This one has the showerhead installed."

She touched my shoulder while circling around me. "I'd give

anything for a warm bath with bubbles. Especially with rose-scented bath oils." Joy flicked the light switch off and on. "At least we have power. I'll be down at the water shortly, but I need to finish one more thing."

Since most of us were still sleeping outside, I had a feeling Tak wouldn't open up the showers to everyone. Packmates would likely get that luxury but not the rest of us. We still had to pay our dues.

I headed down the central hall toward the stairs on the opposite end of the large house. *Mansion* was probably a better word for it, but nothing about it was pretentious. When I reached the first floor, I glanced to my right and didn't see Mercy on the living-room floor where I'd left her. They must have already gone to the water, so I headed toward the kitchen entryway and took a right down the back hall. Once outside, I stuffed soap, shampoo, clean clothes, and a towel into a bag.

"Wait up!" I shouted at Mercy, Archer, and Krys. Public bathing wasn't something I'd ever practiced before, and I sure wasn't about to get naked. But they weren't total strangers anymore. We'd spent a month laboring and breaking bread together.

"I sure hope Bear doesn't pitch a fit about our bathing," Mercy said. "I saw him go down earlier with all the steel pots to give them a good cleaning."

Archer swiped a bluebonnet from the field. "We'll just shove him in."

"I don't think you're supposed to pick those," I said. "Isn't that the state flower?"

"It's private property, cutie-pie. Besides, do you really think they jail people for flower picking?" He tucked the flower behind my ear.

"I don't know," Mercy said. "Humans are strange. I once saw a man smoking a cigar while pumping gas."

As Krys stripped off his shirt, he added, "I once saw a Vampire with gold fangs. He had it sealed on some special way, and they wouldn't retract."

They all tried to one-up one another on the way to the stream. I'd spent most of my time around Shifters and humans, so it was fun listening to their stories about different Breeds.

We'd forged a path around the back end of a large hill to access the stream. Wildflowers were in bloom, scattering yellow and red patterns across the meadows and up the hills. They grew between rocks and danced in the breeze like colorful puppets swaying to their favorite song. White clouds looked like stretched cotton balls drifting lazily across the Texas sky.

The babbling water grew louder as we crested a small hill. We had a favorite swimming hole where massive flat rocks provided a spot for sunning and jumping in. The water was deep and wide, but it became shallower downstream. It wasn't as large or murky as rivers I'd seen, nor was it as small as a creek. The water had a bluish tint in this spot, polished rocks lining the entire bed. Because of that, when our feet touched the bottom, it didn't churn up a bunch of muck that clouded the water.

Tak stood up in the water near the bank and flipped back his wet hair. He widened his arms. "This is the life!"

Melody hollered and leaped from a rock. She tucked in her arms and legs and splashed down right next to him.

Hope wasn't there for swimming. With her hair in a messy bun and green pants hitched up to her knees, she waded in the shallow end. After reaching into the water, she stood upright and examined something.

"Find anything good?" I asked.

She held up a pretty white stone. "I don't want to remove what's here for decoration. It would spoil the natural look. I'm only curious what type of rocks we have on the property." She tossed the stone back into the river. "But it would be nice to find a special memento—something we can treasure."

"You aren't bathing?" I asked.

"I'll be testing out the new shower when we get back."

Farther upstream, Bear continued scrubbing his pots.

"I don't think I've ever seen him without a long-sleeved shirt on," I commented.

"Me neither. But then, I hardly notice with my mate walking around like Tarzan." Hope straightened after pulling another stone from the water. "Where's Catcher?"

"He saw us leaving, so he's guarding the house."

She flashed a smile. "He's a good wolf."

"He sure is."

I waded over to join Mercy and Archer on the largest rock, which stretched halfway across the water. Montana and Lucian were swimming on the right side, deep in conversation. The only ones missing were Salem, Joy, and Virgil. I set down my bag.

It grieved me to think some of us might not make the cut.

Archer took off his shirt and dropped it at his feet. He had grown less shy about his amputation the more he got to know and trust us. I gathered he wasn't that way with strangers or in public, but ours was a safe environment. He backed up, then did a handstand before flipping backward into the water.

"Show-off," Mercy muttered. "Why do men always have to make a spectacle of themselves?" She kept her pink T-shirt on over a pair of stretchy bicycle shorts. After plugging her nose, Mercy stepped off the rock and into the water.

Mercy never stripped down when there were men around. Since she didn't have any problem when it was just the girls, I guessed she might have been insecure about her body. I didn't see anything wrong with her petite size, but maybe it had to do with her small chest or narrow hips. Most Shifter men focused on a woman's hips and ass. For obvious reasons, Shifters couldn't get implants, so it wasn't uncommon for people to have insecurities about things they couldn't enhance or fix. Mercy was a pretty girl with a sparkling personality. Except for the smattering of tiny freckles on her nose, she had flawless skin. She could make a person choke on their laugh, and she got along with everyone. Her radiant smile lit up a room.

As far as I was concerned, she didn't need to cover up a damn thing.

I took off my tank top and adjusted my red bikini. When my fingers touched the zipper on my shorts, I zeroed in on Montana, who was watching me over Lucian's shoulder. He splashed water on his face and ran his hands through his hair, which made his biceps bulge.

God, I love that sexy model pose. Does he know how it drives me wild? Probably not.

Ever since our night of passion, we hadn't gone down that road again. Neither of us wanted to jeopardize our chances of getting into the pack.

Well, that was my reason. I wasn't sure of his.

The awkwardness between us had faded quickly and bloomed into a close friendship. He asked me things about myself—my favorite movies, what my parents were like, my favorite memories while in Dax's home. Even though Dax was a maniacal lunatic, most of his pack were decent people. I'd spent too long there not to have good memories to share.

I'd found out Montana was in his seventies. When he was a boy, he had a pet frog named Jeopardy. Shifters frowned on pets, but he said no one really cared about enforcing those rules on kids. We spent a few evenings together, watching the sunset in quiet awe, Catcher at my side. We talked about places we wanted to visit and wondered what life would be like in another thousand years. Being around Montana was so easy that I didn't always need to fill the silence with conversation.

My shorts dropped to my ankles, and I kicked them aside. After toeing off my blue sneakers, I sat on the rock and let my toes touch the cool water.

Montana waded over to me, the water forming a bowed ripple behind him. When he reached my feet, he tickled them.

I laughed and jerked them up. "Stop that. You're worse than a big brother who loves torturing his sister."

His smile dimmed, and I quickly realized what I'd said.

"I'm sorry. I didn't mean it like that."

He splashed me with water, breaking the tension immediately. "How's painting coming along?"

I showed him the teal paint stains on my shin. "The bathroom's done."

When he touched my leg and wiped at the paint, a shiver ran down my spine. His touch was intimately familiar, and even after a month, I still got butterflies whenever his skin grazed mine.

Lucian pulled himself onto the rock and sat next to me. Like Mercy, he also wore a T-shirt for swimming. As I stared at his stern profile, I could hardly remember the lustrous black hair he'd once had. Nothing but a shadow of stubble remained.

"You need a hat, or that cue ball's gonna burn," Montana quipped. "You're too pale—like a man who just got out of prison."

"I don't spend much time outdoors." Lucian draped Archer's T-shirt over his head. "Better?"

A bee hovered briefly in front of my face before I waved it off. "I've barely seen you in days."

Montana treaded water. "I saw him scaling a tree like a monkey this morning."

After a deep sigh, Lucian leaned back on his hands. "I finished setting up surveillance cameras. It took a long-ass time because I wanted them spaced out all around the property. I can't put them everywhere, but I picked the points someone would most likely enter or cross through. It's important to keep them hidden."

"I guess running around naked is out of the question," I said.

Montana squeezed my pinky toe. "I wouldn't go that far."

As he wrung out the end of his wet shirt, Lucian continued, "They're set up mainly on trails and walkable passes. There's some in front, but they're hidden. Tak said he'll show all his packmates their locations. I also put an alarm on the gate so that he won't get any more surprise visitors."

We had installed a large swing gate at the end of the drive. Not only that, but Tak had hired someone to pave the entire driveway—all the way to the dirt road. Melody was more excited than anyone and broke out a red kick scooter, which made Lakota shake his head. She said she missed riding around the city on it, especially because it was good exercise. Then Lakota suggested anytime she wanted to burn calories, they could go to the bedroom.

"What happens when the alarm goes off?" I asked.

Lucian adjusted the shirt on his head. "It alerts everyone inside the house."

"Like a doorbell."

"Right. Whoever's monitoring surveillance cameras can see who it is. For privacy reasons, I can't install them along the access road. Other packs in the area use it. But I—or whoever works security—will see everything on a monitor. As soon as the gate is triggered, a visual pops up on the screen."

"I'm sure it'll be you working security," Montana assured him.

"That remains to be seen." Lucian stood and dropped the shirt before heading over to talk to Lakota.

Montana pulled himself up next to me, his body glistening.

Stop looking at his body. And quit thinking about words like glistening and sensual.

While wiping the water from his chest, he squinted at the group swimming in front of us. "Are you still worried about Dax?"

I swirled my feet around in the water. "Not as much."

"You heard what Lakota said weeks ago. Dax went home. A guy like him wouldn't want to leave his people alone for too long. They might get ideas. Or his wives might run off."

"They should."

Dax was a busy man and had a million things to do. Most people in his pack liked the security he offered them. After Dax had shot Virgil and Lucian, Lakota searched but found no trace of him in the area. Just to make sure, Lakota called one of his connections to discreetly search for Dax's whereabouts. Dax must have driven straight home after that day, because he was back at work.

Lakota had taken his truck in for repairs. It took a few days for it to sink in. We were all rattled, but in time, Dax was finally becoming a distant memory. I could put all that behind me and focus on the future.

"What kind of car did you drive before you came here?" I asked.

Montana played with the drawstring on his dark swim trunks. "A silver Nissan Altima."

I snorted. "I pictured you as a guy with a badass muscle car. Fat wheels, a loud engine, a cool pair of sunglasses."

He tipped his head and grinned. "Do I look like a bad boy?"

"Maybe."

"When you work undercover, you need an unassuming car. Something that blends in. Nothing flashy, nothing loud, nothing bright. It's easier to tail people if your car looks like all the others."

"Was your work dangerous?"

Melody screamed when Lakota splashed her, and Montana gave her a cursory glance. "Sometimes."

"Do you think you'll do that same work here? If you get in with the pack, I mean."

"It was good money, but I'm not sure how much work there is in Storybook."

"Austin's not that far. You can visit me there when I get kicked out." I jumped into the cold water and stayed submerged.

When I heard a loud splash, I opened my eyes. Montana's face looked different underwater. We stared at each other in a cradle of silence. Sunlight trickled down as if casting a net, and we were caught in it.

As Montana drew closer, he looked through my soul, skimming his hands down my sides. When he curved his arm around me and held me close, we sank to the bottom. Small bubbles escaped his nostrils.

With everyone only feet away, we basked in complete privacy. I glanced up to the left and saw legs kicking, but visibility wasn't so great at that distance.

Montana turned my chin until I faced him, and I did something I'd wanted to do for the longest time—wrap my arms around him. We embraced, and in that instant, I knew without a doubt that the feelings between us hadn't diminished.

I drifted back and held his shoulders, my toes lifting away from the rocky bottom.

This time, he leaned in. Instead of kissing me, he rubbed noses with me and smiled. I was everything in his arms. And in his eyes, I glimpsed my future.

Our future.

He swam backward and away.

With my lungs tightening, I went up for air. When I breached the surface, no one was paying attention. Those few seconds that had transpired between us changed everything. I no longer wanted to put what was between us in the past. I wanted the secret to surface—seen by all.

Just not now.

I treaded toward shore until my feet touched the rocky bottom. The only people not in the water were Lucian, Bear, and Hope, who were each doing their own thing.

This is life. This feels like home.

I slicked back my wet hair, which touched my shoulders. My long hair had once been part of my identity. Perhaps at some point in life, we all depart from our original self to become someone else. My transition just happened later.

"Look what I found!" Hope exclaimed, holding her arm high.

Everyone drew closer, and she met Tak halfway.

"Look." She handed him an object. "It's an arrowhead."

Tak held the shiny black stone in his hand, then kissed it. "That's good luck."

A twig snapped, and I glanced over my shoulder.

Virgil stumbled toward us and stripped off his clothes. His eyes were bloodshot, and his entire demeanor seemed off. He was panting, his cheeks flushed, as if he'd run the entire way.

I took a step toward him. "What happened to you?"

The smell hit me like a sledgehammer. I scrambled out of the water and onto the rock.

He toed off one of his shoes and kicked it twenty feet toward Bear. Two seconds later, Bear started cursing.

"I crawled into my tent to get my soap," he began. "All I wanted was soap! He sprayed me." Virgil waded into the water like a sinner about to get baptized. "I tripped and fell, and he kept spraying me."

Melody gagged and paddled ashore. "Skunk!"

Virgil floated on his back. "I feel so *defiled*."

In a mad rush, everyone scrambled out of the water like in a scene from *Jaws*.

"Why don't you float downstream before you defile the rest of us?" Archer complained.

Holding his shirt against his nose to block the noxious stench, Tak used a stick to pick up Virgil's clothes. "Bear, I need your bag."

After they stuffed Virgil's clothes into a bag and sealed it, everyone collected their clothes and dressed.

"Do you know why a skunk was in your tent?" Tak finished tying his shoes. "Because you keep food in there. Tonight, I want every wolf to mark the area around the house. Predator piss is the best deterrent." He wiped his nose. "Clean your plates. If you're throwing away food, that means you're taking more than you need. And don't store food in your tent. Bear provides enough—especially for those who can't hunt."

Sometimes the wolves hunted at night, and because of that, they were less hungry in the morning. But we still gathered at mealtime, regardless of who ate.

"We're here!" Joy announced as she walked up. "What's that smell?" She pinched her nose and stopped at the tree line.

Tak walked toward her, holding his hand out. "If you want to bathe, go upstream. Way upstream."

"Like a mile upstream," Archer added. "Someone's not sleeping in the backyard for the next two weeks."

Joy furrowed her brow. "Who?"

I joined her. "Virgil got sprayed."

Melody slicked back her wet hair, the turquoise color shining in the sun. "Someone's gonna have to tear down his tent and throw everything away. And I mean *everything*."

Montana's hands shot up. "Don't look at me. I'm not going near it."

Virgil cried out before rolling himself underwater. When he stood again, the water came up to his navel, and Archer tossed him a bar of soap.

"Rub that all over you until there's no more left," Archer instructed him. "That's the heavy-duty stuff."

Fortunately for Virgil, it was laundry day. Most of his clothes were inside the house. We still enjoyed hanging them out on the line, but no one wanted to handwash everything. Ever since they'd installed the washer, we'd been using that instead.

"Someone call a Relic!" Virgil whined. "It's a medical *emergency*."

"Quit your caterwauling and scrub-a-dub-dub." Mercy snatched her shoes off a rock. "I sure ain't riding with you tonight."

Lucian walked past us to the trail. "This is *bad* luck."

CHAPTER 23

Just before sunset, we piled into the trucks and headed out to eat. About fifteen minutes later, we reached a private road. It didn't have a street sign, but Hope referred to it as Juniper Road. Lakota jumped out and opened the swing gate. When I noticed a No Trespassing sign with a paw print, I knew we weren't going to a human restaurant. Truthfully, Breed bars made me uneasy. They always sensed I didn't belong. Besides that, I was only comfortable around Shifters. Theirs were the only places we frequented back home.

Shortly after we passed a place called the Rabbit Lounge, we pulled into a paved parking lot on the left. The building was nestled in a shady area with large trees lit with tiny lights. I didn't see the restaurant name on the building, only a colorful neon sign of a dragonfly.

"What's this place called?" I asked from the back seat of Tak's truck. Melody sat behind the driver's seat with Mercy in the middle.

Hope twisted around. "Dragonfly Bar & Grill. We call it Dragonfly's."

"A friend owns it," Melody added. She leaned around Mercy to face me. "He used to work for my pack and seemed content for a while, but I think he wanted to get out of the city. He's a Vampire."

"A *Vampire*?" Mercy exclaimed.

Melody sat back. "He's not so bad once you get to know him."

Tak finally found a parking spot when someone pulled out. "I've never trusted Vampires. I wouldn't bring us here tonight if I didn't respect him. When he heard about land going up for sale, he contacted Melody since he knew we were looking. He's the reason we're here."

"He also protected my family during a pack war years ago," Melody added. "If you're with us, he'll treat you like family. Who's hungry? Because I could eat a horse."

Hope snorted. "Don't say that around Kevin."

Melody shuddered before opening her door.

"Who's Kevin?" I asked.

As Hope unbuckled her seat belt, she replied, "Kevin's a local horse Shifter who does odd jobs. Sometimes you'll see him trotting around."

We assembled in the parking lot, and as we headed toward the wooden building, a car sped past us from the back, where I guessed they had additional parking.

"Why would he build a bar close to another in the middle of nowhere?" I asked.

Melody strutted beside me in her black-and-purple patchwork jeans. "They're not exactly competing for the same customers. The Rabbit Lounge is more like a saloon. It's a totally different vibe. If you ever go there, you'll see what I'm talking about."

"It's also better to group your businesses together and help one another." Hope tugged Melody's hair. "My sister taught me that."

Confused, I tilted my head at her. "I didn't realize you were sisters."

When Hope smiled, love filled her eyes. "Melody is my spirit sister. We grew up together. We made dreams together."

Melody turned around and walked backward. "We got in trouble together too. Like that time we snuck away to meet these boys at a—"

Hope hushed her and flicked her eyes to Tak, who was striding ahead of us.

Melody fell back a step and flanked me. "We were seventeen, long before she met the hunk of her dreams. Anyhow, we never made it to the lake. Hope's horse got lost, and we wound up on the highway. A state trooper pulled us over. True story."

"Neither of you had a car?"

Melody laughed hard. "My pack let me drive around the property, but they didn't trust me on the open road after I crashed my uncle's bike into a tree. Not my fault. The tree got in the way," she said before skipping ahead of us.

"She speeds," Hope pointed out.

I wasn't sure why, but that didn't surprise me. Melody had boundless energy. I'd watched her flying down the driveway on that kick scooter as if she were racing the wind. She seemed fearless. This was the same woman who'd fired a bow at a man who threatened her Packmaster.

I loved that their pack had female warriors. Not only that, but they had jobs and ran their own companies too. I'd been living a sheltered life among Breed, brainwashed to believe that all packs were run like my former one. Now I finally understood why my mother wanted me to live with a pack. She knew how good they could be with the right leader.

I glanced at the outside of the building, thinking it didn't look that far off from being a saloon.

But I was wrong.

We walked in and faced a counter. When I saw a short menu on the overhead wall, I frowned at Hope.

She took my hand. "It's a cover. In case humans wander in or even law enforcement. You never know. People around here are... inquisitive. The customers in the upstairs restaurant get free meals as an incentive to fill the room."

A man behind the counter smiled at Tak, and they exchanged

friendly greetings. When he lifted part of the counter for us to walk through, each of us had our hand stamped. I didn't see a mark, though.

As we walked single file through the kitchen to a door, I watched the busy cooks and spotted a service elevator opening. When the worker unlocked the door, we descended a wide, lighted staircase. I gripped a handrail to look up at the black lights on the ceiling without tumbling down the stairs. It made some of our clothing and accessories glow.

The light also revealed a dragonfly stamped on my hand. A bouncer stood at the bottom, verifying our stamps before letting us through.

Most of us weren't dressed in fancy duds. Tak had on a sleeveless black shirt and cargo pants, which were a staple for him. He wore a chunky turquoise bracelet that I guessed Hope had made for him. But Lucian looked spiffy. I'd gotten so used to seeing the men shirtless or in sweaty tank tops that I'd forgotten how he'd worn dark dress shirts when we first met. Krys had broken out his leather pants but left his shirt at home. He wore a black blazer instead, which I presumed was his attempt at dressing up. His leather boots with silver chains, however, told a different story. At the end of his long necklace hung a pendant shaped like a shield. A wolf's head was engraved on the surface.

Because of the skunk incident cutting our bathing short, Tak had made an exception and allowed us to use the showers inside. I'd forgotten about the simple pleasures of hot water. Camping outside gave me a newfound appreciation for the little things.

Mercy adjusted her tight black skirt, then pointed at Joy's white blouse. "If they got more of these lights in there, you'll be easy to spot."

When Joy smiled, her teeth glowed like the Cheshire Cat.

Hope stayed by my side as we walked down a hallway toward a padded door. "Tak isn't fond of bars or clubs, but he loves the food."

"Virgil missed out," Archer said, his excitement thinly veiled.

Because of Virgil's skunk fiasco, we had to leave him home. Since

Tak didn't want to leave the house unguarded with only one wolf, it worked out for the best.

Montana snatched my gaze and held it while I walked through the doorway.

My jaw dropped at the scene before me. "This is unbelievable."

What I'd thought would be a cellar with a few tables turned out to be a fantasy brought to life.

Melody looked over her shoulder. "This is the gold room. It's the main restaurant."

Gold chandeliers and pendant lights hung from the ceiling and cast an enchanting golden glow that reflected off the wood flooring and crystal. The booths abutting the wall had private carriage-like structures built around each one. Pillars broke up the room while also stabilizing the ceiling. A central wall on the left created a division with window-like openings high enough that no one could look to the other side without standing. Glass candleholders flickered in each one.

When a server approached us and introduced herself, a blond man tapped her shoulder and motioned for her to leave.

He bowed. "It's always a pleasure to be graced by your visit."

Tak inclined his head. "I have friends tonight."

The man smiled. "So I see."

His hair was so pale that it looked unnatural, and his looks were otherworldly, as if he belonged in another era of men. But his inky-black eyes framed by dark eyebrows chilled my blood.

Montana rested his hand on the small of my back, putting me at ease.

"I'm Atticus Rain," he said, bowing his head to the group. "Call me Atticus. Welcome to my establishment. I hope the atmosphere is to your satisfaction, but if not, you'll discover there are more rooms to explore. Come right this way. I have just the table for you."

Atticus seated us at a wooden table that fit everyone. Since it was close to the wall, we didn't have people all around us. He pulled out

Joy's chair and seated her. Once we were all situated, he asked, "Does anyone have any special dietary requirements?"

No one spoke up.

"Splendid. Should anyone want a glass of milk or a fruit shake, we have options that aren't on the menu." A few people gave him bemused looks, at which Atticus clapped Tak on the shoulder. "I hear it's good for growing boys like you."

Tak rocked with laughter. "You're a good man."

When Atticus crooked his finger, a server whisked in with menus. "I'm not here all the time, but I always greet special guests when I know they're coming. Any time you want reservations, call me directly. I'll be sure we have your table ready, provided it's to your satisfaction." He winked at Melody. "Always a pleasure, young miss."

"Bye," she sang, waving while Atticus made a graceful exit.

Did Montana choose the seat next to me on purpose?

Our side faced the wall, which was decorated with artwork of dragonflies.

Lucian pulled out the chair on my left and sat. Meanwhile, I stared across the table at Mercy, who was rubbing her back against the chair like a dog with an itch.

"What's wrong?" I asked.

"Those skeeters were eating me alive after we went swimming. Right under my shirt!" She grimaced and reached over her shoulder. "Someone scratch my back before I die."

"Here." Archer put his hand behind her back.

She wiggled in her chair. "Don't be so gentle. Scratch me like a lottery ticket." Suddenly, her shoulders sagged, and she rested her arms on the table. "Do you think they have mosquito lotion on the menu?"

When I opened the menu, the prices flashed at me like warning lights. "I can't afford this," I whispered to Montana.

I'd spent the remaining amount of Dax's money on new clothes, including the flowy black dress with embroidered flowers I was wearing. It came from Moonglow—Melody and Hope's store—as did the sandals. And that had emptied my wallet.

Tak knocked on the table. "Dinner is on me. This is my appreciation for the hard work you've done. And today, we completed the barn."

Lakota patted Montana on the back while the rest of us clapped softly. Even though the barn had been Montana's project, I was proud to know they'd used my design. It felt incredible seeing something from my imagination brought to life.

Montana leaned in close and whispered, "I like that lipstick."

The servers whisked in and placed water in front of everyone before taking drink orders.

Once they left, Tak continued, "I have good news." He scooted back his chair. "Montana, rise up."

Montana's cheeks reddened when he got up and stood behind me.

I wondered if he regretted putting on his Montana T-shirt for the auspicious occasion.

Tak regarded him for a second. "You're a man who doesn't want to outshine others. I've watched how you keep the peace, encourage people, and give credit where it's due. It's time someone gives *you* credit. You accepted an ambitious task. Not only that, but you've also built a barn from the trees on our land. And in doing so, you created a solid business relationship with the sawyer who runs the sawmill. *And* you saved me money," he added while flashing a smile.

I twisted in my chair to look up at Montana. He held the same proud look as when they'd put the finishing touch on the barn. I scouted the room to see if customers were paying attention, but they weren't. It was our private moment.

Tak lifted his chin. "You bring stability to this pack. You're a man I can count on. Montana Vance, do you accept this invitation to join my pack? Will you follow my lead, protect your brothers and sisters, help the needy, and stay loyal to this house?"

Montana drew in a deep breath. I caught him biting his lip for a second before he answered, "I'd be honored as hell."

We erupted in cheers. Those who clapped loudly belonged to the pack. But envy and disappointment plagued the rest. We all wanted to join this house.

While Tak congratulated Montana privately, everyone else resumed studying their menu.

Mercy touched her turquoise earring. "I'm so glad I skipped dinner."

"We're *having* dinner," Archer said.

"No, this is supper. There's breakfast, dinner, and supper."

Archer looked at her sideways. "Dinner is called lunch, and supper is dinner."

She swung her gaze to Bear. "Settle this argument. Archer thinks that supper is dinner but everyone knows that lunch is dinner and dinner is supper."

Bear's sonorous laugh rocked his whole body and made me feel all warm and fuzzy. He couldn't have had a more fitting name for a big guy who was nothing but a teddy bear. "You can leave me out of it."

Archer lifted his menu and spoke as if to himself. "I guess someone doesn't need that itch scratched. I bet it's tickling back there. Itchy, itchy."

She wriggled in her chair. "One more time."

"That's a hard no for me."

Mercy slapped the table. "Fine. We're eating dinner. Now, scratch."

When she twisted away from him, he stroked one finger down her back. "And what's that meal we have in the middle of the day?"

She glared over her shoulder at him.

I couldn't help but laugh.

When Montana sat down, he lifted his menu.

"Congratulations," I said. "Looks like you finally get to sleep in the house."

His smile withered.

"A word of advice," I offered. "Pick your room as soon as possible, and move in. Virgil already pulled out the measuring tape and is marking his territory."

"We'll see," Montana replied.

"Tonight." Tak sipped his water. "Now that we've finished most of the interior, packmates can choose their rooms." He turned his attention to the group. "Everyone, order something special for our feast. The sky is the limit."

THREE HOURS LATER, we had eaten our fill. Steaks, ribs, loaded baked potatoes—you name it, we ate it. But the conversation kept us seated for much longer. Then came dessert. Not long after that, we split up to investigate the place.

Beyond the gold room was the red room and the green room. The red room had a gothic vibe with plush red furniture and intimate seating. Low lighting and dance music set the mood, and it seemed to attract a more amorous crowd. Since the bar was full, I kept walking.

Though I'd expected the green room to be a club, it could only be described as an enormous lounge and was tastefully decorated with green furniture. The dark walls were lit with gold sconces, and pendant lights hung from the ceiling. The curved bar on the wall by the entryway only had a few customers sitting in plush green seats, and they were more interested in idle chatter than getting drunk. Most people were scattered around the room in small pockets. Since Tak was a former alcoholic, I could see why he felt comfortable here. Dragonfly's wasn't a party atmosphere that centered on alcohol. Some were drinking, and others were having conversations on the luxurious furniture while smoking cigarettes or nibbling hors d'oeuvres. *Classy* was the word I would use to describe it.

All the rooms were separated by soundproof walls and possibly doors, because I couldn't hear the thumping beat from the red room at all. Jazz music kept the vibe casual. A subtle floral scent briefly caught my interest, and I couldn't discern whether it was perfume or a fragrant air freshener. Then I touched a gardenia on an accent table and realized it wasn't artificial.

After my third drink on Tak's tab, I found a cozy spot on a couch and curled up. I played a game with myself called Guess the Breed, in which I tried to figure out everyone's Breed based on their physical appearance and mannerisms. I didn't spot any Vampires. *How many live around here? Just the one?*

"Robyn!" Bear swaggered over and took a seat next to me. He grinned when I tried to focus on his face. "Someone's feeling mighty good," he remarked. "How much have you had to drink?"

"More than I usually do. It must have cost a fortune to build this place."

"I heard Atticus is loaded. Old money, probably. Can't say I know much about him, except he sure knows how to season his meat."

"The food was good but not as good as yours."

He looked down at his beer bottle. "You're just saying that cuz you're drunk."

"No, I'm saying it because you have a talent." I put my feet down and adjusted my dress, which came to my knees. "Why aren't you with the guys, picking up women?"

He stretched his arms over the back of the sofa. "They're lined up around Archer." Bear spoke with a slow Southern drawl that must have driven some women crazy.

"Really?"

"Seems he's a real ladies' man."

"Huh." I leaned closer to him. "I always thought Breed women were picky about that sort of thing. You know, with his missing arm and all."

"Mating? You bet. Between us, he'll probably never find a mate. It's a dangerous world out there. Women want protectors, and they see him as weak. His wolf is slow. The alpha might take that into account." Bear chewed on a toothpick while staring into the crowd. "But fooling around is a different ball game. And Archer's got game. What about you?"

I traced my finger around an embroidered flower on my dress. "Some guy was hitting on me for a while at the bar. See that man over there with the mustache? Him."

Bear craned his neck to look at the handsome man sitting at a table with a beautiful woman.

I cleared my throat. "He didn't ask my Breed, but I could tell he wasn't sure about me. I think he's a Mage and must have sensed I had weak energy. When I told him I was human, he got up from his seat and left without a word. Just walked right off like I didn't exist."

Bear tilted toward me. "Robyn, all that means is he wasn't the right one. When a good man sees a good woman, he never walks away."

"You're so lucky," I said as the room took a full tilt.

"Why's that?"

"Because you're pack. He'll never pick me. I don't know why he's kept me this long except maybe because I sketched a barn and a stable."

"You've done more than that. You've put in as much work as everyone else."

"*As much* isn't good enough." I glanced up at his bushy beard and eyes like dark chocolate. "I'm human."

"Listen, that man was born and raised in a tribe. He's only been around his own kind. Not just Shifters but Natives. And here he is, building a pack with people who aren't his tribe. He's making his own. Have faith in that. Don't you worry—the fates'll look after you."

"The fates," I mused.

What do the fates have up their sleeves with Catcher? Will he always remain that way? Is it too late to change back? Has his animal assumed control? He needed to let me go, and that would only happen once I found a home.

Mercy took quick steps toward us. Her legs and arms were brown from the sun. She tugged at her tight skirt, which had inched up. Silver eyeshadow made her grey eyes shimmer in the light, but something beneath her sparkling visage made me sit up.

"What's wrong?" I asked.

She sat on an ottoman in front of me. "I was having a perfectly decent conversation with a Mage in the red room when some little worm in a Panama hat grabbed my tush. And I don't mean he gave it a pinch. He got all up in there. I spun around and knocked his arm." Mercy shut her eyes and huffed.

"Are you okay?" I asked, horrified that someone had violated her that way.

"People have no business grabbing a person like that. And if *that* wasn't insulting enough, the man I was talking to laughed at my reaction."

"What did you do?"

She looked down at her hands. "I splashed his drink in the pervert's face and walked off. I should have slapped him, but I was mortified. All I could think about was getting as far away as possible so my wolf wouldn't jump out. Why is it so hard to find a gentleman?"

Bear put his hands in his lap and tucked his fingers into his palms. "We should leave soon. Why don't you two find Tak and see how much longer he wants to stay. We've had more than enough fun."

Mercy dug around in her purse. "Well, I'm not letting that pathetic worm ruin my night. I want to try that peach-flavored cocktail before we leave. Who knows when we'll get another night out? I'll meet y'all in the front in a few minutes."

When I stood, the room spun like a carousel. I grabbed Bear's shoulder before finding my balance.

"Do you need help?" he asked.

"I'm good." Embarrassed, I crossed the room in the straightest line I could walk. My head felt fuzzy from a few gin and tonics. Since I hadn't eaten a big meal, I had assumed it wouldn't hit me that hard.

When I entered the red room, the music pumped in a sexual rhythm. A young couple sitting in a curved booth sipped champagne, and two men were caressing the arms of a woman in a leather top. Her back was against a column, and she smiled at me when she caught me staring. A few people were dancing in an open area in the back.

Walking along the wall, I passed an opening on the right, and someone jerked me inside. The hall curved in a semicircle, the light barely reaching the dead end. When the shadowy figure pulled me closer, I recognized Montana and his sexy hat.

He walked me into a wall and claimed my mouth in a wet, hot kiss. Montana's hat fell off.

Our tongues moved in a sexual dance. The music vibrated against my back, and the deeper the kiss became, the more I ached to feel him inside me.

A strangled moan escaped my lips when he moved down to kiss my neck. I slipped my hands beneath his tight shirt, his feverish skin warming my fingertips.

"I get so fucking hard thinking about you," he said in my ear.

I released a shaky breath. "You think about me?"

He faced me, sliding his hands up my dress. "Every damn night."

Heat pulsed against my flesh when my body remembered his greedy kiss between my trembling thighs. Montana rubbed his hands up and down over my ass, his lips barely grazing mine.

"Do you touch yourself?" I glanced to the left when I heard chatter pick up.

He leaned close to my ear, his breath hot on my skin. "I can't. Too many people sleeping nearby."

I reached down and cupped his thick shaft. Montana pressed one arm against the wall and rested his head against it. I kept stroking him, knowing it wasn't enough—knowing he needed more.

"We can't do this." I licked his earlobe and nibbled on it. "You *know* why. But if we could, I'd want you to turn me around and pull down my panties."

He made a guttural sound, keeping his head next to mine.

A moan escaped me when he slipped his other hand down my

panties and squeezed my bare ass with insatiable lust. His fingers curved deep and grazed my slick opening.

Instead of stroking me, he left them there, and it drove me wild.

I moved my hand down and stroked his thigh up to his groin, teasing him and making him harder as I caressed him.

"I'm *so* wet. It would be so easy. So fast. So hot."

He growled in my ear, "I need to fuck you. My *wolf* needs me to fuck you."

I shuddered, ready to come at his command. All he had to do was slip his fingers inside me and say the word. All he had to do was spin me around and pull my panties to my knees.

The music kept thumping, and I wanted desperately to take it further.

To take it all the way.

A dark hunger gripped me. But I was a Potential, and this wasn't the place for an impulsive act.

I quit stroking him when I realized it would only make him miserable without the release he needed.

He kissed my shoulder tenderly, then my neck. When we fell into a deep kiss again, something changed. The desire was still there, but he wrapped me in a loving embrace.

I'd never felt so adored, so desired, so safe.

He curved one hand around my neck and the other around my back. When the kiss ended, he pulled me in close.

Overcome by a current of emotions, I nestled my face against his chest. In his arms was the only place I wanted to be, taking in his scent, feeling his heartbeat, remembering all the times he'd made me laugh and the friendship we'd built. Thinking about the possibility that I might not be chosen to live in the pack and how that would split us apart.

My stomach twisted into a knot, and I squeezed him tighter.

Montana leaned back and cupped my face. When the fire dimmed in his eyes, another look replaced it, one I couldn't describe. "We'll figure this out. I don't want you to get the wrong idea about what's going on between us."

"What's going on?"

He rubbed his nose against mine. "*This* is going on." He kissed one corner of my mouth, then the other. "Do you trust me?"

I wasn't certain where he was going with the conversation.

Montana tilted my chin up and looked into my eyes. Then he smiled. "Are you drunk?"

"Define drunk."

"That's what I thought. Maybe now isn't the time."

"Time for what?"

Wiping his thumb beneath my lower lip, he replied, "Never mind. Let's fix you up before everyone thinks you made out with someone."

I picked up my small purse, which had fallen on the floor. After handing him a tissue to wipe the lipstick off his mouth, I fixed my makeup using a lighted compact mirror. Ambient red light from the club peered in from around the corner, and I could see *exactly* why these little hideaways had been created.

"You go out first," he said. "I need a minute to, uh... cool off."

I stood on my tiptoes and stole a chaste kiss.

With one hand cradling the back of my head, Montana whispered in my ear, "You're my girl."

CHAPTER 24

IT TOOK A FEW MINUTES for Montana's erection to completely subside, but even when it did, he still ached for her. Earlier, when he'd spotted Robyn walking toward him from the green room, he ducked into a private hall meant for lovers. Montana wanted to make their relationship less ambiguous.

Now all he could think about was how he had told her he wanted to fuck her. He wondered what the hell she thought of him now. *Fuck* wasn't the right word either. What he'd meant to say was *claim*. Montana wanted to claim her with every fiber of his being, and that went beyond sex.

He wanted her as his mate, and his wolf knew it too.

The spirit animal that lived inside Shifters had no desire for humans. With life mates, wolves steered their human counterpart toward their intended. The human side might have doubts or plans, but the wolf ran on instinct. While Robyn could become a Shifter through sex, she was still human. *So why did my wolf wake up when we were in that hall? Why did he sing for her?* And it wasn't the first time that had happened. Only now, it was more intense.

After dinner, when the group had split up, several women had approached Montana. He tried to engage in flirtatious conversation but found himself disinterested and distracted. He couldn't get dinner out of his head. Sitting next to Robyn at the table had felt unexpectedly intimate. All he wanted to do was put his arm around her. And when she laughed or made a hilarious remark, he imagined clasping her hand and kissing it. Each time Montana stole a glance, he wanted to get lost in her emerald eyes. Even her intoxicating scent reeled him in. But they had an audience, so all those impulses had to be suppressed.

During their encounter in the private hall, he'd wanted to reveal his true intentions to pursue her. But she was tipsy, and it wasn't the right time.

Since he had a minute to think, he put on his hat and straightened his clothes. Tak had given him orders to let everyone know they were leaving, so he had a job to finish. When he entered the green room, he didn't see anyone from their group. While weaving through the red room, he spotted Bear pinning a man to a wall.

"Hey!" he yelled, waving his hand.

Bear slowly looked over his shoulder at him.

Uncertain whether he could hear from across the noisy room, Montana tapped his wrist where a watch would be and pointed toward the front. "Gotta go!"

Bear's victim squirmed like a fly caught in a spider's web. He couldn't escape, since his feet were dangling off the floor above a white Panama hat.

Montana headed toward the gold room, deciding not to involve himself in what was clearly a personal dispute.

Lucian approached from the right. "Is everyone coming? I'm ready. This is too much peopling for one day." He suddenly leaned in and took a deep breath.

Montana gave him a sharp look. "Keep your nostrils shut."

An elfin smile curved up his cheek. He tapped his finger against his jaw and said, "You have a little something right here."

Montana wiped his jaw.

Lucian's golden eyes glittered with interest, and though it wasn't clear how much he could tell by the scent, he obviously knew Montana had made out with someone.

"Bear's right behind me," Montana said. "Let's go."

They joined the group out front. Montana branched apart from Tak's group and followed Lakota to the black pickup. Joy sat in the front seat with him, while the other women rode with Tak.

Except for Lakota and Tak, most of them were pretty buzzed. Tak had one rule about going out: designated drivers weren't allowed to drink.

On the ride home, Montana took off his hat so that it wouldn't fly off in the back of the truck. Salem sat beside him. He was a reticent man when it came to small talk about personal things. Archer, on the other hand, gave a play-by-play of every woman he'd verbally seduced.

Archer was a cool cat, but he was a shit pool partner. They'd competed against Krys and Lakota for money. Despite having one arm, Archer convinced him he could play using his foot. Montana had no reason to doubt after seeing him work his ass off on Tak's house. Eventually, it came out that Archer and Krys used to hustle people, with Archer sitting against a wall, hiding his disability, while Krys picked out a couple of chumps. After winning, Krys would play against his partner, then split the money with Archer.

"I'm gonna buy my new lady friend a big, juicy steak," Archer said with a wry grin.

"That'll be the last dinner on me," Montana fired back.

Archer laughed. "Once is all I need, sucker."

"Is that Lucian?" He shielded his eyes from the headlights beaming from Tak's truck, which followed them.

Lucian was standing up in the back of the truck, banging on the roof and yelling something, but Montana couldn't make it out. Tak's truck quickly accelerated and shot by them.

Montana stood. "Something's up!"

Lakota's truck picked up speed, and after another minute, Montana smelled something, like chimney smoke in winter.

Then he saw it—a glow in the distance. All the blood drained from his head, and he pounded on the truck roof, shouting, "Go! Go! Go!"

Lucian must have smelled the smoke with his keen senses.

Montana held on while they hit bumps in the dirt road. His heart galloped like a team of horses, and he got a sinking feeling in the pit of his stomach.

The house.

When the truck took a hard left turn, they almost tumbled out. As soon as the dark house came into view, relief washed over him. But that feeling only lasted a few seconds before it dawned on him what else could be in flames.

A cacophony of shouts sounded from the back, and when the truck slowed, the men jumped out. His feet clashed against the pavement, and he ran so fast that he thought his heart would explode. As soon as he rounded the corner into the backyard, his heart splintered.

The barn he'd spent a month building was an inferno. From the top, a large vortex of fire circulated. Everyone was running back and forth from the well and pump, putting water in containers and splashing it onto the building.

"Where the hell is the hose connector?" Lakota shouted. "Find it now!"

Buckets of water couldn't save the barn.

Robyn's voice drew his attention to the path leading to the barn. She frantically called for her watchdog.

Montana jogged up to Virgil. "What happened?"

"I don't know. I've been at the river all night, trying to wash off this skunk. I came back once to get a lantern and more soap. That's where I've been." Sweat trickled down Virgil's beet-red face. "I swear I didn't do this. When it got cold, I headed back. That's when I smelled smoke." He slicked back his wet hair and gasped for air. "I ran as fast as I could."

"Did you see anyone?"

He shook his head.

"Where's Catcher?"

Virgil shook his head again. "I tried putting it out. The hose wouldn't reach."

When Montana turned back to the barn, terror crippled him.

Robyn opened the barn door and disappeared into the flames.

"CATCHER!" I shouted, panic flooding my veins like poison. When I heard a loud bark coming from inside the barn, I pulled the sliding door.

Acrid smoke billowed out. Covering my nose and mouth, I searched the fiery-hot building. The fire was concentrated in the loft on the far end, embers showering down like confetti.

My lungs rejected the filthy smoke, and my eyes burned.

"Catcher!" I called out. "Catcher!"

The heat was unbearable. He yelped from the storage room, and I flung open the door. The fire hadn't penetrated the walls, and it was easier to breathe in there. Catcher was lying in the center of the room, surrounded by spatters of blood on the polished floor.

"Get up!" When I put my hand on his side to shake him, he yelped in pain.

Since he was too heavy to carry, probably nearly two hundred pounds, I grabbed his hind legs and dragged him out. Heat scorched my skin, and the urge to flee consumed my thoughts.

Then part of the ceiling caved in, bringing fire with it.

"Robyn!" Montana yanked me away from Catcher and flung me toward the door. "Get out! I got him."

Blinded by smoke and flames, I ran out of the barn and fell to my knees. Someone helped me up and ushered me far enough away that I didn't feel the searing heat anymore.

Once I landed on the grass, I coughed, struggling to breathe.

"Get it all out," Mercy said, patting my back.

Despite the pain, I sat up and faced the burning structure. Lakota had connected the hose and was spraying the monstrous flames at the base. Others ran around to the back with buckets of water.

I spotted Salem kneeling over Catcher.

My heart stopped. "Montana?"

He staggered toward me and dropped to his knees. My god, he was burned badly. His clothes were on fire. "Are you okay?" he croaked.

I patted out the flames. "You need to shift!"

He morphed into his wolf and then back to human form. His skin was less raw, and he repeated the process six more times to fully heal. When he finished, he collapsed onto the grass.

I threw myself over his back, horrified and profoundly moved by what I'd just witnessed.

"Robyn, your hand," Mercy stressed.

When I sat back on my ankles, I stared down at Montana. "He almost died."

She gave me a knowing look. "He'll be fine. You need to go to your watchdog. If he doesn't shift, I don't know. Salem's looking at him. But your hand..."

I jumped to my feet and ran to Catcher. "What can I do?"

Salem sat back. "By the looks of the abrasions, someone assaulted him. No burns. Possibly smoke inhalation."

"I found him locked in the storage room."

Salem stroked his beard. "If we're lucky, he didn't breathe in too much smoke. We don't have oxygen tanks."

"Why not? We should have a full medical unit here!" With a trembling hand, I brushed my hair away from my face and gathered my thoughts. "Help me carry him inside, away from the smoke."

Salem looked over his shoulder. "Get a large piece of plywood. We'll put him on that."

I felt nauseated but pushed it down to search for plywood. When I found one, Mercy helped us transfer Catcher onto it.

"On the count of three," Salem instructed us. "One, two, three."

We lifted Catcher and carefully walked toward the house. The shouts grew distant as we moved farther away from the chaos. I was torn in so many directions. I needed to be with my watchdog, but Montana was all alone out there. The others also needed help extinguishing the fire.

Carefully, I walked up the steps onto the deck, the edge of the board digging into my palms. Someone had gone inside and left the door open, so we turned right and moved quickly down the hall toward the kitchen.

"On the counter," Salem said, directing us to the island.

We each blew out a breath when we set him down, and Mercy switched on the light.

"I'll get your bag." She disappeared out the doorway.

Stepping in front of Catcher, I looked closely at his face. His teeth and the fur around his mouth were stained with blood. The cuts on his snout and paws were nothing compared to the tear in his right ear. "What happened to you?" I whispered.

He whined again, keeping his eyes closed.

Mercy's shoes tramped against the floor when she flew into the house. "I got it! Anything else you need?"

Salem opened his bag and took out his stethoscope, and we waited silently for him to listen. "He needs oxygen."

"I'll be back in a jiff." Mercy took off down the hall.

Salem moved his stethoscope around. "He doesn't seem to have rapid breathing or any sign of pneumothorax, but it sounds like there's fluid in his lungs. Can you get him to shift?"

Crippled with fear, I stroked Catcher's face. "You need to shift. You hear me? Please, Catcher. I know you understand. You're hurt bad. *Please.*"

When he opened his eyes, he gave me a doleful look. His hazel irises were missing their usual sparkle.

"This wasn't a wolf fight—someone bludgeoned him." Salem set his stethoscope on the counter. "He could have multiple internal issues. I don't know how extensive the damage is without the right equipment. My advice is to get him to shift. That's the only guarantee he'll live."

Tears welled in my eyes. Never had I imagined that death would be the thing to separate us. Even though watchdogs fought to the death, I'd never found myself in mortal danger. It wasn't supposed to happen that way.

I kissed Catcher's nose. "Please don't die. Stay with me. I need you." I stroked his soft fur without applying any pressure that might hurt him. All those nights at the foot of my bed, all those afternoons when I'd taken him outside to play chase—in the span of thirteen years, Catcher had become my only real family.

I'd never seen him so vulnerable, and the thought of him being in pain wrecked me. "Tell me what to do," I said, fighting an onslaught of tears. "Give me an answer that won't destroy me. I can't do this, Catcher. I can't let you go. Not like this. Not on this table, in this kitchen. I should have been here. You were fighting for your life while I was having dinner. I'm so sorry. This isn't fair."

Salem pulled out a syringe.

Alarmed, I grabbed his wrist. "What's that?"

"It's to ease his pain. We don't euthanize wolves, if that's what you're thinking. But he shouldn't have to suffer. If we're lucky, the alpha can force him to shift." Salem gave me a sobering look. "If not, you should say goodbye now, while he's conscious."

I draped my arm over Catcher and pressed my face to his. Our eyes met, and I held his gaze. "Remember that time you followed me to school? A teacher grabbed my arm to haul me to the principal's office because of my short skirt. The next thing I knew, you were tearing off his pants. I yelled at you and called you a dumb dog. That's not what I think of you, Catcher. I was a teenager who had lost her parents and was scared of losing you. It wasn't my finest hour, but that was the first time I knew I loved you. When I realized how quickly you could be taken away from me."

Catcher groaned, and his tail flapped once.

"I love you. I never told you that before because I feared loving anyone. You weren't meant to stay with me forever, so I didn't want to get too attached. But I love you, Catcher. You honored a dying woman's wish to protect her only child. Even if you did it for money, you stayed." Tears ran down my nose and spilled onto his face. "You'll never know how much your service and companionship meant to me. There's no better watchdog. I love you so much. You're my family."

Someone pulled me back while Salem injected him with pain medicine, and Catcher's eyes closed. To my relief, his chest continued to rise and fall, but he must have inhaled more smoke than I had.

I coughed several times until the urge subsided.

"He's a strong wolf," Montana said from behind me.

I wiped away my tears. "I know."

He captured my wrist. "Salem, her hand."

Salem rounded the island and looked at the burn on the back of my left hand. He then led me to the sink and turned on the water. "Hold it under running water for at least fifteen minutes. We've probably waited too long, but it'll clean the wound and slow down any further tissue damage."

"Is it bad?" Montana asked with concern.

"Pretty nasty second-degree burn. It'll probably scar, but she needs to keep it clean. Pat it dry, then I'll bandage her hand. You'll need to change the dressing once a day."

"And the pain?" Montana asked.

"I'm fine." I glanced over my shoulder at Catcher. "It's not that bad."

"I happen to know a burn hurts like hell," he bit out.

My face heated with embarrassment. "I'm so sorry."

"I didn't mean that, Robyn." He showed me the brand on his hand, and it seemed strange for a man who had run through fire to relate to my pain through an old scar.

"If anything changes with Catcher, come get me." Salem's voice grew louder but more distant as he walked down the back hall. "I need to make sure the others are all right. I'll send Tak in when he's available to see if he can get Catcher to shift."

My back ached from hunching over the sink, and my arms were trembling.

Montana set something down behind me. "Sit on this."

Between my legs sat a wooden stool. After helping me onto it, he reached around me to hold my arm up.

I leaned against him. "I thought you were dead."

Resting his chin on my shoulder, he said, "I didn't mean to scare you."

"You shouldn't have gone in." The horror of seeing him burned so badly was something I would never get over.

"Don't you know? I'd run through fire for you."

I closed my eyes. "Thank you."

"Think nothing of it."

We both turned to look when the back door slammed. Tak appeared in the kitchen while staring at a piece of paper in his hand.

Was it possible for Catcher to shift if he was still unconscious? "Salem said you could get him to shift."

He lowered his hand and walked toward us.

"What is that?" Montana asked.

Tak set the paper on the counter, and I read it.

Honeybunch,
Thought you could use a housewarming gift.

"It was taped to the door," Tak said. "This wasn't an accident. The fire was deliberately set."

Montana picked it up and looked at it. "Who's this from? It's not signed."

"It doesn't have to be," I replied. "It's from Dax."

CHAPTER 25

After Salem dressed my injured hand, we carried Catcher to a large storage room in the back hall. Tak thought a quiet room would be better in case Catcher woke up agitated and lashed out. I laid beside him and held his paw until I fell asleep.

At some point in the night, someone carried me outside. The hazy memory mingled with my dreams.

Birds chirping pulled me out of my slumber. The red fabric on my tent glowed from the morning sun. I flipped the blanket off. My dress still smelled like smoke, so I put on a pair of grey sweatpants and a navy-blue shirt. Outside, a handful were gathered at the firepit.

"Where's Salem?" I asked groggily, looking around at their weary faces.

Joy stretched as she stood. "They took Catcher."

I swallowed a lump in my throat. "Took him where?"

"There's a Relic in a nearby town. They have all the equipment Salem needs." She touched my shoulders. "Come sit down, honey. Eat something."

My eyes were swollen from all the crying I'd done. I winced when electrical shocks stabbed at my burned hand, the raw nerve endings mercilessly torturing me. "I can't eat."

Handing me a plate of bacon, Bear said, "You need food. If you keep this down, I'll make you something else."

Everyone stared glumly at the fire. Unable to look back at the barn, I chewed my food.

"I bet Montana sleeps for three days," Mercy said. "I once knew a guy who shifted twelve times and wound up sleeping for a week."

I glanced around the yard. Virgil wasn't in sight, but because of his new cologne, he was probably isolating himself. "Where's Lucian?"

Mercy curled up her legs in the Adirondack chair and looked at her pink nail polish. "He's still sleeping. He was up all night, reviewing footage. I guess you didn't see him in action. He was flashing back and forth with the water, and that helped get it under control."

Melody slurped on her coffee. "Hope and I have been through this before with our shop, and it taught us a valuable lesson."

"How to keep assholes off your property?" Archer muttered. His hair was usually styled nicely, but today it was a mess.

Melody set her empty cup on the grass. "That, too, but we should discuss how to prevent and put out fires. We don't have the luxury of the fire department out here, let alone fire hydrants. That's why they built the barn away from the house, so it's less likely to spread. We could install fire sprinklers in the house, even if it means tearing things up again. And fire extinguishers in all the rooms, including the barn. They might have giant-sized ones. We're just lucky Catcher fended them off."

I flicked my eyes up. "What do you mean?"

She tapped Lakota's arm. "You saw the video. Tell her."

A burst of wind rustled Lakota's long brown hair, and he threaded his fingers through it. "After the fire was out, Lucian looked at the footage. I knew he'd finished installing the cameras, but I didn't think he had them wired to anything, since we don't have computers. He has a laptop and phone, and somehow, it's connected. He doesn't have an alert set up yet, so that's why he didn't know what was going on when we were out last night." Lakota rubbed his face. The exhaustion reflected in his voice and the dark circles under his eyes.

I handed my plate to Bear, who was collecting empty dishes. "Thanks. I don't want anything else, though."

Lakota finished his coffee and let the empty mug dangle from his fingers. "The video shows Dax rolling up to the front gate and opening it. That's when it triggered the video, but Lucian set it to record five minutes before it was activated. Dax cut the lights on the vehicle, and a couple of his wolves ran out. He somehow knew we'd left. Cameras caught one wolf tangling with Catcher while the other shifted to human form and searched around the house. That one ran back to Dax and gave the green light."

I hugged my middle while the scene played out in my head.

Lakota set his empty mug on the grass. "There were four of them plus Dax. He held that paper in his hand while checking out the property. Catcher fought them all. Every last one. Only two of the men shifted. The others carried gasoline. At first, it looked like they wanted to burn the house, but his men couldn't get close enough. When they headed around to the back, Catcher chased them. One tripped, and Catcher tore into his arm. The guy didn't shift back."

I accepted the water Bear handed me. "If he had a job to do, Dax wouldn't have let him. He controls his pack. They're not allowed to heal without his consent."

Lakota shook his head. "That's fucked up. When they were out here, Dax pointed at Catcher, and Catcher bit his hand. There's no audio. Only Dax cupping his hand and shouting."

"Why didn't they shoot him?" That seemed out of character for Dax, who guarded his reputation. "They had all those guns before."

"Because they didn't want to wake anyone in the house," Lakota snapped. "I think they counted on someone being home. Catcher taunted them until they chased him into the barn. We don't have footage in there."

"He lured them," Melody pointed out. "In a confined space, he could have taken them down. Something must have happened."

The tools in the barn happened.

I shut my eyes, refusing to imagine what Catcher had gone through. *He could have fled. This isn't his pack. But he stayed and fought.*

"They lit up the barn with Catcher inside," Lakota went on. "Then they all looked toward the field. I think they heard Virgil. He must have yelled, thinking we were home. They took off after that. The alpha stuck the note on the front door, and they scurried off like a bunch of mice."

I chewed on my thumbnail. "If he didn't burn the house, he's not done. Not by a long shot."

A vehicle sounded from the front, and Lakota stood.

When I jerked forward, Mercy captured my wrist. "It's fine. Krys is out front. If it were anyone else but Tak, he would have shouted."

Catcher.

I flew out of my seat and jogged around the house. By the time I got there, they were unloading Catcher from the back of the truck on a makeshift stretcher. "Is he okay?"

No one answered, and I followed them into the house, where they set him down in the oversized storage room in the back. Someone had laid out a thick comforter for him and put a dim lantern in the corner.

"It's too hot in here," I argued. "He'll suffocate."

Tak put his hand on my back. "You needn't worry. They're coming out today to install the air-conditioning units. I called and moved our appointment up. Catcher must stay in a confined space. When a wolf is vulnerable, he'll fight to protect himself from perceived threats. I don't want anyone getting their fingers chewed off by accident," he quipped.

"Is he going to be okay?"

After Salem finished listening to his heart, we stepped out of the storage room and closed the door.

"He needs rest," Salem advised. "His broken ribs need to heal, so I don't want him getting excited and moving around. Tonight, he should be able to eat. If he accepts food, I want him on a high-protein diet. No snacks, no fillers."

Tak adjusted his braid. "I lined the floor with plastic, so he can piss in there if he likes."

"I'll clean it," I offered.

Tak patted Salem's shoulder. "When Doc here thinks he's stable enough, we'll put him in your tent. That way, he can do his business outside. There are too many steps on the porch for us to walk him in and out. A wolf belongs outside."

My shoulders sagged. "Thank you."

Pursing his lips, Tak glanced out the back door. "The little one rode on her scooter she calls Daisy. Men name their cars, so I can't judge. She came home with an oxygen tank strapped to her back. I don't know where she got it, and I don't care. That helped Catcher breathe easier, but I couldn't make him shift. Even when he was looking right at me. He's a stubborn wolf."

I rubbed my eyes and wondered if the nightmare would ever end.

Tak opened the door. "Come. Let's talk outside."

Once we returned to the firepit, Tak claimed his chair by the back steps.

Salem didn't look like he'd slept a wink all night. When he sat down, he slumped in his chair and yawned. His disheveled brown hair had come loose from the elastic band he usually kept it in. Bear offered him coffee, but he waved it away.

"Shifters heal faster," Salem assured me. "Even in animal form. We ran all the tests, and it looks like someone kicked him. There's a blow to his head, which likely split his ear. That's what knocked him out. If I had to guess, I'd say they used a gardening tool. From there, they beat him. There were signs of internal bleeding, but by the time we arrived at the clinic, it was under control. He needs lots of rest and pain medicine."

"No work today," Tak ordered us. "I want the house quiet so he can rest. Once Doc here says he's stable, we'll move him to a private tent."

Archer glanced over his shoulder. "Should we clear out the debris?"

I finally mustered enough courage to peer at the charred remains of what had once been a beautiful barn. Part of the front was still standing, much to my surprise. I wanted to burst into tears. *All that work Montana and Lakota put into it...*

Tak heaved a sigh. "We need to rent a flatbed trailer first. That comes later. The barn wasn't meant to be. It's not good to dwell on the past, unless there's something you can learn from it. We will build it again, only stronger."

"Melody suggested fire sprinklers," I said. "Can you also put those in the barn?"

He snapped his fingers at me. "Those are ideas I like to hear. The barn is a dangerous place because we store hay there."

"We need fire extinguishers too," Melody added while tying her blue hair up in a ponytail. "Lots of them. In every room and in every building we erect."

"Including the heat house." Hope cleared her throat deliberately.

A smile flickered across Tak's face. "That's one fire I don't want to extinguish."

"How is your hand this morning?" Salem asked me.

"It's fine."

It was far from fine, but I didn't want the attention, with everything going on.

"I'll change the dressing later and assess it myself," he said. "We need to keep it from becoming infected. I have more painkillers. You shouldn't have to endure pain. It causes the human body undue stress, which can affect your overall health."

"What do we do about Dax?" Lakota asked.

Tak turned his gaze to the barn. "Make a few calls and find out his location. Either he's nearby, or one of his men is watching us. The snake slithered away the first time because he wanted to strike and see if it would weaken us. He doesn't realize who I am and what my ancestors have fought." Tak rose to his feet. "We live in the country, and my pack is small. In his eyes, we're weak. The alpha underestimated us because he doesn't think we're a threat. He never imagined a country pack would have high-tech surveillance cameras." Tak squinted at the tents. "Lucian!" he roared.

A moment later, Lucian sleepily crawled out of his tent in a pair of black sweatpants and a tank top. When he joined the group, he remained standing.

Tak gave him a thorough appraisal. "I usually plan this, but nothing could have prepared me for last night. When Lakota mentioned a Chitah would be knocking at my door, I laughed. Why would a Chitah want to live with wolves? But I gave you the benefit of the doubt." He rounded the firepit and stood a few feet away from him. "When you mentioned putting cameras around my property, I laughed. Why would I need so many cameras on this beautiful land, except to record my handsome backside?"

Everyone chuckled.

Tak was momentarily distracted by a butterfly that flitted around me and landed on my bandage. "I grew up in a large community," he continued. "Our land was always secure. We had strength in numbers. So I took for granted how vulnerable a smaller pack is. There are also your laws to consider, which are all new to me. Because of your video, I can legally challenge that Packmaster." He erased the distance between them and put his hand on Lucian's shoulder. "Without your footage, I wouldn't have been able to prove it was Dax. He conceals himself from culpability. That's what snakes do. They hide in the grass."

"Do you need me to make a copy?" Lucian asked with a yawn.

Tak grinned. "Not now. You're ruining my important speech."

Lucian's golden eyes snapped awake.

After clearing his throat, Tak said, "You have proven your worth and earned a seat at my table. Lucian Cross, do you accept this invitation to join my pack? Will you follow my lead, protect your brothers and sisters, help the needy, and stay loyal to this house?"

Lucian inclined his head. "On my word as a Chitah, I will."

Since Catcher was sleeping, everyone clapped quietly.

After a quick hug, Tak swung his attention to the group. "I'm going to war. A Packmaster trespassed on my land, destroyed my property, and threatened the lives of my people. He intended to burn the house without knowing whether my packmates were asleep inside. Under the laws that govern non-Native land, that entitles me the right to challenge him in any way I see fit. The video will protect me. Since not everyone here is pack, I'm offering you a free pass to sit this out. It's dangerous, and I understand if you're not ready to offer your life for an alpha who hasn't claimed you as a packmate. Once Lakota confirms Dax is still in the area, we need to devise a way to lure him out of hiding."

"I know a way," I interrupted.

He stared down at me. "And what is that?"

"Use me as bait. I'm the reason he's here. Dax is used to getting his way, so he doesn't think you'll fight back. None of the packs back home ever did. All it took was one encounter with Dax, and they gave up. He could have burned down the house on his way out, but he wants us to be afraid of him taking it a step further. And he will."

Tak knelt before me and gripped my chair. "You're still human, and your watchdog is wounded. I can't promise to keep you safe from a pack of wolves."

I was so tired of Dax's games. It needed to end. "I'll do whatever it takes to bring that man down, even if it costs me my life. He'll follow me until I'm either dead or back in his house, and I can't live like that. He's hurt enough people. If I don't fight back, he'll hurt more."

"Then it's settled."

Up close, I could tell that Tak's tattoo was intricately designed across his face like artistic shadows. His angled eyebrows gave him a countenance that hovered between dangerous and playful. But when he smiled, his eyes weren't cold and empty like Dax's. They didn't make me recoil or tense with fear. Tak was the embodiment of a true Packmaster with honor and integrity.

Instead of looking at me with blame, his brown eyes showed me kindness, compassion, and respect.

"Just let me know what you need me to do," I said. "Can you excuse me? I want to check on Montana."

Tak rose up and swaggered toward a cooler. "Bear, you can move your food into the kitchen tonight. They're delivering the air conditioners and appliances today."

I distanced myself from the group and headed toward Montana's tent, then froze in my tracks when I saw Virgil sitting in the grass wearing nothing but a pair of Speedos.

He dunked his hand in a bucket and spread a pasty white substance all over his chest.

"What *is* that?" I asked, tickled by how he looked like a powdered donut.

"Baking soda, peroxide, soap, and Bear's peppermint extract. Don't tell him I swiped it."

I wrinkled my nose. "That makes it smell worse."

"Don't be a hater." He slathered it all around his neck. "At least I'm not the one with dead animals outside his tent."

I jerked my head back. "What are you talking about?"

Virgil bent over and dipped his hair into the bucket. When he flipped it back, water shot near me like a sprinkler, and I jumped out of the way. "The rabbit. Don't worry. I got rid of it. But what I wanna know is... who the hell hunted for you? It sure wasn't Catcher."

"Are you sure someone killed it?"

He scooped his hand in the bucket and slapped the thin paste onto his stomach. "Maybe it hopped over and took one whiff of your dirty laundry before it died of natural causes." He added more paste to his neck. "I hope it wasn't that maniac sneaking onto the land again. I saw him on the video. He creeps me out."

"Did you see anything last night?"

When Virgil finished covering his face, he looked like a mime. "They were leaving when I got here. I tried to find Catcher." He swirled his hand in the bucket. "I didn't think he was in the barn. The last thing I'd want is someone dying on the property, especially under my watch."

My attention wandered to Montana's tent. Memories of his burned body flooded my mind. How could I ever forget that image of him saving my best friend? That was the most selfless act I could imagine.

Virgil gave me a desperate look and held his hands together in a prayerlike gesture. "Can you do me the biggest favor in the world?"

"What's that?"

"Sneak into Archer's tent and bring me his coconut lotion."

The delivery people arrived that afternoon and installed the air-conditioning units, refrigerators, and a couple of deep freezers. Since they were a company of Vampires, lifting heavy appliances was right up their alley. Bear moved his cooking supplies inside, even though he still planned on using the firepit until Tak finished selecting his packmates. We left the barn alone, though a few of us walked around to check it out. While the inner room remained intact, heat and flames had scorched everything else. Archer and Krys walked through the mess and recovered all the equipment.

After folding up their tents, the packmates selected their rooms. Lakota and Melody chose first, since he was the beta. Instead of picking a room on the ground floor near Tak, they took one of the smaller ones upstairs with a view of the front yard, which faced east. Since it was a corner room, they also got a south-facing window. I thought that was considerate given how betas always received extra privileges within a pack.

Lucian discussed what he needed to monitor their security system. Though they could have created a surveillance room, Lucian didn't think it was necessary. He said he could hook everything up in his own bedroom, provided it was bigger than the ones upstairs. That put him on the first floor in the hall by Tak's room.

Salem and Joy wanted a room nearest the bathroom. I didn't think that would be an ideal location, but she said that would allow her to be the first one in there in the morning. Joy didn't wear much makeup or do her hair any special way. In fact, she didn't look much like a morning person at all, from what I'd seen.

That left Montana, who'd been asleep all day. Bear didn't even bother putting lunch or dinner in his tent. We just left him alone to rest.

Crawling into Catcher's tent, I asked, "How are you feeling?" We'd put him in there after the delivery people had arrived. Even though wolves couldn't smell Vampires, we still thought it was a good idea to get him out of the house, especially since they weren't exactly being quiet. "I brought you something. Bear made you a steak dinner. I cut it up, and it's rare, just the way you like it."

I set the tin bowl in front of him. Ambient light shone in from the house, and his eyes sparkled when he opened them.

Catcher stood and stretched his front legs before shaking his head, apparently forgetting about his stitched ear and broken ribs for a moment, and he whined. It felt so good to see him standing, and my heart warmed when he sniffed the bowl and tasted his food. The steak would give him strength.

"Bear put rice on the bottom," I said. "Tak didn't want you eating anything but protein, but I think Bear was afraid your stomach would shrink."

Most wolves hunted their meat, but Catcher had developed a taste for certain human foods, including cooked meat.

I checked his water bowl to make sure it didn't need a refill. "The pack moved into the house today, so it'll be quieter out here. I'm going to keep your tent open so that you can walk around and use the bathroom. Don't run off. You need to lie down, okay?" He knew the words *lie down* for sure.

While looking up at me, Catcher smacked his lips.

"We have cameras set up now, and the wolves are guarding the property. I promise you won't be left alone again. You just need to take it easy and heal up."

Suddenly, Catcher stepped over his bowl and rested his head on my shoulder. That was his way of hugging me. I curved my arm around his large neck and gently stroked his soft fur.

"You're the best watchdog a person could ever want. I'm going to make sure Dax never does this to anyone again."

Catcher grunted and stepped back. His pensive stare made me uneasy. Surely he didn't understand every word. Then I remembered he knew Dax's name.

Crickets trilled, and the house looked different with the lights on inside. It made us outsiders, but at least we weren't alone.

Archer squatted at the tent opening. "How's he doing?"

"Better."

"His eating is a good sign. We found the remainder of a hand in the ashes."

My eyes widened.

He chuckled. "Who knows what else we might find? He put up a hell of a fight."

It got really quiet except for the sound of Catcher gobbling down his food.

"It's a little weird with half the group inside now." Archer scratched his chin before looking over his shoulder at the house. "I don't know what else I gotta do to prove I deserve a spot. Maybe fight off a pack and lure them into a burning building." He pointed at Catcher. "If anyone deserves to be in that house, it's you. But I guess it doesn't work that way, since you guys come as a pair." He squeezed my shoulder. "Looks like it's all up to you, cutie-pie."

"I thought hard work and my sketches would be enough, but here we are."

Archer touched the thorny tattoo around his neck. "Tell you what. If it doesn't work out for either of us, why don't we group together and find another pack? Catcher's one hell of a wolf, and you're not so bad yourself," he said with a playful wink. "If one of us gets lucky, we can put in a good word for the other. I'm tired of drifting."

While Catcher finished his meal, I turned toward Archer and glanced at his empty sleeve. "Have you ever lived in a pack before?"

He nodded.

"Did they kick you out because of that?" I subtly jerked my chin at his arm.

"I don't really wanna talk about it."

"Can I ask you something unrelated?"

"It depends."

A smile touched my lips. "Why do immortal men dye their hair?"

Archer covered his face and laughed. "Girl..."

Since there wasn't a harsh line between colors, it wasn't a bleach job that had grown out. The lightened ends faded seamlessly into the brown roots.

"Well, obviously you're not a natural blond," I pointed out. "I know it seems like a dumb question, but my former packmates never dyed their hair. Humans do, but usually, it's just the kids. I didn't meet too many different Breeds where I come from. When we were at Dragonfly's, there were a lot of men with dyed hair and unusual styles. Don't women judge you on other qualities? Like your animal type or height or eye color? That's all women talked about in my old pack."

"Some of us are old," he explained. "After a while, you get bored staring at the same reflection. Same as you. I once tried long hair. It wasn't me." Archer gave me a patient smile. "Let me know if he needs anything."

I touched his left shoulder. "Thanks."

Giving my hand a sideways glance, he backed out of the tent.

While I was halfway curious about whether Archer was disguising himself, I really wanted to break the tension after my awkward question about his old pack. I couldn't invite myself into people's personal business—especially immortals. Their lives were far more complicated, and many had a dark past. Archer obviously wanted to join a pack, and it didn't make sense that he would have left one voluntarily, so they must have been bad or thrown him out.

Once Catcher was done with his food, he groaned and walked back to his blanket. After turning in circles and pawing at the fabric, he lay down.

I hovered over him and kissed his nose. "Sleep. Even if you hear the wolves howling." When I tickled underneath his front leg, he smiled at me the way wolves did. "Good night, big brother."

After leaving him alone, I carried his empty food bowl back to the kitchen. The evening was pleasant, and the fire had already burned out. I picked up a cup someone had left by a chair and set it on a wire shelf where Bear kept his dishes.

When a shadow approached from the side of the house, I jumped in surprise. Tak's ebony wolf approached me with a heavy-footed gait. He was bigger than all the wolves. Though his animal watched me, I had to remind myself that alphas were always awake in there.

Then I saw his smiling eyes. He nudged my arm and licked my hand.

"You scared me."

He bumped against me, pushing me away from the house.

"I was just putting up Catcher's bowl."

Hope walked out the back door. "Tak, I think we need a screen door. There's a fly in the house after someone left it open." She untied her blue robe. "Hi, Robyn. We're going for a run. Everyone, that is. Well, except for Lucian and Joy. Lucian's still recovering, and Joy went to bed early." She drew in a deep breath. "My gosh, it feels wonderful tonight."

"Is there anything you need me to do?" I asked, stumbling when Tak nudged me toward the tents.

She padded down the porch steps, the slit in her robe revealing her curvy thighs. "Keep an eye on Catcher, I suppose. Tak wants us to mark the territory and check every square inch."

I chuckled. "So that's why everyone was drinking so much at dinner. Is someone watching the road?"

She swept her long hair off her shoulders and gave me a reassuring look. "Krys. His wolf seems to find humans tasty, so good luck to anyone foolish enough to trespass. You have nothing to worry about. We'll be surrounding you from all directions." She flicked a glance down at the bowl in my hand. "I'm glad to see he's eating. You can leave that bowl out here for tomorrow morning since it's his. I'm sure he licked it clean."

Then Hope shrank as if the ground had swallowed her. She had such a beautiful wolf. Her silver coat looked like someone had sprinkled sugar on her head and shoulders. But her front paws were the sweetest, like little white ankle socks. After greeting me with a push of her nose, she frolicked with Tak. They circled each other with cheerful faces before racing into the night.

After setting Catcher's bowl down, I picked up her robe and draped it over a chair. It seemed quieter without the gathering that usually lingered into the late hours. Fewer tents, and the existing ones were spaced apart. Virgil had moved to the side yard, but once in a while, I heard him singing.

Concerned about Montana, I headed over to his tent. "Are you awake?" I asked quietly.

When he didn't answer, I unzipped the tent and peeked inside. Unable to see, I crawled in and patted around. When fur brushed against my palm, I sucked in a sharp breath.

"I'm sorry," I breathed.

His animal jumped to his feet, and I froze. Wolves could see better in the dark than humans. Since I was on all fours, I lowered my head submissively. Spooking a wolf in the middle of the night hadn't been my intention.

The only sound in the tent was his loud sniffing as he buried his nose in my hair. The wolf moved his attention to my armpit, and I tittered when his wet nose touched my belly where my shirt hung loose.

As soon as he went to investigate my rear end, I sat down. "No, sir. Not even my watchdog is allowed to sniff back there."

He licked my jaw and neck. It felt humbling to have a wild animal accept me, especially when I knew how unpredictable and dangerous they could be.

"I just wanted to check on you, but it looks like you're doing all right." I stroked his soft face. "Did you get locked in here? You can go. Door's open. All the wolves are out tonight."

On cue, two wolves howled in synchronicity.

Montana's wolf startled me with his loud, distinctive howl. It soothed my soul, and I lay down on the blanket, waiting for him to dart out to join the others.

"Thank God you're okay," I whispered.

One of his paws stepped on my leg as he moved around. Then he got really still while sniffing my bandage.

Instead of rushing outside, he stretched out beside me and groaned. I buried my face in his fur and realized that he was the first wolf besides Catcher I'd ever been close to—close enough to take in his personal scent. Wolves didn't stink. At least not with Shifters. They didn't smell like dogs, even when they got wet.

He was so trusting in the way he rolled over, allowing me to scratch his belly. I smiled, thinking Montana's wolf was so similar to him—brave, calm, caring, and affectionate.

When he twisted his head toward me, he licked my neck. They differed in one way: Montana's wolf was a silly creature, more so than his human counterpart. Catcher had his moments, too, but he didn't engage in belly rubbing. Nor did he snuggle with me for the hell of it.

I thought about my encounter with Montana in the red room. *What did he want to tell me?* Everything was so fuzzy after all those drinks I'd had.

Then the wolf sniffed the air as if he'd caught a scent.

I gasped when he flipped over and stood astride me. Afraid he might attack, I shielded my throat. But as soon as my hands went up, his full weight collapsed on my body.

I wheezed from the sudden weight. Montana had shifted to human form.

"What the—?" He flipped off of me faster than a fish jumping out of a fisherman's boat.

When he knocked his head against the lantern, I erupted with laughter.

"Robyn?"

A snort escaped, causing me to laugh even harder.

"What the hell were you and my wolf doing?"

I choked on my laugh at his outlandish remark.

The light switched on, revealing a confused man with the corner of the blanket covering his manhood. Montana gave me a bemused look.

Once I caught my breath, I released a few stray chuckles and explained, "I just came in here to see how you were feeling. Your wolf wanted a belly rub."

He arched an eyebrow. "Did he, now?"

"I thought he was about to maul me. Next thing I know—"

"He jumped on top of you and shifted?" Montana scratched his head. "That's not like him."

"*Sure,*" I said teasingly. "Is that how you seduce all your women?"

"I'm serious." He cocked his head at all the howling. "Who's out there?"

"Everyone except Catcher. Lucian and Joy are upstairs."

"And you're rolling around in my tent with my wolf." Montana sprawled out on his belly next to me and propped himself up on his elbows. He didn't seem shy at all about showing me his bare ass. "How's your hand?"

"I just took a pill, so it's helping. Whatever Salem has in his bag works better than the stuff in the store." I turned on my side and rested my head in my palm. "Can I ask you something?"

"Sure."

"What's your craving?"

He scratched under his chin. "None of your beeswax."

"Come on. Is it M&M's?" I reached above my head and shook his bag of candy. "Is that why you buy the *jumbo* bag?"

He snatched his candy and tossed them to the other side. "No."

"Then what? I promise I won't tell anyone."

He rubbed his eye as if embarrassed. "It's radishes."

I stirred with laughter. "Sorry. I didn't see that coming. It's always fun to learn what everyone craves. Why do you think Shifters have cravings when they go back to human form?"

"Beats me. Might be the last thing we ate in a past life."

"I doubt it. I knew a three-hundred-year-old Shifter, and I'm pretty sure they didn't have Fruit Loops in the Middle Ages."

He tenderly touched my face. "You're beautiful when you smile."

Shying away, I replied, "Don't say things like that."

"Why not?"

I gave a one-shoulder shrug. After the amusement tapered off, I broached a topic that risked his throwing me out of the tent. "Can I ask you something else?"

"Sure."

"What happened to your hand?"

CHAPTER 26

When I'd asked Montana about his hand, I fully expected him to shut me down and switch topics. Older Shifters in particular didn't open up about their past. But I wanted to know everything about him—I wanted him to have someone he could confide in.

"Help me bridge the gap," I said.

"What gap?"

"The one that exists between us because you've held back. I've told you everything about me. Well, maybe not everything, but you've heard all the meaningful parts. You're like a puzzle that's put together, but there's one piece missing—the most important piece of all." I stroked his shoulder with my fingertips. "I've called you Montana because it was your choice. You wanted to start over with a new name. But I want to know about James. Who was he? What did you mean before when you said I deserved a better man? What happened to your sister? Because when you talked about her, it was in the past tense. You said she disappeared?"

He ran his fingers over the brand, which looked like the letters *CH* linked together. "My job took me out of town. One day, I came back to visit Tammy. You remember I told you she was living with my old pack?"

"Yes."

Montana turned onto his back and used the corner of the blanket to cover his privates. "She talked about becoming independent for a while and working, so needless to say it shocked the hell out of me to learn she was living with a different pack. When my former Packmaster told me which one, I wanted to fucking strangle him."

Turning onto my back, I drew up my knees.

"He wouldn't give a reason," Montana continued, "so I asked around. Some of the packmates clammed up, but a good friend of mine said there were rumors the other Packmaster was threatening a hostile takeover. He thinks they traded Tammy to make sure that didn't happen. The thing is, you don't just walk up and knock on the door of the Bear Creek pack and ask if you can talk to your sister. They're more of a gang than a pack. They did a lot of shady stuff, usually drug deals and shit that didn't involve us."

"What did you do?"

He scraped his bottom lip with his teeth. "I did what I do best—infiltrated them. Pretended I wanted to join. I made pals with a few packmates at their bar, talked up some shit I'd done, and cast the line. It took three months, but eventually, one of them invited me on a drug run with him."

I furrowed my brow. "What kind of drugs?"

"They negotiated the purchase of drugs and had people sell them to humans."

"Like a cartel?"

Montana drew up one knee and put his arm over his forehead. The dim light painted soft shadows on the contours of his body like a work of art. "It turns out they bought cheap shit and had a team of Sensors spiking the drugs. Anyhow, after that run, he asked where I was staying. Said he'd put in a good word. The next thing I knew, I was talking to the Packmaster."

"Weren't you nervous?"

"My job is dealing with guys like him. I was only nervous about seeing Tammy and her blowing my cover. After an initiation, I was in." Montana raised his left arm and displayed the brand. "They brand you like cattle and seal it with liquid fire."

"What's it stand for?"

"It's the Packmaster's initials."

When he dropped his arm to his side, I held his hand.

"They kept me busy doing illegal stuff," he confessed. "When the Packmaster assembled everyone for introductions, I finally saw Tammy. She didn't look like herself." He withdrew his hand from mine.

"In what way?" I asked.

"She had a thousand-yard stare, and it fucking eats me alive. I expected relief, excitement, perhaps even fear. But not that. I had to play it cool and wait before we had a moment alone. She told me to leave and said her life was over—that she belonged to them now." Montana shot up to a sitting position. "I think he threatened her."

That sounded like Dax, only he was less direct.

I sat up and put my hand on his back. The right words had left me.

He stared at the lantern. "One night, I joined them on a job. Something felt off. We wound up behind an abandoned warehouse, and the Packmaster showed up in his car. He confronted me. Said he found out that Tammy and I were related. They beat me, shot me, and left me for dead."

So *that* was where he'd gotten the scar on his abdomen.

"Someone found me two days later."

"Why didn't you shift?"

"The bullet had lodged inside, so I couldn't. I spoke to the Council about Tammy, but they said if it was a fair trade, there was nothing they could do. If she thought it would save our old pack, that's something Tammy would have done." His top lip curled up. "I told them she was in fucking danger, so they joined me on a surprise visit. I think they were scared of him. The alpha didn't expect me to show up at his door, but he gave us the grand tour. Her room was empty. He told the Council she'd left on her own, but when we had a private moment..."

His breath hitched as he struggled to fight his emotions.

"You don't have to talk about it," I whispered.

Montana took a breath. "When she found out they shot me, she ran. His men caught up with her, and he dealt with it." Montana wiped his face. "I asked what he meant by that, but he refused to give me any details. Instead, he told me about a house he'd once wanted and how the alpha wouldn't sell. So he took it by force. Instead of keeping it, he burned it to the ground and made the alpha watch. He said his only regret was that I wasn't there to watch." Montana hung his head, his voice broken. "Tammy's gone, and I couldn't save her."

Unable to sit behind him any longer, I crawled around him and onto his lap. Then I held him while he broke down.

"You did everything you could." I stroked his back with one hand. "She knew that. Don't you see? You didn't fail her."

"Bullshit." He leaned back.

I put my hands on his shoulders. "Your sister wasn't waiting for you to save her. She was protecting you. If she had left before all that, her Packmaster would have found out who she cared about most. That's how men like him think. And that would have led them to you. So she stayed with him, and that was *her* choice."

"I should have killed the bastard."

"And what? Go to jail? Be executed by the higher authority? Do you think she could have lived with that guilt? Even if you had fled with her, he would have destroyed whatever life she created. Her only choice was to stay. When she thought you were gone, she had no reason to anymore."

Men weren't always allowed to be vulnerable, especially Shifters. They were expected to pack up those emotions like luggage and put them away.

If it hadn't been for Catcher all those years ago, I might have turned all that rage into something dark. Sometimes, we need to fall apart before we can be put back together.

"You shouldn't have to carry this pain alone." I lifted his chin. "You told me that you weren't the right man to turn me, but you are. Even though I had a watchdog, you've watched out for me since day one. After almost losing Catcher, I never want to leave anything unsaid. I never want to doubt my feelings. Or hide them." I searched his eyes for understanding—for acceptance. "It's been more than a month, and I've slowly been falling in love with you."

He shook his head.

"You're kind, you make me laugh, you work hard, you stick up for me. And you don't think my drawings are a waste of time." I stroked his handsome face. He had such a stern brow, and I hated to see the pain in his eyes. "I've never met anyone more tone deaf, but I still love hearing you sing to yourself when you're working. Accept my love."

He adamantly shook his head. "No. I can't."

"Why not?" I asked in frustration. "It's yours. Why won't you take it?"

"Because I don't deserve it!"

The air stilled. Even the wolves quelled their barking.

"The hell you don't." After forcing him onto his back, I sprawled across him. "I love you, whether you like it or not. I'm not asking you to reciprocate. It's not fair to make you say something you don't feel, but *I* feel it. That's all that matters. We have chemistry. You know it, and I know it." I gently rocked my hips, and his eyelids fluttered. "Years ago, I made a pledge that I'd only turn if I loved the man. That mattered to me. Now I realize why. I've been with human men, but becoming an immortal? That only happens once."

When I kissed him softly on the mouth, his lips were salty with tears.

"Be my one and only. Make me a wolf."

He tunneled his fingers into my hair and kissed me back—kissed me like I meant something more than sex.

I worked my mouth down his bristly jaw to his warm neck. Then I raked my teeth against his skin and sucked the flesh until he groaned.

His hands rested over my sweatpants, but he made no move to pull them off. Unlike our previous encounters, Montana relinquished all control. I slid down and drew his nipple into my mouth, teasing the small tip with my tongue.

Montana's scent drove me wild. I trailed my kisses down to his abdomen. While he didn't have a six-pack, he was everything I desired in a man.

All the while, he gently petted my hair.

"Robyn," he pleaded, bending his left knee.

Leisurely, I kissed my way to his hip, doing my best to avoid his lengthening appendage. He fisted the blanket beneath him. I licked his groin and moved lower to the soft patch of skin inside his thigh.

He panted, and every few kisses, his breath hitched. I stroked his other thigh, grazing his balls with my thumb.

It wasn't about me anymore. Montana had suffered after running through fire for my watchdog, and I wanted to give this courageous man the pleasure he rightfully deserved.

So I licked him and licked him again, in all those soft places until he spoke my name more urgently.

"*Robyn.*"

I stroked my palm up to his belly, still avoiding contact with the one part of him that needed my touch.

But I never stopped kissing, stroking, licking, or touching. I memorized his pleasure points. Whenever my tongue teased him in a new place, he tensed and groaned.

Sitting up, I stripped off my shirt. Montana gazed at me with heavy-lidded eyes while I took off my bra.

Rising onto my knees, I said, "Take off my pants."

He shot up on command and hooked his fingers around the waistband of my sweats, then he slid them down so slowly that I came undone. After they moved over the curve of my ass and rested in a bunch at my knees, he leaned back on his hands.

Montana looked at me differently from other men because there was a wolf in his eyes.

I stood up. "All the way off."

When Montana looked between my legs, he wetted his lips. Obeying my command, he tossed my sweats and panties aside.

"Lie back."

He complied. I didn't want this to be about me dominating him, but it was important that he knew the decision was mine. He would never have to wonder if he had pressured me into it.

I sat next to him. "Wolves like it from behind, don't they?"

"Yeah," he breathed.

I was wet and aching to feel him inside me. While stroking his stomach, I said, "I'm going to suck you, okay?"

His breathing was labored. Instead of answering, he watched, enraptured, as I moved my hand down to his erection.

From base to tip, I stroked it with my finger. "When you can't take it anymore—when you need to come—I want you to flip me over and take me from behind. Then I want you to come inside me."

I lay down on my side, putting my legs by his head. When I bent down and took him in my mouth, he made a guttural sound.

Twisting my wrist, I built up the momentum. I teased the head, taking him in shallow strokes until his hand cradled the back of my head. He gently grabbed my ass with the other hand.

Montana stroked my slick opening with one hand and fisted my hair with the other.

I went deeper, faster, until I was choking on him.

His body seemed to vibrate, and I was worried he might shift.

I pulled it all the way out. "*James,*" I whispered, uncertain what was happening.

He growled and turned me until I was flat on my stomach. When he pulled me to my knees, I braced myself.

Montana pushed the head in and kept it there.

I cried out, not bothering to silence myself. The howling outside grew louder as they drew nearer. I wanted him, and waiting was pure torture.

"Are you sure you want this?" he asked with a smoky voice, bracing my hips with his hands.

"*Yes,*" I whispered, staring at the blanket.

He pushed in another inch. "There's no going back." When he pulled away, I thought it was over. But then he teased me with shallow strokes. "I want to claim you," he said as if to himself.

I peered at him over my shoulder. "Make me a wolf."

Carnal fire burned in Montana's eyes. He anchored his hands against my hips and guided me, our skin slapping faster and faster as he climbed the edge.

The tent moved as wolves circled it. Their barking and howling intensified, as if coaxing out my wolf.

"Are you sure?" he asked more urgently.

"*Yes.* James, *please*. I want it. Hurry!"

He pounded harder until the friction hit me in all the right places.

My orgasm happened so fast that I shouted.

"*Fuck,*" he growled. His thrusting grew frantic until he fell across my back and roared with pleasure.

The wolves' cries became deep howls that overlapped one another.

I stayed still with him inside me. This was how it had to happen, and I didn't want to break the connection.

Montana nipped my shoulder with his teeth, then kissed it.

Panting like two marathon runners, we remained that way for another minute until our hearts slowed to an acceptable pace.

"Are you okay?" he asked.

"I think so."

He pulled me up and cradled me in his arms. "I usually last a *lot* longer," he said with a chuckle.

I was trembling, nervous about the unknown, uncertain what to expect.

A wolf brushed against the tent.

"Is that normal behavior?"

"No," he said, his voice a soft caress. "They know something's about to happen. Something magical."

And it was.

First, it ached like cramps. Then it felt as if someone had shoved a hot iron into my uterus. My body locked up, and I screamed.

Montana held me tight. "I got you."

Those three words anchored me. Had he panicked and raced out, I wasn't sure what I would have done.

Growling from the pain, I dug my nails into his chest. My legs curled inward, putting me in a fetal position. Nothing lessened the ache, but Montana's unwavering embrace gave me the strength to endure it.

"*God, it hurts,*" I whispered.

"You can do this. Just breathe. Like all those lessons you give everyone. Slow, steady breaths."

It felt like I was giving birth to my spirit wolf except in reverse. For a second, I thought I would die.

"Look at me," he commanded. "Robyn. Robyn! Look at me."

I turned my gaze up.

"You can do this." Montana tipped his chin, keeping his eyes on mine. "You're a fighter."

I nodded, my courage spiriting me away from the pain. Montana wasn't there to rescue me. He was guiding me every step of the way.

"This is the most beautiful moment of your life," he said with reverence.

Then came the tremors, like an earthquake within the layers of my skin. A hot flash hit me next.

"Just go with it," he said calmly. "Don't fight your wolf. She wants to come out. Let her take control."

Something pressed against my being with an urgency that was like nothing I'd ever known. My body folded within itself, which felt similar to sliding down a long tunnel. Montana's hands weren't around me anymore, and my feet felt different. I looked up at him, but it was like looking through a telescope.

He smiled at me. "Hey there, beautiful."

I snorted, then barked. Fur covered my body, and my paws were awkward and big. The world was noisier and filled with so many smells. I fanned my tail back and forth, and in that moment, I realized I wasn't alone in my head anymore.

What a strange feeling.

Not only was the wolf in control, but her familiar spirit circled mine as we became acquainted. It seemed as if we'd always known each other. While I couldn't hear her thoughts, I knew her intent, her emotions, her curiosity and boundless energy—her love for Montana as she licked his neck and jaw.

Then I felt her fear as she heard and smelled wolves circling the tent.

She growled low in her throat when a long-haired Native man peered inside.

"Knock, knock," Tak said in a friendly voice. "Maybe I should take over from here."

A minute later, I slipped into a peaceful sleep.

In the aftermath of passion, Montana was awestruck by Robyn's transformation. Skin like satin had changed to fur. Her beautiful heart-shaped face had transformed into a long snout with sharp teeth. Though her emerald eyes remained the same, they were like two luminous jewels glittering in the darkness.

She was midnight black from head to toe and average size with large ears. Though her bandage had fallen off, it was hard to know if she would heal from her first shift.

Many Shifters experienced their first change alone. They could feel it coming on like a fever and isolated themselves. So Montana had never witnessed a newborn wolf entering the world, especially not in that way, in his arms.

After Tak stepped away from the tent, Montana held her head in his hands.

"Trust me," he said, looking into her inquisitive eyes. "I won't let anyone hurt you."

If someone so much as growled in her direction, he would end them. The thought of that crazy-ass Krys meeting her put him on edge.

He lovingly stroked her ears, her face, and her neck, allowing her to take in the unfamiliar smells. Montana wanted her memories of him to be filled with love and safety. It was her first experience in the world—her first outing. She wasn't yet acquainted with the thrill of racing full speed across a meadow or the anticipation of hunting prey.

After putting on his pants, he gave her a pointed look. "Ready?"

When Montana stepped out of the tent, he saw that Tak had lit several lanterns. The porch lights on the deck were also on, even though the moon provided enough light. The pack stood nearest their alpha, and the rest of the wolves spread out.

Robyn's black wolf lingered by the tent opening, sniffing the air and drawing in their scents.

Catcher stood a few feet to the side and looked worse for wear. The other wolves danced around and yelped, but none made any moves toward her.

Finally, Robyn's wolf emerged from the tent.

Catcher approached her first, and his head lowered as he sniffed the air.

"Ease up," Tak warned Montana. "He's more likely to jump you than her."

When Robyn caught his scent, she whimpered. Her tail flapped uncontrollably as she curled her body and assailed him with wolf kisses.

Catcher raised his head to the sky and released a long and mournful howl. It tugged at Montana's heart. In that moment, Catcher must have realized Robyn didn't need him anymore. She had her own wolf to protect her now.

"Robyn," Tak called out, his voice firm but gentle. "Come."

Her wolf gave Catcher one last lick on the snout before obediently trotting over to the alpha. Cautiously, she watched the wolves when she passed by them. Wolves didn't usually attack females, but Montana followed her to be safe.

Tak bent over and smiled. "A newborn wolf on my land is a blessing. And a black one—that's a good omen." He stroked her head. "Pleasure to meet you." Then he spoke words in his Native tongue while touching her face. Montana wondered if he was blessing her.

When Tak straightened up, he supervised while the wolves introduced themselves. They jumped on one another, licked faces, wagged tails, rolled over, and even growled. It was all typical behavior—wolves getting overly excited and establishing their dominance. When one of them got out of line, Lakota's wolf straightened him out.

Tak joined Montana's side. "She's a pretty girl."

When the sound of footfalls reached him, Montana looked over his shoulder.

Lucian plodded down the steps. "Who's the black wolf?"

Tak glanced back at him. "That's Robyn."

After a blink, Lucian frowned. "How did that happen?"

Tak laughed and patted Montana's shoulder. "Ask Romeo here."

"You work faster than I gave you credit for." Lucian ran his hand over his bristly scalp after sitting on the step. "I figured it might take you until July before you got the balls to chase her."

"You knew?" Confused, Montana drew closer. "Because of our encounter at the bar?"

"Hit rewind," Lucian said. "I knew something was going on when I heard you two the night of the cold front."

Tak waggled his eyebrows at Montana. "Why do you think I put you in that tent together to keep warm? Sometimes, destiny needs a nudge."

Robyn rolled in the grass while the wolves circled. They had lost interest in the new wolf and were restless for a run. Krys had returned to his post.

Beneath the moonlight, she was pure magic. Robyn had chosen this world because of her love for him. She had relinquished the burdens of her human life and now walked among them as a proud Shifter. He had given her that gift, and it didn't fill him with fear or entitlement. All he could do was stand there and admire the grace in which she walked the earth. He knew now what his wolf must have always known—she was his life mate.

Tak put his arm around him. "Why don't you shift? I think your wolf would like to meet his intended."

CHAPTER 27

NOTHING COULD HAVE PREPARED ME for how restful I felt after my first change. My wolf stayed out the entire night and into the morning, and I only remembered a fraction of it before blacking out. She and I were still getting used to each other. Like discovering a bee in the car while driving down the freeway, part of you wants to scream. But the bee is just as scared as you, so the best move is to stay calm.

My hand got a bit better, but Salem said it was too late to completely heal and I would always carry the scar.

When Bear sounded the gong to announce lunch, I cringed at the thought of facing everyone. *Were any of them conscious inside their wolves when Montana and I were having sex? Do they remember my screams of passion?*

Tak sure did.

In fact, anyone in a ten-mile radius probably did.

I sat close to Tak while he finished eating a tortilla wrap.

After wiping his mouth, he stood. "Come walk with me." Tak set his plate down and then led me to the edge of the house. "I've seen the mark on Montana's hand. I don't know if he chose to brand himself or not, but now you carry the same pain."

"It's just a coincidence."

"Coincidence is when a nonbeliever witnesses magic."

I watched the group putting away their dishes. "I don't know what's going to happen between us, if anything. Those aren't the promises we made to each other. We haven't talked about it. I..."

He tapped my arm. "Speak the truth."

While cupping my arms, I stared at his turquoise bracelet. "I don't want you to think I'm pretending to like Montana just to get into the pack."

He tossed back his head and laughed. Then he leaned in and said quietly, "If that was pretend, you deserve an award. Let me allay your concerns about my thoughts on the matter. It's not my place to decide who people choose to love or lay with. When a packmate chooses an outsider, the alpha decides whether their union will create conflict or harmony in the house. My job is not an easy one and comes with the responsibility of always putting the pack first. Becoming a wolf didn't increase your odds of being chosen."

"I know."

Boy, did I know. It complicated matters far worse than I'd imagined. Everyone was probably gossiping about my motives. While last night hadn't been planned, I had no regrets.

Tak bent over and plucked a yellow dandelion. "I knew I wanted you in the pack after our conversation the night Deacon left."

I looked up in surprise.

"You put aside your desires for the sake of others. While you didn't want to leave, you were willing to if it meant keeping others safe. That's what a true wolf does." He turned the weed in his fingers. "But you were still a human. I also wanted to see how serious you were about Montana."

"Nothing was going on back then," I assured him.

He tucked the flower behind my ear. "That's what Lakota and

Melody once told me. You can pretend all you want not to like someone, but the eyes never lie. Your eyes were all over each other." Tak gave me a wolfish grin. "Did you know his wolf hunted for you? Wolves don't do that for just anyone. That's why I can't invite you into my pack if you deny him. There's too much history between you two for harmony to exist."

I watched Catcher poking his head out of the tent. "I don't know what Catcher wants. Now that I'm a wolf, I can tell he's different somehow."

"You don't need him anymore, and he knows it. Though you might love him, that doesn't require his services. Catcher proved himself a steadfast packmate by defending my home with his life. But I can't ask him to stay. He needs to know where you're going, and from there, he'll decide."

"What are your thoughts? About me, I mean."

He wiped the corners of his mouth and glanced off at the group. "Tell you what, Robyn Wolfe. Once you figure out your relationship with Montana, come see me. If you choose not to mate, you'll always have me as an ally. I can help you settle somewhere and perhaps find a job. But don't force a mating for a spot in my house, because in the end, you'll make each other miserable. You'll make *me* miserable." He lifted my chin with the crook of his finger. "Love takes courage. That also means loving yourself enough to know the right choice."

"Thank you."

He put his hand on my back and led me to the fire. "Your wolf is quite the entertainer."

"What's that supposed to mean?"

"After running through the ashen barn, she rolled around in the mud. We laughed for a solid ten minutes."

I jerked my head back. "Everyone saw?"

Grinning, he replied, "It happened at dawn. After we got dressed, you jumped all over our clean clothes."

I face-palmed. "So much for first impressions."

"Montana put you in the washtub and bathed you. Rubbed all that mud and ash out of your fur. Even cleaned between your toes. That's love. My mate won't even clean my toes."

"Thanks for giving me time. I won't tell anyone about your loose offer. I don't want them to think—"

"Who cares what they think?" He stopped short and faced me. "Don't take too much time. Indecision isn't making a choice. That's what we do when we're afraid. Give me your answer soon."

I sighed. "One crisis at a time. Right now, I want to focus on Dax."

"Do you have his number?"

"Memorized."

"Good. I want you to call him. Beg him to stop. He's used to beating down his enemies, so you need to look weak and afraid. That's what he's counting on. He's expecting your call. But be yourself. Say nothing out of character."

I noticed the lace on my boot was untied. "Yes, I can do that. What's the plan after?"

"If he wants you to leave with him, we'll set a trap and make sure he never leaves town."

"Then what?"

"We slay our dragons."

I sucked in a sharp breath. "But killing a Packmaster is illegal."

"An alpha can challenge him," Tak pointed out. "It's a graver offense if someone of lower rank kills an alpha, especially if they kill the man. I don't plan to fight as men. We needn't worry about these things. Dax violated the laws that govern him, and that means I can challenge him to the death."

After Tak assembled everyone by the porch steps, he addressed us. "As I mentioned last night, those of you not in the pack can sit this one out. I won't count it against you, since this is pack business. I don't require a reason. We're planning an attack. If you wish to stay behind, you can go inside now. Some work still needs to be done in the master bath. Aside from that, I would appreciate anyone who guards my home and watches over the wounded wolf."

Joy branched away from the group but nervously looked at Salem.

Hope hooked her arm around Joy's. "Come on. I'm sitting this one out too. You can help me work on the grout."

The rest of the group looked at one another. When I noticed Montana wedging himself between Archer and Lucian, I smiled.

He smiled back.

Then everyone else caught us and did the same.

Tak chuckled. "If we can get back to business. After Robyn contacts the alpha, I'll have the rest of our plan laid out. Wherever and however we ambush him, we won't rely solely on our wolves."

"What the hell do you mean by that?" Krys asked.

Montana joined Tak's side. "We don't know how many he has with him. We saw four on the camera. That might be it, but it might not. Lucian and I can tell you firsthand that Dax isn't a man who fights honorably. I've got a spare weapon. Who's a good shot?"

"I am!" Virgil called out from beside his tent, raising his hand.

"You're staying here," Tak ordered him. "You'll give up our location."

Virgil's expression soured, and he put his toothbrush back in his mouth.

Salem lowered his head. "I can shoot."

Someone in the medical field being skilled with a weapon seemed a contradiction, especially since Shifters didn't use weapons to go hunting.

Not for food, anyhow.

Melody sat on the porch steps and squinted in the sunlight. "I've got an extra bow if anyone knows how to use it."

Archer kicked the dirt. "I can use a machete."

"I can throw an axe," Lakota boasted. "No one can beat me at our games."

Tak canted his head. "If you start up with that nonsense, I'll give you a spoon to fight with. Everyone knows I'm the reigning champion."

"Any other weapons around here?" Montana asked. "It's too risky to buy or borrow without word getting around. Not everyone needs to be armed, but we should prepare for the unexpected."

"Is Dax still in town?" I asked.

Lakota nodded. "He's camping out in unclaimed territories. But he's moved locations twice."

Montana touched the brim of his hat. "I'll say it because no one else will. I don't like using Robyn as bait. Not if it puts her close to him."

I didn't like it either, but it had to be done. "If anything happens, I'll run. I'm not armed, so I won't have a choice."

"But what if you shift? It's too dangerous to put a new wolf in that position. She has no fighting experience. You have to teach a new wolf to fight through play and hunting."

"I have to do it. Even if I leave this pack to get away from him, he won't stop. Tak interfered. He'll take out his wrath on this pack just for the fun of it. Especially if he knows there's a video of him burning the barn."

Tak turned around and stared up at the house. Black beads hung from the leather band at the top of his braid. "Bear, I want you to stay here."

"I can fight," Bear insisted.

Tak faced the group with a growing look of concern. "That's why I want you here. Keep Virgil near the house. I won't leave my people vulnerable. Lucian, show Hope how to monitor your surveillance cameras. We can put Catcher in the cellar."

"Don't do that," I blurted out.

Tak gave me a pointed look. "He cannot fight."

"If Dax's men show up and burn down the house, he won't survive in the cellar. Besides, he can keep watch for intruders from the back. I'll tell him not to fight, but he's a wolf. He'd rather die fighting than suffocate in a dark room. Alone."

Tak nodded in acquiescence. "We must make the first move. Robyn, if you were going to beg him to stop, how would you do it under these circumstances? We have no landline, and you have no phone."

I gave it some thought. Clearly, Tak wanted every step of the process to be genuine so that Dax wouldn't grow suspicious. *How* would *I do it?* I tugged on my earlobe. "Well, Dax wouldn't want me calling on someone else's personal phone. It would put his number on their call log. I'd probably get a ride to a nearby bar or place of business and use their phone. So I'd have to hitch a ride with someone when they were leaving."

Lakota scratched his neck. "I need to rent the trailer again to haul off the debris. I could use a few extra hands to pick up supplies."

"Where's it located?" I asked.

He sat on the steps next to Melody. "Same road as Dragonfly's. There are a few Breed shops down there."

"Play it out," Tak said with a wave of his hand.

"Can I tag along?" I asked. "You can drop me off at the Rabbit Lounge while you do business. I really need a drink."

Lakota rested his arms over his knees. "I don't want you going alone with that crazy asshole out there."

"I'll go," Montana said without hesitation.

Tak studied him for a beat. "No. That wouldn't be wise. Too distracting. If she has to separate from you, then you'll get left behind."

Lucian raised his hand. "I never got to finish that beer."

"Shouldn't I have a car?" I asked. "If you want to lure him into a trap, it won't work if you're the one chasing him."

"Would you steal my truck? Is that in your character?" Tak paced. "We'll split up in separate vehicles. Only two main roads lead in and out of this territory."

"I have Daisy," Mercy piped up.

Tak met eyes with me. "If he comes for you at the bar, we'll have time to move in. If he sends someone to retrieve you, we'll follow. Dax won't leave this county. That much, I can promise. We'll shoot out his tires if he runs."

In a fluster, Montana took off his hat. "You want her to go to him? He could use her to hold us off."

Tak gave him a swift smile. "Robyn is one of us now. He doesn't know that. If she senses he wants to play that game, she can shift and run. He won't have too many of his men chase her if it means leaving him unguarded." Tak hiked up the steps. "Get ready. We leave in twenty minutes."

We piled into Lakota's truck—Lucian and me in the front, Melody and Krys in the back bed. It was so warm outside that I'd dressed in shorts and a tank top, but I immediately regretted my choice when the air-conditioning blasted me.

When I walked into the Rabbit Lounge, I chortled at the saddle barstools. It wasn't as Western-themed as the bar in Dallas, but it had its own unique charm, like the pair of pants hanging on a hook by the front door.

After ordering a bottle of beer, Lucian walked past the pool tables and took a seat in a booth. I stayed at the bar because I had work to do.

I signaled to the bartender. "Can I use your phone?"

The tough old biker-looking guy smirked at me. "What's wrong with *your* phone? Did it come unglued from your hand?"

"I lost it after a shift."

I'd never seen anyone with grey hair that long. He pulled a corded phone from the counter behind the bar and dragged it over. Then he slammed it in front of me.

"I never should have ripped out the pay phones." He stood there, not giving me an ounce of privacy.

Something about him didn't give me a wolf vibe. His aquiline nose made me think of a bird of some kind, but he didn't give off that vibe either. It felt strange that I could sense Shifters differently.

"Do you serve food?" I asked, trying to get rid of him.

"Nope."

Gin and tonic was my preferred drink, but I needed to keep the guy busy so that I could have privacy. "Could I get a margarita?"

"Fucking women and their margaritas," he grumbled before walking off.

And the worst bartender award goes to...

Before he fired up the blender, I dialed Dax's number.

"Who could this be?" Dax answered.

I swallowed hard. "It's Robyn."

"Well, hello, Robyn!" he said gleefully. "Are you calling me on a business phone? Because I sure don't recognize this name."

"You need to stop this. They have nothing to do with us."

"No, they most certainly do not."

I twisted my body away from the bar and lowered my voice. "What do you want?"

"You know what I want, honeybunch. I want my *wife* to come home."

Sickened by the sound of his voice, I continued the charade. "You can have any woman you want. You don't even love me."

He laughed haughtily. Then he started talking to one of his posse. "She wants love. Isn't that the sweetest damn thing you ever heard? Robyn, I crisscross my heart that if you come home, I'll give you *all* the love you need," he said suggestively.

My stomach turned.

"Humans are such timid creatures, but I don't think you realize what you're running from. I pamper my wives. That's something you won't get with any other pack. You've seen how far I'll go to protect what's mine. Think about it, Robyn. Cold feet, I can handle. But disloyalty? Well, that's something else *entirely*. Things might be happy-go-lucky with that Packmaster, but do you feel safe with him after what just happened? Now, let's stop this charade and go back home, where all your friends are waiting. You've got your own private room from the other wives. Did I tell you that? Oops. Forgot to mention it to the little lady," he said to his buddy again, his voice getting even more jovial at the thought of my crawling back to him. "I haven't done that for my other gals. You're special."

I put my head down and released a sigh. Dax was good at wearing people down.

"I promise if you come with me now, I'll leave your new friends alone. They can go back to tinkering on another rickety barn in the middle of godforsaken nowhere. All will be forgiven. It'll be like none of this ever happened. But if you take off and run, I will *hunt you down.*"

"But I don't love you. I can't do this."

He chuckled softly. "I don't care if you love me. But I'll still treat you better than anyone else. Luxury vacations, all the designer clothes you could dream of. Hell, I'll even build you a walk-in closet."

Something in his voice shifted, the sound of him getting irritated.

"You're legally bound to me," he pointed out. "And let's not forget that I've financially supported you since you were a kid. Do you think your odd jobs were enough? Hell no. Come back home with me. You can stay long enough to pay off all the debt you owe me. If you want to leave after that, you're free to go. Easy peasy, nice and easy. But you won't want to—not once you realize how good it feels to be a Packmaster's bitch. What do you say, Robyn? Do we have a deal?"

I silently wept while listening to him, not just for the destruction he'd unleashed, but also the fear he instilled. Tak was willing to fight for me. So was everyone else in our group. It dawned on me that I could save lives by just going home.

When the bartender switched on the blender, I sat up straight and sniffed.

"I'll make it real easy," he said in a honeyed tone. "Where are you?

We'll come get you. We can even stop off and get a tasty chicken salad with lots of red peppers. That's right. I *know* what my girl likes."

In order to make it sound like he was influencing me, I sighed and waited a few beats before answering. "Someone's with me. I don't want there to be a fight. You promised."

"That, I did."

"I also need to go back and get Catcher. Then I'll figure something out."

"He can't come," Dax said firmly.

"I can't just leave him!"

"You don't need a watchdog anymore, honeybunch. Once you're mated, they have to leave. You know it, and I know it. He's better off with this pack you hooked up with. Ever think of that? Maybe he's the one who belongs there, not you. He was willing to lay down his life for those people. Can you say the same?"

"You almost killed him!" I shrieked.

The blender suddenly cut off.

"Now, I had nothing to do with that," he said coolly. "My boys got out of hand. Speaking of hands, you didn't happen to find one around there, did you?" He chuckled again. "Don't you worry your pretty little head. I'll be sure everyone receives fair punishment. You have my word on that. Whoever you're with, you tell them you're out. You're done. I promise they won't bat an eyelash that you're leaving. In fact, I bet your alpha will be as happy as a clam. They don't want you, Robyn. Men like him don't want trouble. I just reminded him of that. Exposed his soft little underbelly. Did you know he killed a woman?"

Dax had done his homework.

"You don't want to mix yourself up with an alpha like that," he continued. "I bet that's why he got kicked off his reservation. Banished to live in the middle of nowhere with a bunch of misfits, including a Chitah." Dax scoffed. "You weren't born into our world, so I can't hold this against you. But now that you know what it's like to live in a weak pack, you'll appreciate what I have all the more. Was he making you sleep outside in one of those tents? Tsk." Dax heaved a sigh. "Catcher's better off with them than by himself. Forget your things. There's nothing at that house worth one iota of your time. I'll buy you new drawing pencils and paper and whatever your little ol' heart desires."

"One margarita," the bartender said gruffly after setting my glass down. "Can I have my phone back?" When he raked his fingers through the side of his hair, I noticed his left ear was missing.

"I have to go," I said to Dax. "What do you want me to do?"

"That's my girl. Where are you?"

Without knowing the name of the street, I fired off the location in relation to Tak's house.

"What a coincidence!" He emphasized the syllables as if he were teaching kindergarteners how to read. "One of my boys just happens to be on that very road. You go on and tell whoever you're with that you're done with that pack. Tell them you're leaving of your own free will. I don't need any Council coming after me for driving my wife home. Make it crystal clear. Then go outside, take a walk up the road toward the gate, and I'll have my boy pick you up."

"Okay," I whispered, staring at the bartender's hands reeling in the cord.

"Good girl. And Robyn?"

"Yes?"

"I've *missed* you."

I hung up the phone and shuddered.

"Hey, Calvin! Fix me up again," a woman called out to the bartender.

After leaving a few bills on the bar, I carried my liquid courage to Lucian's table and drank some of the icy beverage. Paranoia set in as I scanned the faces in the room, wondering if Dax's man was spying on me. Dax would want someone to stay by our house—in a place where a person could blend in. It made me uneasy to think how close his group was staying to the property—close enough to watch us going in and out.

I sat across from Lucian with my drink.

His golden eyes bored right through me, his nose twitching when he picked up my emotional scent.

"I'm leaving," I informed him. "This isn't the right pack for me. Especially after what happened with Catcher."

His dark eyebrows drew together.

"Don't have Lakota coming after me. I've hitchhiked before, so it's nothing new. I'd rather not deal with all the long goodbyes. It's better this way." When I slowly winked my left eye, which was shielded from the room, he played along. We carried out the conversation at a normal volume in case one of Dax's men was in the room.

"It's your call," he replied. Lucian scooted against the wall and twisted his body to see the room. While he nursed his imported beer, he scanned the pool players and people at nearby tables. "What about Catcher?"

"I think he already made his choice to stay. You can toss all my stuff. There's nothing worth keeping, and it's time for me to start over." I stood and touched the rim of my glass. "Tell Tak I'm sorry about the barn, but I appreciate the chance he gave me. He was never going to pick a human anyhow. Bye, Lucian."

He saluted me with two fingers.

I weaved around tables and noticed one guy in a white T-shirt staring hard at me from a nearby table. If Dax wanted someone to spy on me, he would pick a person I'd never met.

My wolf calmed me while I marched across the parking lot, as if she were telling me that nothing bad would happen with her around.

Since Lucian had a phone, he was in charge of keeping everyone in the loop. Tak had selected him to accompany me for good reason. If Dax sent one of his men to pick me up, Lucian could run at Chitah speed to either track me or catch up with Lakota.

While heading up the long road, I thought about my mom. *What would she think about my choices?* Though her friend had placed me with Dax, I'd chosen to stay all those years. She would never have wanted that life for me. I only stayed because I was young and didn't know any better.

A couple of cars drove by. When I was a short distance from the gate, the distinct rumbling of a motorcycle engine closed in from behind.

After it pulled up next to me, the rider lifted his face shield. He was the white-T-shirt guy from the bar.

"Get on," he said before rolling the throttle.

I swung my leg over the seat and held on. Instead of lifting the gate, he drove around it. Once he hit the main road, he took off like a streak of lightning.

How can they possibly keep up with us? Oh my God, I need to get off this thing.

My nerves were jangled. I might be going home with Dax for real if we lost Tak and his people. In our discussions, no one had anticipated a motorcycle. The wind plastered my hair back as we flew down the road.

After two quick turns, he slowed the bike and steered off the road. We bounced on the uneven trail, and my stomach dropped when I looked at the terrifying distraction of rolling hills and steep drop-offs on my left. The narrow path wasn't wide enough for a car and had so many sharp turns that I wanted to jump off.

"Slow down!" I yelled at him.

The hill on my right sculpted into a high cliff armored with tall rocks. When we neared the base of the cliff where Dax was standing, the motorcycle finally slowed. My Packmaster leaned against the front of the van, his arms crossed. Instead of the passenger van he normally drove, it was a large cargo van. Behind him, the path was wider and led to an opening that could have been a road. Judging by the makeshift parking spot and view, I guessed it must be a popular spot for teenagers to make out—or for people to commit murder.

He casually removed his plaid outer shirt and tossed it at his packmate. There were three of them. Four, including the biker. One had a bandage wrapped around the stump where his hand used to be. Dax dusted off his white undershirt as if he were straightening himself out to meet the queen.

As soon as the motorcycle came to a full stop, I stumbled off it. The adrenaline coursing through my veins had me winded and dizzy.

"*There* she is!" Dax greeted me with mirrored shades that concealed his true emotions. "I hope Chess here took it easy with you on that bumpy trail." He put his arm around Chess, the scrawny man with the goatee. "You didn't scare my bride, did you, Chess?"

"No, sir. Brought her here, just like you told me to."

Dax patted his cheek. "Good boy. I wouldn't want you to end up like poor old Richard. Remember him? He scared my first wife in that car of his. What kind of car was that?" Dax asked his men.

"A Corvette," one of them replied.

"*A Corvette!*" he parroted. "Now he's buried in that car." He shoved Chess aside and walked toward me. When he pushed his aviators to the top of his head, he gave me a sardonic smile. "Got something for me?"

Oh shit. What does he want?

Dax bent forward and tapped his cheek.

God no. Please, not that.

With his men watching and the uncertainty of whether the plan had backfired, I stalled. Then I decided to give it to him.

When Dax closed his eyes for his kiss, I sucker punched him. He held his jaw and belted out a laugh. Then his soulless eyes met mine. "I like 'em feisty!" he growled.

He struck my face with the back of his hand so fast that I didn't see it coming. I hit the dirt, a sharp pain radiating across my cheekbone. Staring at the ground, I swiped my fingers across my cheek to look for blood.

"Now that we've kissed and made up, *never* do that again."

I grabbed a handful of dirt and threw it into his eyes.

Dax bellowed like a grizzly bear. When I jumped to my feet, I had nowhere to go. His men were spread out, trapping me against the cliff wall.

"You wanna play with the wolf?" Anger and humiliation dripped from his tongue. "Let's play."

I laughed, unable to control myself.

Dax ran his fingers through his salt-and-pepper hair and knocked his sunglasses off. "You think this is funny? Do you have any idea what I'll do to you? Can you even conceive it in your tiny human brain?"

I laughed even harder. "You're too late."

Dax lunged and pinned me to the rock. He squeezed my throat so tight that I couldn't breathe.

Panic surged beneath my skin when my wolf made a desperate attempt to come out. I fought hard to keep her subdued, knowing that she was no match for a powerful alpha and four wolves. As flashes of light glittered in my vision, I clawed at his arm.

Dax tilted his head and took a deep breath. After a moment, he searched my eyes. "You did it. You really fucking did it."

Not everyone could tell humans apart from Breed, but some wolves had acute senses. He could probably smell my wolf and see it in my eyes.

It pissed him off.

"Whore!" He let go of my throat and paced away.

I gasped for breath, my heart pounding against my chest.

"You know what, Robyn? You don't mean a thing to me anymore. But what a fucking *waste*. Who was it? The cowboy? The Chitah? Or all of them?" Dax spun on his heel. "Did you really think I'd want sloppy seconds? Did you *actually* think I'd take you back after you gave away the only thing I wanted from you?"

His men looked at one another in confusion. Clearly, he'd kept my unique DNA to himself, even at the expense of his reputation for marrying a human.

"I never wanted to go home with you, Dax."

He widened his arms and looked upward. "Then what the fuck are we even doing here?"

"So that I could tell you in person. This moment deserved more than a phone call. I wanted to see the look on your face. That one. Because that's the look of defeat. Your packmates have seen it now. How does it feel to know they'll be talking about this behind your back for years to come? You can't do anything to me anymore, Dax. I've already won."

Dax blinked, and a hollow smile touched his lips. After a stretched silence, he said four words that chilled me to the bone. "Chess, get the gasoline."

An incessant beeping drew everyone's attention away. Mercy's blue Vespa purred as she slowed it to a stop. Lucian sat behind her with a menacing gaze. His golden eyes were pulsing with black.

Mercy took off her white helmet and beamed. "Hey, y'all!" She noticed the man holding a gasoline canister. "Did I interrupt something?"

CHAPTER 28

Montana pointed at a coyote crossing the dirt road. "Look out!"

Tak blared the truck horn, which scared the animal off.

After Robyn had left the bar, Lucian called Tak and let everyone know what was going down. One of Dax's men had followed her out the door, so instead of leaving right behind him, Lucian exited through the back. The last thing they wanted to do was tip off Dax or his men. Lucian stayed out of sight and followed them to the end of the road. When she mounted a motorcycle and they sped off, he sent another quick update so that they could get into position.

Montana was riding with Tak, Salem, and Archer. Melody and Krys were with Lakota. The only one who'd gone alone was Mercy, who insisted her Vespa could hit highway speeds and go places a truck couldn't. They had all three main roads covered.

When the motorcycle had abruptly jumped onto a walking trail, Lucian tried to follow but couldn't run Chitah speed on the rocky terrain. The last update they received was from Lakota, who said Mercy was attempting to traverse the hills.

Lakota's number lit up Montana's phone, so he put it on speaker. "What's up?"

"They're heading to Casper Cliff."

Tak yanked the wheel, and they whirled around like a ride in an amusement park.

"They took the trail," Lakota continued. "I'm heading on the north end of Ranch Road. The trail leads right to it."

"On my way to the south end," Tak informed him. "Let's block him in."

The call ended.

Montana held the grip above the door while Tak punched the accelerator. When he hit the pavement, the truck skidded sideways, the tires screeching.

Tak looked as cool as a cucumber and turned up his metal music.

"I shouldn't have eaten that sandwich," Montana said to himself.

Tak turned down the music. "What was that?"

"What's the plan after you sandwich him in?"

The engine roared when Tak's truck jumped onto a dirt road. "If he's on the main road, we'll blow out his tires. If he's still on the trail, we sneak attack."

When the truck hit a bump, they jostled around.

Archer poked his head between the seats. "I bet your mechanic loves you."

"There's Lakota." Tak pointed at the black truck parked at the top of a hill. His vehicle blocked the road, with dense trees on either side. Tak slowed to a stop, then turned his truck sideways to block the narrow road. "Keep your voices down."

Montana got out and checked his weapon.

Tak left his door open and met up with them. "The trail's there, beneath that tall cliff." He pointed at an opening on the right between them and Lakota. He continued speaking in a hushed tone. "There's a place to park when you pull in, but he can't drive the trail. It's meant for hikers, so we've got him blocked in." Tak searched the grass until he found a rock. After lifting it, he dug a shallow hole and hid his keys beneath it. "Old trick I learned. If you shift, all they have to do is find your clothes to steal your keys."

When Montana's phone chimed, he cursed and quickly answered.

Lakota waved at them. "Everyone is circling the cliff. Mel is checking out the angle from above while the others flank them. He can't be but fifty feet from the road. What does Tak want us to do?"

Montana relayed the message.

Tak stared up at the trail entrance, then glanced over his shoulder at Salem. "I want you positioned in front of the trail on the opposite side of the road. Don't let anyone out. Lakota and I will shift and come at them from the woods. Montana, follow us and get as close as you can without revealing yourself. We can't move in if it puts Robyn in danger. When you have a clean shot, fire." He clapped Montana's shoulder. "Don't shoot my wolf."

"You got all that?" Montana asked Lakota.

Moments after they'd hung up, Lakota's silver wolf emerged from the trees next to them. Salem ducked behind the ones across from the trail entrance and made his way into position.

Archer held up his machete. "I'll come around behind them."

Montana suddenly felt an overwhelming sense of panic. Something wasn't right with Robyn. All he could think about was getting to her as fast as possible.

When Tak shifted, he and Lakota's wolf entered the woods. The uneven ground was difficult to navigate. Because Archer wanted to do a sneak attack, he skipped farther ahead. When Tak's wolf stopped, Montana took his cue to change direction and move stealthily toward the base of the cliff. It didn't take long before he spotted the white van. The doors were closed on the side facing him.

Then he heard voices, shouts, and a wolf yelping.

"Fuck it." He moved in fast.

When he reached a clearing, he spotted Lucian lying on top of a Shifter. The man beneath him was bleeding at the neck and suddenly shifted. Chaos ensued. Mercy was engaged in a tug-of-war over a red gas canister, and one of Dax's packmates fled the scene.

Montana caught sight of Dax. He had a clean shot until Tak and Lakota jumped into the fray.

Robyn, where are you?

A scrawny man in a white shirt pulled a weapon and fired it at Lakota's wolf. Montana shot him four times until he fell. Lakota's wolf picked up a scent and took off.

When Dax heard the gunfire, he fled toward the van like the chickenshit he was.

Montana aimed at the moving target and fired only once because Tak's enormous wolf jumped in the way. It looked like the bullet had struck Dax in the shoulder or chest. He instantly shifted to wolf form, hit the van, and spun around to fight Tak.

Montana ran onto the scene. "Robyn!"

Her clothes were lying in a pile near the cliff wall.

An arrow whistled by. Montana swung his gaze up to Melody leaning over the edge. The cliff was at least three hundred feet tall. While Melody had a great vantage point, she couldn't see anyone's faces. He waved his arms at her so that she wouldn't fire at him again.

Archer unleashed a primal scream while running onto the scene with a machete over his head. Mercy let go of the red canister and reeled back. Bringing it down, Archer buried the long blade in the man's shoulder. When he pulled it out to strike again, the wounded man shifted.

The gas can spilled, and a gun fired from the woods.

Montana directed his attention to the wolf attacking Lucian. He couldn't fire his gun, so he rushed at them and knocked the animal off.

Turning on him, the wolf bit his wrist, thrashing until the gun flew out of his hand. Montana beat that animal in the head, every blow powered by the rage he felt at the men for taking Robyn. The wolf's jaws locked, his sharp fangs piercing Montana to the bone. Shifter wolves often dismembered their enemies, so once they latched on to an arm or a leg, it could be hard to get them off.

When Lucian kicked the animal in the stomach, it yelped and then sprinted into the woods.

Krys took off. "The fucker's mine!" He shifted midstride and disappeared into the brush.

Montana pivoted just in time to see Dax's animal take off. Tak's ebony wolf shook his head and staggered, unable to put weight on his bleeding foot.

Then a gunshot popped from Salem's location.

When Tak shifted to heal himself, Montana realized he might need help, so he changed form and joined him on the hunt. His wolf picked up their enemy's scent, and they followed at lightning speed.

My head was swimming at how fast everything was unfolding.

Dax had planned to set me on fire with gasoline, but before he could carry it out, Mercy and Lucian sped onto the scene. A verbal altercation followed, then Lucian flew off the bike and attacked a man who reached for a gun. Mercy saw the gasoline can and sprang into action. The next thing I knew, multiple guns were firing. I shifted and ran so fast that I didn't know where I was going, only that I had to get away from Dax before he turned his rage on me.

It was only my wolf's second time out, and Tak had warned me against fighting. A newborn was too inexperienced to take on a pack, let alone an alpha. If she were attacked at a young age, it might alter her behavior—make her aggressive and difficult to trust.

Though my wolf thirsted for blood, we needed to find safety. I weaved around Dax and slid beneath the van. My heart lurched at the sight of Montana firing his weapon.

Dax shifted and slammed into the front of the van. The chilling sound of two alphas fighting to the death stilled my wolf. I could smell

Tak and see his legs as the two tangled. Dax's white animal had distinctive brown legs. Packmates used to remark that it looked like he had walked through mud.

Tak ripped at the white fur, staining it red as he attempted to get at Dax's belly. Eviscerating a wolf made it nearly impossible for them to shift back without human intervention. Dax lowered his head and chewed on Tak's foot.

Why would he chew on his foot?

My wolf jolted forward and snarled at him. It startled Dax enough that he let go and scurried away.

When Tak didn't immediately follow, I realized why. My former Packmaster wanted to buy time to escape, so he'd attempted to cripple his adversary. Tak shifted twice to heal before racing off with Montana.

I felt myself slipping from consciousness, so I changed back to human form and crawled out.

Another gun fired several times in the woods.

Naked and confused, I grabbed the first T-shirt I saw on the ground.

My hands shook as I surveyed the gory scene. Archer stood over a wolf with a bloody machete in his hand. The motorcycle driver stared vacantly at the sky, blood soaking through his white shirt.

I hustled over to Mercy, and we hugged. I'd come so close to being burned alive by Dax's men.

Melody ran onto the scene with a bow in hand and a quiver filled with arrows over her back. Out of breath, she leaned against Archer. "I swear to the fates I'm never doing that again. I almost fell off the ledge."

"You almost shot me in the ass," Lucian grumbled from the ground.

"Let's see *you* fire at a target from a hundred yards. I've never been out here before." She squinted up at the cliff's ledge. "It's too high."

I knelt before Lucian and noticed that his eyes were pulsing black. "Are you okay?"

He examined his bloody arm. "I'll live." Then he looked me over. "Are you hurt, female?"

I gave him a half-hearted smile. "I'll live."

Krys emerged from the woods without a stitch of clothing, unless the dead wolf draped over his shoulders like a shawl counted. It had a missing front paw, and its throat was torn out. He threw the animal down next to its packmate.

Melody looked around. "Where's Lakota?"

Salem joined our group. "He's still in the woods."

"There's one missing," I said, looking around. "There were four of them."

In a flash, the men shifted and raced into the woods to Lakota's aid.

"Where's Dax?" Melody asked.

"He ran that way." I pointed toward the van. "Tak and Montana were close behind."

Mercy picked up a gun. "Let's go hunt us a wolf."

Lucian stood and cleared his throat. After three deep sniffs, he puffed out his cheeks and drew in all the scents. His gift was incredible to watch, since he picked up not only personal scents but emotional ones too. We jogged behind him, past the van, until we reached a dirt road.

He ran at Chitah speed from one side to the other, following the scent. "It goes both ways. I can't tell if they circled back."

"Listen!" I hissed.

In the distance, the wind carried the ruthless barking of wolves.

Lucian crossed the road toward the cliff and drew in a breath. "Up there."

The only way up the cliff was from the side or the back. We ran a little up the road so that the climb wouldn't be as steep. Melody had the best shoes for running and sprinted ahead of us with Lucian.

"Why didn't you shift?" I asked Mercy. "When you first got here."

She panted as we struggled to keep up. "He had the gasoline in his hands. If I let go, he would have poured it on me or you before I could bite him. Too dang risky."

I'd always thought Shifters relied on their wolves as weapons. All those years with my old pack, and they had taught me nothing. Since I was alongside a fighting pack, I was learning how to live and think like a warrior. They used common sense. Unfortunately, my common sense had me running up a steep mountain with no shoes on.

"Why don't you shift?" Mercy asked when she noticed me falling way behind.

"Because I'll be naked!"

She cackled. "You're so adorable. I'm the only one who can see you, and I'm not even looking. Go on and shift. I'll carry your shirt. Just go!"

I ripped off my shirt and balled it up. As soon as I flung it at her back, I shifted into my wolf.

Mercy bent down to pick up the tee. "Go get 'em!"

My wolf picked up Dax's scent immediately. She raced ahead, leaping over roots and clawing her way up steep inclines. Tak's scent was musky and entirely unique, making the two easily distinguishable.

I flew past Lucian, who was helping Melody up a rocky hill.

My nails helped me power up the hill, twigs snapping beneath my thick paws. Though my wolf had never hunted before, she instinctually knew how to track a scent. The thrill of the chase moved through me like an ancient song. The lyrics were bone deep, and I knew every word.

I reached the top of the hill and followed the powerful scents to where the wolves must have tangled. Through her eyes, I noticed marks in the dirt. A few drops of blood snagged her attention, and she lingered on them before taking a right.

I cocked my ears at the sound of the others catching up. My wolf took off up the hill, where the fighting sounds grew fierce. I was struggling to stay conscious, my periphery growing darker.

She followed the sounds of snapping, snarling, growling, and barking. Then she caught another scent—*Montana*.

When the ground leveled out, my wolf weaved around trees so fast that my head spun. Then she skidded onto the scene, her front legs splayed. Clouds dotted the sky, and beyond the cliff were rolling hills of endless trees and land.

Three wolves were engaged in a fight, gnashing and snarling, bodies colliding and tangling. Montana's wolf bit Dax whenever he attempted to flee. Tak's massive animal hunched his shoulders, every hair standing on end. My wolf wanted to jump in, so seconds before I blacked out, I shifted to human form.

Kneeling on one leg, I watched the tumultuous assault. My heart pounded against my chest when Tak and Dax rose on their hind legs.

Melody and Mercy caught up to me, huffing and panting. Lucian wasn't as winded, but his face was flushed.

When Mercy handed me the shirt, I scarcely moved.

This fight would seal my fate.

As they drew nearer to the edge, I clenched my hands. Blood and dirt mottled Dax's white fur. When he tried to flee, Montana charged. Because Tak was the Packmaster, he got the honor of challenging the alpha. All Montana could do was keep Dax from running.

Quickly, I put on the shirt and stood. We watched in silent awe as two beasts, once mythical to me, battled to the death. *What if Tak loses?* Thoughts of his grieving life mate ran through my mind.

Tak vaulted at Dax and shoved the wolf closer to the edge. Dax pivoted, causing Tak to graze the cliff's edge with his back legs. I clutched my chest as if that could stop my racing heart.

Like a tornado, Tak circled around. He sank his teeth into Dax's throat from the other side so fast that the wolf yelped with surprise.

Dax skidded backward until his hind legs slipped off the edge. Then Tak released his hold and growled at the white wolf, who struggled to climb back up while blood gushed from his throat.

Before he bled out, he shifted to human form.

Dax's arms desperately gripped the ledge. "Pull me up!" he shouted. His wound wasn't entirely healed. "I'll make a deal."

Tak shifted and rose to his feet. "A man without mercy has no right to beg for it."

"I'm slipping!" He desperately clawed at the dirt.

I'd never seen him look so weak and helpless. Part of me wanted to see him as a person who could change, but that would never happen. He would become obsessed with erasing the embarrassing moment where he'd begged for his life. Dax would come at us hard, with everything he had.

"Robyn! *Help me.*" He looked right into my eyes. "You owe me! You're my wife!"

My wolf pulsed against my skin.

In a move too fast to track, Montana's wolf lunged and wrapped his jaws around Dax's face. He shook violently, making Dax scream.

I ran forward, terrified that Dax would drag Montana down with him, but someone held me back.

A second later, Montana let go, and Dax plummeted to his death.

Tak peered down at the corpse, then kicked dirt off the edge. "It's a shame he only learned humility in death."

Montana shifted to human form and scanned his surroundings. After glancing at the body below, he looked around until he spotted me.

I rushed into his arms. Montana's embrace wrapped around my entire being.

"Are you okay?" he asked against my neck.

"Yes." Tears of relief slipped out. "I'm free."

"What a shame his wolf slipped," Tak remarked. "Is that what everyone saw?"

Those behind us verbally agreed.

"Lucian," Tak continued, "do you know any cleaners in the area who can assist?"

"I do," Melody offered, raising her hand.

When Montana let go of me, I saw his wrist had healing wounds from a nasty bite, as did his shoulder, face, and leg. But after one or two more shifts, there wouldn't be a scratch on him.

Melody hooked her bow over her arm. "I left my phone in the truck. The number's in my contact list."

"Call Hope," Tak said to Lucian. "Right this minute. I want to know that she's safe."

Lucian did as he was told, then gave Tak a curt nod to let him know that all was well with his mate.

Melody headed down the hill. "I think I burned a million calories today."

I peered over the steep edge and looked at the bodies far below. The van was farther to the right. The white body directly below took me by surprise. Dax was in wolf form. "I don't get it. His wolf wasn't the one who fell."

"Correct," Tak said. "He changed form while falling."

"That's a coward," Montana stated. "He made his wolf feel the pain of death."

"The wolf was braver than the man." Tak ran his fingers over a grisly bite on his arm that was only partially healed. Then he approached Montana. "Because he was in human form when he fell, I don't want that used against you by the law or even his pack. He's a wolf in death, and that's all that matters. No one will know. But as far as this pack is concerned, yours was the death blow." Tak closed the distance and gripped the back of Montana's head. Their foreheads touched. "You're a true warrior. You stood by your alpha and fought with honor and courage."

After a friendly wink, Tak shifted and trotted off.

I walked into Montana's arms and fell into a deep kiss. His scent filled my nose, and his taste covered my tongue.

He lifted my shirt over my head.

Mercy stirred with laughter. "We'll just leave you two lovebirds alone."

Montana tossed the T-shirt over the ledge. "Shift. I'll follow you."

Our wolves ran swiftly past the others, racing each other as if they were old friends. I envied those who could hold their consciousness the entire time—feeling every moment through their animal's senses. It was exhilarating but equally frightening since she was in complete control. At least mine gave me a few minutes' worth.

When we reached the bottom, we entered the trail and trotted past the van. The rest of our group had gathered by Dax's animal at the base of the cliff. I shifted by my clothes while Montana searched for his pants. I'd become more comfortable with my nudity when I realized no one else cared. No one leered or stole glances.

"Don't touch the body," Montana instructed them. "Lucian and Melody are calling in the cleaners."

Tak returned from the main road with his trousers on and his shoes and shirt in hand. "Is anyone injured? Give me the status."

"One of those jokers shot my wolf three times." Lakota collapsed in the dirt, overcome with exhaustion.

Tak gestured to Krys and Salem. "You two can carry him to the truck."

After putting on his shirt, Krys flipped his long hair out from beneath the collar. "Does he need a stretcher?" he asked, shoving his foot into one of his boots.

Lakota tossed a pebble at Krys's head. "I can walk."

After a sonorous chuckle, Tak finished putting on his shoe. "A breeze could blow you over, brother. You need more stamina if you want to keep that mate of yours happy."

"I've got plenty of the stamina that counts," he fired back. Lakota wobbled as he climbed to his feet. "I shifted *five* complete revolutions, and that excludes my first shift."

"Is that so?" Tak began braiding his hair. "I once shifted eight times and walked three miles in the snow."

Lakota strode by him. "Did the horse buck you again?"

Despite the otherwise-somber moment, we laughed. Alphas and betas could shift more times than the rest of us without getting as worn down. It always seemed like a competition existed between those two.

Hope hiked toward us from the road. "Here I am, thinking my mate is dead. And I find you out here laughing like it's a party."

Tak held her in a tight embrace. "How did you get here so fast?"

She stepped back. "Lucian called me earlier to tell me you were on your way here."

"And why would he do that?"

"In case something happened, I'd know where to find the bodies." Hope's eyes glittered with tears. Her emotions quelled when she noticed the bodies littering the base of the cliff. "My gosh. Is everyone all right?"

"Mostly."

Virgil ambled up behind her. Instead of joining us, he leaned against the side of the van. All he had on was a pair of white swim shorts and sneakers. "Corpses everywhere, and all you two want to do is kissy-kissy."

I smiled at Hope. "You let him in your car?"

"Guilty as charged." She lifted her collar and smelled it. "He insisted on protecting me, and knowing my mate would never want me to venture to a dangerous place alone, I agreed. The windows were down."

Archer snorted while tying his shoe with a method I'd never seen. "You might need to blowtorch the seat."

"Someday, I'll laugh at your jokes," Virgil said, "but today is not that day. Who's in the van?"

"Nobody," Archer informed him.

Virgil pressed his ear against the side. "I disagree."

CHAPTER 29

Aiming his gun, Montana noiselessly approached the van. Because of the wide parking space, there was enough room for us to create a semicircle near the side doors.

Tak peered through the driver's-side window before heading to the back.

I braced myself when Lakota slid open the side door.

"Oh my god," I breathed.

A woman lying on her side stared at us. She was muted by a ball gag that was strapped around her head. Her hands were bound behind her back, and her ankles tied with a belt. She couldn't sit up because of a metal collar around her neck attached to a twelve-inch chain bolted to the floor.

Tak climbed in. "Lakota, help me."

Montana lowered his gun while Lakota unlatched the belt from her ankles. She couldn't have slipped out of the restraint because of her boots. Tak ran his fingers around the collar while Lakota worked on freeing her hands.

Her gaze darted around.

Hope covered her mouth and whispered, "We should call a Relic."

The woman mumbled something unintelligible. Drool leaked from her mouth.

"Look down," Tak said. She did as he commanded until the collar clinked open.

Wiggling to a sitting position, she swung her legs out of the van. She wore green camo leggings and a long tank top. Her wavy reddish-orange hair curtained her face when she leaned forward while Lakota cut the ties with a pocketknife.

When her hands flew forward, she rubbed her red wrists. She tried to remove the gag, but Tak was still unlatching it.

As soon as the buckle freed, she spit out the gag and took several deep breaths. After wiping her mouth, the woman slid her jaw from side to side while rubbing her cheek.

"You poor thing," Mercy cooed.

The woman rolled her shoulders. "I'm going to kill that fateforsaken fleabag with my bare hands. Are you little bandits in league with him? Well, breaking news—I'm not going anywhere with you. I've been tied up for three days, so if you don't mind, I'm outta here."

Archer scratched his jaw and gave everyone a puzzled look.

"You're not going anywhere," Tak said from inside the van. "We'll call the local Council so that you can speak with them."

"About what?"

"Kidnapping."

She hopped out of the van. "Is this a rescue mission?" She beamed from ear to ear and looked like the Joker with her makeup smeared across her pretty face. "Well, holy shitballs! I hit the jackpot."

"We weren't here for you," Tak said matter-of-factly. "We came for him."

She dusted off her clothes, which had bloodstains on them. "So, where's Dax? I have unfinished business with him."

"It's finished now," Virgil informed her.

She put her hands on her hips. "You let him get away? I didn't spend the last eighty-odd hours trussed up like a roasted hen only to be sent walking."

Tak jumped out of the van and towered over her. "What's your name?"

"Magic."

"Why were you chained up?"

She scratched the back of her head. "Because my father hates disobedient children."

"Your *father*?" Virgil exclaimed. "That troll was your father?"

"I was his dirty little secret." She fanned the air in front of her face. "Who has the stinky cologne?"

Archer shoved Virgil. "Is that my coconut lotion I smell?"

Magic snorted. "Your lotion isn't masking anything, Pepé Le Pew. Try some laundry detergent in your hair the next time you take a bath. I heard it works better than shampoo to get out skunk."

Virgil curled his dirty-blond hair around his finger and held it beneath his nose.

Krys glared down at Magic. "You talk too much."

"Am I too verbose for your liking?" Magic sauntered up to him. "Would you rather I put the collar and gag back on? I bet you'd like *that*, wouldn't you, Mr. Tough Guy?" She bit her bottom lip and smiled at him. "Cat got your tongue?"

Krys's expression blackened, and he stepped away.

Magic spun on her heel. "So, where's the jerkhole? Don't tell me you let him get away."

"He's dead." I pointed to the right. "Over there."

Magic's shoulders sagged, and she headed over to the wolf's body. She squatted and spoke to Dax, but I was out of earshot.

Tak lowered his voice. "Robyn? Can you verify her claim?"

"Some of his daughters lived in the pack, and the rest were married off, but I knew them all. I don't remember her."

Magic finally returned to our group, her red hair a tangled mess, tears in her eyes.

Tak inclined his head. "My condolences for your loss."

"My loss?" She angrily yanked open the passenger door. "The only loss is not getting everything I've been holding in for the past thirty-seven years off my chest." She rummaged around the seats and retrieved a wallet. After emptying it and stuffing the money into her tight leggings, she felt underneath the seat. "That man deserved an award for all his efforts in ruining my life." Magic reappeared with another wallet and emptied it.

Her behavior was clearly making Tak suspicious. "You say you're his daughter? What proof can you give us?"

"No offense, but you guys are complete strangers. I appreciate your setting me free, but that doesn't mean I'm under any obligation to provide credentials."

"I lived with Dax," I chimed in. "And you definitely weren't one of his kids."

"You're the one he came for, aren't you?" She pinched her chin and studied me for a moment. "I remember you now. You had long hair, didn't you?" She closed one eye and tilted her head as if trying to imagine it. "You were smart to leave before he sunk his claws into you. Aren't you the human?" Magic slammed the door and leaned against it, crossing her arms.

"What did you mean by your being his dirty little secret?" Tak pressed.

She sighed. "I didn't realize I was going from kidnapping to crash-course therapy, but seeing as I'm outnumbered, here we go. I wasn't allowed to live with the pack because my mother wasn't his wife. It would have stained his reputation if anyone knew he'd had sex with a Sensor. Double strike because I was a girl. Triple strike because I'm a hybrid."

For two Breeds who could procreate to conceive a child was uncommon. When they did, the gifts usually canceled out or were weaker. I'd heard stories about hybrids. Some called them crossbreeds. Others called them mutants.

"Don't look so surprised. Not all of us care about hiding our identities." Magic touched the red marks around her neck and winced. "Does anyone know a good masseuse? I think I have a permanent crick in my neck."

Tak shook his head and gestured to the metal collar in the van. "Why would a father do this to his child?"

She tilted her head, still rubbing the back of her neck. "He's been trying to get rid of me since my birth. He paid my mother off, but it wasn't enough. Meanwhile, his legitimate kids are living in the lap of luxury while I'm eating a bowl of Cheerios for supper. What did he care? To him, I was no better than a human child. One day, my mom left to ask him for more money. She was sick of the Sensor jobs." Magic pushed away from the door. "She never came home."

"Dax killed your mother?" My heart broke for her. "Just for asking for money?"

Magic tried combing her fingers through her matted hair. "I used to think that. It wasn't until years later that I realized she probably blackmailed him. Threatened to tell everyone about his defective, illegitimate child if he didn't give her more financial support. My uncle raised me, and he wasn't a nice fellow." She blew out a breath and warily looked around. "Who are you guys?"

"Someone he tried to fuck with," Lakota replied.

"That sounds accurate. Dear old Dad was never one to make friends."

Dax's daughter climbed into the back of the van and dragged a cooler toward the open doors. After lifting the lid, she pulled out a beer bottle. Water dripped from the brown glass while she cracked off the cap and guzzled it down.

She gasped for a breath and wrinkled her nose at the beer label. "When I turned twenty-one, I shocked my uncle by going through my first change. Dax found out. Don't ask me how, but the man knows everything. *Knew* everything. Past tense is wild." She sat down at the edge of the van and peered over at the body. "I think he was thrilled that I could shift, but it probably scared the hell out of him at the same time that I might join his pack or talk. So he mated me off to a Shifter in another pack. I had little choice in the matter. When Dax shows up at your door with a posse, you can't exactly say no."

Montana slanted his eyes toward me. "Sounds familiar."

Hope sat next to her. "How in the world did you cope at such a young age?"

Swinging her legs, Magic replied, "I skipped town when I found out my mate was a royal douche."

Virgil sputtered with laughter.

After finishing her beer, she put the empty bottle in the cooler. "I wound up in Cognito. It was like moving to Mars. I met a bounty hunter named Boots, and she taught me everything I know. After that, I moved to Houston. Since they don't have many people in my line of work, I stayed busy."

"And what exactly is your line of work?" Lakota asked.

"A little of this, a little of that. Things were great until Dax found me."

"After all those years, he was taking you back to your mate?" I asked in disbelief. "What a monster."

"Not exactly." She scoffed. "Let's just say he was less than thrilled to find out I was the one locking up his business partners. Dax was deep in criminal activities. He probably shielded that from you, didn't he?"

I shrugged. "Everyone knew he had the home-building company. There was some talk about other things, but none of us knew."

"He was a disturbed man." When she rubbed beneath her eye and noticed eyeliner on her finger, she lifted the end of her long tank top and cleaned her face. "Dax made problems go away. As in... *poof*." She snapped her fingers. "Scumbags paid him good money. He also moved people on the black market by locating buyers. Ask me how I know."

Tak crossed his arms. "He was going to sell you?"

She straightened one leg and turned her ankle in circles. "I used to love these boots. I got so many compliments on how sexy they were. Now they're ripped. And the heel is coming off this one after I pegged his packmate in the chest with it. That's the only reason I'm taking his money," she said, patting the bulge in her waistband. "He owes me a new pair of boots."

Hope touched her shoulder. "Why was he going to put *you* on the black market? His child?"

"Does it really matter?" Despite Magic's portrayal as a strong woman unaffected by her father's torments, I noticed a slight quaver in her voice that suggested otherwise.

From what I knew about the black market, there were dirty dealings that happened through a special place on the internet where Breed had access, like the immortal version of the dark web. But Dax selling his own daughter made me want to strangle his corpse. Now I got the full picture of just how deplorable a man he was.

Magic waved her fingers like a magician casting a spell. "Lose the sad faces. My father was a maniacal wolf with a horrendous wardrobe. I've never seen his closet, but I bet there's nothing but plaid. Am I right?" she asked me. When no one laughed, she continued with the story. "He found out that I locked up one of his buddies and got paid good money for it. Word got out that I was his daughter, and he was humiliated. To be fair, it didn't exactly help my reputation either. Try getting away from *that* legacy," she said, pointing at the dead wolf.

"How did he catch a bounty hunter?" Lakota asked, his suspicion thinly veiled. "Assuming that's what you are."

"Because he's a smooth talker. Or was." She scratched her nose. "He wanted to get together and explain what really happened to my mother. Dax knew I wouldn't miss that conversation for the world. They ambushed me. I'm not entirely sure what his original plan was, but then he discovered something I'd kept a secret my whole life."

"That you're a crossbreed," Hope guessed.

"Having a wolf in me was a miracle, so he automatically assumed the Sensor part was defective. My mother always wanted me to keep that a secret, so I did. Not even my uncle knew." Magic hopped onto her feet. "Suddenly, I wasn't the worthless daughter he always thought I was. I was *special*. But not special enough to take home for Thanksgiving dinner. Nope. He decided he could make some good money off me and recoup what he lost with his business partner. You know what he said to me before he tied me up and threw me into that van?" Magic faced the body. "One man's trash is another man's treasure."

Everyone shifted their stance.

"You should report to the Council what happened," Hope suggested. "What he did to you was criminal. He's gone now, but it might entitle you to some of the inheritance you were denied."

She scoffed. "And ruin my reputation? I'll pass. The fewer people who know about this little incident, the better." Magic approached me. "So, why did you leave?"

"He forced me to mate him."

Her eyebrows slanted down. "If anyone deserves to die twice, it's him. Sorry he did that." Magic strutted toward the van and dragged the cooler out. It splashed water onto the dirt when she set down the container full of beers. "You guys look thirsty. My treat." She slammed the doors. "Are the keys inside?"

"You can't just leave," Tak said, frowning at the woman. "Cleaners are on their way."

"Sorry, but I gotta get back to saving the world. I'm a nomad, and that means I play by a different set of rules. If I stick around, that'll spell trouble. I won't give my father's ghost the satisfaction." She picked up the ball gag and tossed it to Krys. "Something to remember me by." Magic circled to the driver's side. "I'm taking the van. It's the least I deserve for my father trying to sell me like cattle."

The idea made my stomach turn. I'd been so focused on my troubles with Dax that I'd never given much thought to others he might have hurt. And to think it was his own flesh and blood.

Everyone walked toward the bodies to give her enough room to turn the van around.

Before she straightened it out to face the other way, she stuck her head out the window. "I owe you one, big guy. You're a wolf, right?"

Tak crossed his arms.

"Thought so. What's the name of your pack?"

"Arrowhead," he called back.

She waved while speeding off to the connecting road.

Virgil stuck his thumbs into the waistband of his shorts. "That girl has bats in the belfry. I suppose it's genetic."

"Arrowhead?" Hope asked.

Putting his arm around her, Tak replied, "I've been thinking about it for a while. When you found the black arrowhead in the river, I knew it was meant to be."

Lakota gave him a wry grin. "I was really holding out for the Tak Pack."

Virgil bent down and picked up a long black cord. The large stone pendant hanging from it shimmered like the aurora borealis.

"That must belong to her," Hope said. "It's labradorite."

He swung it around his finger. "It's mine now. Finders keepers."

"You can't keep what isn't yours," she pointed out.

He slipped it over his neck and admired the stone against his bare chest. "There's an unwritten rule that anything you leave at the scene of a crime is *bona vacantia*. Do you really think the cleaners are going to return it to Crazy Girl?"

"Don't call her that." Hope shook her head. "Not everyone deals with their trauma the same."

Melody walked into sight with a phone in her hand. "The cleaners are on their way! We moved the truck to make room for them. Who was that woman driving away with the van?"

THE CLEANERS WERE the legit kind who reported their findings to the proper authorities. When they arrived, they questioned everyone and collected information. The five of them worked efficiently to clean the mess. Before collecting the bodies, they combed the entire area and eliminated all traces of blood spatters, clothing, gasoline, and body parts—basically any evidence that hikers might stumble upon and report to the police.

Virgil didn't want to stick around, and since neither he nor Hope had witnessed the carnage, they headed home early.

After I finished my lengthy and private interrogation, I hiked down the trail and met up with Tak, who was putting on his black tank top.

"Do you think we'll get in trouble for this?" I asked.

He tucked his tank into his pants and watched the men work. "They make it sound more serious than it is. They're cleaners. That's their job."

"To scare people?"

He chuckled and leaned against a tree. "Basically."

"What about the fact that we killed a Packmaster?" I asked quietly.

"Without an alpha to take over, his pack will dissolve. It'll be messy, with the distribution of property, money, and business. His people will have no place to go and may struggle to find a pack who will take them in. They don't deserve to suffer for the mistakes of a bad leader, especially if they had no idea what he was up to."

"What about the beta taking over? He wasn't here today."

Tak shook his head. "A beta isn't fit to lead. He'll always have packmates challenging his position, and it makes the pack unstable." Tak jumped away from the tree and slapped his back. "These ants want to eat me alive."

Joining us, Montana stroked my back. I still had no idea where our relationship was heading, but I felt his concern.

"Did you speak to the Council?" he asked.

"The Councilwoman is fine with it," Tak replied. "It's *his* Council I have to work this out with." Tak watched the cleaners bag up Dax's wolf. "Eden contacted them, and after they notified the pack, they called me on Lucian's phone. I explained what happened."

"What did they say?" Montana wiped blood off his hand. "Does his pack want compensation?"

Tak kept his eyes on the cleaners while they worked. "He said most of his pack were eager to leave but felt trapped. The Councilman was new and not yet swayed by Dax's influence. But many were. Dax was a loose cannon, and from what I understand, they won't be having any parades in his honor."

I turned away and stared at the scenic view.

"What troubles you, woman?" Tak asked.

"Am I really free of him? We're legally mated. If I want to move on, do I have to go back and nullify the document?" I faced them, deciding they couldn't possibly understand my valid concerns. "There's a lot I don't know about Shifter laws. Is there a difference being a Packmaster's widow? Am I going to have to worry about one of his brothers showing up to claim me and there's some archaic law that entitles him to do so?"

"Let's not worry about all that right now." Montana petted the back of my head. "What's that thing you like to say? One crisis at a time."

Tak pinched his chin, pretending to look serious. "That's a good motto. I should carve it on wood and nail it over our fireplace."

I chuckled. "Or stitch it on Virgil's tent."

Wrinkling his nose, Tak said, "He will stink for weeks. Wolves and Chitahs are more sensitive to smells than other Breeds, including humans. Hope let him in her car, so she might be due for an upgrade."

"I think we all need upgrades," Montana added. "I could use a set of wheels. Maybe we should build a large garage. I heard Texas gets a lot of hail."

"That's why you don't need those fancy cars." Tak gave him a friendly pat on the back before walking off. "Better yet, buy a horse. They never run out of gas!" He rocked with laughter as he distanced himself from us.

"I'd love to see you on a horse." I smiled at Montana, who seemed amused by the idea. "You have the hat for it. Does everyone in Montana wear a cowboy hat?"

"I wouldn't know. I'm not from Montana."

I blinked in surprise. "Yes, you are. You said—"

"I never said I was from there. Don't you buy T-shirts from places you've traveled to?"

A laugh slipped out. "I feel like I don't know you anymore."

"I'm from Colorado originally. Grew up on a ranch. After I left the pack, my job took me all over, including Montana." He scratched his jaw. "Sometimes when you're undercover, it helps to look like a tourist."

I poked his belly. "Good thing you weren't wearing a Mississippi shirt when we met."

He glanced up at the cliff, then gave me a curious look. "How do you feel about what happened with Dax?"

"I know Tak had to be the one to challenge him, but I'm glad it was you. Your wolf did what I couldn't."

Montana cupped the back of my neck. "That devil would have dragged you down with him out of spite." He caressed my cheek with his thumb. "You're my girl. I can't let anything happen to my girl."

Butterflies stirred in my tummy when he gave me a hot look. Montana's whiskey eyes always held a smile behind them. His wolf danced in his gaze, and it was as if our wolves were communicating on a level beyond our comprehension.

What are they saying to each other?

Perhaps what we weren't saying.

"What do you crave?" he asked. "Do you know? Some people never figure it out. They go years without knowing—especially if it's a food they're not familiar with."

I licked my lips when my stomach rumbled. Yes, there *was* a craving after my shifts. It was more of an insatiable desire. The more I thought about it, the hungrier I got. "I want shrimp." My mouth watered just saying the word. "And I'm not even a fan of shrimp."

The corners of his mouth turned up. "You are now. I'll see if Tak wants to swing by the store on the way home. I think we deserve a feast."

"Don't forget the radishes."

Putting his arm around my neck, he kissed the top of my head.

Dax had thought turning me would make me love him—make me loyal.

Make me *his*.

But that didn't happen with Montana.

I was his before.

Since I was part wolf, the answer couldn't have been clearer—Montana was my life mate. *Does he know? Can he feel it? Does he even want a lifetime commitment?*

One certainty I felt in my bones, knowledge so deep that it couldn't be denied, was that regardless of where our relationship was heading, I knew without question that I would love him for as long as I drew breath.

CHAPTER 30

Two weeks later.

"I NEED MORE CAULK!" I announced, holding up the empty gun I'd been using to seal gaps.

Melody sputtered with laughter. "Don't yell that so loudly. It sounds like you're saying something else."

I put the caulking gun in the grass. "Does this mean I can quit?"

Melody set down her paintbrush and tied her turquoise hair into a ponytail. "Nobody gets off that easily." She pinched the front of her blouse and pulled it away to circulate air. "The last time I told Tak I was all finished with work and needed to shower, he made me wash his truck. True story."

"I guess that killed two birds with one stone."

"He's a good Packmaster. Nobody wants a lazy pack, and I was looking for an excuse to quit that day." She stared at a loose tendril of hair. "I'm thinking about dyeing my hair again. What color should I go for?"

"Purple?"

"That's the last color I had. What about something lighter? Or maybe a different color underneath. That would look pretty in a ponytail, don't you think?"

"Sure. What does Lakota think about it?"

"I've been dyeing my hair since I was a teen. He probably doesn't remember what it used to look like." Melody peered around the corner of the barn toward the house. "I'll bring back a few cold drinks. Just stay here and keep working so that he doesn't make us rebuild the well or something. I'll tell Hope you need more *caulk*." She gave me a cartoonish wink and headed off.

We had worked around the clock to erect a new barn. Since we already had the design, they just had to make adjustments for a sprinkler system and a hay elevator to lift the hay up to the loft. Tak planned to use it, but he also didn't want to become dependent on machinery.

Tak thought a red barn would be an eyesore, so he had us stain the wood to weatherproof it. The layout was the same as before. An enclosed room inside provided an ideal space for an office or additional storage. Installing an air conditioner in the window would be simple. The rest of the barn would be used to house tools, equipment, and machinery.

I wiped my sweaty brow and sat on a bucket turned upside down.

Virgil leaned against the barn and fanned his face with his hat. "I'd give my left kidney for a swimming pool."

"I thought you couldn't swim."

"Lots of people go skydiving even though they can't fly. I don't understand why he's against it. Look at all this. You could build an entire resort out here. What's wrong with a pool?"

"We have a stream."

He swept back his tousled hair. "I need a golf cart to get there. Too many ticks crawling up in sacred places."

"Did you finish installing the flashing?" I asked.

"Hours ago." He put his hat back on. "Once I get the weathervane up, she'll be done."

We'd spent the day weatherstripping the barn, not only sealing the wood but also filling in gaps so that the wood wouldn't rot and water wouldn't get inside. Tak said moldy hay would make his horse sick. All the windows and doors had to be checked, and Virgil took it upon himself to point out everyone's mistakes.

I glanced down at my tan line, which was noticeable where my jean shorts had cinched up. The stains on my white tank top were permanent, but they were my outdoor work clothes.

"Do you think he'll pick the rest of his pack soon?" I asked Virgil. "Ever since we took care of Dax, he's been making us finish this barn. What's he waiting for?"

Virgil admired the colorful stone around his neck. "Beats me, sugarplum. He didn't let me fight with you guys, so I need to make water into wine to get noticed around here."

Until Montana and I decided how serious our relationship was going to get, I couldn't give Tak my answer. I didn't want to rush things when it had been so good between us the past few weeks. If Montana found out about the conversation I'd had with Tak, he might jump to make the wrong decision—or worse, get spooked by the pressure. Even though he'd chosen a room in the house, we'd been sharing my tent. After waking up each morning, we ate breakfast together, worked all day, and bathed in the stream. Sometimes, after the others left, we made love in the shade.

Heaven.

He already knew how I felt. It was up to him to decide how serious *he* wanted to get.

Catcher had grown more distant, but he stayed around and helped wherever he could. It made me sad, yet it was the natural order of things. His freedom was more important to me than anything, and maybe he was trying to figure out his place in my life the same way I was figuring out my place in Montana's.

"How are things with Romeo?" Virgil asked. "Have you found a flaw in Mr. Perfect?"

I picked a weed. "He kicks the covers off in his sleep."

"Freak." Virgil put his hat back on. "I'm so glad I don't stink anymore."

"That's up for debate," Tak said, rounding the corner. "I could smell you from across the yard."

Virgil stretched his arms. "That's just the masculine scent that is Virgil Nightingale. Aphrodisiac of the gods."

"Your aphrodisiac attracted your girlfriend with the white stripe down her back. Go to the house. There's a delivery for you." Irritation flashed in Tak's eyes. "It's gigantic."

"If I had a nickel for every time I've heard that..."

"They want you to sign for it."

Virgil stepped backward. "'Scuse me."

After he took off running, Tak gestured for me to stand up. He always wore cargo pants and a tank top and never seemed to break out in a sweat. Instead, he glowed. I dripped. It was obvious I hadn't spent as much time outdoors, let alone doing manual labor.

"I came to ask about your decision. Weeks ago, I offered you a place in my pack, but you needed time. It isn't lost on me that you two have spent a lot of that time in a tent together. All that screaming is making me look bad. I have a reputation to uphold in my own bedroom."

I should have been mortified, but I wasn't. After living with a pack, I'd learned that Shifters couldn't keep their sex lives quiet. "If he doesn't want me as a mate, I won't stay. That much, I've decided. But I'm not going to pressure him into a relationship. He needs to make up his mind in his own time."

Tak folded his arms and gave me a peevish look.

"I'm not giving him an ultimatum. That's not fair to either of us."

"An indecisive wolf can't be trusted. And if he's ignoring his wolf, perhaps he's not ready for commitment. Maybe you aren't life mates. I was in love once before. Since I wasn't ready for the responsibility of love, the spirits cursed us." Tak watched a red cardinal that had landed in a nearby tree. "On the other hand, some people need a push. You should fly away, Robyn. See if he follows."

"You should give *him* words of encouragement—not me."

Tak unleashed a boisterous laugh. "I'm not here to direct your love life. I only need to know if you'll have a seat at my table. The rest is for you to decide. Come. Let's talk over lunch."

"Uh, let's not," I said, walking alongside him. "I'm not discussing my complicated love life in front of people."

"Love isn't complicated. Women are."

"I dare you to say that in front of Hope."

He nudged my arm. "I have no wish to be sleeping in the new barn tonight."

I looked over my shoulder at the beautiful structure. "It's better than the first one."

"Once we get the stable set up, I can bring my best girl back home. She misses me. My stubborn father-in-law refuses to relinquish my horse until we have a suitable home for her. I think he enjoys making me work for his approval."

When I focused on the house, I jerked my head back. "What's everyone standing around for?"

Not just standing around—they were in a row, putting a wall between us and the house. When they branched apart, I stopped in my tracks.

Picnic tables had been pushed together with pink vinyl tablecloths neatly flattened out. There were plates, gift bags, and what looked like a large sheet cake.

"What's all this?" I asked.

Joy gave Tak a worried glance. "Are you sure you got it right?"

Montana didn't have a shirt on, and I fixated on his chest for a hot minute as he strode toward me with that sexy black hat. "Robyn, you know what day it is."

"It's Wednesday, isn't it?" I scratched my head. "Or maybe Thursday."

Then it hit me.

"My birthday," I breathed. "How did you know?"

I'd been so busy that I hadn't given it much thought, especially when we didn't have calendars outside. In fact, I'd rarely given the date much thought in the past ten years.

Tak had a guilty look on his face when he grabbed something from the table. "I did a follow-up call with the Council. Not ours but your old one. I asked about the paperwork you signed for your mating ceremony." Tak walked up and handed me a yellow envelope. "They sent over the original form that had all your information on it. Happy birthday."

When I opened the envelope, I pulled out torn-up pieces of thick paper. Looking at the seal and other writing, I recognized the mating certificate. Dax had wanted everything to be legal and signed, as if he were buying a piece of property.

"It's a shame it got torn up in the mail," Tak said. "I've heard those machines at the post office can really chew up those envelopes."

"Thank you." When I realized I was officially free of Dax and our forced union, my heart filled with gratitude. "This is the best thing you could have given me."

The torn-up certificate erased the ceremony as if it had never happened.

"You haven't seen *our* gift." Melody hugged Lakota's arm and pointed at a large bag on the table.

Tears stung my eyes.

"What's wrong?" Montana asked quietly.

I wiped my nose. "The last birthday I celebrated was before my mom died. They didn't acknowledge birthdays in my old pack. The little children received gifts, but no one celebrated birthdays. You didn't have to do this for me. Even if this is the only one I ever get, it's really special. Thank you, guys."

Mercy wiped her eyes. "Now you're gonna make *me* cry." She'd worn a pink shirt that matched the tablecloth.

My birthdays had once been filled with childhood memories of family—family I never thought I'd have again. I opened the yellow bag from Melody and Lakota, thanking them for the new sketchpads, pencils, charcoal, pens, sharpeners, and erasers.

Joy smiled at me while I opened her and Salem's gift.

"I see you wearing pajamas all the time," she said, adjusting her red scarf. "They're a little hot for summer, but you can wear them in the fall."

I held up a pair of blue flannel pajamas. "These are great!"

Archer snorted and sat on the bench. "From what I hear every night, I don't think she's been wearing pajamas much lately."

Not everyone gave me a gift, but being there was enough. Krys hung back and listened to Melody talk about her trip to Austin with Lucian to pick up the yellow cake with white icing. She sulked about a delicious pineapple cake she wanted to get, but no one in the group could agree on a flavor.

Bear announced his gift would be catfish and fried shrimp for lunch. Mercy had caught the fish.

"Wait!" Virgil said before jogging out of sight.

"Did they really leave that storage container in our yard?" Hope asked. "He can't keep it there. It's an eyesore."

We listened to strange sounds coming from the side of the house. Several people sat on the benches while we waited.

Virgil returned with a large, flat cardboard box. "Your gift, madam."

Mercy put her hands on her hips. "This should be real good. I can't *wait* to see what you dug out of that metal box you parked in the yard."

"Second-hand gifts are the best kind," he said with a winsome smile. "It's sealed up, so you'll need a knife. Be careful."

Montana pulled a switchblade out of his pocket and sliced open the edges.

"I can't take something that's yours," I said, hoping it didn't turn out to be a tapestry of naked women.

He flicked his hat onto the porch and shook out his long blond hair. "I've been staring at it for years. I think you'll appreciate it since you're an artist."

Montana pulled out a large canvas painting and faced it toward me.

I gasped. "It's beautiful. It looks like—"

"The stream by the house," Virgil finished. "Pretty bizarre, isn't it? Like it was destiny."

The painting depicted a peaceful river with trees flanking it. The water was so clear that I could see the rocky bed.

I bent over and squinted at the signature, which read *Dawn*. "Do you know the artist?"

"No idea who painted it." Virgil tried to sit on the edge of the empty cardboard box. "I bought it ages ago at a human resale shop. She'd be old or dead by now. Bet she never guessed how far her art would travel. You should sell your sketches. They might be around longer than you."

Montana chuckled. "Not anymore."

The empty box collapsed, and Virgil fell onto it. "I bought it because of my impeccable taste in art. It called to me."

"It's really beautiful, Virgil."

Archer rested one leg on the long bench seat. "What else do you got in there, Taz? I didn't have you pegged as an art collector."

"It just so happens I've posed nude for artists. Just think—a naked version of me is hanging in someone's living room as we speak."

"What did you do that for?" Mercy asked, her disapproval painted all over her face.

Still sitting, Virgil crossed his ankles. "Money. I've had some rough patches, but as the song goes, a country boy can survive. You just have to take off your pants sometimes."

She cackled. "Boy, you are about as country as the New York subway."

"Don't be a hater. I was born in the South." Virgil stood and offered his hand to Archer. "I've got a ticket stub collection of every concert I've ever attended. Wanna see inside my compartment?"

Archer licked icing off his finger. "That's a hard no for me."

"I can add to your ticket collection," Melody said while straddling a bench seat. "My dad still plays with his band, but they don't do as many concerts as they used to. Everything's gone digital."

"I'll hold you to that," Virgil replied.

Hope took the painting away from Montana. "We can store this inside for now so that it doesn't get ruined."

"Thanks, everyone," I said, blown away that they had planned a party without my knowing. "This was so unexpected, and I can't wait to taste Bear's gift."

"Me too," Tak agreed.

Catcher brushed against me, so I scratched his ear.

"Are you ready for some fish?" I asked him.

"We're not done." Montana took off his black hat and held it. "There's one more gift I have, but I'm not sure you'll want it."

"Why wouldn't I? It's the thought that counts."

He pressed his lips tight in a nervous smile. "Yeah. Um... When I first met you back in that motel in Nebraska, I thought you were a pretty girl who'd walked into the wrong place. You looked as lost as I felt. But I haven't felt that way since the first time we kissed."

From the corner of my eye, I saw Mercy clutch Melody's arm and gasp, and my chest tightened at the sincerity in his eyes.

Montana got down on one knee and set his hat on the grass. "I don't know how to do this, and I'm not so good with words. But I need you to be my forever. I think my heart is gonna bust open if I don't ask you to be my mate. I've been planning this for two weeks."

"*Two weeks?*" I exclaimed. "You mean you wanted to ask me this *two weeks* ago? I thought you weren't sure about us—that you needed time to think."

"Not sure?" He stood and cradled my neck in his hands. "I was always sure. But you were born human, and it's not in your nature to rush things. Humans do all that dating and..." He snapped his fingers three times.

"Engagements," Melody offered.

"It was killing me to wait," he admitted. "But I wanted to make it special. Your birthday was coming up, and I couldn't think of a more special day than the one you were born on. I was worried like hell you might change your mind in the meantime."

"So you decided to ask me when I'm sweaty, dirty, and looking my worst?"

"I can give you a bath, if that'll help you make up your mind." He gave a crooked grin. "You're my chosen. There's no other. But it's up to you."

Standing on my tiptoes, I kissed him passionately. Montana knew how to kiss a woman, and I didn't care how many times he'd practiced until he mastered it. All I knew was that I was the lucky one who would get to kiss those lips forever. Every nerve ending in my body tingled with excitement when he wrapped his strong arms around me and held me the way I liked.

Finally, I broke the kiss. "I've been looking for home all these years, and I finally found it." When I placed my hand over his heart, I gave him a look that said everything. Montana had offered me something Dax never did: a choice.

A few watchers whistled and howled, reminding me we had an audience.

Tak said, "Just so everyone knows, Robyn's not joining my pack through a mating. I already asked, but she wasn't certain where love would take her."

"Is that true?" Montana asked me.

I shrugged. "I wanted to see where this was going. Without any pressure. If you weren't ready, I would have left. Staying would have caused problems for both of us."

"So it all hinged on me?" Montana's brows knitted. "You said no because you were waiting on me," he said to himself, working out the choice I'd made—the choice to leave something I'd always wanted if that meant his happiness.

"If you didn't want to get serious or just weren't sure, I couldn't join the pack," I explained. "You know the chaos that would cause. Especially if we started dating other people. But I also didn't want to tell you about Tak's offer because that might rush you into making a decision you weren't ready for. Everything happened so fast between us."

He kissed my neck softly and whispered, "Not fast enough."

"Does anyone know if there's a nearby storage rental?" Virgil asked, breaking up the romance. "The guy was going to jack up my rates, so I had no choice but to close the unit and ship it all down here." He sniffed his shirt, then grabbed a can before spraying his armpit.

"That's not deodorant," Archer informed him. "It's bug spray."

Virgil set the can on a table. "Smells citrusy to me."

Mercy put the can on the porch steps. "I think that skunk damaged your olfactory nerve. You should have a Relic look at that."

"I'll move the container off the property as soon as I can," Virgil promised, ignoring Mercy's remarks. "I just need a cheap place to store my things."

"Funny you mention that." Tak climbed the steps and sat down at the top. "Some of you have been waiting for my decision, and today, you will have it. The ones who arrived here before you were sent home. All but Bear. Some individually and others in groups. I needed help building my house and used this as a way to weed out the weak."

Archer lowered his leg and straddled the bench.

"Some refused to work," he continued. "They were sent home. We had a few insolent wolves who slept in my house, and I sent them packing. One disrespected my mate, and—"

"He got an ass beating," Lakota finished.

Tak laced his fingers together. "Not everyone is strong. Not everyone can build a house. Some took credit for work and craved attention. Others refused to help those who were struggling. Watching each group has been eye opening. Before I could store food here, I saw wolves who hunted without sharing their bounty, even with someone too lazy to hunt for themselves. I sent three people home who bragged about the rabbits they caught but didn't share with those who were unlucky. It is not up to you to decide who doesn't belong in a pack by exposing their weakness. All it does is expose your vanity and selfishness. A good alpha will see it."

Montana and I drew closer. People were shifting around, averting their eyes, and waiting for the hammer to fall.

"Some of you set deadfalls and traps. Without telling anyone, you gave your winnings to Bear. This was smart for two reasons. You can't always rely on your wolf to hunt for you. But most importantly, a stronger wolf always looks out for the weak. If you take care of the pack, the pack will take care of you." Tak looked at his hands. "I have considered many qualities unrelated to building my home. Others before you were sent away for selfish behavior, and for that reason, my expectations are high."

"Too high," Hope added while sitting next to him. "My alpha has high standards for good reason. I look for those with good hearts. We have spoken about this at great length, and I've offered my thoughts based on my experience living with a stable pack. I have personal experience with flawed traits that lead to problems. We can't know everything about you; we can only judge you based on what you've shown us. The more you reveal about yourselves, the better. Including your negative traits."

"Those are the most important traits of all," Tak said. "It's easier to show the best parts of ourselves than it is to reveal our weaknesses. You have shown me enough to know who I want as packmates."

Archer stood and paced toward the tents.

"And where are you going?" Tak asked. "Sit back down, Archer. I'm not done with my speech. When I finish, you can leave."

Archer's face reddened when he sat, and I couldn't tell if he was angry or embarrassed.

Tak pulled a black arrowhead out of his pocket and held it up. "Hope found this in the river. It's a sign that warriors once lived here. They hunted and fought in battle. I believe the spirits have guided my decision. There's a reason why most of you were on that last bus. Robyn was meant to be here. She brought us Dax, and that tested me as a Packmaster. I don't think the wolves in the previous groups would have gone to battle, let alone won. It was *this* group who took down an enemy, including those who aren't even packmates. The fact you were willing to die for one another reveals all I need to know. You believed in this place and in me. Now I want to show that I believe in you."

Tak set the arrowhead in Hope's palm before he stood and descended the steps.

I clutched Montana's arm, nervous about who wouldn't make the cut.

Tak gestured to the empty spot in front of him. "Archer, Krys, Mercy, Virgil—line up in front of me, and I'll tell you who's going home."

All four of them ambled over and stood in a row. Mercy tucked her fingers into the back pocket of her capri jeans. Krys, who stood on her right, crossed his arms. His black shirt and jeans had a white paint stain from where he'd leaned against a wet wall.

Tak eyeballed each of them. "Mercy, you're small. A single female joining a pack with unmated males will often cause trouble. But you get along with everyone equally. You lift spirits and bring joy to others, and that's what a home needs. I'm going to edit my speech because you know what I require. Will you accept a seat at my table?"

She bent over and huffed out a breath. "Holy mackerel! You really had me going for a minute there. *Of course* I'll be your packmate!"

Hope gestured for her to sit on the steps. After taking a seat, Mercy gave her a quick hug but kept a somber expression since the unchosen were facing her.

Tak glared at Krys and arched an eyebrow. "Your wolf is the most unpredictable and vicious animal I've ever seen. But I understand him, perhaps more than I do you. He doesn't trust people, but he's fine with other wolves. He survived our introductions, and I still have my handsome face. Your wolf reminds us that boundaries are important to learn —that we are still wild by nature. You are temperamental but honest. Perhaps too honest," Tak said with a chuckle. "You work hard and fight hard, and there's always room at my table for a warrior. Do you accept my offer to join the Arrowhead pack?"

"Shit." Krys tipped forward to look past Virgil.

"Take it," Archer said. "Don't base your decision on me."

Breaking away from someone you cared about wasn't an easy choice. While I couldn't see Krys's face, his hand went up as if he were rubbing his forehead.

"We came in this together," he argued.

Archer stepped forward to look at him. "If you turn down this opportunity because of me, I'll personally beat your ass."

Krys sighed. "Yeah. Okay," he finally said.

Tak laughed and patted his shoulder. "Don't look so excited. Take a seat."

Archer whispered something to Krys before clapping a hand on his shoulder and returning to his spot. It must have been killing him to see his cousin accepted, knowing his odds weren't good.

Tak turned to stare at Virgil. "I have been on the fence about you most of all. Sometimes a man uses jokes to hide something about himself. What are you hiding, Virgil?"

He shrugged. "My marvelous robe collection?"

"I suppose I'll be seeing more of it. Your knowledge of construction has given me what I lacked with this endeavor. Just keep the skunks away from my house."

"Is that an official invitation?"

Tak shot him an icy stare and held it until Virgil quit fidgeting. Then his lips eased into a grin. "Have a seat at my table, Mr. Nightingale. Consider this your formal invitation."

Virgil strutted like a peacock toward the steps and snatched up his fedora. When he sat, he stretched out his legs and leaned back on his elbows. "I've already picked out my room."

Tak cleared his throat and stepped in front of Archer. "I suppose you've waited for your answer longer than necessary. The charming bus driver who brought you here called me on the morning of your arrival. She told me about her one-armed passenger."

Archer made a fist, then splayed his fingers.

"Before meeting you, I had made my decision. Tripods are physically weaker and can't keep up with a pack. They're easy targets."

"We can save the speech," he said. "I really don't need to hear this."

"That's up for debate." Tak leaned on the porch railing. "She told me about the one-armed man who tackled the gunman. Then I heard about the two men—the ones I sent home—who were taking all the credit. You never mentioned this when you arrived. Why not?"

"Didn't seem important."

"When Robyn was sick, you brought her your clothes to wear. You are kind to the women here and compassionate by nature. But you try too hard to prove yourself as a man. I thought you were going to chop your leg off that first day when you started swinging that axe." He paused, thoughtful. "I sometimes wonder if you were born a warrior or made one. Your wolf may not be fast, but he's brave. He's not resentful of his weakness, but you are. Careful that you don't let that turn into something dark. So long as you keep my advice in mind, I would be honored to have you in my pack."

Archer's attention snapped up. "Are you fucking with me?"

Tak leaned in. "I'm a funny man, but do I look like I'm making a joke?"

Flummoxed, Archer looked around at our reactions. "You told us to line up so that you could tell us who was going home."

Tak grinned. "I like to build up the suspense. So, what's your answer?"

Archer threw his head back. "Fucking hell, *of course* I want to be in this pack."

Everyone clapped and whistled for the newest packmates. Tak gave him a brief welcoming hug while everyone jumped to their feet and congratulated one another.

I smiled up at Montana. "It feels like a family now."

"That's exactly what a pack is supposed to be."

Tak crossed the lawn. "What about him?" he asked, pointing at Catcher.

Shaking my head, I replied, "I don't know."

"When will you know?"

I stroked Catcher's head. "When I move into the house. Right now, he thinks I'm still an outsider. But once I settle my things in a room, he'll decide."

Tak squatted in front of Catcher and stroked his face. "You know you have a place in my pack. Tell that to your human. Maybe he'll come out someday. If he does, he'll need a pack to guide him. He's been wild for too long. Or maybe he won't. Either way, you're a brave wolf I'd be honored to have as my packmate. Do you want me to be your alpha?" He searched his eyes for an answer.

Suddenly, Catcher wrenched away and torpedoed across the yard.

I watched him until he disappeared in the distance. Not once had he stopped to look back. He was upset about something, and there was nothing I could do.

After collecting my thoughts, I joined everyone at the picnic tables while Bear served delicious catfish and shrimp. I set aside a plate for Catcher for whenever he came back.

At the end of the table, Tak gulped down a few swallows of iced tea. "I called Eden to come out later and make it official. I want it to be known to all the locals who belongs in the Arrowhead pack. Your ancestors live in your memories, in your blood, and in the way you honor them. You are my chosen family, and because of that, I will honor your beliefs as you honor mine."

"I don't know if I can learn to speak another language," I admitted.

"I flunked Spanish in school."

He dipped his shrimp in sauce. "The younger generations will learn, but we must respect one another's cultures."

"What should I know about tribes?" I asked. "We didn't learn much about them in school, and I never met any Natives where I lived."

"Human Natives have different cultures from Shifter ones. We've always lived alongside them but separate, so our traditions and beliefs are different. Most tribes are separated by animal type. That's not always the rule, but this is how it all started. Each has their own history with different beliefs and customs. I can only share stories from my tribe, and Hope will share stories from her pack."

"I didn't live in a tribe," Hope explained to us. She finished sipping her tea and wiped her mouth. "My parents were from different backgrounds and taught us their ways. For instance, Lakota and I believe dreams are powerful messages sent to us from the spirits."

"Funny you mention that, sister," Lakota said. He was sitting at the opposite end of the table. "The night before the last bus arrived, I had a dream I was standing on a cliff with my pack."

Melody examined her shrimp. "I had a dream that my mate picked up all his dirty laundry from the floor."

Montana chuckled beside me.

I used to sit across from the men I dated. But when Montana sat beside me, we could speak intimately and touch. During the conversation, I sometimes squeezed his leg. He responded by stroking my back or shoulder. Montana was open with his affections, and I loved that about him.

Having a birthday lunch with my new family filled me with unspeakable joy. Though my parents had been gone a long time, I knew they would be proud of the life I'd chosen. We weren't the perfect pack, and in many ways, we were still strangers. But we'd bonded.

Maybe it really was meant to be.

CHAPTER 31

"Is it straight?" Montana glanced at me over his shoulder.

I leaned against the bedroom wall—our bedroom wall—and tilted my head to the side. "A little higher on the right. That's it. Perfect."

He stepped away from the painting Virgil had given me, which would hang above our bed. It seemed as if the painter had seen the place it would one day travel to—a land with aging trees, winding streams, and spectacular sunsets.

After my birthday lunch, we'd spent the rest of the day snacking and hanging out before everyone went for a swim. Instead of going with the group, Montana and I enjoyed our first hot shower in the new house. One of the upstairs showers was designed for two people.

We toured each room while discussing ideas for décor or lighting. After dinner, we packed up their tents, cleaned the yard, and moved their things inside. Nearly everyone had items still in storage and talked about needing to ship them down. But I was starting from scratch, like a blank sheet in a sketchpad.

It felt strange to see the backyard without all the tents, but those early memories of our pack had left an indelible mark on my heart. The firepit remained, since we enjoyed gathering there, but once we got a dining table, we would start eating inside.

"Do you think we can fit a queen bed in here?" I measured the bedroom in my head, trying to figure out how much space we would have based on mattress size.

"If that's what you want." He snaked his arms around my waist and growled into my neck. "But I like cuddling. The smaller the bed, the better." His kisses set me on fire as he walked me into the wall.

I curled my fingers against the nape of his neck and moaned when he squeezed my ass. "Do you think Tak will hear us from down the hall?" I kissed his soft mouth.

"Lucian's right next door. We can ask him tomorrow morning."

"I bet he'll switch rooms."

Montana chuckled and tucked my hair behind my left ear. "We put soundproofing material between the walls, and the closets also create a buffer. His is on the right side of ours. Lucian's a night owl, so he'll probably be out of his room at night anyhow. Once we get a heat house, we can go there if you feel like getting loud."

Montana gazed at me, the wolf pacing behind his eyes. He cupped my breast, never once breaking eye contact.

God how I loved it when he did that. The connection between us was so powerful that it wasn't even about sex. We were drawn together like two magnets, and when we opened that channel, it empowered my wolf.

"Help me make the bed." I weaved around him and grabbed a folded comforter.

He took one end and I the other as we spread it onto the floor.

Our bedroom door was on the wall opposite where the bed would be. The wall on the right had a large window that faced the front yard. Since our bedroom was on the southeast side of the house, we also had a corner window. I fantasized about setting up a drawing table since we would have plenty of natural light. Fire sprinklers and smoke detectors had been installed throughout the house, but I was still relieved that Montana had chosen a ground-floor room with windows. After what happened to Montana and Catcher in the barn, the idea of being trapped in a fire scared me.

Neither of us had much to unpack. We shared the closet, which was on the wall to the left of the door as you came in. Our clothes barely made a dent.

"We can build a shoe shelf in here," I said, peeking at the space to the right.

"Shoe shelf?" He snorted. "How many shoes do you think I have?"

I shut the door. "You could also fit a bed in there if you'd rather sleep alone."

"Not gonna happen." He put his arm around me, and we stared at the painting. "If we have a fight, we work it out before we go to bed. I don't like going to bed angry."

I hugged his waist. "Me neither. Can I tell you something?"

"You can tell me anything, sweetheart."

"I've never lived with anyone before. A pack, yes. But not with another man. I'm a little nervous."

Montana stroked my back and kissed the top of my head. "There you go again, worrying about nothing."

"I can't help it. We've never even talked about kids."

"So let's talk about it."

"Do you want them?"

He looked at me softly. "Yes."

"How many?"

"One."

I chortled. "One? I thought you were going to say twelve."

"You're the one pushing them out. If you give birth and still want more, I'll happily impregnate you."

I pinched his chin. "So I guess that means we'll see."

"There's no rush," he promised. "You're a Shifter now. That means you're fertile for hundreds more years. We've got all the time in the world to be ready for a family. Time to build a career or travel. If you want them now, we can start. If you don't want them at all, we can talk about it. This is you and me for the long haul."

I wrapped my arms around him. "You always say the right things, even if you don't say everything."

He was quiet for a minute. "What does that mean?"

"Nothing."

"Don't say 'nothing.' It's only our first night, and I don't want to sleep in the closet because you're mad at me about something."

I stepped back and scratched my neck. "You asked me to be your mate, but you've never even told me you love me."

He dipped his chin and leveled his gaze at me. "Haven't I?"

Then I thought about all the sacrifices he'd made. "You're right. I don't need to hear the words."

Montana walked me backward into the wall and leaned in so close that our noses touched. "I love you, Robyn Wolfe. I love you something fierce. It's been that way for a long while now. It just scared the hell out of me for all kinds of reasons. In the beginning, I wasn't sure if you loved me back. Not until you looked at me across the campfire."

"When?"

"The night Deacon left. That's when I knew I wasn't feeling this thing all by myself. But I couldn't do a damn thing about it. If Tak picked you and not me, you'd have to make a choice. You needed this pack."

I shook my head. "I needed *you*, James. All I ever needed was you."

He kissed my mouth so sweetly that I melted against the wall. Then he rubbed his nose against mine. "When you told me how you felt the night of your first change, I didn't want to say it back. Maybe I wasn't sure if that was what you really needed to hear in that moment. Not as a reply anyhow. I wanted to show you. I guess that's how I am. But it doesn't mean I'm not feeling it."

When Montana ran his hand over the light switch, the overhead light turned off. Then his breathing changed.

"Not until we get curtains," I said, wriggling free. "It's one thing if they hear us, but this is a big window. Anyone could drive up at night and flash their high beams on us. Not to mention wolves have good night vision."

He patted my ass. "I never thought I'd mate with a shy girl."

"I'm only human."

He kissed my head. "Not anymore."

After I tossed our pillows against the wall, he helped me shake out another blanket. The nightlight on the wall provided enough light to see. Tak didn't want to run the air conditioner so early in the season, especially while the nights were pleasant, so I opened the window and let in a breeze.

"I haven't seen Catcher all day," I muttered, staring at the darkness outside. "Not since lunch. He's gone."

Montana zipped up a bag behind me. "You can't worry about him anymore. He's got to make a choice for himself, and that's not something he's done in a long time."

"I know. I was just hoping we could see each other before he left."

A cricket trilled in the front yard and lulled me into a trance. The idea of life without Catcher was unfathomable. He was family. Would I ever see him again? Would he shift back to human form and go about his life as if I never existed? Would he even remember me?

I listened to Montana taking off his shoes and changing out of his clothes.

"I'm the third-ranked wolf in the pack now," he said. "I talked it over with Tak and Lakota."

I spun on my heel. "You didn't tell me. That's wonderful!"

"Gamma wolf isn't a term most of us use, but ranking helps keep the peace. That way, everyone's not trying to bite one another's heads off for control. Most wolves are born an alpha or beta, so the other positions, you have to work for. Even the betas have to earn their spot in the house if there's more than one. Now, if Lakota goes out of town, I'll take over his duties."

I kicked off my shoes and knocked them into the corner. "I'm eager to start working on the stable."

"So is Tak. He really wants his horse. I just want to finish it so that we can build a garage."

"Can we buy one of those tiny Smart cars?"

"Not gonna happen."

"You're the one who insisted a detective has to blend in with his surroundings."

Montana shot me a look. "That's not blending in; that's disappearing. I hope you're not serious. One of these pickups out here could squash you like a bug."

"It would take up less space," I retorted.

He put on his white sleep shirt. "Good. Then we'll put it in the closet."

Sitting on the windowsill, I asked, "Do you think I'll be able to find a good job? One that won't embarrass the Packmaster?"

"Embarrass?"

I stared at my feet. "There aren't many jobs out here."

Montana crossed the room and knelt, resting his hands on my legs. "Hope asked me earlier if you were going to hold regular classes for yoga and meditation. She said it's helped her, and she thinks other packs might be interested. You should do it, Robyn. Not only are you good at it, but Tak would see it as a valuable contribution as well."

"I'm not sure I could make much money."

"The money isn't the goal. You can always adjust your rates later, but getting to know the locals is exactly what we need. Country packs isolate themselves. If you help others, it'll go a long way with making allies."

"What about just having a peace party? Isn't that what packs do to get acquainted?"

"If they have them out there, maybe. But gaining their trust first would be better." He gazed up at me in earnest. "Robyn, I don't know what the hell Dax told you about earning your keep in a pack, but it doesn't always have to do with money. Especially for a self-sustaining pack. Shifters over fifty aren't all familiar with the new things you crazy kids are doing these days."

I chuckled, remembering that Montana was in his seventies.

"Look at it this way: you'll be starting your own business. You never know where it could lead. People might commission you for art once they get to know you better."

"They're just sketches."

"No, they're fucking beautiful. They're an inspiration, and you might do the same for other Packmasters who are looking to build on their land. The only limits you have are the ones you make for yourself. Now that you're a Shifter, you have all the years in the world to work on your craft. You can even go to school, if you want."

A knock sounded at the door. "I hate to, uh... disturb anything," Tak said from the hall.

Montana rose and answered the door.

"You need to come with me." Tak peered inside. "Both of you."

When we followed our alpha, Montana took my hand. It wasn't the way a sweetheart holds your hand, soft and gentle. His firm grip assured me that no matter what happened in our lives, we were in this together.

We reached the end of the short hall where the bathroom was located and took a left down the back hall, passing Tak's bedroom. I thought we were going to the kitchen until Tak stopped at the back door.

I glanced out the window and gasped when I spotted Catcher's tan-and-black wolf pacing on the deck.

Brushing past everyone, I swung open the door. "Catcher!"

He licked me like crazy, as if he hadn't seen me in seven years.

"Where have you been?"

He whined excitedly. When I walked onto the deck, he jumped up so that his front legs were resting on my shoulders.

"He was pawing at the back door but wouldn't come inside," Tak informed me.

I fell to my knees and kissed Catcher all over his big head while he showered me with sloppy kisses. Tears of joy wet my cheeks, and I squeezed him tight.

"Thank you for coming back," I whispered.

Montana knelt beside me and held his hand palm up.

Catcher sniffed it before biting down but not aggressively.

"He likes you," I said, watching Catcher play-biting Montana's arm before jumping onto his shoulders.

Montana scratched his side and growled into his neck.

Catcher froze, barked twice, then jumped off. He trotted around the porch and barked several times before howling into the night sky. Then he hopped excitedly over to Tak and bumped against him.

I stood and watched with gratitude. Catcher hadn't returned to say a last goodbye—he was asking his pack to join him beneath a rising full moon that was cresting the treetops.

Archer strutted past us and shifted to wolf form. Then Lakota followed suit. Virgil did a running leap over the steps, twisting in midair before transforming into his white wolf.

Moonlight spilled onto the porch and illuminated those who joined us. Some chose to stay behind and guard our home.

"My pack is complete." Tak looked proudly at his packmates before shifting into his black wolf.

Montana cradled my neck and kissed me softly. "It looks like Catcher was saving his present for tonight."

"It seems so." I stroked his bristly jaw, wondering if he might be jealous of my attachment to Catcher. "Does this make you uncomfortable? I'm not sure if he'll ever shift back or not, but—"

"He's family," Montana answered. "Your brother is now my brother. But I have one rule."

I searched his eyes. "What's that?"

"He can't sleep in our bed. The only Shifter you get to sleep with is me."

I laughed before giving him a hug. "Sounds dreamy. Can I still wear my flannel pajamas?"

Squeezing my ass, he growled in my ear, "Only if I get to take them off."

My lips found his neck, and I kissed my way to his jaw while the pack howled all around us. It made me remember our first encounter. I nipped his whiskery chin and stepped back.

Montana stripped off his white shirt. "Come on, sweetheart. Let's run with the family."

When Montana shifted form, the pack greeted him. I watched them circle around Catcher, who had his eyes locked on mine. It felt as if the world was moving in orbit and we were stationary stars. I wanted to thank him for all the years he'd served me—for all the comfort he'd given me during difficult and lonely times. Yet somehow, he knew. In that glance, we shared a lifetime of emotions.

The howling overlapped as the pack beckoned me to join them—to run through the dark woods and hunt. I slipped out of my skin and into my wolf so that she could share in my joy.

The joy of love.

The joy of family.

And most of all, the magic of finally having a home."

Love Takes Courage

Made in the USA
Columbia, SC
04 January 2025

c52dd4bf-94ba-45d2-9a0c-ac663171a586R01